Praise for *The Vampire Hunters*

All the elements of a great adventure. Texas teenagers looking for thrills, a faithful dog, a doofus nice kid who wants to join the gang. But wait! It gets better . . . Is a former film star a vampire?

The author launches readers down Texas back roads, across some quiet lakes, through harmless teenage fumblings with young love, and toward a different kind of gang. A delicious mix of evil and homespun goodness.

The Book Reader

It's up to Scooter and his friends to clear the innocent and trap the real vampires. The atmospheric writing, the harrowing quest, and the emphasis on action . . . will make the book a good choice for reluctant readers.

Booklist (American Library Association)

When Scooter is asked to join the Graveyard Armadillos, he is thrilled, even when he learns that to be accepted he is expected to 'prove' that moviemaker Marcus Chandler is a vampire. . . good ingredients (with) an albino moviemaker, a group of teens, a smart dog, first love and a crazy vampire . . .

School Library Journal

More Praise for *The Vampire Hunters*

This is a young adult vampire thriller about a group of youngsters who decided to solve the mystery surrounding a series of gruesome deaths. They unwisely pursue their investigation and encounter Mr. Shade, a nasty vampire . . . There is a lot of adventure in Hill's tale.

S.F. Site

. . . the appeal of *The Vampire Hunters* is not in gratuitous novelty but in a few kids' determination to overcome the odds and set things right.

Vampire's Crypt

PRAISE FOR THE VAMPIRE HUNTERS STALKED

"Scooter and his friends thought they were rid of Lucius Shade for good but when a vampire comes to town looking like Shade, the Vampire Hunter's gang and their trusty dog Flash has to go and find out the truth. The only question on everyone's mind is will they survive? Adventure, romance and a startling discovery makes this one of William Hill's best books for all ages."

Caitlynne in Pottsboro MS, TX

An Otter Creek Press
Book

TITLES BY WILLIAM HILL

Fiction for the young and young-in-spirit

THE MAGIC BICYCLE
CHASING TIME: THE MAGIC BICYCLE 2

Young Adult Fiction

DRAGON PAWNS
THE VAMPIRE HUNTERS
THE VAMPIRE HUNTERS STALKED

Fiction

CALIFORNIA GHOSTING
WIZARD SWORD
VEGAS VAMPIRES
DAWN OF THE VAMPIRE
VAMPIRE'S KISS

Dedicated to:

Ellen Hill, my mom, who claims to have little imagination, but supported mine through Dr. Seuss, comicbooks, and more. She didn't believe in all that fantastical stuff, but she believed in me. Thank you for forcing me to learn to read.

Acknowledgments:

My novels are greatly enhanced and embarrassment is saved through the help of volunteer editors.

Thanks, again, to the students of Pottsboro MS. They have been helpful with pros and cons, but only because Pat Mace, a wonderful librarian, was willing to share my rough writings with interested students: Hunter Sloan, Caitlynne Davis, Lydia Hill (and mom, Vickie).

I appreciate the in depth analysis by Erin Bechtol, of Whittell HS, Lake Tahoe, NV. Also thanks for your confidence.

Nadine Allen, for pointing out confusion, commas, and helping me realize where I had left unintended loose threads.

My family, Dad and Mom, for support in every way imaginable, and Kat, my beloved for time and understanding. My son, Brin, for his belief that Dad is 'famous'. Don't just dream it. Be it.

The Vampire Hunters Stalked

BY

WILLIAM HILL

ISBN 978-1-890611-41-5
ISBN 978-1-890611-42-2
Library of Congress Card Number - pending
Retail Price: $14.95 (trade softcover)
$22.95 (hardcover)
Copyright© by William Hill 2006
All inquiries should be addressed to:
Otter Creek Press
3154 Nautilus Road
Middleburg, FL 32068
(904) 264-0465 phone and fax
(800) 378-8163
e-mail: otterpress@aol.com http://www.otterpress.com

Cover Art: Pete Pilcic

First Printing - November 2006

Printed in the United States of America

THE VAMPIRE HUNTERS STALKED

by

WILLIAM HILL

Otter Creek Press

ONE

LIGHTNINGSTRIKES

Scooter's hopes sank when the aluminium boat's motor shuddered and died. The summer day had gone wrong early. If this young writer had crafted the story of today— a glorious reunion with friends who had survived a vampire—it would have turned out better.

Nothing compared to confronting the undead, but a thunderstorm could be just as deadly, especially when caught adrift in the middle of Lake Tawakoni, along 'Tornado Alley' in northern Texas.

Sunny, scorching, and muggy had changed to cloudy by afternoon. The temperature plunged to chilly. Lashing winds brought a violent storm. Lightning flashed, and Scooter's hair bristled. "That was too close for comfort!"

He patted his dog, who shivered in agreement. Flash hated lightning and pressed against him. The wet golden Labrador wore a canine life vest with a blinking light. It glinted off his collar, a leather circle set with studded silver crosses.

"No kidding!" At the back of Grandpa's Starlite 12 Riveted Jon boat, Russell worked to restart the outboard. He wore his dad's Rains County Sheriff's baseball cap and a clear rain poncho over his emergency orange life vest, a U. of North Texas t-shirt, and faded denims. It all looked too tight on his muscular frame. Scooter thought of nicknaming his formerly skin-and-bones best buddy the Incredible Bulk.

"What now, y'all?" Kristie asked. The minister's daughter was a fantastic girl unlike any other. Because Scooter hadn't seen her in weeks, he found himself staring. Redheaded and freckled, Kristie Candel looked miserable, obviously cold with a runny-nose. Her yellow rain slicker seemed like an unheeded warning.

"Don't give up the s-ship," Russell quipped.

"Can it suck anymore?" the new kid moaned.

With each passing minute, Scooter's similar question of how the day could get any worse had been repeatedly trumped, starting with the addition of Kellen 'the Intruder' Redgraves to their fishing party. Scooter had assumed they would have a fantastic time together. That was before the Intruder had rocked the boat.

"Don't look at me. It wasn't my fault," the Intruder blurted his motto. His pink eyes peered from under his flat-brimmed hat. It flapped in the wind like the wings of a clumsy albatross.

The Intruder appeared distantly related to Scooter's writing mentor, Marcus Chandler. Both looked like albinos with ghostly pale skin and disturbingly red eyes, but the similarities ended there.

Scooter mentally listed the accusations levied against the Intruder. To begin, he caused them to start late, then he squandered prime fishing time when he lost his hat, forcing them to hunt for half an hour. To make matters worse, the Intruder lost Russell's Penn Pro, a fine rod and reel, and hooked a tree with his best bass lure—a handmade piece crafted by Russell's great-grandfather.

His easy-going bud went ballistic, looking ready to shoot the Intruder. It was a good thing Russell didn't carry a gun.

Scooter felt a rain drop and groaned. The weather forecast called for isolated squalls. With the Intruder aboard, a ten percent chance of rain became a certainty. The gusty winds bullied the black and blue clouds to spill their guts. The silence of the motor was loud because of the keening wind and the smattering of rain.

"Good news! One gas tank ran empty, that's all. We have two," Russell said. He flipped a switch on the connecting hose to draw gasoline from the other five-gallon can, then he yanked the starter cord. The Mercury 50 HP outboard turned over, the prop spinning.

Kristie cheered. Flash barked.

Russell steered the aluminum boat to slice across the waves. The swells quickly roughened. The greenish crests gained white caps. Water splashed over the bow, dashing Scooter and Flash. The lucky dog cuddled with Kristie.

The boat porpoised, the bow riding airborne then splashing back down. Scooter gripped the gunwales and braced himself, hunkering down. With each bucking, he was bludgeoned, banging knees and elbows.

"You look like a masthead!" Kristie laughed.

"I was wondering if maybe we should let you drive," he replied, sharing a quick over-the-shoulder smile with her.

"Would a song help, y'all?" she drawled.

"Sing? At a time like this? Is this a musical disaster?" the Intruder interrupted. "How about the soundtrack to *Titanic*?"

"We've survived worse, thank God," Kristie retorted. With her Texas twang, the Almighty could be named G-awed.

"Worse than this *The Ten Commandments* weather?"

"Do you relate everything to movies?" Scooter asked.

"Yeah. A lot of disasters happen in film. They either take

the worst real life stuff or use it for symbolic reasons."

"There are books full of spiritual stories where disciples are beset by storms while fishing," Kristie said.

With the next bashing wave, Scooter's feet flew airborne. Another pounding wave tore his grip loose and sent him flying. His heart lurched, fearing he might tumble overboard. Kristie grabbed him, and he fell back onto them.

With his weight off balance, the boat slowly tipped.

"Whoa!" Russell adeptly steered them starboard, throwing them to the bottom of the boat. They hit a wall of water that drenched them as the craft sliced bumpily but safely through. "Sorry! I'm making for the closest shore," he said and turned.

Scooter saw where he would take them. In an effort to save time, Russell headed uncomfortably close to the destroyed vampire's lair. A sharp neck pain reminded Scooter of where he had been bitten. He stared angrily at the tree-spiked hump of land that had once been called Fisherman's Island. Thank Heavens and Kristie, Shade was truly dead.

The air suddenly smelled of sky-high ozone. Just two weeks ago, he had been outside working with Judge Grandpa on the reconstruction of the lake house when a typical Texas thunder-boomer blew in. Lightning struck a tree across the back cove about thirty yards away. The old oak had exploded, sending debris across the water. He had dropped the hammer, feeling a twinge like he had been holding onto a hot spark.

After that, he had checked into lightning. An average bolt lasted .2 seconds and could travel up to eleven or twelve miles. Was the number 360,000 the speed or the degrees of heat generated? Just as then, the hair on his neck stiffened.

"I feel . . . I don't know, y'all, how to express it. That I'm speeding and yet not going anywhere," Kristie replied. Scooter thought she was talking about the helpless moments when you foresaw disaster but discovered it too late to stop.

Russell shot the gap between islands and steered around the haunted isle, using it for protection against the howling wind. In the lee, the boat planed across the slight chop, speeding closer to the thrashing breakers.

"What's that?" Scooter asked, pointing ahead. The waves suddenly looked beaten down. Flash barked an alarm.

"Looks like machine gun fire in *Saving Private Ryan*," the Intruder doom-and-gloomed aloud.

The surface boiled and churned. The rain changed to sleet, then it grew to stinging, bb-sized hail. The ice pebbles ricocheted off the gunwales, splattered on benches and shattered on the outboard. A golf ball-sized stone dented the toolbox lid, clanged off the bow, and whizzed past their heads. Scooter grabbed the cooler lid and gave it to Kristie for protection.

"Hang on!" Russell yelled. He steered them to port with a tight 180 turn, almost riding on the lower gunwale to return to the lee of relative calm. The icy hail receded to rain.

The worst of the storm swept toward them, now chasing them. Hail as big as golf balls could kill them. They had all heard tales of baseball, even grapefruit-sized ice meteors.

"Where do we go from here?" Russell asked.

"Are you crazy! Make for that crappy fisherman's shack over there! Half a roof is better than none!" The Intruder shoved a finger at the ruins of the vampire's lair.

Scooter's cross bit into his hand. He looked to his friends. They hesitated. Even with Shade destroyed, the island filled Scooter with a clawing fear, causing a full-bodied clench.

"I could use a sign," Kristie admitted.

The Intruder flipped his hat back to share his incredulous smirk. "You don't call this *Perfect Storm* weather a sign?"

Her reply was to quietly sing a prayer.

"I think I would rather be b-beaten to death by hail than go back inside S-Shades shack, but we could get under a tree or h-hide under the dock," Russell stammered.

"Wouldn't one of the other islands do?" Scooter asked, then he looked to Kristie. She tried to smile, her lower lip quivering. Her hair seemed to crawl from under her hood.

Scooter tingled all over. Before he could warn them . . .

A bolt of lightning lanced down.

The fulgence blinded everyone. The dazzling light reflected off the water, making all the world blaze blue-white radiant. Every detail was overwhelmed, leaving only stunning brilliance.

The deadly charge caught the jon boat between the water and the sky. Scooter felt seized and shaken violently, similar to when he had bumped the electric fence around his Uncle Bob's garden. Every muscle herked and jerked in a wrenching seizure as time seemed to stand painfully still.

The frenzied stabbing of the lightning drove away all thought, until a charge surged off Flash. Light and dark seemed reversed, then the world jiggled, trying to come back in focus.

The crack of thunder resounded, bringing back a sense of weight and time. The day returned grim-gray and gloomy. The wind lashed the rain, but Scooter hardly felt it. "Did you feel that?"

"Touched by God," Kristie said, her voice reverent. She reached under her shirt, pulling out an empty necklace. "My aunt's cross. What happened to it?"

The minister's daughter had been radiant before. Now

she blazed beautifully with a golden and royal purple whole body halo, much like the earth angel Scooter believed her to be.

Since being bitten by the vampire, he had been able to perceive auras around people. Although the scientific proof was questionable, the light allegedly represented spiritual energy and physical health.

The others were surrounded in a similar but less incandescent nimbus. A silvery blue glow colored Russell. The Intruder glowed angry yellow and orange with a dark core, like livid flames were burning around a wicked soul.

Flash suddenly licked him, letting him know he was all right. His light blazed brighter than any of them.

"I love you, too, boy. If you can believe it, I think we were just struck by lightning." Scooter petted his beloved dog. He could feel his companion's heart race, just like his own pulse.

"I think we just had the mother of all jump starts," Russell whispered with awe. "Good thing aluminum is nonconductive."

"There's a sign if I ever saw one! Unless you think they're filming another *X-Men* movie here!" the Intruder yelled, wild-eyed. "Russell, if you won't take us there, I will."

Hail fell sporadically among the rain, making up Scooter's mind. The three friends looked at each other, reaching a wordless agreement. Flash whined.

The outboard had died, so Russell yanked the starter cord. Nothing happened. "I hope the lightning didn't fry it."

The air seemed to sizzle like a fuse on its way to release nature's fireworks. Lightning wasn't supposed to strike twice in the same place, but it did more often than people dreamt.

After another futile effort, Russell removed the cover and sprayed the motor with B-12 Chemtool. His next yank succeeded in getting the engine running.

"Yee-haw!" Russell cried. He turned the tiller and twisted the throttle, leaving it wide open. The jon boat bounced and lurched. The pelting rain hurt.

"This was fun. I'm glad I came along on this three-hour tour. Why are y'all scared of that shack?" the Intruder asked.

"Mr. Shade stayed there. He murdered Jo, Missy, and Debbie. He and Garrett messed up my sister," Russell said flatly.

"Oh, I have goose bumps," the Intruder replied.

Russell frowned, then asked, "Hey, Scooter how about over there?" He pointed to a humpbacked section of the dock where the boards had buckled to form a protective arch. It still stood despite Kristie using it as a boat-launching ramp.

Scooter gave him a thumbs up.

As if the skies had been ripped open, it still hailed unmercifully. Frozen marbles battered them, making it hard to see and hear over the smacking and metallic pelting. Russell slowed to dock. Scooter groped for a pile to guide them, leaning far out.

"I can't take it anymore!" the Intruder cried. He lunged onto the dock, leaving the jon boat rocking wildly. Scooter danced, wobbling back and forth. Water lapped over the gunwales. It would have sunk if the crazy boy's departing weight hadn't buoyed them. The Intruder scrambled onto the warped planks, stumbling and staggering before disappearing inside the lopsided door frame and behind a blue tarp.

Idiot. Then Scooter realized the Intruder didn't know any better. Judge Grandpa said good judgment was often created by adverse experiences. Well, the rest of them were experienced.

They guided the boat under the wooden planks. Russell used a docking rope to lash them to a pile. Scooter grabbed a post, then slipped, pushing the boat away. He held on, stretched across the water, inches from falling in.

"Got ya, and I'm not letting you go," she said, grabbing his shirt. He drew the boat closer, making it easy to tie up.

Lightning forked, then the fulgence cracked the sky. It shook the dilapidated dock and the air around them. The fusillade of hail increased. Bullets seemed to give way to cannon balls splashing in the water and pounding the planks. Icy flak exploded through the cracks where the rain poured through.

But the thunder couldn't drown out the Intruder's screams.

Scooter tried not to assume the worst—that Shade had returned—and held tightly to his blest cross.

TWO

STRANDED

The three friends looked at each other, torn over what to do. "Y'all just can't sit there!" Kristie cried.

"The hail will kill you before you can get there!" Scooter yelled over the din of the ice chunks crashing on the dock.

"It can't be Shade! You saw him turned to dust! And if he wasn't, it's still daylight!" Russell shouted.

"Ya call this daylight?! It's as black as night, darker now than sunset that day!" Kristie's words froze them. The stormy gloom might be dark enough. A bitterly cold wind sheared under the dock. The gusts whistled like banshees.

"We know what happened last time, so we know better than to go charging in," Scooter said gently. He took Kristie's cold hands, warming her chilly fingers, then he kissed them.

She stared into his eyes as if they were alone in the world. "I have a responsibility. I brought him along to have fun."

"But . . . ." Scooter began, lips working, tongue tangled, trying to think of something, anything to say.

Being a good buddy, Russell stepped up. "I'm not going out without football gear, Kristie. In my emergency care class, I learned a f-first responder's duty is to k-keep himself safe. Wait until the hail s-stops."

"We can't just leave him," Kristie pleaded.

Scooter rubbed the twinge of pain in his neck. "We won't leave, but we can't rush into danger. Let's think first. That's how we survived this place last time."

Shortly, the barrage lessened, then changed to rain. During the gentle pattering, they heard laughter.

"A vampire could be tickling him to death," Scooter said.

"Not funny. We're on this island. I'm freezing," Kristie shuddered. She had told them she had never felt such darkness and desperation, not even helping the homeless, or visiting the dying. She lifted her sunny yellow umbrella to shield them.

Now that he wasn't scared to death, Scooter realized they were soaked to the bone, making them oblivious to the water in the bottom of the boat. A layer of icy shards floated on top. While Scooter bailed, Russell tried their cell phones. All three were dead.

They were lucky to be alive. Or were they? If they were stranded here, they might wish they were dead.

Bailing gave Scooter a headache, and his back slowly knotted. Kristie rubbed away his pains as she sang 'I've been bailing out the boat' to the tune of *I've Been Working on the Railroad*.

"Good thing you've been chopping cords of wood," Russell joked, then took over for him.

Kristie shivered. "I feel watched. How about y'all?"

Scooter nodded. "No place seems safe since I learned about vampires."

"They seem to stir up the weirdoes in Bluff County. Not to worry, though, I'm ready for all kinds," Russell replied ominously. The fierceness around his eyes and the tightness of his face transformed him into a stranger.

Kristie removed her hand from Scooter's shoulder, and he missed it. "Thanks. I'm much better now," he replied. His headache was gone, and his senses seemed heightened, expanding out and taking in more. He clearly smelled rain, ozone and sensed lightning dancing unseen through the air. Along with wet dog, he detected Russell's nervous sweat and Kristie's rose-water perfume.

"Look! This explains why my hands are sore," Kristie said. Her palms and fingers were bruised with ugly discolored blotches. Scooter held the umbrella so she could compare.

"Do they hurt?" Scooter asked.

She nodded. "I was gripping the edges of the boat when the lightning hit."

"I held the tiller with this one," Russell said, presenting his right hand. It was bruised as if he had slapped concrete.

Scooter looked at Flash's paws. All four were singed.

The Intruder bellowed a snort and a long chuckle.

"I wonder why Redgraves is laughing," Scooter stewed.

"There's a boat hidden over there." Russell pointed. A small, tan fiberglass canoe had been flipped over and tucked in nearby bushes. The wind and hail had beaten down some of the foliage, revealing its hull.

The next rumble of thunder sounded distant and retreating. A minute or so later, a glory hole appeared. The clouds parted even farther, allowing warming shafts of sunshine to grace the island. It splayed through the planks above them like the dawn. The bugs returned, especially the mosquitoes. Their high-pitched buzzing sounded loud under the dock. Kristie selected a bottle out of her bag, and they hurriedly applied repellant.

Despite the insects, the warm sunshine was a blessing. If they must face the ruins of Shade's lair, they would do it under the dazzling countenance of the sun. The wind still carried a few scattered droplets, until it shifted and brought a wall of choking wood smoke blowing from the ruins.

"Oh, God! The shack's on fire!" Kristie cried. She jumped up, rocking the boat.

Scooter hung onto the dock to prevent the boat from

capsizing. "Easy, Kristie! Look again. Someone has a campfire burning." He lifted Flash onto the warped planks of the humpbacked dock, then he climbed up. Kristie took his hand and hauled herself up next to him. "Russell, be ready to fly, if something happens to us."

His bud glared, but he tossed a pewter cross to Kristie, arming her.

Wincing with every step, Flash carefully maneuvered around the broken boards. Scooter's feet ached. His dog stopped about ten feet from the ruins and barked twice.

"Hey!" Scooter cried. Underfoot, the boards broke, giving way. He fell through, catching himself with his arms. The planks squeezed closer, making it hard to breathe. He could feel splinters through his shirt. "It's trying to eat me!"

"Don't panic," Kristie said. "Together now, Russell." Taking his arms, his friends pulled him to his feet.

"We'll do this together. I'll stay outside," Russell said.

The roof looked like a tree had fallen on it, but the angle was wrong, as it would have to come from the water. Scooter knew a boat had done the damage. Using the dock for a ramp, Kristie had launched Marcus' boat to crash atop Shade's lair. The collapse had let in the sunlight, saving them and others by destroying the ravenous vampire.

Before, the cabin had looked like a malevolent spider hunched and ready to vault. Now the predator seemed wounded, partly squashed. The shack's front room was obliterated, but some of the walls and the ceiling of the back two rooms remained intact. The smoke billowed from the rear, beyond a crooked doorway. A blue light flickered through what looked like a sheet of writhing shadows.

"Kellen?" With her cross ready and warding, Kristie glided deeper into the ruins, pushing aside the blue plastic.

Scooter hesitated, a little embarrassed by her courage and his lack. But then he had been trapped inside . . .

As soon as he stepped inside, spider webs entangled him. The remaining enclosure was suffocating. The memory of what it felt like to have Shade's cold dead hands around his throat had left an unforgettable mark on his life—proof of the impossible. Since then, the world seemed darker.

"About freakin' time you showed up. It's a heck of a lot drier in here," the Intruder giggled.

"Howdy. Strange meeting y'all here. Or not, I guess." CJ Mochrie stood to greet them. He stank of whiskey and tobacco.

Calvin Jefferson was just about the last person Scooter expected to find here. He adjusted his glasses, looking unhappy in a camouflaged hunting jacket, blue jeans and snake-hide cowboy boots scuffed from running away from home. His aura was faded, matching his ashen face. Less than two months ago, most people would have sworn CJ was incapable of doing anything wrong. Now his once bright eyes were sadly darkened. Seeing a vampire had stolen his youthful bliss and carved worry lines.

"What are you doing here?" Kristie asked.

"Camping," CJ replied. He had lived here with shelves set up inside his makeshift shelter along the back wall. A trio of tarps and blankets created a wind-proofed space. Flash sniffed around a bedroll and sleeping bag spread across the floor boards. He pounced and snapped up an ugly black beetle, pitching it over for Scooter to stomp.

CJ had a camping stove, but he was burning the roof's wooden shingles in a sunken fire pit lined with rocks. The hole in the ceiling, the one that reminded Scooter of falling inside, let smoke billow out. The smell of Cutter repellent, and the citronella candles kept mosquitoes away while the No-Pest Strip trapped flies, bees, gnats, and mosquito hawks.

"Like in *The Shining*, I can feel the memories here."

"How would you know!" Scooter shook a fist.

Kristie stepped in his path, keeping him out of the Intruder's face. "Scooter! I'm safe. Go breathe."

Scooter left both reluctantly and eagerly. When he stepped outside into the warming sunshine, the phantom hands left his throat. He could breathe freely again.

Russell had donned a camping headlamp. It was dark enough inside. "Are you okay?"

"Now I am. Redgraves is drunk."

"Did I hear CJ?" Russell asked. Scooter nodded. Clutching a cross in one hand and a can of pepper spray in the other, the Incredible Bulk pushed through the tarp.

"Ah, *Inspector Gadget*," the Intruder giggled.

"Ah, the sheriff's boy. You've gotten big. Would you like to dip?" CJ asked, holding up a round tin of Skoal.

"No thanks. Why did you hide your boat?"

"I don't want anyone to know I'm here. I'd appreciate it if y'all would keep this to yourselves. Yeah, right. The infamous vampire hunters. As if y'all can keep a secret!"

"Camping? Ya ran away from home, again," Kristie said. She disliked liars. "Has it slipped your mind what happened here?"

"Yeah. This place gives me the heebie-jeebies, but my bro won't come back here. That's all I need to know."

"He's peeved again?" Kristie asked. The brothers fought constantly, but the peas in the pod hated to be separated, until the vampire proved to CJ that 'his bro' only cared about himself.

"Worse, he's possessed," CJ said. His voice tugged at Scooter. He had seen CJ shaking in his boots before. He shivered as if bugs were crawling all over him.

"Like a pod person in *Invasion of the Body Snatchers*?"

"I'm telling ya, Byron Jefferson ain't my brother no more. Next time y'all talk to my bro, y'all understand exactly what I'm talking about," CJ continued, ignoring the Intruder.

"What's different about him?" Kristie asked.

"Everything. He just looks like my brother! That's all. He doesn't think, act or talk like my brother. He doesn't even dress like BJ. He's wearing a bow tie."

Scooter almost burst out laughing but held back.

"Like the assassin roach in *Men in Black*?"

CJ paused, hugging himself. He looked at each one of them before saying, "He wants me to be a Bible thumper."

"And what's wrong with that?" Kristie asked, obviously insulted. After all, she was a minister's daughter. Flushed and enlivened, she was beautiful when she was mad.

"Oh, that's right. Your father's a minister. Yours is the sheriff. And your grandfather is a judge. Rough lives."

CJ had no idea of the pressure to not embarrass a high-profile parent. It was enormous.

"They do kind of represent Law and Order, don't they? Establishment. Authority," the Intruder snickered.

"Yeah, they do, don't they?"

"You were talking about BJ," Russell growled.

"It's the way it happened that scares me witless. BJ just woke up different, like someone had flipped a switch. Ma might die of rapture if she can convince me." He lifted up his shirt, showing the painful welts across his ribs.

The sight of CJ's back affected them all far more than any words. Pearl Mochrie was more than harsh, horrifying Scooter. But what could he do about it? Because of the near lynching of Marcus, Scooter knew that people could be more monstrous than monsters.

"Ma's wicked with a belt. There's more on my legs. My bro used to hate to watch me get switched, because he knew he was next. Now, Bro enjoys it." CJ said, mocking his brother.

No one spoke. Outside, the wind whistled and moaned. The tarp flapped loose and snapped at them.

"Once when I looked closely at BJ, seeing if there was

any hint of him inside, I saw him," CJ whispered. "His eyes were like they used to be, except he looked trapped. I've seen that look, when he was stuck with a filly he didn't like anymore, or when Ma made him do something he couldn't wriggle out of. Don't ya see? His mind is caged in a body no longer his. I want no part of this."

Scooter shivered. One would think a Bible-thumping and bow tie wearing BJ would be a big improvement. Still, such an about-face must seem alien to CJ.

"Perhaps the encounter with Shade opened his eyes to the Good Book," Kristie suggested. "My experience with a vampire certainly made me think about my life. It proves that there is more to it than we know—what science tells us, and what meets the eye. When you're afraid ya don't have a future, you start thinking of what might have been, and with a second chance, what could be."

"Yeah, but . . ."

"I have seen trauma change people, encourage them to set their days to a more purpose-driven life. But I don't believe there is any excuse for what was done to you. Hear me?" Kristie looked as if she wanted to heal him.

CJ nodded. "I'll survive. Listen, I don't remember what happened here. Will you tell me?"

They really didn't want to talk about it, fearing it would disturb ghosts. And yet, keeping it quiet wasn't helping either.

"All right. Kristie, Racquel and I followed Garrett to you. Y'all were k-kidnapping the LaRoche kids. You brought them here, to this island. To S-shade," Russell began.

CJ must have heard the story. Yet, he acted befuddled.

"We ran out of gas. Fortunately, Scooter and Mr. Chandler found us and brought us here," Kristie continued.

That was the short of it, Scooter thought. They had fled

his grandparents' place in a boat with Shade chasing them. That's when they discovered that moving water hurt the undead. The next morning, they had been awakened by Russell, Racquel and Kristie. Together, they searched for the vampire, finding it holed up here.

"Racquel and Russell were tricked inside. I fell through the roof," Scooter admitted. Sometimes, he had two left feet. Trying to be cool usually backfired. "We were all going to die at Shade's hands when Kristie crashed the boat into the shack."

"You did what?" the Intruder asked. The news of destruction peeked his interest.

"It was the only thing I could think of. I was divinely inspired," Kristie replied.

Finally, when CJ had digested their story, he spoke, his voice barely a whisper. "The last thing I remember, before waking up in the hospital with Ma looking down in disgust, was the Pinto breaking down and meeting a honey outside the Pilot Point graveyard. Everything else is all busted up. What I do recall seems like a nightmare, where I'm a puppet doing a clumsy two-step. I'll die before that happens again."

"And you think it's happened to BJ?" Russell asked.

CJ nodded. "I know it."

Scooter wished the sheriff had let them torch the place. "I think we should leave now, while we can. It looks like more nasty weather is on the way."

"Let's go" Russell said.

Flash woofed, heading out the door. His tail wagged excitedly, glad to be leaving.

"Y'all, we can't just leave CJ," Kristie said.

"Why not? I have food, clothing, shelter and medicine. I'm not in any danger here. I am if I go home," CJ pointed out.

Scooter struggled with indecision. He knew it was

wrong not to tell anyone about CJ, and yet, he worried about him.

"County services," Russell said thoughtfully.

CJ hopped angrily afoot. He seized Scooter by the shirt, ready to fight. "They would send me to my Uncle Bart. That's worse! That's why we never mention Ma whippin' us."

"Hey! Easy! This place will drive you crazy," Scooter replied. He kept quiet about the dock trying to eat him.

"Slugging Scooter isn't the way to solve this," Kristie said.

"Are you trying to make me run? What don't you understand?!" CJ asked, shaking him. Scooter's shirt tore.

"Enough," Russell said. He pried CJ's hands free.

"Come with us," Kristie cajoled sweetly. Scooter would have gone in an instant. CJ was too frightened to be calmed.

"Would you want to go home? Huh?! Think about it?" CJ snapped. He lifted his shirt to display his welts.

Scooter and Russell shared a long look. They both knew what Sheriff Knight and Judge Keyshawn would do. But they knew that even adults weren't always right. After seeing how the town had reacted to the murders and disbelief over Shade, he realized what his grandfather had told him was true. Just because you were older didn't mean you stopped overreacting, making poor decisions, or incorrect assumptions.

"You're going to tell, aren't you?" CJ assumed. Keeping an eye on them, as if they might tackle him, he hurriedly packed, stuffing clothes into trash bags. "I'm outta here."

"CJ . . . " Kristie began.

"Just go!" CJ snarled.

The Intruder needed help from Scooter and Russell to get to his feet. Flash assisted, shepherding the tipsy boy outside. As soon as they stepped on the ruined dock, Scooter felt a raindrop. Lightning flashed, summoning a violent deluge.

Despite the rain, Scooter was tempted to go for shore.

Russell placed a hand on his shoulder. "I don't want to stay here either, but hail like the last might kill us. "

"All right! All right!" Scooter gnashed, hating it. He desperately wanted to be far away from here.

"Hey, hey! You're back!" CJ chuckled. He stoked the fire, throwing on more shingles, making it pop, crackle, and blaze. "Good! Maybe convince you not to tell anyone." He flipped out his pocket knife, and it snapped sharply open. Reversing it, he began to trim his nails.

Scooter dreaded the thought of staying here any longer. What if they had to spend the night? This place would kill them, or cause them to kill each other.

THREE

SHADE'S CURSE

Russell was entangled, tied down with spider webs. Black widows with hundreds of eyes and legs scuttled across his skin. He thrashed and flailed, but he couldn't escape the sticky mess. More and more spiders gathered, covering him from head to toe. No matter how hard he tried, he could do little more than wiggle like a worm on the end of a fish hook.

He hated being powerless and a puppet. This wasn't right. He was having a nightmare. With all his will, Russell wrenched awake.

The gloom seemed deathly quiet. The rain had stopped. The last of the thunder died, leaving a frightening stillness.

Something skittered across Russell. He jerked and squashed a big black spider on his soggy chest. "Oh man!" he breathed, then realized he had fallen asleep in wet clothes.

In the dimness, he couldn't make out anything but bodies. Scooter and Kristie were heaped together. They looked much alike, tall and slender with reddish hair and freckles. He thought they belonged together, but this could be trouble. Flash lifted his head to look at him and winked.

He felt watched, looking around for everybody. He thought he saw CJ. Where was Redgraves?

What had he been doing before falling asleep? They

had played music to lessen their fear, having fun and wearing themselves out. He had grabbed a pair of sticks and drummed on a cooler. When Kristie chimed in to sing, Flash and Scooter had acted as woofers. Along with the rain, Kristie's voice sounded like one of the elements, giving them courage.

"Russell, did you see Freddy?" Redgraves whispered. The new boy spooked Russell by popping up from a shadowed place into a swath of pale gloom slanting. He puffed on a cigar, reddening his eyes. Two squashed bugs decorated his twitching cheek. *"Nightmare on Elm Street* Freddy."

"You are n-not funny." Russell checked his watch, finding it was six. They had more than two hours of daylight left. "Where's CJ?"

"He left as soon as it stopped raining. He said you would rat him out," Redgraves replied. The way the chubby boy looked at him and handled the all-too familiar Bowie Pocket knife to peel an apple caused Russell to freeze. Redgraves' cool detachment reminded him of Garrett.

"I hope you don't mind that I borrowed your knife."

Redgraves had been in his backpack! Anger and worry flared. Russell had the momentary urge to slap the boy, then he noticed the kid peering at his right hand. "Next time, ask. Did you cut yourself?"

"It's just a flesh wound, pronounced the black knight!"

The blood smelled fresh, hanging in the hot and smoky air inside the ruins. Unable to think, Russell grabbed his pack and hurried out. "Come outside. I'll help you."

Redgraves trudged out, peering up blearily at the patches of blue sky. His eyes were glazed, as if he hadn't slept. Russell cleaned the boy's shallow wound before wrapping it with bandages.

Meeting Mr. Shade had taught him that it was stupid to be ignorant of first aid. A body had working parts, kind of like a car, except that automobiles could sit idle with dead batteries and still be fixed later. People couldn't. Sometimes, though, you could jump start a life.

"Man that Rebel Yell was tasty," Redgraves crooned.

"How much did you drink?"

"Not more than two shots, CJ said because of the pills."

"The pills?" Russell asked, concerned.

"For pain. I was complaining. It's been a hard day and my back and neck ache. He gave me a Vicodin."

"Oh. I see. How do you feel?" Russell asked. Drug use could create all sorts of trouble. People already assumed 'The Vampire Hunters' were on drugs.

"Spacey. You dropped this," Redgraves said. He handed him an empty, Ziploc-snack plastic baggie.

"Uh, it's not mine," Russell almost stammered.

"I just found it near you. No biggie."

A little panicked but concealing it, Russell hoped, he checked the secret zipper pocket on his backpack. It sat wide open and unzipped. Fingers searching frantically, he found his spilled pills. He counted them, twice, short one. Did Redgraves have it?

While Redgraves sat down and stared at the lake, looking melancholy, Russell downed a Mexican bean with a slug from a water bottle. He almost popped a Greenie, but he would wait until later, when he must stay awake tonight.

He noticed CJ's canoe still sat onshore, stashed among the greenery of a patch of weeds, a clump of bushes and two twisted mesquite trees. Mochrie hadn't left. Maybe he waited to see what they would do. He turned to a dark stand of trees and stared. "CJ?"

His headlamp highlighted a chattering chipmunk. The scavenger seemed to be the voice of the ruins, mocking him. The shack had withstood the storm and, oddly enough, appeared even more organized. Could it be rebuilding itself?

He stripped to his swim trunks, then waded to the boat. From this angle, he would swear the planks looked more crooked. Scooter thought the dock had tried to eat him.

The jon boat floated with only a few inches of water in the bottom. As soon as he touched the outboard, he knew they were stuck on the island. He could feel the congestion, preventing the Mercury from drinking.

He confirmed his feeling through trial and error, finding the intakes mud-packed. The motor couldn't draw in water through the impeller, so they were stuck. He cursed quietly.

Russell gathered driftwood and broken boards, including shingles to start a bonfire. The wood was a little wet, but he finally ignited it by using handfuls of brown pine needles and gasoline from the boat. The driftwood caught, setting the shingles afire.

The thick black smoke stank and carried tarry ashes. The polluted cloud swept along the shore, cinders and ash drawn away on the balmy wind. He knew it might remind Redgraves of what had happened to his home in Killeen, but he didn't stop. Russell suggested fishing, but Redgraves just stared out at the lake. Finally, he sighed loudly and hefted himself afoot for a walk.

As if waiting for him to leave, the clouds broke, letting the sunshine through.

"Glorious sunshine," Kristie announced, cheerily popping out of the ruins. "Thank the Almighty." She broke into *Good Day Sunshine*. Russell could see why Scooter was crazy about her. With her song and the wonderful sunshine, Russell almost forgot their problems.

"You sound good."

"I'm alive and lively. How about you?" she drawled.

Russell envied her smooth, silky accent, the way she said 'you' sounded like yew.

"I'm glad the storm has passed, but I'm nervous about tonight. The m-motor doesn't work. We're s-stuck."

"That's not good news," she replied, rubbing her hands gently. She held them up for him to see. The bruises had spread, darkening to her finger tips. "How are yours?"

He showed off the bottom of his feet. They were yellow-bruised. "We were lucky." Russell mentioned nothing about having a sense about the motor's failure. People already thought he was crazy.

"I think we were blest. I don't know about you, but I have prayed for a way to protect myself against vampires. This could be an answer to our prayers."

He had made that plea and listened. Russell still waited for a reply. "How so?" he asked.

"Either we're lucky, or blessed for a reason." She looked around. "Have you seen CJ?"

"No, but his boat is still here. Kellen went for a walk. They might be together."

"Well, the island is tiny. I'm going to find them."

"S-separating is usually a b-bad idea."

As if from thin air, Flash appeared. The dog slid under her hand, then leaned against her leg, tail batting in constant cheer and defense. "Wonder dog, here, will protect me."

What could Russell say to that? "Well, oh, all right. If you're not back in ten minutes, I'm coming to look for you."

"Fine. Flash, let's go find CJ. All ya, all ya, in come free. Hide and seek is over," Kristie sang as the pair set off.

Trying not to worry, Russell kept building the fire. He made sure to stay out of the smoke, but it seemed to pursue him, intent on choking him.

A couple of minutes later, Scooter staggered out into

the smoke and sunshine. He coughed and rubbed his eyes. "Air. Sweet air. I can't believe I slept. Where's Kristie?! I thought I heard her scream! Oh, never mind, I hear her."

Russell strained his hearing, concentrating. He heard nothing. "She's out with Flash looking for CJ."

"And you let her go?"

"If I went looking for him, he would just hide. He might t-talk to Kristie. Flash is with her."

"Let's go find her. I don't trust this place," Scooter said as he looked around. "You've been busy and out to the boat, haven't you? Why . . . oh, no. We can't leave, can we? That's why you're setting up outside." His best friend was frightened. He abruptly stilled, then raced off. "Come on! Hurry!"

"What?" Russell had heard nothing.

Flash barked urgently. Kristie screamed.

Scooter sprinted like a greyhound. His best friend was one of the fastest kids in the county, having achieved his nickname by outracing a motorized scooter.

Kristie kept screaming.

Waving away the bugs, Russell arrived to find Scooter trying to pull Kristie out of the ground. She hung about waist deep, trying to get a foot out of the maw. It looked like the earth had swallowed her, then he realized she had just fallen in a hole. His imagination was running wild, almost as fast as Scooter's.

Working together, they lifted Kristie out, dragging fragment of boards along. The stench reminded Russell of his visit to the county morgue. She had fallen into crude graves. His father had said that decomposing bodies stank as badly as rotting fish.

"These graves weren't here a month ago. Dogs searched the island for bodies. I was here," Russell said.

Kristie shook. "I heard Flash barking. I wish I hadn't

looked, then I fell. Lord be merciful, those poor kids. I'm gonna be . . . ."

Scooter held her as she doubled over and spasmed, but managed to hang onto her guts. Eyes watering, she stood tall. Scooter guided her away, but left Flash as a bodyguard.

"Thanks for keeping me company," Russell said. What would his dad do? Investigate and discover the truth. Did he ever get the willies?

Russell smeared some eucalyptus and aloe lip balm under his nostrils, then he pulled a bandana from his back pocket and held it over his nose and mouth. He steeled himself, realizing there might be someone he knew.

With a booted toe, he flipped over the board to open it like a casket lid, revealing a grave. The eye-watering stench almost overwhelmed him, making him stagger back. He kept a tight grip on his stomach and clamped down on his throat. If it hadn't been for the awful photographs from his emergency class, he would have hurled.

Above the corpses, the air seemed to dance and writhe with the no-see-ums and other swarming Texas-sized bugs. He fought down his gorge and tried to study the five bodies in a detached way, more like a mechanic, noting their clothes, hair color and gender. He forced himself to look for ID and medical alert tags.

He found no bracelets, but each had twin holes in their necks along the carotid artery, the vessel that took blood to the brain. The deep slashes on their wrists left dried blood scars.

Like a vision, the image swept down on him. Redgraves played with his knife and the look in his eyes. It reminded him of Racquel when his sister talked about suicide. He had heard the same in Redgraves' poor-me attitude.

Suddenly certain that Redgraves was going to kill himself, Russell sprinted flat out. He caught his friends as they reached the shore. Scooter yelled after him.

In the dying light, taking on a bloodied crimson and battered purple, the ruins seemed to gather the darkness and smoke around it. Rushing against death, Russell sped by the fire. Anger drove him. Suicide was stupid. He hoped he wasn't too late.

He burst through the tarp just as Redgraves ran the blade along his wrist. Blood welled from the slash. "Ow! Damn that hurts! No wonder people blow their brains out!"

Russell kicked Redgraves' arm. His large Bowie Pocket knife flew out of his hand. "You need help, Kellen," Russell said. Could this place have triggered his death wish?

"Why did you do that? I want to die!" Redgraves sprawled on his knees. Blood dripped onto the wooden floor. It soaked up his sacrifice, leaving a dry stain.

"You might want to right now, but you probably won't the day after tomorrow!"

"What's happening?" Scooter asked, rushing in.

"Redgraves almost made a huge m-mistake."

The suicidal boy curled up and wept. "I can't even kill myself without screwing up. Failing sucks. Living sucks."

Kristie immediately grabbed the first aid kit. She placed a bandage across his cut. She stanched the oozing blood with a 4x4 gauze pad, then wrapped white cling around to hold it.

Russell closed the knife and pocketed his Bowie Special. Would he get in trouble since Redgraves had used it to try and kill himself? It had cleaned lots of fish, and he would miss it, if it was confiscated. He coughed, tasting ash and a rotting foulness worse than fish dying in the sun. "I think we should drag him out of here. The smoke might be affecting us all."

They agreed and worked together to guide the heavyset boy outside. He felt pity for Kellen Redgraves.

"How did you know?" Scooter asked him.

"He had the s-same look in his eyes as Racquel. All the dead bodies had slit wrists. I guess I just f-figured that this place would add to his despair."

"It's not safe on this island. We must tear this place down. Burn each and every piece, then watch it from a safe distance, preferably out on the water," Scooter urged.

"I was thinking the s-same t-thing until Kristie found the bodies. My father and the deputies will want to search for evidence. I'm going to t-tell CJ that. He can decide what to do."

"A forensics team already searched this place!"

"But they didn't find the bodies! You, a judge's grandson, should know better than to destroy evidence. I don't think this was here before. Do you?"

Scooter was unhappy, but he agreed, knowing better. "I guess you're right. But who are they going to convict? Your dad doesn't believe us. He thinks this was a small time gang-cult thing led by Garrett Brashear."

"It follows profile and rational," Russell replied, sounding so much like his dad he scared himself. Dad casually dismissed the thought of vampires. Men were monsters. Wild creatures didn't need to exist. "The murdering stopped as soon as Garrett and the Gunns were busted. What we told him was too far out for my dad. This time, there's proof: bodies with bite marks."

Scooter paled, and Russell knew how he felt. Nothing seemed as carefree, and each day seemed short. Nights stretched intolerably long.

"There, that should do it. Would you like a sling?" Kristie made a cloth support out of triangular bandages.

"I don't want to live! My life is like a bad movie, the lowest grossing movie of all time. I want to be pirate-worthy!"

"Kellen, why do you want to die?" Kristie asked.

"There's nothing to live for. My mom's dead, and so's my old man. And my brother, Karl, was the one I went to movies with all the time. The fire took them! I thought Karl was behind me, but I am such a screw up! When I turned to go back in, a fireman grabbed me. I should have gone straight to my parents room!"

"Then nobody would remember them and honor their lives. That's up to you now," Russell said. He had attended too many funerals.

"You were born in your parents' and the Almighty's likeness. What you do still reflects on them," Kristie said. She cocked her head and examined his other hand, finding a small round wound. "What happened to your finger?"

"I don't know."

The air inside had cleared, so Russell went back inside and searched CJ's bedding. He found a diamond lapel stick pin. The sharp point was bloodied. Had Redgraves stuck himself, then decided to commit suicide?

"So we're stranded here?" Scooter groaned.

"Until rescued."

"This place inspires nightmares." He shuddered.

"I know. The c-curse of Shade lingers here. It seemed to me the s-shack and dock are shaped differently from the last t-time I was here. It's almost like it c-can move on its own."

"Animated?" Scooter squeaked. "That's crazy." Russell didn't like the word, so he glared. "Sorry. No crazier than vampires," he apologized as he fed the fire. "Won't your father be upset?"

"Dad will forgive me, eventually."

"The bonfire will make a great signal. That's a perfect excuse to burn this place!" Scooter laughed. They halfheartedly high-fived. "You don't look quite right."

"To be honest, I haven't felt right since we were hit by

lightning. I feel . . . wired, like I drank a six pack of Mountain Dew along with a package of Oreos," he replied. They had done that to stay up late to watch creature double features on the Sci-Fi Channel.

"How are we going to get off this island? Do you think we can row to shore?" Scooter asked.

Russell walked outside, onto the dock to draw in the fresh air. Across the flat plane of green water, he could see green and red boat lights coming toward them. The distant whine of a motor grew louder.

Hopping gaps in the planks, Russell reached their boat. He unpacked the binoculars and looked across the water. He expected to see lights identifying it as the sheriff's cruiser, but it remained dark except for its stern and aft lights.

"Who is this?" Scooter asked.

"I don't know. But it isn't a sheriff's boat," Russell replied. If it wasn't his dad, who might it be?

FOUR

THE EX-DIRECTOR

The boat sped directly toward Scooter. Still shaky, Kristie joined them upwind of the toxic bonfire.

The firelight's red-orange blaze gleamed luridly off the stern railing and its white hull. The cruiser abruptly slowed, the bow rising. Swampy waves washed onto the muddy shore, just before the v-hull ramped onto land. Scooter didn't recognize the craft, but it looked like a twenty footer, a bow rider, almost new with a canopy.

Someone jumped into the water, landing mid-shin deep. The figure wore all black. Due to his luminous and pallid skin, Marcus Chandler seemed disembodied—a floating head and ghostly hands. Both were scarred from a fire.

Scooter was thrilled to see his writing mentor. His elderly friend had a knack for timely, even heroic rescues.

Kristie breathed a sigh of relief and ran to hug him.

"Well, hello, Kristie! Scooter and Russell. Wow, what have you been eating? Big pills?" he asked. Russell blushed. "You didn't, perhaps, feel summoned or drawn, did you?"

Marcus now believed in vampires and the supernatural. Mr. Lucius Shade had wanted the retired director of Hollywood horror films to make a biography of his undead life. The vampire had threatened Scooter, hoping it would convince Chandler to make big screen pictures again.

Way too many mistakenly believed Marcus was a

vampire. All here, except the Intruder, knew better. Flash counted Marcus as a friend. That was a high enough recommendation. The old guy had even risked his life to save Judge Grandpa.

"No. We were driven here by a storm. Now our motor won't start," Scooter replied.

"Then it's a good thing I decided to come out. I waited for it to rain, so the whole island doesn't go up in flames."

"Excuse me, Marcus. Do you have a phone or a radio? Kellen is hurt and needs medical attention," Kristie said.

Except for the burn scars, Marcus and the Intruder looked like time-lapsed versions of each other. Both were bone pale, nearly translucent. In the bright firelight, their albino eyes blazed an even brighter red. Upon seeing the Intruder, Scooter's mentor had the look of a man who had been in a foreign country for a long time and had just met someone from his homeland. He smiled friendly, then he pulled out his cellphone. "What should I tell them is wrong?"

She hesitated, so Russell stepped in. "A deep wrist laceration. We stopped the bleeding, but he's lost a lot of blood and probably needs stitches."

"Where's your phone?" he asked Scooter.

"It's dead. Funny, huh?"

"We think we were hit by lightning," Russell said.

Marcus studied them. "Then you may all be in need of immediate medical care. Anyone feel strange or ill?"

"I always feel strange on this island," Scooter replied. He didn't feel like talking about his heightened senses, or his newfound awareness of Flash. Marcus smelled of gasoline.

"I sense . . . hopelessness," Kristie whispered.

Without any more questions, Marcus dialed 911. He gave his name, location, and what was going on. After listening, he said, "The paramedics will meet us at the Pickup Ranch. Your father is on a boat, but we can be there before he can get here."

"Who's the dispatcher?" Russell asked.

"Here," Marcus said, handing off the phone. When he approached the Intruder, the boy just stared at him.

"Hello, Kellen, I'm Marcus Chandler."

"You look like me, related to the Grim Reaper in *Bill and Ted's Bogus Adventure*. Are you sick, too?" Marcus nodded. "Do you have porphyria?"

"No. I have vitiligo. Porphyria and vitiligo are similar in ways. And as you can see, I have lived with it for quite some time, and quite well, despite the recent harrowing events. Here, let me help you up," Marcus said. He stuck out a hand, pulling the new boy to his feet.

"Thanks. I have done a buttload more today than I usually do in a week," the Intruder said.

Scooter hadn't thought of that. It might explain why the Intruder was tired and grumpy.

"It's good to get out, especially at night. Although it's cold in winter, I like it because I can be out earlier since the days are shorter. Are you ready for a boat ride?" Marcus asked.

"As long as you're not going *Overboard*."

"I can tell you like movies. Well, so do I," Marcus said.

The Intruder smiled in such a genuine fashion that he looked like an entirely different person. It unnerved Scooter, perhaps because it transformed the new boy. Marcus had learned more about him than the rest of them had during the entire day. An inexplicable jealousy welled within him.

After Shade, Scooter found it almost impossible not to be wary of newcomers, and in some ways, those who were different. He tried to believe he disliked the Intruder because of what he had done, not because of what

Redgraves looked like. At least he wasn't frightened of his lack of pigment and red-pink eyes, as he would have been if he hadn't already known Marcus.

Scooter wouldn't be surprised if the Intruder was tainted by Shade's curse. His aura shared a lot in common with CJ's aura. Marcus had been stained, too, along with Russell and himself. Although, now that Scooter scrutinized everybody, he realized that neither Russell or Kristie looked tainted anymore. Had the lightning cleansed them?

"Scooter, is anyone else with you?" Marcus asked.

"CJ Mochrie is hiding somewhere," Scooter replied, gesturing helplessly everywhere. He quietly explained about the younger Mochrie's abusive home life and suspicions.

"A monster?" Marcus asked, concerned and jumping to the same conclusion. They had talked before about assuming the worst. Marcus, like Judge Grandpa, cautioned him not to presume someone was lesser because they looked unusual. "What kind?"

"A Bible thumper," Kristie replied tightly.

"Yes, dad. We found five bodies," Russell continued talking on the phone. "Kind of in the middle, in a clear area."

"You found bodies here?" Marcus asked, crestfallen.

Kristie nodded, unable to find the words.

"Shade has returned, or there's another vampire. Or somebody who thinks they are a bloodsucker is killing kids. It doesn't matter right now. We must get off this island! The longer we're here, the more bodies I'm afraid that Sheriff Knight will find when he gets here," Scooter said.

"Let's go," Russell said as he returned Marcus' phone. "Dad said to leave CJ to them. He might be armed."

"CJ! It's Marcus Chandler! It's dangerous here. I'll tow your canoe and drop you off anywhere between here and my ranch!" He waited for a reply, giving CJ half a minute, then he turned to them. "Let's cast off in The Muse, my almost new Stingray 220 LX. It replaces my old Baja. Silverscreen wasn't designed as a battering ram, but it did a great job."

Kristie blushed.

They shoveled mud onto the coals, stirred, and left. Scooter and Russell pushed the red and white boat to no avail. "You're stuck. You came in too fast," Scooter said.

"I know. The gear shift is stiff and tricky. That's my story, and I'm sticking to it," he laughed lightly. "It's gonna take all of us to get off this island. Are you willing, Kellen?"

The Intruder was stronger than he looked, but Marcus had firmly beached the boat. When Kristie hopped out and shoved, too, Scooter thought they would move it, but it remained stuck.

"We might as well leave the fuel. I was planning on torching the shack," Marcus said. "I apologize for taking the law in my hands. I'm willing to pay the fine to sleep easier."

Scooter smiled wryly and gave his buddy the thumbs up. That's why his mentor stank of fuel. "We'll have to wait. It's become a place of evidence again," Russell said.

They set up a fire brigade to unload four 2-gallon plastic jugs of gasoline. With everyone out and pushing, they managed to inch the Stingray 220 LX off shore. Scooter swam in the warm, green water to turn the boat around, then he climbed up the stern ladder.

"So you were planning on burning the shack to the ground," the Intruder said. "Why?"

"It was a monster's lair."

"You believe that, too? I thought they were trying to scare me with that vampire B.S.," the Intruder replied.

"Believe them. I am not afraid of dying, but I was

frightened for my immortal soul. In fact, I still am. Vampires like to torment the living, much as a cat plays with its food."

"It sounds like a cool movie," the Intruder said cheerily.

"Perhaps. Today there are many who would like to see the vampires win. Perhaps the American Civil Liberties Union would get involved, calling for legislation to protect them from 'hate crimes'," Marcus said, sounding bitter. "Be that as it may, Kellen, it takes far more than a good story to make a good movie."

"It does? Like what?"

"Memorable characters set in conflict with powerful themes. Some action, adventure, mystery and romance. An intriguing setting. Those kinds of things."

"That sounds cool."

"Thank you. I think it's cool, too, neato and groovy. Scooter, what's the job of a writer?" Marcus quizzed him.

"To create memorable characters and put them in conflict and under duress."

"Why's that?" the Intruder wondered.

Marcus stared at Scooter, so he would answer. "So we find out what they're made out of by testing their mettle."

"Well said. That's true about our lives. We are the main character in our own stories. What we do can affect other people's stories."

"*It's a Wonderful Life?* I didn't think his life was that great. He had a bum ear, and he didn't get to chase his dreams."

"You could look at it that way. Scooter, how is your grandfather?" Marcus asked kindly.

"Recovering slowly."

"We're old. It takes a lot longer than for you young bucks. I can remember when a skinned knee healed in a day or two. Now it takes a month," Marcus replied. "Russell, would you like to drive? I want to chat."

"Of course! Ow!" Russell cried. He hopped up, digging

frantically into his pants pocket. As though it were red hot, he tossed his bandana on the floor. A golden needle tumbled out.

"What's that?" Scooter asked.

"A stickpin I found in the shack, in CJ's bedding." Russell checked his leg. "I'm bleeding."

Anything of Shade's that drew blood was reason for concern. They all knew it.

"Did you poke your finger with that?" Kristie asked Redgraves. The Intruder looked puzzled, then he gazed at his hands. Marcus turned on the cabin lights. The diamond stickpin winked wickedly.

"You took evidence, after telling me not to burn the place down because your father would want to search it! What's that all about?" Scooter pointed.

"Toss it overboard," Kristie shivered.

Flash barked, then wagged doggy encouragement.

"I can't. As you said, it's evidence. I took it because I was concerned it wouldn't be there later," Russell continued.

What if it's cursed? Scooter almost said, biting his lip.

Russell and Marcus traded spots. The Incredible Bulk dwarfed the wheel. He jumped up as soon as he sat in the driver's seat. "Yeow! It shocked me!"

"I'm glad that we unloaded the gasoline. It can explode in such situations. Something like that happened on a set of *Night of the Unliving*."

"That was a great movie!" the Intruder gushed.

Russell touched the wheel. When nothing happened, he sat down and resettled. His eyes closed fractionally and something about him seemed to change.

Helmsman Russell turned the key. Nothing happened. He frowned and tried again. On the third twist, the engine turned over, caught and started. "There we go. Hang on."

The bow rose as they roared away. The nose slowly lowered as they sped to plane flatly across the glassy lake. What a difference a few hours could make.

"You're quiet," Kristie told him.

"I'm glad we're finally leaving the island behind," Scooter replied. He gently took her hand. "Since I heard you scream, well, I haven't been thinking straight."

She squeezed his hand. "Those poor kids. How horrible!" She closed her eyes, tears streaking her cheeks. "This summer makes me question everything. I still wonder why some of us lived and others died."

"I talked to Judge Grandpa about it. He says that's human nature. It's called survivor's guilt."

"My father says I am looking at the event with human eyes, and thinking with human thoughts. He says if I keep praying and reflecting, spiritual guidance will come to me."

"Hey!" Scooter cried. Flash jumped into his lap and sprang off his chest. The golden Lab snapped at something.

Scooter felt it at the last moment and ducked. His hair was snagged and some of it yanked out. "Ow!"

A chill swept across the boat, jolting everybody. "Brr! What was that?" Kristie asked.

Scooter followed his dog's pointing. Flash fixated on a winged creature darker than the starless night.

Everyone in the boat was alive, their radiance illuminating the night. Whatever had strafed him was lifeless.

"Where did that chill come from?" Marcus asked. Everyone shuddered in a visceral reaction.

"Flash saw a vampire," Scooter replied. His words invoked a nervous, fear-laden quiet. Only one thing Scooter knew fit such a description, a vampire turned giant monster bat. "I think I did, too. It reminded me of the thing that chased us across the lake."

"We are in peril. Flash knows vampires. Remain wary, pray for CJ, and keep your crosses handy," Marcus told them.

Russell throttled up, and the boat raced across the star and moonlit sky mirrored in the placid water. Scooter felt hunted, an unpleasant sensation he'd had before. The clouds seemed to take on winged shapes that stared down and stalked them. Crescent points down like teeth, the moon peered out from between the clouds.

"Shade?" Kristie whispered.

"I don't know. But I don't see how. I saw him fall to ash. Will you sing a song to lift our spirits?" Scooter asked.

She radiated light and love. The lightning had touched Kristie's voice, making it golden, evoking strong emotions with every song. Her inner beauty was expressed through her dazzling voice. When she took his hands, despite the weariness of the day, Scooter felt reinvigorated.

He avoided thinking about caring too much for her. She was almost family, more than a friend and yet even more.

Kristie blessed them, singing all the way to the Pickup Ranch dock. The roofed stall and lone pier sat west of the dam. A single sentinel waited, a lovable black dog named Beauty, although she looked like a pointy-eared devil dog. Marcus had selected her from the pound. Beauty ran, her tail wagging her entire body.

Taking the binoculars in hand, Scooter surveyed the Pickup Ranch. Everything looked normal, if one discounted the front-end buried pickups surrounding the shoreline ranch in a semicircular fence of trucks. He saw no vampires in hiding, but then they usually found you first.

"Keep your crosses handy," Scooter said.

Despite the Intruder's help, the docking went smoothly. Marcus let Russell steer them into the hanging straps attached to the overhead winch. Scooter hopped onto the dock, rubbed on Beauty, and then he flipped the lever up, setting the cable spinning around an axle as the winch drew up the sling straps cradling the boat.

"No vampires, yet," Russell said. "Race you dogs!" With a challenging cry, he ran with Flash and Beauty to Marcus' new pickup truck. The duel-wheeled white, one-ton Ford replaced the red Dodge destroyed in the lynching. Marcus reached the truck last, taking over the driver's seat from Russell, who had started it.

"Why are the pickups like that?" the Intruder asked loudly over the bellowed croaking of the frogs.

"My father was odd for a rancher, which is probably why I ended up a strange geezer. He said he wanted to have a visible history of the truck, one of the main staples of ranch life in Texas. That along with a fishing pole and hunting rifle. Frankly, I think he wanted to do a workman's version of the Cadillac Ranch."

"Then it isn't some kind of barrier against vampires?" the Intruder asked.

"If so, it doesn't work," Russell said.

"This place was built long before all the intrusions. My father dug two of the ponds. I named the larger one Thomas' pond after him. It's the best for fishing, especially brim and blue gill," Marcus said. In the moonlight, the ponds gleamed like watery eyes staring out from the earthen facade.

Inside the pickups, split rail fences ran to and beyond a wide, one-story ranch house with a front-screened porch and a stout chimney. The fences continued on past a garden to the barn and its lone star weather vane, chicken coop, and green-metal horse corral. A single light fell on the front of the barn and its door, still in need of a final coat of paint to cover the streaky red with white.

The last time they had driven in from the boat dock,

their truck had been mobbed. Frightened people driven by the Gunns had nearly hung Marcus. Nobody was here tonight, but that didn't mean it was deserted.

"I know a vampire is here," Scooter muttered.

They turned to park in the rear at the carport just off the garden. No outside lights were on, making the bone-white house a dimly distinct structure. It was easy to see into the kitchen through the large window and the open back door. The screen kept out a mob of frantic moths and mosquitos.

Marcus drove under the carport and parked. The driveway looked deserted when the motion sensor lights flicked on to flood the night. A swarm of moths swirled in the brilliance.

Scooter noticed the frogs and crickets had fallen silent. Flash snarled and lunged against the side window. A second later, Beauty joined him, acting frantic.

Scooter was almost paralyzed by dread, barely able to grip his cross amulet. He knew it! A vampire was here. It had probably circled around to follow them home.

The night was spiky and sharp. He could smell a horrible stink, worse than a dead skunk. A smoky tang, like a stale cigar, tried to sweeten the gut-twisting stench. He didn't see any glow of life to explain the light or the smell.

Russell futilely locked his door. "Let's get out of here!"

Scooter tried to calm his dog. "Flash! Quiet! I know! Thanks, boy. We all know now. Please, quiet down! I can't think!" His dog stopped barking, but every muscle quivered. His nose heaved, breathing hard. When Beauty kept barking, Flash nipped her to quiet her.

Marcus restarted the engine, then he turned to Russell. "When I get out, you take the wheel. Be ready to drive fast and far. Here's my cell phone."

"You're not going outside, are you?" Kristie asked.

Beyond concerned, she was frightened, now drawn and appearing ill. Scooter worried about her.

"This is my property, and I value my privacy. I want to know if someone is trespassing," Marcus said, then he rubbed his chin. "Who knows? It might be kids up to mischief. I might make some new friends like last time. Hey!" When he opened the door, Flash pushed by, darting out first, a golden blur followed by a black streak.

"Who's there? Show yourself!" Marcus shouted.

Scooter tried to hop out of the car. He eluded Kristie's grasp, but Russell snagged him, surprising him with his strength. "Not so fast. You're not going out there."

"I am not leaving my dog."

"And I'm not leaving you," Russell said. With his other hand, he grabbed his backpack. "Kristie, you drive."

"Oh, all right. How come I'm always left to drive?"

"I was left last time," Russell snapped. Opening his backpack, he withdrew mirrored glasses and put them on.

"Well, I'm staying here! I'll drive like I'm a stuntman in *Fast and Furious*, or *Gone in Sixty Seconds*. You can bet I'll be gone a lot faster than that," the Intruder rambled on.

Kristie slid into the driver's seat. Scooter knew she wouldn't hesitate to flatten a monster.

FIVE

THE DARK BEAUTY RETURNS

From the cover of a big tree he'd climbed, CJ watched the boat leave. Good riddance, do-gooders. After he was sure they were gone, he climbed down and jogged to his canoe. He uncovered it and hauled it to the water's edge, readying his escape. He should be able to slip away under the cover of darkness. Chances were minimal that anybody would run over him. He couldn't risk a light, not now that he was a hunted man.

He was certain Scooter and Russell would rat him out to the authorities. Kristie would feel it was her duty to find him help. She meant well, but she needed to live in the real world. Although, Calvin Jefferson wasn't sure what that was nowadays.

Just two months ago, he thought the world of his brother. Now he wanted nothing to do with his bro. BJ had deserted him several times, caring only for himself.

Wondering where to go next, CJ walked back to the shack. He had a feeling it was watching him. Sometimes the pills made him feel weird, but most of the time Ma's painkilling medicines helped with all his bruises.

When he entered the ruins, CJ noticed the chill, then he was startled by more company. She was back, almost sending him to his knees in worship of the most incredible woman he had ever seen. With a welcoming smile, the dark beauty slipped out of her clothes. Her pants slipped down with a whisper of promise, then Tai peeled off her shirt, exposing a super model's eye-popping figure in Victoria Secret underwear. Her black bikini strained as she glided to greet him. "Good evening, Calvin Jefferson. Have you forgotten me?"

"No, Tai." CJ knew he should run, but he couldn't, held helpless by her supernatural allure and the promise in her voice. He could think only about wanting her to touch him, kiss him, and more, making him sweaty and willing. Yet, even if he wanted to let his gaze roam her body, he couldn't pull his attention from her eyes. Nothing could describe them, except they seemed to be a deep, dark secret. She lavished a little attention on him, making him feel like he meant the world to her.

"They said you were dead."

"That is true, but then I am undead. It is time, CJ. For what they did to Lucius Shade, Gunstock must suffer. You, my lover, are going to help me."

CJ's heart was ready to explode from his chest. Had she said lover? Why had she ever left? It didn't matter. She was back, and he would do anything for her.

When she kissed him, nothing else mattered. He smelled lilies and tasted blood when she bit his lip, making him her servant, again.

SIX

THE UNDEAD REPORTER

A bone-shivering breeze sliced through the steamy summer night and bit into exposed flesh like a cold, sharp knife. Russell shivered violently, his teeth hurting.

At the edge of the floodlight's beam, an ice-pick thin figure stood aloof. He was clad in the blackest of suits, crowned with a fedora sporting a white feather. The stranger seemed to have appeared out of nowhere. The sudden travel left him smoking. "Good evening."

The visitor drew on his cigar, then exhaled a dragon-sized cloud. Russell noticed he wore gloves. The brim of his hat and its odd white feather kept his face in the shadow.

He just knew it had to be a vampire. The way the stranger invaded your space and made everything else seem unimportant but him was uncomfortably familiar. Russell would have shouted a warning, except his lips and tongue were quivering. It was worse than stuttering.

"Interesting collar you have there, Flash. Are you Marcus Chandler's ferocious guard dog?" It seemed there was nothing beneath the suit and hat but darkness with a voice.

The golden dog hunkered low and faced the strange visitor. Barking as he backed up showed the depth of his fear. Beauty stood quivering, keeping a safe distance.

"*Rest*. You are in no danger from me."

Flash sneered, then he snorted disbelief. Russell agreed. Fear had its hooks buried deep, making it difficult to breathe.

"Who are you? Why are you here?" Mr. C asked.

"Pardon the intrusion, Mr. Chandler. I am Will Ripley with the *L.A. Times*. I am pleased to meet you. I have seen all of your movies." He didn't step any closer or offer a hand in greeting, but he bowed his head in a gesture of respect.

"I still read the paper, and I don't recognize your name, Mr. Ripley. Are you with *The National Inquirer*?"

"I am an inquiring soul. Does that count?" Ripley replied. "I'm pleased to find you all together. It makes my job easier."

"You report on the rich and famous?" Scooter asked.

"I am an investigative reporter. Please, those of you in the car, *step out*," Ripley said. Forgetting he had promised to be gone in less than a minute, Redgraves hopped right out. Kristie hesitated, but she exited moments later.

Russell recognized the powerful, cajoling tone of voice. Scooter described it like that in *The Vampire Hunters Club*.

"I am looking for Lucius Shade. He sent me a note, saying there would be a big story here," Ripley sneered. The visitor reminded Russell a little of Racquel's beau, Garrett.

"Shade is gone," Mr. C said flatly.

"Is he?" Ripley asked, focusing on Scooter. "I thought you might have seen him as recently as tonight."

Mr. C stepped in. "About a month ago, he grew angry when I refused to make a biography of his life . . . so to speak. I told him I no longer direct feature films."

"You made movies! A director? Wow! That's too cool-rad-groovin' for words," Redgraves said.

"How angry was he? Lucius Shade isn't renowned for his patience," the reporter pressed.

"He kidnapped me. When I tried to escape, he got a serious sunburn," Scooter snapped. As much as Russell hated Shade, Scooter's loathing went deeper because his grandparents had nearly died when their house had burned.

Ripley's gaze lingered on Scooter. Russell remembered the vampire's hypnotic gaze. Eyes grew from the shadow, engorged and enlarging to dominate.

"I see. The hero is actually a heroine. Are you the vampire slayer?" Ripley turned his attention on Kristie. She stood her ground. "Such faith gives me chills," Ripley said. His attention passed over Redgraves but lingered on Russell, blinking as if bothered by the mirrored sunglasses, only to settle again on Kristie.

She reached for the cross hanging around her neck and came up with only a chain in hand. "I saved my friends. I was desperate." Kristie teetered. "Whoa. I don't feel so hot."

"Do you wish to be a vampire?" the reporter asked.

"What kind of crazy question is that?" Scooter asked. He hovered protectively about Kristie.

"I have read that you are self-styled vampire hunters."

"We're survivors," Scooter retorted.

"Dizzy. Scooter . . . ." Kristie murmured. She fell limp, and Scooter caught her.

"Stop whatever you're doing to her!" he pleaded.

Russell checked her breathing and pulse. Her heart beat too fast, but she didn't appear injured. And yet, with the lightning, who knew? She could just be suffering shock.

"Leave," Mr. C commanded.

"I have done nothing to harm you. I just ask questions."

"I don't believe you!" Scooter drew out his cross.

"Obviously. You have all been changed by your

experiences this summer, especially today. Your days and nights will be fascinating, in the Chinese sense of interesting times. That is why I will be watching you." With a swirl of his jacket, the vampire turned and disappeared, his feather lingering like doubt.

SEVEN

THE AUTHORITIES

"I don't think I like the sound of that," Russell said. He studied the others. Right now, they all appeared related to Mr. C and Redgraves, as white as cadavers. Russell was glad he'd had some medical training. Now he didn't feel so helpless, although all he could do for Kristie was treat her for shock.

"Let's get Kristie inside," Scooter said. "What do you think, boy? Was it similar to Shade?" His tail tucked close, Flash whined. "Ripley was a vampire," Scooter announced with certainty.

"I feel like I stepped into *The Twilight Zone*." Redgraves appeared unnerved but not shaken to the soul.

Mr. C held the back door open, inviting them in.

The storm door was layered in crosses welded together. The wooden door stood engraved and studded with iron crosses, just like every outside door. Russell could relate. His room's door and windows were similarly protected.

Using the art of old horror and Sci-Fi movies, Scooter had helped Marcus decorate. Looking a little like a metal version of the Michelin Man, Robby the Robot stood in the kitchen holding a tray of glasses and a bunch of napkins.

Russell heard a hum. He couldn't place it, as it seemed to be coming from all over, vibrating through the house.

Through the kitchen, Scooter carried Kristie down the

hall. He turned sideways to get past the old-fashioned Mummy and a scaled down version of the shiny silver robot from *The Day the Earth Stood Still*. It guarded Nirvana—the writer's name for the computer workroom. The posters along the wall came from scary movies.

"Did you know Ed Wood? Oh, I loved *White Death*." Redgraves rambled, reading on. *"The Fly, Frankenstein Meets the Wolfman, Attack of the 50 Foot Woman, and The Invasion of the Body Snatchers."* An egg-like pod sat on the floor next to the couch where Scooter laid Kristie.

Russell knelt next to her, then he rechecked her vitals. Her heart's rhythm pounded steadily and strong.

"Horror and crosses. They do seem to go together," Redgraves said. "Are you Catholic?"

"I no longer attend church. My presence disrupts the services. But my faith aids me here at home," Mr. C replied.

"You know you are always welcome at the community church," Scooter said.

"Do you have a light blanket?" Russell asked. He found paper and marked down her breathing and pulse numbers. "That will keep her warm."

"Here. When was the last time y'all ate?" Mr. C brought in a quilt, then headed for the kitchen.

Russell's stomach growled like a starving lion. The Mexican beans and Greenies made him hungry and thirsty.

Light flooded the kitchen and spilled into the hallway as Mr. C flipped a series of switches. "I heard that. I have tasty strawberries and a couple of cantaloupe. I'm afraid I don't have any Coke. Sweetened tea or lemonade?"

Russell's heart still raced, and he could hear a loud hum. Again he wished for last spring when it was just him, his best friends, a fishing pole, and a box of bottle rockets. He wanted to go back to before his home had become such a confusing place of predators lurking in shadows.

"Do you think the vampire did something to Kristie?" Scooter asked while he paced.

"Kristie could just have heat exhaustion, but we were struck by lighting," Russell said, staring at his burned hand.

Mr. C brought in fans. Scooter placed a cool damp rag on Kristie's forehead.

"I wonder why that vampire left us alone?" Russell asked.

"They can't just go around slaughtering everyone. It would alert the authorities," Mr. C replied.

"Why would someone be looking for Lucius Shade?" Scooter asked. "I don't know about you, but when the vampire stared at me, I thought about every time I've seen Shade, including tonight when I felt that cold, lifeless breeze."

"I wonder what he was after?" Mr. C asked.

"Come to think of it, he never did say he was a *friend* of Lucius Shade," Russell added. The more he thought about it, by the tone of Ripley's voice, he had a feeling they weren't kissing cousins. "He said he was an investigative reporter."

A brisk knock sounded from the front door. Through the windows, red and blue lights from an ambulance swirled down the hallway. Mr. C peered out, then threw the door wide open. "Come in, please."

"Bruce! Conchita!" Russell knew just about everyone who worked for the county around Lake Tawakoni. Bruce Harlan was big and quite hairy like a cuddly bear. He taught a first responder class at the community college. Russell had taken that course before sitting in on the EMT class.

"They say lightning struck near their boat, and they have the burns to prove it," Mr. C replied. "Kristie Candel passed out just a few minutes ago."

Bruce moved immediately to check on her. Scooter

answered his questions. "I'm going to bring in oxygen and a gurney," Bruce told his partner.

Conchita Rodriguez examined Russell. The stocky woman with the charmingly uneven smile was his mother's close friend. "Tell me about the lightning."

Russell relived it as he told it, the blinding fire raging through him. It had felt like falling into a hill of fire ants. Incredible pain, then the thunder had ended it, leaving an echo of burning, as though his muscles—all his flesh—had been stretched to the limit.

"I'm fine, Conchita. You might want to start with Kellen. He has a nasty cut," Russell said, finger-slashing at his wrist.

"Okay, but if you collapse on me, your mother might stop baking me key lime pies!" she said, then settled on her new patient. "Who are you, young man?"

"Kellen Redgraves. I just moved here from Killeen. I'm diabetic and suffer from Porphyria," he stammered as she took his hands, turning them palm up.

"And now lightning. You have some challenges," Conchita said. She palpitated the purple-black flesh. "Tell me about that cut on your wrist. How did that happen?"

"I'm sorry, I know this sounds strange, but I don't really know what came over me. I've been extremely sad. I thought being alive was more painful than being dead, but I couldn't stand the pain. Bill Paxson in *True Lies* is tougher than me."

"So you cut yourself?"

Head down, Kellen Redgraves wept as he nodded.

"Are you on any medication?"

"I missed my insulin shot this afternoon. But I took a Vicodin for my back pain."

Russell wished he hadn't mentioned the drugs. He had been undecided, because now they would be suspicious.

"I see. We have three passengers," Conchita told Bruce

as he returned with a gurney. "Kellen needs some guidance. I would like to take Russell to get examined, too."

A heavy knock on the kitchen door frame announced his father. He was a big man, a former A&M football standout. Stern and grim, he looked every bit the weary and wind-blown Lawman, as Racquel called him.

"Come in, Sheriff Knight," Mr. C said, opening the door to invite him in. The men shook hands.

"Since you returned, Mr. Chandler, I have been busier than a dog guarding a chicken coop." His dad was frustrated and upset. Even so, he gave his son a shoulder hug. "Bruce updated me. Are you all right, young man?"

"I'm okay, Dad."

They placed Kristie on a backboard and strapped her down. Conchita set up the face mask and oxygen tank. Scooter looked ready to weep. Russell couldn't think of anything to ease his suffering. He clapped his hand on his best friend's shoulder. "Hang in there." Together, they lifted her onto the rolling cart and followed it to the ambulance. Bruce slid her inside, then he ushered Redgraves to get in.

He paused next to Mr. C. "Uh, excuse me, sir. It was a pleasure to meet you. If there's room, could I join you and Scooter, please? I would love to learn about making films. I still have my dad's video camera. Please? All my life I have dreamed of making movies."

"I'll talk to your counselors," Mr. C said.

Russell glanced at Scooter. If he hadn't been concerned about Kristie, he would have been up in arms protesting.

EIGT

MEDICAL ATTENTION

While driving to the hospital, Dad asked them what happened. Russell and Scooter had to speak up over the windshield wipers while it rained. They took turns telling the tale, and neither mentioned Ripley. Their story lasted into Gunstock.

Thinking for some time after they were done co-narrating, his dad finally said, "Well, we have to be careful about making assumptions, but we can start with what we know. CJ was on that island, but we never found him or his canoe. We can assume he's hiding elsewhere. He doesn't want to be found, but we'll keep looking."

"I wish we had hogtied him," Russell said.

"Who found the bodies?"

"Flash, then Kristie," Scooter said.

"There were five, just like you said, a pair had these left on them." His dad pulled two crosses out of a pocket. "I recognized them as yours, Russell. You have been carrying them since you encountered Shade."

"I laid them there, hoping it might help their souls rest."

"Then I'm sure you noticed that they each had wounds on their neck, like a vampire had attacked them?" he asked. Russell nodded. "Their wrists had also been slit. Autopsies will tell us which killed them, but somebody either thinks they are a vampire, or wants us to believe one of the undead is at fault," his dad finished, shaking his head sadly.

"Redgraves would be dead if Russell hadn't gone charging in," Scooter finally said, speaking up for him. He really appreciated that Scooter reacted to his dad as his best friend's father rather than the High Sheriff of Bluff County.

"Good job, Russell. I know I can count on you to make a well thought out decision," Dad said.

He remained silent, basking in the praise. His dad was miserly in handing out compliments. It made Russell twist a little with guilt.

"If it hadn't been for Redgraves, this wouldn't have happened to Kristie," Scooter said. Anger crept into his words.

"Easy, Scooter. Before you start worrying, let's see what the doctors in ER have to say. Okay?" Dad said.

Russell hated seeing Scooter this way. Dad called on the radio, finding out Kristie was awake and alert.

"Well, that's good news. So much has been bad. Five dead kids. CJ running off. Our PE teacher involved with the Minutemen and hate crimes," Dad began. "Now we can add drug dealing."

Russell didn't want to hear it. He liked Mr. Martin, both as a teacher, and as a scout leader from years back. Since working out at the same Y.M.C.A., Mr. Martin had been very supportive in Russell empowering himself.

"Just too much bad news," Dad murmured.

Nobody had recovered from the last batch of deaths. Everybody around Gunstock felt they should have done more. None of the reporters would let anyone forget, especially Jimmy B. Little. He thought the High Sheriff could have done a better job, blaming his dad's decisions for the deaths.

"What do you boys think happened?"

"I think you really don't want to know what I think," Russell replied. He wondered what to tell him about Ripley.

"What is that supposed to mean?" his dad snapped.

"You don't believe us about Shade, but there are nine witnesses, ten if you count Flash."

"Russell, I know you are not lying to me. You never have before, so I don't have reason to disbelieve you."

Russell immediately felt better. "Thanks."

"I also know that life is a matter of perspectives and perceptions, including assumptions and worse, jumping to conclusions, and seeing what you wanted to see. In the Shade case, I have three distinctly different descriptions, including gender. I can't help but wonder if there were several people leading this Cult of the Vampire.

"I understand you two almost died. Almost dying is a traumatic experience, especially the first time. Every time I go to check on a suspicious car, or worse, get dispatched to a domestic dispute, I know it may be my last call. It makes you look at life differently."

Russell fumed, barely containing his frustration. You had to 'experience' a vampire to understand.

"Son, think about what happened to you from someone who wasn't there. Someone lacking an imagination. Or, better yet, a pragmatic person. Scooter's and Kristie's explanations are wild, and if I publicly believed them, it would open me to ridicule, which I could live with. That comes with leadership.

"But worse, it would cause a panic. That goes against the job and common sense. Lastly, along with conflicting eyewitness reports, there's no evidence."

Dad held up a hand to stall their protests. "I know someone scared y'all something terrible. It must have for Kristie to crash the boat into that cabin. It has changed y'all. Stolen your innocence, making you suspicious. I hate that."

"Who was suspicious first?" Russell countered. They had reluctantly consented to drug tests to prove they weren't under the influence of psychedelics. At moments like this, he would have liked to choke some sense into his dad.

"I'm sorry. Guilt by association with the Graveyard Armadillos. Did you see anybody else on the island?"

"Not there, but a reporter was at the Pickup Ranch. He said his name was Will Ripley with the *L.A. Times*," his best friend said. "He was dressed in an all black suit and dark hat with a white feather. His eyes were red and bloodshot."

"I'll check it out. I can believe that reporters are vampires."

Russell doubted that Dad would find anything. "I have something for you," he said as he unrolled the stickpin from the bandana. "Redgraves found it on the island. We remember Shade wearing it. I doubt you'll find anything, but . . . ."

"I'll have it examined and tested. Good work, junior detective."

At the Tawakoni Regional Hospital, they waited in separate rooms. Russell kept his cross handy. He would be ready if the vampires were bold, recalling some changed shape.

The examination rooms were spartan and plain, except for boxes of gloves, tissues, and a biohazard bag. A blood pressure machine hung from the wall, the cuff dangling. Posters displayed the human body, muscles in one and the skeleton in the other. They were similar to the posters covering up the Grateful Dead on his walls. He only recollected for a moment on how a vampire had altered his life.

Again, a loud hum affected Russell's hearing. He had noticed it from the moment he walked through the electric door. Tinnitus was a ringing of the ears.

He paced, not wanting to be here. He feared what the tests might show. He hadn't expected to get examined so soon.

Russell waited another minute, then he peeked out the door. The hall was empty. As he stepped out, another door opened. Scooter joined him. They had called his grandparents to convince him to be examined.

"Do you know where they took Kristie?"

"What are you boys doing out?" Nurse Gabby asked.

"I am getting claustrophobic, and I'm worried about Kristie," Scooter snapped.

"I don't know anything specific about Ms. Candel, but unlike you, she is resting comfortably. Now, go back inside your rooms and stay there. The doctor has ordered tests. Russell, your mother is on the way. I'll be coming back soon to draw blood, and you should hope I'm in a gentler mood by then."

"I've been trying to avoid having my blood taken all night," Scooter jested.

It was just like his best friend to turn a phrase. Russell cracked up, laughing so hard he could barely stand. They supported each other during the laughing fit.

Nurse Gabriella had no idea and looked at them in disbelief, then she left in a huff.

"I bet the shots are going to hurt," Russell finally said. His laugh was somewhat forced and uneasy. The blood test might embarrass his dad. Perhaps he could blame it on the lightning.

"No more than you deserve," said a familiar voice as a nearby door opened. CJ's brother stood there, staring down on them, acting superior despite appearing ill. BJ's blue eyes were narrowed in pain. His rodeo good looks had faded, his flesh gray and his blond hair white. Byron Jefferson Mochrie perspired profusely, so he loosened his silly-looking bow tie.

"BJ, are you all right?" Russell asked. He was shocked to see him, both here and in his condition.

"When you walk with God, you are always all right," he replied, sounding like a complete stranger. Even his voice was different, deeper. His arrogance over his girl-attracting looks seemed to have changed into a vest of self-righteousness.

BJ's eyes were abnormal, the pupils constricted. Russell was reminded of a trapped animal, then he remembered CJ's words. His brother was possessed. Then he fell back on his recent emergency training. "Do you feel a sense of doom?"

"Since you put it so well, yes," BJ said. His knees gave way. They caught him before he could fall. Groping to lean on the wall, he shook free of them. "I don't need help. I've got God."

Russell could hardly believe his ears. This was not the Byron Jefferson of the Graveyard Armadillos. When he collapsed again, Russell caught him.

"Do you have something for my headache? I feel like someone is pounding on my skull, trying to get out."

"Well! I thought I told y'all to go back to your rooms," Nurse Gabby began, then she saw BJ. She rushed to their side, helping them carry him to an examination table. Russell feared that what was wrong with BJ couldn't be examined. He also worried about what they would find when the doctors looked over his lab work.

A flash of lightning, the hospital shaking, and the lights flickering awakened him. He wasn't alone.

The thunder sounded like an introduction. A dark figure stood quietly in the dimly lit examination room. Someone had turned off the lights, leaving a thin illumination coming from under the door. For a moment,

Russell thought Shade had returned as Tai, the woman that BJ and CJ remembered. He fumbled with his cross.

"Hello, little brother. Still having childish nightmares?" Although her voice had changed, he recognized the scornful tone of his sister. Usually Racquel just sat in a dark room, depressed over Garrett. "You shouldn't have gone boating. I told you so."

"Yep, you told me so. What do you want?"

In the darkness, her eyes grew more luminous with curiosity like a cat's. She studied him as though having him under a paw, then she said, "You went back to Shade's island, didn't you?"

"We had a man-made disaster—Kellen Redgraves— with us, and we ran into a storm that made us seek shelter."

"Man-made, natural and supernatural disasters. What an interesting day. Did you see Tai?" Racquel studied his eyes, getting nose-to-nose close. Her expression of scrutiny unnerved him. "Yes, you saw her all right."

"Enough!" Russell held back a blow, furious at her. She had no right to treat him like that. Fighting his anger, he grabbed her wrists. Just a month past, he would never have been this brave. He loved his sister, but he didn't trust her.

"You are stronger, but the fear in your eyes is telling," she said. Her eyes widened, hope bright in her eyes. "She will free Garrett soon. I must be ready and look my best when he comes for me!" Combing her hair with her fingers, she rushed out of the room as if she were going to immediately put on midnight make-up. "He's up."

Mother followed in Racquel's wake. Upon seeing Russell awake, she smiled. "You look all right. Your papa is worried."

"He was worried about me before this."

"Mamas and papas often fret over their kids."

"It's more than that. He doesn't believe us about the vampire."

Mama patted him on the shoulder. "Your father is a loving but practical man. He knows something terrible was done to you, and it bothers him that he hasn't caught the perpetrator." She squeezed his shoulder. "He has no idea how to catch a vampire, so he is trying to find a real world explanation."

"Do you believe me?"

"Russell, I believe you saw a monster. I find it hard to believe there are creatures more monstrous than kidnappers, murderers, racists and rapists. We already have terrorists, tyrants, and serial killers. That's why we need more loving parents and honest officers than exorcists and Men In Black. What matters is that someone harmed you."

Russell felt like he was trying to describe colors to a blind man. "Then you don't really believe me."

"Dear heart, in Mexico, we have a day to celebrate the dead. It is much different than Halloween. I believe in spirits as a part of everyday life. There are evil spirits, and good ones, too, like Mama Q, blessed Mary watch over her soul."

"I'm only half of that land, Mom," Russell replied.

"I know. And as you say, we live here, so speak English. But my belief in spirits doesn't change just because the language and culture is different," she said.

"Hello, Maria. You're just in time for his EKG," Nurse Gabby said as she rolled a device in on a cart.

The sticky glop was cold, even before she pinched the electrodes to his bare chest. When she turned on the monitor, he felt an electrostatic shock all over, making his hair rise. It tickled mostly, but hurt a bit as it surged off his nose, ears, and fingers. The Electrocardiogram monitor blinked, then the machine went blank. "Am I still alive?" he asked.

"When did you get a smart-mouth?" the nurse asked.

"I picked it up hanging around writers, mechanics, and emergency personnel."

Nurse Gabby's chuckle was short lived, because hitting the reset button changed nothing. She was going to get help when Russell touched the EKG machine, and it came on.

The humming was the electricity. He could hear it and feel it sizzle on the air. He wouldn't be surprised if his test results came back abnormally weird. Perhaps it would help him keep his secret.

NINE

A VISIT TO THE VET

Feeling relieved and yet guilty, Scooter trudged out of the hospital. He was mad they hadn't let him see Kristie. Despite this, he kept in mind Ripley's words and stayed alert for vampires.

He inhaled the muggy night air, taking in the rain and pine-scented breeze. Scooter felt Flash coming, splashing through the puddles with clumps of cottonwood seeds.

His wonder dog tiptoed to greet him on tender paws. Flash always made him feel safer. To answer his look, Scooter said, "Russell and Kristie are doing all right. They are going to stay here tonight. Okay?"

Flash nodded, then, despite sore paws, he galloped about. Scooter examined his dog's aura, finding it entangled with his own. "How do you feel? Should we call Dr. Daniels?"

"It's already arranged. He promised to meet us there, now," Judge Grandpa said. His favorite grandfather squinted at his watch, then he resettled his spectacles.

"Excuse me! Aren't you Jonathan 'Scooter' Keyshawn, one of the Vampire Hunters?" Jimmy B. Little asked. The reporter wore coke-bottle glasses and a smile that made you sick the second time you saw it. Unfortunately, they had encountered the stout and rumpled representative from the *Dallas Daily*. The jittery reporter wore a white suit, matching hat, and bright tennis shoes. As if he were always on the run, he perspired profusely.

"Were you out fishing with Russell Knight and Kristie Candel? Or hunting vampires? I heard you were out on an island and somebody tried to commit suicide," he said.

"That's wrong. Lightning hit the water near our boat."

"Hey, that's a great headline. *Vampire Hunters Survive Lightning*," Little said as he gestured.

Scooter disliked the name the reporter had given them. "My dog has a vet appointment. Good-bye."

They ignored Little's questions all the way to Judge Grandpa's white Buick. He started it remotely, hurrying along to escape the parasitic reporter. They drove off, ignoring the questions he shouted.

"Are you all right, Jonathan?"

"Just worried, Grandpa."

"Never enough worries, are there, that we can't create more? The reason worry kills more people than work is because more people worry than work."

"If it's true, then you will live a long time."

"Thank you." Judge Grandpa patted him on the back and chuckled heartily. When he did, his blue eyes twinkled, and he looked a little like Santa Claus, if you looked past the burn scars, taking them for wrinkles. He was much skinnier now, like St. Nick on the Atkin's Diet.

"You know, in stories, the bad guys can be stopped and the threat ended. In real life, it just goes on and on."

"That's a rather pessimistic point of view. I've seen civilization and reason triumph often enough to remain a believer that we can stagger forward," Grandpa said.

"I don't know. Marcus said that deep down, people aren't much different now, mentally and emotionally, than they were three thousand years ago. The town gossip now has a job as a reporter."

"What were you talking about?"

"Characters and characterization and how to make them seem realistic and relatable."

"Well, there's a lot of truth in what he says. Are you sure you feel all right?"

"I don't think I'll ever feel all right again," Scooter said. While he petted his dog, he just stared out the window. A month ago, they had driven this same route.

The wound on his neck had disappeared. That's why he had been certain Shade was destroyed. On everybody the vampire had bitten, its mark had faded to nothing. Although he still felt tainted, he didn't feel controlled like a puppet.

Scooter was starting to believe he had made a wrong assumption. "Do you believe me about Shade?"

"As I've said, I remember very little about that night."

"But you saw him! He tried to kill you and Grandma."

"I don't think you're lying to me. I just don't recall much. It could be so horrible that I can't remember. My memory needs upgrading."

"Sheriff Knight doesn't believe us," Scooter said. If his grandpa didn't believe him about that, there was no reason to tell him about seeing auras, or his unusually close connection with Flash.

"He doesn't believe because the witnesses contradict each other. Many times people see the same thing and describe it differently. They make quick assumptions, then become sure of them. As a judge, I'm not allowed to assume anything, except that the defendant is innocent unless proven otherwise. We are required to rule on evidence and facts."

"What if we can't get the facts?"

"Don't take it to court and expect to win. And even if you have facts, there is always someone who will dispute or spin them. Was it Mr. Shade or the lynch mob that made you pessimistic?" his grandfather asked.

"I had higher expectations of adults, that's all."

"That's all? You should have high expectations of adults. Just don't expect them to be heroic or altruistic."

"I think I'll lower my expectations."

"That is sad, my boy. I hope it doesn't lower your expectations for yourself," he said.

Scooter remained quiet.

"It is very, very difficult to do the right things when other people see them as wrong from their perspective. There was a time when nobody interfered with the right of a parent to beat their children as discipline. We don't allow that, or slavery anymore. Things are better, but we're still human and selfish. But it would never improve if good men despair and lower their expectations. If you have to be like anybody, be like Flash."

The golden dog softly howled in agreement.

"Once again the voice of reason has spoken," Judge Grandpa joked. "Just remember, a few rotten blueberries don't spoil the whole bunch. Just pick them out."

"Grandpa, have you ever wanted to break the law?"

"Yes, I would dearly love to speed."

"Really?" Scooter asked, surprised.

"Sure. But I drive extra carefully for you. So, are you talking about big breaks, or in the rule-bending category?"

"I want to burn the ruined shack on the island."

"Oh, my. That wouldn't be a good idea because it's a crime scene. Why do you want to burn it down?"

"There is a curse there that keeps hurting people and ruining lives," he replied honestly, despite knowing it sounded inane.

"I see. That's not enough for a court of law."

"I know. I think the shack draws like to it," Scooter persisted. He looked out, wondering where Ripley might be? It could be flying right above them, out of reach of Flash's senses.

"An unsavory element?" Judge Grandpa asked. Scooter nodded. "Well, we can readdress this issue when it's no longer a site of evidence. It might become a public nuisance, bringing thrill-seekers to the place."

"By then it might be too late. There's just so much I don't understand," he finally mumbled as he scratched.

"Well, you either believe people are innately good, or basically bad, and go from there."

"Marcus said the same."

"Did he now? He has an outstanding mind. Most people don't know it, but a long time ago he did a lot for this town. You should look into it some time. Ms. Ophelia Emmitt might help you," Judge Grandpa said. He paused and then smiled. "Now there's a story that needs telling. Well, here we are."

He turned into the driveway. The illuminated sign read: *Armadillos to Zebras. Vet. Hospital. Kennels. Dr. Leroy Daniels.*

Set in front of the small complex of structures, fences, and pens, the main building sprawled long and wide. A porch surrounded the front of the building, while a railed walkway led up from the side. Old-fashioned gas lamps hissed and provided light along the stairs.

Flash liked Dr. Daniels, but he dragged his tail up the steps, so Scooter scooped him up.

Dr. Daniels swung open the door. The vet was big, round-bellied, and elderly, with graying temples crowning his darkly bald pate. His beard was gray, looking almost white against his swarthy complexion. Judge Grandpa said he had been a veterinarian in these parts for a long time, back when people were shocked to see a black doctor. Some had slighted him until their favorite animal had an emergency, then they relented, only to find that Dr. Daniels was gifted in treating four-leggeds and the winged.

"Well, this is something you don't see every day. Jonathan Keyshawn carrying his dog." The vet lowered his bifocals and got eye-to-eye with Flash. "How's my favorite good-for-nothing hound dog?"

Flash chuffed, less enthusiastic than usual.

"His feet were burned when we were hit by lightning," Scooter replied.

"You're lucky to be alive. You been checked out, young man?" the doctor asked. Scooter nodded. "Are you sure this mangy mutt is worth keeping?"

"Yes, sir. He's still the best dog in the world."

"Well, Flash, you have him bamboozled. Bring him over here. We'll find out what's wrong with him," Dr. Daniels said. He guided Scooter through the deserted entry hall, past the empty chairs and benches into a side hallway, then held the doors open to the examining chamber. Scooter placed his furry friend on the shiny silver table. The vet listened to his heart and lungs, moving on to check his ears. They were red, the flesh looking inflamed.

Trying to ignore the tingling in his ears, Scooter held his dog as still as possible while Dr. Daniels dabbed medicinal ointment in his ears. It hurt Scooter's ears.

The vet examined Flash' paws, finding the flesh reddened underneath charred hair. "I can understand your reluctance to walking," he told Flash while he rubbed cream into the pads of his feet. "He needs rest, time and medicine for his ears and paws to heal. Three times a day, both medicines," the vet said as he handed over a white tube and a gray one. "If they get worse, I will have to wrap them in gauze and tape. For starters, I suggest white tube socks."

Flash whined pitifully.

"It's that or bandage and medical tape. Don't chew either." He gave them a stern look over his bifocals. "Everything else seems fine. Should I keep him over night?"

"No. I would miss him too much. Now that I know he has a dry nose because of an ear infection instead of lightning strike, I feel better," Scooter replied. He stuffed the tubes of medicine into his jeans pocket. He felt something else and fingered a pill.

"What's that?" Dr. Daniels asked.

"I don't know. I found it loose on the ground in the ruined shack on Fisherman's Island. I didn't want Flash to eat it, so I scooped it up. I forgot to give it to the paramedics," he said over Judge Grandpa's snoring.

"Would you like me to take care of it?" the vet asked. Dr. Daniels noted the numbers and letters. "I don't recognize it, but I can research it. Give me a couple of days and then call me. Okay?" He nodded. "If it's illegal, then I'll have to report it."

"Sure," Scooter thought it might be. Russell had mentioned Redgraves had taken a painkiller. He thought over his next question, remembering Grandma Mae mentioning the vet had a little Dr. Doolittle in him. He seemed to be able to communicate with Flash. "Do people ever get close enough to animals that they can hear, see, and smell through their pets?"

"The Native Americans thought so. Remember we are a land of animal totems. And when I was younger, visiting Aunt Geraldine, I saw a Voodoo woman in New Orleans do some amazing things that I still can't reconcile. Science would debunk it, I'm sure, but even so, when I have been with an animal a long time, I develop a close rapport so that I empathize with it."

"Thanks for telling me I'm not being a stupid kid."

Scooter gently awakened his grandfather, then they said good-bye. Judge Grandpa looked plumb-tuckered out. "Tomorrow we should go get my boat before something else happens to it."

Scooter dreaded returning to the island.

TEN

THE HIDEOUS ARTIFACT

At dawn, Scooter awakened itching all over. He smelled a strange visitor over the heady aroma of eggs, cheese, and bacon. The undercurrent of Old Spice told Scooter his grandfather was awake.

The other scent was flowery but not his grandmother's peach hand cream. He heard another woman's voice. It might be Mrs. Harlan, paramedic Bruce's mom, coming to check on her house. It had a nautical theme. Taxidermic fish mixed with rods and reels lined the walls. They had been living at the Harlan's for six weeks. Scooter loved staying on the lake during the summer. The Harlans were wonderful neighbors.

The shoreline location allowed them to walk down the peninsula, leaving the other six homes of Siete Hombres behind, to his grandparents' house under construction. The new place sat atop the old foundation near the end of the grassy point of poplars, willows, and cottonwoods.

Scooter crawled out of bed. His entire body felt like he had worn scratchy clothes too long. He grabbed a pair of clean old jeans, his towel, and lumbered to the bathroom. In the shower, he discovered hundreds of chigger bites covering his entire body. He recalled the bugs in Shade's shack. Grandma Mae would know what to do.

Scratching like a dog with fleas, he ambled downstairs.

"Good morning. I smell food," Scooter said. Flash greeted him briefly, then his snuffling nose returned to the kitchen.

"Ah, there you are. We're ready to go. The sheriff's boat is here," Judge Grandpa said. Despite wearing his fishing clothes, his expression held the gravity of a work day. "Don't look so stricken. I packed a cooler and just finished making breakfast burritos. You can eat as we go. Jonathan, this is Agent Pryde."

"Good day, Jonathan." the woman said. She looked like a policewoman—with an air of authority in the way she stood, even at ease. The military cut of her blond hair furthered the impression. Her hooked nose had been broken and gave her a vulpine look. She wore a plain gray pants suit and what looked like black combat boots. A U.S. Marshal or a lady Texas Ranger?

Agent Pryde stirred a travel cup of steaming coffee, sugar, and butterscotch cream. It all mingled with the scent of lavender perfume.

Scooter was amazed by all the smells. He stuck out his hand to shake. Her hand engulfed his meager grip. "Hello."

"I have heard about you and your friends, Russell Knight and Kristie Candel. Some have called you vampire hunters."

"Have you seen them?" Scooter asked. He itched.

"Young Mr. Knight is eager to leave. Ms. Candel was sleeping. I hope they're well enough to speak to me later," she said, flashing her Federal Bureau of Investigation ID badge. Special Agent Noelle Pryde.

"Investigating the 'Cult of the Vampire?'"

"Yes, do you want to talk about vampires?" she asked.

"Are you open-minded?" he asked as he scratched.

"I don't know about vampires, per se, but I would like to talk about creatures of darkness, those with the charismatic power to turn people into sheep. Will that do?"

"That's a start," Scooter said. His stomach grumbled as Flash's rumbled loudly. The golden Lab barked. "Oh, yes. Sorry. How rude of me. This is my best friend, Flash." His furry companion folded his front paws, making it look as if he were bowing.

"He's a better person than most people. Let's go, Flash," Judge Grandpa gestured with the cooler to the dock.

Scooter talked with Grandma, and she gave him fingernail polish to cover the bites. The relentless itching was going to drive him mad.

The sheriff's county boat bobbed in place, lashed to the grommets. The water craft was an olive and tan rig, twenty-two feet long with an open wheel under a hardtop canopy. Two long antennae stuck out. Extra racks of lights covered the bow and were mounted along the side and back.

Once Agent Pryde and Judge Grandpa boarded, Scooter helped untie the lines and cast off. Deputy Al steered them into the main body of Lake Tawakoni. The green water rested uncannily serene after yesterday's onslaught of whitecaps. The low eastern sun created a gleaming streak of gold running toward the islands. The dark humps wavered like mirages atop a watery highway.

Scooter fed Flash, woofed down a burrito, then pulled off his shirt and rolled up his pant legs. He dabbed fingernail polish over the chigger bites. He thought about shellacking himself.

"Good Lord, Jonathan. What happened?"

"This is what comes from napping in Shade's shack."

"Jonathan, while you work, please tell me about Shade?" Agent Pryde asked.

He was thoughtful, recalling what he had read. "Didn't a cult of vampires kidnap kids somewhere out west?"

Her expression turned stony and angular.

"Mr. Shade claimed he came from Hollywood and knew

Marcus—Mr. Chandler—through an actor he had directed. I don't remember his name." But it sparked an idea. He would have to ask his mentor about the man. "Shade wanted Marcus to direct and produce a biography of his undead existence."

"My grandson is perturbed that few believe him."

"Assume I don't know anything," Agent Pryde said.

"Only those who were there believe me. Anyway, this sounds kind of stupid, but I wanted to join a gang called the Graveyard Armadillos. My buddy, Russell Knight, introduced me to the leader, Garrett Brashear. Jo Gunn, BJ Mochrie and his young brother, CJ, and Racquel Knight were already members. My initiation involved taking a picture of Marcus Chandler—owner of the Pickup Ranch and a former Hollywood director of horror flicks."

"And a fine actor," Grandpa interjected.

"The Armadillos thought he was a vampire instead of suffering Vitiligo, as reported in the newspaper. They figured by taking a picture they could prove Chandler was a member of the undead, and the reason kids were disappearing."

"Brilliant strategy. Show a picture of the background, a blank, or a bad photo and you have your proof that vampires can't be photographed," Pryde said.

"They were boozin'," Judge Grandpa added.

Scooter frowned but continued, "Marcus is such an odd-looking man that he scared me witless. He thought I was with the *Paparazzi* to get photos of him mourning his parents.

"In retribution for harassing the man who would direct its biography and make it infamous, Mr. Lucius Shade killed Jo Gunn. It said it would keep killing until Marcus relented and made a film of his unlife."

"Describe Lucius Shade."

Doing so perturbed Scooter, because he could see him clearly. He had to clasp his hands together to stop them from shaking. "I don't know how much help that will be, because it can change shape. It looked male, thirty-ish, tall and waxy pale with a sharp nose and cruel expression. Its hair was cut short, like a page in olden days, and it had distinct eyebrows. Shade's black eyes turn a deep red like hot coals when it stares at you."

"Why do you keep referring to the vampire as it?"

"It can be male and female. It isn't human anymore, now a shapeshifting monster that lives on the blood of others. Shade kidnapped Judge Grandpa, Grandma, and me." Scooter explained how Marcus struck Shade with a cross, setting its flesh on fire, which ignited everything else.

"Judge, is he serious?" Agent Pryde asked.

"Grimly so."

Undaunted, Scooter summarized what had happened, telling her about Shade, as a giant bat, chasing them across the lake. How they would have died, but they hit a sandbar, throwing the vampire into the water, injuring it and driving it away. The next morning, they were found by Russell, Kristie and Racquel.

They found a boat on Fisherman's Isle. When they landed, vicious dogs attacked. Flash fought them off, while Racquel shot them. Garrett lured her in, then Russell. Scooter admitted falling in while trying to chop a hole in the roof. "Mr. Shade was there," he finished in a hoarse whisper.

Flash licked his hand, then laid his head on his lap.

"Thanks, boy," Scooter said, patting his friend. "I thought I was dead when it bit me on the neck." He touched the spot. The skin was smooth, his bite marks gone.

"What did the doctors find?" Agent Pryde asked.

"Just bruising," Scooter replied.

"How did Shade's bite feel?"

"Worse than his bark," Scooter suddenly burst out laughing. "I'm sorry. I'm nervous about going back out there. Shade's bite was sharp all through me, into my mind," he said through clenched teeth. His hands were white-tight gripped, reliving the spiking agony. "I could feel my memories fade away with all hope.

"Then there was a loud crash. The shack shook and shattered like there was an earthquake." The agent watched with an intense focus, and although Judge Grandpa had already heard this story, he listened as if he were trying to find changes. "Sunlight filled the room—incredible beauty and brilliance—and I watched, thrilled, as Shade disintegrated."

"How so?"

"It decomposed into ash and dust. Kristie had launched the boat and crashed into the shack, destroying the darkness with daylight. She saved me. She saved us, though Garrett believed that *it* still exists as Tai."

"Tai?" the agent asked.

"As I said, Shade could shapeshift. It was some kind of superior vampire, a Trueblood, I think, so it could alter its undead flesh to look like anyone or assume animal forms."

"I see," Agent Pryde sounded doubtful.

"No, you don't, but I'm afraid you will."

"Why do you say that?"

"Another vampire is here, in Gunstock. It called himself Mr. Ripley, a reporter for the *L.A. Times*. It is looking for Shade."

"That is quite a tale," Agent Pryde said.

"I don't want to believe it either," Scooter mumbled.

They fell into silence, mulling his words. Flash clamored on the seat, sticking his head beyond the windshields into the breeze. His long ears flapped like wings on a Norseman's hairy helmet.

The perfect water and the hum of the motor lulled Scooter. What a difference a day could make. The moments between calm and stormy, life and death, could be seconds.

When he looked at Judge Grandpa, he could see the passing of time. Not minute by minute perhaps, but day to day he watched as his beloved grandfather grew older. Afraid he was going to cry, Scooter changed his thoughts.

They were already into the dog days of summer. The hint of coolness in the air warmed early with the gigantic blazing ball of the sun barely thirty minutes above the horizon. Soon it would be stifling, then the thunderstorms would pop up, forming black anvil thunderheads.

Scooter shuddered, getting a chilling flash. His skin crept as if trying to leave bone and muscle behind, knowing they were nearing Shade's Island. His bites ached acutely, so he took an antihistamine and an ibuprofen. When he squinted, he saw what looked like a dark mist hanging over the spiky-looking chunk of land.

Flash growled. Scooter smelled the stench wafting across the water. It seemed toxic, a mix of wood, chemicals and old bones, making everybody cough.

"Not a lot left of the cabin." Judge Grandpa wheezed while he pointed.

Scooter had seen the ruins just yesterday. Today it looked like an ogre had stomped on it. Except for a few shattered planks sticking up like broken bones, the shack rested low, an oversized lid of a casket set shallow in a deserted grave.

"Did Mr. Chandler ever tell you there was a cult that plagued him once in Los Angeles?" Agent Pryde asked. Scooter shook his head. "They thought he was revealing hidden secrets in his movies. A plot to kidnap him was foiled about a decade ago. The assigned agents were certain they had caught everyone involved, but I'm having serious doubts."

Scooter would ask Marcus. It sounded like quite a story.

Russell's father waited for them along the shore and waved in solemn greeting. Deputy Al directed them along what was left of the dock. Judge Grandpa's Starlite 12 Aluminum Riveted Jon boat had been tossed ashore. Upside down, the prop stuck up like a symbolic tombstone.

"Oh, no," Scooter exclaimed.

"It looks like the hull is intact. We'll tow it back," his grandfather said, clapping him on the shoulder. Even forgiven, Scooter felt awful about abandoning it.

Deputy Al cut the engine, letting them coast in. With a gentle bump and soft, sandy grind, they beached it. Scooter hopped out to help his grandfather. Just setting foot on the tainted soil caused him to shake. Flash walked gingerly, and Scooter wasn't sure if he was just sensing his dog, or if the ground really caused his feet to ache. His bites buzzed, as if a horde of sharp-toothed bugs gnawed on me.

"Good mornin' everyone," Sheriff Knight said. He seemed uncomfortable.

"Sir, how's Russell?" Scooter asked.

"Restless. His blood work was abnormal, so more tests. I almost get the feeling he knows what's going on, but he won't tell me. Maybe he'll tell you."

"I'll call soon," Scooter promised.

Examining it, Judge Grandpa strolled around the aluminum boat. Scooter spotted a shiny object on the ground. He recognized Kristie's opal cross, a gift from her grandmother, and pocketed it. He smiled, imagining her delight.

His radio squawked, interrupting them. "Sheriff! Sheriff!" In the background, they heard someone retching. "You've got to come see this!"

"Don! What? Where are you?" the sheriff asked.

"Go, Flash. Find them!" Scooter said. His dog bolted,

becoming a golden streak. Before anyone could stop him, Scooter was in hot pursuit. The trail seemed familiar, heading toward where the bodies had been buried.

"It's horrible! Decker has lost it!"

Flash reached the stench and the deputies first.

Big Deputy Ross was on the ground, hunched over and dry heaving. Skinny Deputy Don thrashed about like he was having a seizure.

When he saw the green-black statuette set in the tree trunk, he forgot everything but the hideous idol. Even with his eyes closed, Scooter could still see it. Blood streaked the half-human beast—naked with male and female aspects—as the statuette crouched ready to spring into a feral attack. Four arms ended in claws that seemed to have paused from incessant clutching. Its face was weasel-like and pockmarked, oozing a black oil that dripped off its goatee. Four eyes sat deep as in despair. Instead of stone, its hair looked like moldering serpents.

The stench was gut-churning, worse than the graves. Dizzy and nauseous, Scooter reached for a tree to ground him while the world spun.

"Look away! Sheriff, I've seen this reaction twice before, every time the Gibbering Darkness idol is found."

Scooter struggled to keep down his gorge. He dropped to his knees, wondering if he should just surrender and puke.

"Pull your men away. It seems to have a radius affect even if you're not looking at it," Agent Pryde said.

Flash grabbed Scooter and dragged him along. The vertigo eased to nothing. "That's good, boy. Thanks."

Scooter saw Judge Grandpa coming and leapt to his feet, waving at him to stay away. The smell and sight might cause him serious harm. Even back here, Scooter could smell the stink, then he realized it clung to him.

His grandpa signaled he would wait.

Scooter jogged near. "It's horrible, Grandpa. I can smell the stink on me. I'm going to swim." Wanting to feel clean again, Scooter stripped to his swimsuit and ran into the lake.

He dove and glided, until he bumped into an obstacle and pulled back, treading water. It hadn't felt like a log, but it wasn't some kind of flotation device either. At first he thought it was a bloated black bag of trash.

Then he noticed an arm and leg. Scooter's skin goosebumped to pins and needles when he realized it was a floating body.

Unable to scream, Scooter kicked away. The corpse pursued, and he swam harder, feeling it grab at his legs. Scooter glanced back, stunned to see Lucius Shade reaching out.

Scooter screamed, sucking down a mouthful of water. He choked and coughed, on the verge of drowning

Flash snagged him by his shorts and dragged him to where he could sit and hack and spit until he could breath normally. He watched the body and realized it was just the waves and his imagination that moved it.

It was a corpse. A dead one, so it couldn't be Shade. Vampires were undead and disintegrated in the sunlight.

"Scooter, are you all right?" Grandpa asked.

"Yes, thanks to Flash. Call the sheriff. I bumped into a body," Scooter replied. He rubbed his neck, looking for scars. The skin felt normal, but could he be wrong?

ELEVEN

FORBIDDEN

Kristie awakened groggily in the dim light of monitors, wondering what had disturbed her. Her neck hurt, kinked and pinched, like she had rested wrong. She must have fallen asleep waiting for Scooter to come visit.

Outside, it was raining, pelting the windows. A flash of lightning startled her. She wasn't alone.

"How are you feeling?"

Kristie jumped. Gasping, she looked over, expecting to find her father.

A doctor stood in the shadows. His white jacket seemed mockingly bright when the lightning flared again. "I'm Dr. West."

At first, Kristie couldn't find his eyes in the darkness of his face. She was thinking he was the blackest man she had seen. His irises were pitch dark surrounded by red-jaundiced eyes.

"I'm okay. A little groggy. What time is it?" she asked while she continued to rub her neck.

"Just after nine. I studied your X-rays. Good news. No broken bones. The imagining scans shows bruising, but you will be fine, perhaps even better than before."

"Better?" she drawled. Dr. West's cool manner and tone seemed disturbingly familiar. She reached for the cross at the end of the filigreed silver chain she wore. Her fingers found irritated flesh and minor burns, but they stuttered when they kept missing her keepsake. It was gone! That's right, her cross had been melted.

"The lightning favored you. Most of the time it destroys what it touches. Occasionally, it transforms."

"I don't think I understand."

"You will with time. You're a bright young woman. Frankly, I stopped in because I heard you were a vampire hunter."

"That's ridiculous. I'm not a hunter. I'm a . . . singer."

"Tell me exactly what happened yesterday and last night." Dr. West's voice was warm, compelling and encouraging, letting her know he supported her.

Kristie explained about the mishaps, the weather, the haunt of the vampire, and finding the bodies, drawling on until her voice was raspy, her throat dry. She hadn't planned to say that much, but she didn't stop until she recalled Ripley's stare. It brought her back, staring into the odd doctor's eyes.

Dr. West never raised an eyebrow but simply said, "Vampires. A scientific conundrum. Is this supposed vampire, Mr. Shade, truly dead?"

"I don't know. I didn't see it with my own eyes," she said. She realized that she was going to sound silly or like a gossip. "Scooter saw him disintegrate in the sunlight, and I believe him."

"Could he have escaped?"

"If you didn't believe Scooter. Dr. West, do you believe in anything unscientific?"

He nodded. "Yes. People laugh at what they don't understand. Remember, at one time, they believed evil spirits caused diseases and stress caused ulcers. Now we know better. While studying in Hungary, I saw vampires. Because of that, I have taken care of people injured by them. Do you have any interest in being a vampire?"

This was the second time she had heard this question. "No. Why do you ask?"

"A colleague once mentioned that vampires were drawn to someone interested in wanting eternal life."

"I am already eternal. Just this body wears out." She paused for a drink of water. When she looked up, she said, "Dr. West, do I look like I've been injured by a vampire? Dr. West?"

Lightning flashed, revealing the room was empty. Just when she was beginning to think she had imagined him, the toilet flushed.

"How are Russell Knight and Kellen Redgraves?" she asked when the door opened.

"According to the doctors, Russell is doing fine. He's restless. Wired, I think his mama said," her mother replied, exiting the bathroom.

"Mother?" Kristie gaped. Where had Dr. West gone?!

Mother Candel wrinkled her noise. Her mother leaned heavily on her cane, shaking and limping to the bedside. As though she were sixty instead of forty, she wore a shawl. "Kellen is still under watch, and he will be for some time to come. They put him on around the clock watch and medication."

Kristie wondered. Had she imagined Dr. West?

"Blessedly, the doctors say you're fine. We can go home. There's a change of clothes in the closet. You might want to put on some make-up. You look a sight."

Kristie was excited to be free. Just the thought made her feel better. She could go visit Russell and Scooter. How had the lightning affected them? "Did y'all meet Dr. West? He was just here, checking up on me."

"No, dear. Is something wrong?" her mother asked as she cradled her daughter's hand.

Kristie wondered if she had still been asleep. Then she

had a paralyzing thought. Could that have been a vampire? She checked her neck, feeling for marks. It felt swollen. "No. I'm fine. Did Scooter ever come by?"

"Not today."

"What about Russell?"

"He's staying overnight again for observation and tests. They know the lightning affected him, but they're just not sure how. Thankfully, y'all are going to be all right, despite your boating misadventure."

That Scooter hadn't visited bothered Kristie. She was certain he would have tried. Was he sick? What else would keep him away? The bodies? With everybody else in the hospital, the sheriff would want Scooter to go back out to the island. She sent him a prayer.

"It was a long, strange day. Bad luck. Bad weather."

"We're in one of those patterns. A tornado hit around Mesquite with grapefruit sized hail. We were lucky it skipped past," her mother said.

"Lucky? Or blest? When I was struck by lightning, I felt blest, touched by the Almighty. I have never felt anything like it," she said, groping for a way to describe it as the memory surged over her, burning like a star. "After that, everything kind of pales, except for finding the bodies. That was horrible. They felt used and discarded."

"It's awful, simply awful. We can take comfort that their spirits no longer feel pain, resting in the Almighty's hands now."

"You look tired."

"My spirit is willing, but my flesh is weak," Mother complained with a smile. "It is difficult to interpret the divine mystery of life when we react with our bodies and think with the human mind. We must see with spiritual vision."

Mother believed she had been challenged so that she

would foster empathy and understand others' infirmities. When she was strong, they realized they could be strong, too. Now she helped others whose bodies had betrayed them. After time, they realized that they were more than flesh and blood.

Kristie could only imagine what it felt like, her mother shaking all the time. How frustrating might it be? Maddening to be let down by your body. If she could make a wish to heal anyone, it would be her mother. Oftentimes she hoped that if she sang the right song, Mother would be free of disease. Then Kristie could give up her junior mother duties.

"Would you look at my neck, please? It aches."

Mother peered and rubbed gently. "It looks puffy and bruised. Kristie, sweetie, is there anything you want to talk about?"

"What makes you think that?" she replied.

"You're my child. Kids spend all their youth trying to manipulate their parents, while parents watch their children trying to gauge reactions to get the best out of them. Why don't you talk to me any more? Since the school year ended, you're not yourself, running around all the time."

She sounded like BJ, Kristie thought. "I'm bored. I haven't been anywhere for the last month, except church. The only reason y'all let me go fishing today was to take Kellen out."

"Your father takes you along with him on his calls. And you went on a retreat to Arkansas."

"I meant around here. I feel trapped. Y'all didn't even let me go to the singing competition."

"You were a wreck, Kristie. You are young, not invulnerable. You had just crashed a boat into a shack and been mobbed. You needed time to recover."

While others doubted, her mother at least believed that

she had faced evil. She claimed to feel the lingering fear and had commented on her daughter's loss of innocence.

"I need to sing, and I like to hear others sing, too. I could try out for American Idol."

"Now look at you," her mother said, shaking. She was visibly upset. "These boys, Scooter and Russell, I know they come from good families, but . . . they seem to be getting you into a lot of trouble. Running with boys is rough business and unladylike."

"It's not their fault, Mom. Y'all just assume it is."

"Well, then it must be your fault. I felt better when Racquel was with you!" Mother huffed.

"Racquel?!" she blurted. How could Mother be so dense? "It was because of Racquel that I ended up on the lake. She drinks and smokes. But it was either hop in the boat or let her go alone, and that felt wrong. So did pushing her out of the boat, but I was tempted! Yes, I was!" Her anger made her neck throb.

"Well, she wasn't with you this time, and look where you are—in the hospital. Kristie, boys will be boys, regardless of whose sons they are."

"We didn't intend to be gone so long."

"That's exactly what you said last time. You know what they say about the road to perdition."

"Y'all just told me the Almighty works in divinely mysterious ways. I don't set out to do these things," Kristie said, feeling persecuted. "How can y'all blame them for me getting kidnapped?"

"The Gunns were looking for Scooter. And saving you once doesn't give them the right to keep putting you in danger. Dear, I'm just trying to protect you. Please, look at it with my eyes for a moment. You go out fishing, and you wind up in the hospital with a hickey!"

"What?!"

"On your neck. You have a hickey."

"Mother, I don't have a hickey. If I had, I wouldn't ask you to look at it!" she snapped. "If you're looking to cast blame, then step up. You 'suggested' I bring Kellen Redgraves along," she began, then she explained the wonders of Kellen, including his suicide attempt.

"That makes me wonder even more about Russell and Scooter."

"What do you mean? Russell saved him!" Kristie started to screech. She barely held her tone. Her smothering mom could be infuriating. "Blaming Russell and Scooter is just as unfair! Y'all are prejudice because they're boys!"

"I'm *discerning*, because I'm your mother. You might understand that someday. I think you should stay away from them for a while."

"But Mother, it's not their fault."

"Whether it's just their nature, or a bedeviling, you stay away from them unless it's a church function. Now stay away from those boys, do you hear?"

"I did. All of June and half of July."

"And nothing bad happened to you dear."

"Nothing good happened either!" Kristie snapped. Keeping her away from her friends was worse than physical pain. The carnival, the dances and the music would seem less merry without her best friends. "I'm not a porcelain doll. Besides, I promised Scooter I would go with him to the Elk's Club fair."

"Well, we'll see."

"We'll see. Maybe. Perhaps. Later. Does that come in *The Guide to Moms' Doublespeak*?" she asked harshly. "And you wonder why we haven't been talking?"

"Kristie, you sound like you need rest. But we'll work it out. Go ahead, change. I'll get a wheelchair."

Working things out meant doing what Mother wanted.

There was more to life than taking care of kids and singing in the choir.

Kristie dreaded the future. What had she done to deserve this? She just wished her mother was healthy, so she could mother the kids. Then Kristie Candel could live her own life.

TWELVE

OUT AT THE PICKUP RANCH

Scooter placed Judge Grandpa's cell phone in the car's cup holder. Nurse Gabby had told him Russell was asleep and Kristie had checked out. He cradled her grandmother's opal cross, having looked forward to returning it and her happy reaction. Now he would have to wait. He and Grandpa had wasted all day on the lake and at the sheriff's department.

"We're here," Judge Grandpa said.

Scooter looked out the window for the first time since driving away from the county offices. He had wanted to tell Marcus all about what had happened.

At the entrance to the Pickup Ranch, the moon sulked on the western horizon, a red eye glaring at them through the tree tops. It created a ruddy glow around the long wall of half-buried pickups and sparked a gleam in their taillights, giving the impression they could roar to life. Shadows gripped the steering wheels, and because of the wind, the tires slowly spun, dirt clouds billowing as if they had thrown the pickups into reverse to escape the grave and go 'hell-razin'.

It was going to be dark in a few minutes. Night time was vampire play time, when people became prey. Scooter couldn't help but feel paranoid. Bumping into the body had scattered his brain.

He got out to stretch and scratch, then he unlocked the gate. He punched a code into a numbered pad. The solid metal partition slid smoothly aside. It had been installed just three weeks ago. With all the trucks around him, it reminded Scooter of a security gate to a huge, surreal lot where they parked the automobiles vertically.

Judge Grandpa drove through the entrance, underneath the archway of steering wheels, then beyond where he parked, waiting for him. When Scooter climbed back inside the truck, Grandpa put the truck in gear and headed down the gravel road, up the first of two knolls toward the ranch house. In the silence, the stones clattered noisily underneath like a rock polisher at work. "Are you thinking about seeing Ms. Candel tomorrow?" he finally asked.

"Sometimes you are scary, Grandpa. I'm trying to figure out what to say to her. I probably won't have long, and there's a lot to tell her. A lot has happened."

"Does Mrs. Candel disapprove of you?"

"What makes you say that?" Scooter asked, startled.

"I can tell by the way she watches you. It makes your grandmother as mad as a hornet that Kristie's mom is suspicious of you."

"I feel like I'm being punished and it's not my fault. I didn't plan to stay out late. In fact, we left early to be back before the weather got bad. It's Redgraves' fault."

"Ah, well there it is. The denial reflex. Have you ever noticed that people have a tendency to blame who they dislike, not who's at fault? They assume *those* people intentionally do things to make life more difficult. From what you have told me, you dislike Kellen Redgraves."

"Grandpa, he's a walking disaster! If you think you've just finished with a problem, wait a minute, another is coming!"

"You blame him for ruining yesterday?" he asked.

Scooter nodded. "Do you blame him for being struck by lightning?"

Scooter hadn't realized it, but he did. "I guess so. If he hadn't kept delaying us, we wouldn't have been there."

"With that line of thinking, perhaps you are at fault. Who scheduled the boating date? Wait a minute, it's actually my fault. It's my boat. I let you use it. Hmm. Well, I don't like the sound of that. It can't be my fault."

Scooter remained quiet. This was drama Judge Grandpa had learned from the courtroom.

His grandfather hummed while he contemplated who was at fault. "Ah, I know who's at fault. The manufacturer of the boat. If Starlite hadn't made it and sold it to me, I would never have loaned it to you, then you couldn't have been on the water to be struck by lightning. I'll file on Monday."

"Grandpa, you are funny," Scooter said. "Okay, Redgraves is not at fault for the lightning, but he is the leading contributor to making the day a disaster."

"Don't blame Redgraves for being different. It's nearly impossible but try walking in his shoes."

"No way. He makes Inspector Clouseau of *The Pink Panther* appear suave and debonair."

"Jonathan . . . ."

"See, you find it annoying, too, when I act like Redgraves."

Flash barked reproachfully.

"Well said. You are being childish," Grandpa said. "We must always do our best to understand people. Doesn't mean we have to agree with them. Or like them. I believe it makes the world seem less meaningless when we find connections and commonalities."

"That's what Marcus says, too. But when I see things like the Gibbering Darkness idol, I wonder." Scooter shuddered.

"Do you think it represents a danger to Mr. Chandler?"

"Yes, and everybody else. Too bad Agent Pryde doesn't believe me."

"She believes there are demented and dangerous individuals terrorizing this county, especially now that Lucius Shade's body has been found."

"Well, it could be a Lewis Shade, but it's not the Lucius Shade. I saw him decompose to ash. Sometimes, I think I'm going crazy," Scooter said. He realized he was scanning the shadows in the trees, looking for Ripley.

"You can't live in this world and think about it without that happening sometimes. Let me know if there is any way I can help."

When they crested the last rolling knoll, Scooter saw a car parked out front. It had a governmental, officious angularity to its style.

The front gate opened. A stout, balding man in a tan suit walked out ahead of Marcus. They shook hands, then the official departed with a wave toward them.

"Who was that?" Scooter asked.

Marcus smiled as he walked over to greet them. He shook Judge Grandpa's hand. "James Dandy. He works for the county's social services. What's wrong? You look like someone who lost his last friend."

"Too much to think about," Scooter replied. Not only did he feel chewed upon, but he also felt scrutinized.

"Better than not thinking at all," Marcus countered, causing Judge Grandpa to chortle.

"You know, if it would help, you should write about what happened yesterday and today," Grandpa suggested.

"That sounds like a good warm up exercise. It will give me some time to write, too," Marcus said.

"You're writing again?"

"Scooter has inspired me."

"Glad to hear it. I appreciate you helping him."

"What's was Mr. Dandy doing here?" Scooter asked.

"Checking to see if it would be a good idea to let Kellen Redgraves create with us. He's recovering," Marcus replied.

Scooter felt ill and angry as he bit back his retort. Even when assuming the worst, you could still be disappointed.

"What's wrong?" Marcus asked.

"Do you remember when you told me it was important to have unbroken imaginative time and a positive environment to be creative?" Scooter asked. He tried to be tactful. "I don't feel . . . creative when Redgraves is around."

"Kellen needs a reason to live. I sympathize with being different, and suddenly being alone. He needs a friend. Friends would be even better."

Scooter didn't know what to say. The Intruder had already messed up his day with Kristie. Now the new kid from Killeen was intruding into his friendship and his creative time. "Couldn't we do it on different days?"

"It will do you some good to read someone else's writing."

Scooter couldn't take it. Adults were allowed to avoid people, why wasn't he? "It's going to screw up everything!"

"Jonathan. Apologize," Judge Grandpa said.

"And you wonder why people aren't honest, grandpa? Honesty is not the best policy, it just leads to having to issue an apology. Thanks for teaching me to be honest."

His grandfather looked taken aback. "Then just apologize for being rude."

Scooter felt mulish. "I'm sorry that I forcefully expressed my opinion about having this rammed down my throat. Kellen Redgraves is going to ruin the creative environment."

"Scooter, I think I can understand your first impression," Marcus said. Scooter doubted it. "My first thoughts of you were unkind, to say the least, but I took a chance and gave you a second opportunity. Look what happened! Can you deny Redgraves a second chance?"

Scooter stewed, disliking the thought because it went against what he wanted to happen. Even so, Marcus had a point. "I didn't like it, but at least I came back and apologized for intruding and being an idiot."

"Would you like to explain this grudge? It's not like you," his mentor continued.

"I don't understand why this is being shoved in my face! My opinion on Redgraves isn't just a first impression," Scooter said. The bite under his left arm throbbed, distracting him. "You and I first met for thirty seconds, if that. I spent an entire miserable day with Kellen Redgraves. Grandpa, if you go fishing with someone who ruins the day by scaring off all the fish, do you invite them to go out again?"

"Unlikely."

"Well, I don't know Kellen that well. Maybe he hates to fish," Marcus replied. "But I know he likes movies, so I invited him to join us. As we know, it's good therapy."

Scooter figured it would be wiser to say nothing at all.

"I see. Well, let's go do a little writing. Perhaps unleashing some creativity with help you think more expansively. We'll feel better and be able to plot what we would like to happen," Marcus said.

"Why? It never does. That's why I like to write fiction."

In Nirvana, Scooter lost himself in the writing. He mentally relived and replayed yesterday in his mind and let it out through his fingers.

He didn't even notice that Marcus had hooked up a third monitor until he had finished a draft of yesterday's and today's events. Scooter proofed his work twice more. When he reworked a scene, he made lots of minor mistakes. The same was true with drawing, when he left sketch marks.

While Marcus read, Scooter went searching through Nirvana's closets. In a chest of drawers he found a different kind of collection, a mixture of old black and white Texas photos, newspaper articles and an unfinished scrapbook of Marcus' career. He couldn't put into words how much he appreciated his help. But, he could turn the man's life into a comic book! Judge Grandpa mentioned it was a story worth telling.

His perusal lasted a short time, as Marcus came looking for him. "A body, the Gibbering Darkness idol and the Cult of the Vampire. I haven't thought about them in quite a while."

"Agent Pryde said you had been harassed."

Marcus smiled grimly as he sat in his Thinking Throne, a black leather recliner that sat in front of a cold wood-burning stove. "There was a cult so named after I worked on a film of the same title. They believed the script to be true. It was a B- movie directed and produced by a friend of mine. Come to think of it, Micah was in that movie."

"Micah? That name sounds vaguely familiar."

"That is the actor that Lucius Shade claims he transformed into a vampire. Micah supposedly sent Shade to see me. I must admit that I had forgotten. I don't think I've been clear-headed since I discovered that vampires were nonfiction."

Scooter nodded sympathetically. "I know."

"And what about this body floating in the lake? If it isn't Lucius Shade, who is it?"

Scooter shrugged. He had no idea.

"A mystery we might, I stress might, have to unravel, but currently, just food for thought," he said, handing Scooter back his writing draft. "Go put the last two days into an impersonal news story. An investigative expose' that answers little but poses many questions. I'm going to call Micah."

Scooter crafted the article, pretending to write like Jimmy B. Little. Marcus barely glanced at the work, saying, "Now, write it from Kristie's point of view."

It took longer, but he managed it. She was willing to put aside her own joy to help others. She believed Kellen should get a second chance and a fresh start.

"One more version. Do it from Kellen's perspective."

Scooter groused, then did as he was told. This crafting took much longer. He had to take what little he knew about the Intruder and expand on it, referring to as many movies as possible. As revenge, he made Kellen Redgraves of Killeen, Texas, born with the family curse of turning gold into brass and silver into lead. When he wrote about the guilt he felt about his family dying in a fire, Scooter could identify with him. For a moment, back when the lake house caught fire, he had believed his grandparents were dead.

While Marcus read all his versions, Scooter went outside. A garrote-taut web almost took his head off, and he had to fight his way through by swinging his arms and imagining a machete. He sprayed mosquito repellent on himself, recalling an old Texas saying, "If it grows it will stick you, and if it crawls, it will bite you." They could add sting.

The humidity swelling from the black clouds made it feel like breathing through a soggy blanket. Lightning flickered distantly, but the rain fell elsewhere.

He felt spindled by vampire stares while playing frisbees with the dogs. Fear and sweat made his chigger bites itch crazily, so even his bones buzzed. He almost shouted at the woods for any bloodsucker to come out, then he realized he would sound looney. To cool off, he turned the hose on himself. He wondered if running water from a hose bothered vampires.

"Feel better?" Marcus asked as he came out the door to join them. He handed him an ice-cold glass of lemonade.

"A little. Thanks," Scooter replied.

Marcus held out Scooter's writings. "This is the best thing I think you've written to date. Quite gripping, a little raw, but with good emotion and detail. I'll admit it appears like Kellen is the root of all evil, but you would be just scratching the surface of the story, if you assume he's just like all the other troubled kids."

"I once thought Garrett Brashear was a cool, walk the edge, kind of guy. I think wanting to be a vampire is atypical."

"Don't be so sure about that. I've seen some odd results on teen surveys on who would like to be a vampire. *Psychology Today* has even covered the topic. Live forever. Stay beautiful. Be powerful. Be in charge and above the law. People don't know what it's like being excluded from the sunshine. "

"What are we going to do about the vampires?"

"Nuthin'," Marcus drawled out the word.

"Nothing?! You're just going to sit here?"

"I am safer here than out there. A man's home is his castle. We have guard dogs and crosses to protect us. I am not a vampire hunter by profession, habit, nor vocation. I am a writer with more dark experiences than I would recommend. Last time, we defended ourselves by going on the offensive because we knew we were going to be attacked that night by Mr. Shade. Ripley didn't attack us outright, so we should give him the benefit of the doubt."

"Shade showed up peacefully, but it had already murdered Jo Gunn."

"I'm hoping that in the world of vampires, there are Gunns, Chandlers, and Knights."

"Huh?" Scooter was confused. Because he felt like he had a thousand splinters, the itching made it hard to think clearly.

"The Gunns are the troublemakers. The Chandlers are the Joe Blow citizens, unproductive types who entertain and relate stories, while the Knights are the peace keepers."

Scooter's mind was spinning, trying to make sense out of it. "You mean, you hope that Shade was atypical."

"I do. Vampires might all be evil, but I doubt they're all intrusive. Otherwise, more would be known about them. Secrecy, like darkness, is their greatest ally."

"Then you won't do anything."

"I will defend myself and my friends. I will not go hunting the darkness in the shadows. This isn't an *X-files* rerun. We can die. We were lucky last time. Please, promise me you won't go out hunting vampires again."

Scooter promised, unless forced by extenuating circumstances. "I wish this would all go away, but since I know the truth, it's hard to do nothing. Agent Pryde is certain it has to do with that L.A. cult from years ago."

Marcus appeared thoughtful. "That's possible. But I have taken what precautions I can, since barbed wire won't keep them out and I won't use razorwire. I have been researching vampires online, far beyond what I used to do for movies, and I can't find anything useful."

Scooter scratched. "I have trouble sleeping."

"Enough grim chat! Follow me."

He walked with Marcus across the gravel and hard pan dirt to the barn. The hens clucked and murmured from the coop, making a little more noise as he slid open the large wooden barn door.

"Scooter, motivation must make sense. It helps us understand the reason why things happen. Do you see why I can't refuse Kellen?" Marcus asked.

His mentor wasn't going to let it go. "Did someone give you a break when you were young?"

"You hit the nail on the head. Many have given me help when I least expected it, but needed it most. That is why I still have hope. That is why I must help Kellen."

"Can I just think it through?" Scooter asked as he followed Marcus to one of the empty stalls.

The Pickup Ranch stabled two horses and an old milk cow named Maybelle. The barn would have been stifling without a breeze. The wind carried flecks of hay and dusty seed into a low cloud. Scooter listened, hearing with Flash's dog ears."Puppies?"

Five rested asleep with a tawny cocker spaniel mother. Scooter gently stroked the five fuzz balls. They looked healthy with bright glows, but the mom was scrawny.

"She's a stray that wandered in a few days ago. Beauty lets her stay, and now I have puppies. Want one?"

"I already have the world's best dog."

Flash perked up, the happiest of canines.

"Would you help me find homes for them?"

"Sure. I can post signs and talk to people," Scooter said. Just seeing puppies made him feel better.

"Great. I know it's a lot to ask, but will you help me help Kellen?"

Scooter pondered the Intruder. He almost said no. "Only because you asked. I wouldn't want him to end up in a mental hospital like Garrett Brashear."

"That will have to do," he replied.

Marcus' cell phone chimed. "Hello? Yes. Micah? Glad to hear from you, sonny boy. What? What do you mean they're coming? Who? Micah?" he asked, his voice stricken. After several more unanswered questions, he hung up. "The network dropped the call, or we were cut off."

They waited, but Micah never called back.

Who was coming? Scooter wondered.

THIRTEEN

NO ASYLUM

Sitting in the corner of his padded room at the Bluff County Mental Hospital, Garrett could feel the darkness swell like the sky before a Texas twister. Night inevitably followed sunset and twilight, but this time the coming dark bristled with deadliness.

The heat cooled abruptly, giving him a sweaty chill. Not that any of them would help him against a vampire.

Could it be Tai?

It must be! Nothing else thrilled him, beyond any drug or high. Anticipation ran her fingers along his naked flesh. He had never believed that the she-immortal had died.

He was just as sure that Tai and Lucius Shade weren't the same creature. Why would he believe a backstabber like Scoot Boy the Superzero? Or the sheriff's lap boy, Racquel's hapless and stuttering brother, Russ?

No, he was certain Tai had survived. She thrived in secret while the idiots presumed they could destroy her.

There could be two reasons Tai was here at the luxury apartments of Club de Bluff County Brainworks. She might be angry that he had been unable to escape on his own. While the leader of the Graveyard Armadillos was stronger than mere mortals, he wasn't strong enough to escape. The staff was prepared to deal with maniacal strength.

Was she here to make him suffer for not stopping the boat? That had been BJ's and CJ's fault.

Four steps across and six paces wide, he paced impatiently from wall to padded wall. After the first week, he had mustered patience. Now, with his mistress here, his impatience reared, breaking loose after . . . How long?

He foolishly hoped Tai had finally come to reward him for his loyalty and faith—to unleash him from these mortal trappings. He leered. Surely she would gift him with his most fervent desire: the ultimate kiss of the vampire.

Who would pay first? Scoot Boy, absolutely, and your little mutt, too! He laughed out loud. Russell and his father, the Lawman, certainly. He relaxed when he recalled the patience he would need to thrive as a vampire. Vengeance was best served cold, someone had said, probably one of the undead.

First, he would find BJ and CJ. Discover why they hadn't come to visit. None of the Graveyard Armadillos had, only his mother and father. He wasn't nothing, nor a nobody. He wasn't an embarrassment, and he wasn't crazy as a loon.

He was handsome, cool, calm and collected. Why? Because he knew the truth. Vampires thrived beyond life. They had risen above the cattle of humanity.

Tai! Come release me. Unleash me!

His words became a chant, then a mantra of affirmation.

Moments before the storm unleashed driving rain, the sharp crack of the lightning awakened Garrett. With the musky odor of overturned earth, Tai drifted in on the breeze, smelling as sweet as a field of lilies.

Another flash of lightning highlighted her. Magnificent beyond beautiful, she was busty and shapely, seductively clad in a simple, short black dress. Her hair and eyes were so dark they seemed an exotic deep purple. "Hello, Garrett, my faithful one."

"Mistress. I've been eager to be with you."

"I'm sure you have. I know you have been faithful."

Her opaque eyes grew larger, bringing the weight of the world down on him. "Do you know why I am here?"

"To keep your promise to turn me into a vampire!"

"You assume too much. Presume that you are deserving, when in truth, you are a failure. The vampire law is very clear on what happens to familiars who fail their master. While I was punishing Scooter Keyshawn, you were supposed to be guarding me. What were you doing instead?"

"Getting Racquel ready for the transformation."

"Ha! You were fondling her! For your inattention, you will suffer until you break down and kill yourself." Her hard-edged stare cut him to the quick. "I cannot make you suffer for an eternity, but I can make it seem that long."

Garrett's fear of her was overwhelmed by his utter fury at being betrayed. He hadn't failed Tai! He had done his part. The Mochrie boys were the failures. "What about BJ and CJ?"

She paused to let the thunder boomers roll through, shaking the cell and the air around them. "Worry not. They are suffering, too. I looked deep into BJ and saw what he despised most were religious hypocrites like his mother. In other words, I turned him into his mother, a stern, spare the rod, spoil the child zealot. He was already whuppin' up on CJ, so all I added was a compelling to read the Bible and pedantically preach it in his pretentious 'know-it-all' way."

She watched her prey, playing with her victim like a feral feline. "And all this time, BJ knows exactly what he's doing, but he's powerless to do otherwise." She chuckled. "He has free will, as long as it follows my compellings. His destiny is to eventually die of a self-induced heart attack, stroke, or seizure. But it usually takes a while. I recall a servant who had to develop bone cancer to die. It was long and painful. But BJ is a showoff kind of boy, so I expect him to go in a dramatic way."

The horror of it struck Garrett. BJ probably wished he was already dead.

"Oh, he wishes all right. But the only way he can escape is to will himself dead. With the human survival instinct, that's very difficult. He'll have to put all his heart into it, one might say. I expect you to give a 110%," she chuckled throatily. "I know you have a lot of heart and will faithfully hold out. But if that's not enough motivation, here's your chance to prove you are tougher than the other Graveyard Armadillos. I expect you to live longer, your pain far outlasting theirs."

He gathered all his rage and threw it at her. *"You must keep your bargain!"* he yelled fiercely, fighting against the mesmerizing.

She blinked. For a moment, she didn't look like the Tai he had known. A second blink and the power of her disdainful stare slapped him down, a gnat struck by a sledge hammer. She ground a stiletto heel into his chest as she loomed over him, claws unbarred.

"Now. What will you hate most? Hmm," Tai mused aloud, pondering the possibilities. *"You will give up everything you love — all those wonderful vices. No nicotine. Bye 'bye cigarettes. No booze. No beer. Nothing experimental. Absolutely no sex. It's abstinence for you. Think of it as purifying your soul by cleansing your body.* And yet, that's not enough. That's not herculean enough for a Texas-sized stud like you! You can handle more."

He saw nothing but her eyes.

"You will become a health and exercise fanatic, treating your body to only the best. Running will become your joy. Hiking a thrill. Nature calls to you, and you want to save it. Do you like the sound of your new life?"

Garrett wanted to puke.

"*You will request, plead, even beg, to join the volunteer wild fire fighting crews. Failing that, you will get on with the brush cutting crew.* You just want to be outside. Sweat and fresh air will make you a new man."

Garrett could think of no worse.

"When you realize it is utterly hopeless and when your body gives up its ghost, then you can die."

"No," he managed through clenched teeth.

"I expect even more. *You will become a straight A student. Go on to college.* What shall you become? Hmm? How about a teacher? There is poetic justice, but then, I am a poet laureate, so that fits, doesn't it? What do you think? Elementary school kids?"

"No!" he wailed. The thunder echoed her demand.

"Yes! *You shall get your teaching credential and instruct kids.* Tonight is the first darkness of the rest of your life, as you become a changed man. *You will be healthy and fit, a respectable member of the community. You will be kind, even chivalrous to women, opening doors and helping them whenever a task is too arduous or unladylike.* Yes, *you will unselfishly help people.* They will call you a saint when they finally bury you.

"Death will come slowly because you will stay healthy and fit, living a lie, hating every minute of it. Or, you know, you can survive by embracing it."

Even after Tai disappeared in the darkness, her laughter haunted him. It seemed to live in the fire that branded her commands into his brain.

Garrett fought it, but he couldn't wait to get outdoors. Before he knew what was happening, he was doing jumping jacks, sit-ups and push-ups. He paused to puke, then went back to building the brand new, nature-lover and bleeding heart: St. Garrett Brashear.

FOURTEEN

ODDS AND ENDS ON THE CHURCH STEPS

When Scooter saw Kristie standing impatiently near the bench in front of the First Community Church of Gunstock, he felt rushed and uptight. He had obsessed about this moment, so he barely noticed the large crowd. He had a lot to tell Kristie, but most importantly, he wanted her to know how much he missed her.

Kristie was dazzlingly beautiful and glistening, despite the weary shadows in her face. She looked serene, but her coppery hair betrayed her, the spiky locks bristling angrily. In a way, she seemed a perfect match for the day. The glorious morning sun was already besieged by dark clouds on a soon-to-be stormy day. Even so, he wouldn't have to worry about vampires until dusk.

She glanced up, her gaze on her mother's back. Mrs. Candel talked to the assistant mayor of Gunstock. Russell had been right about Kristie's mother. Mrs. Candel appeared much healthier, standing straighter and shaking less. Her aura was brighter with less crimson streaks than before. Even so, her smile seemed forced by the weight of her daughter's glare.

It still amazed Scooter that he could see their lights. Each person's aura was different and unique, like glow-in-the-dark paintings found at the Ft. Worth Museum of Art. He wished they could see as he did. It might change their outlook. Those who were angriest not only saw red, but their auras ranged from crimson to bloodthirsty-screaming scarlet, bleeding onto others, probably making them mad.

Kristie's expression changed when she saw him. Scooter grinned as she lit up, her golden-purple aura brightening.

"Hi, Kristie! It's fantastic to see you!" On your feet again, he almost finished. He was disappointed and confused by her perfunctory embrace. He had expected a bear hug.

"Thanks, Scooter," she said coolly, despite the tight anger around her eyes and in her gaze.

"You look . . . good, if a little mad."

"A little?" she growled.

"Last time I saw you, I was really, really worried, but then, you had passed out."

"Oh, yeah. I'm just tired. Tired of tests. Tired of Mother. Tired of not being able to do anything," she bemoaned, then she perked up. "I'm glad to see you out and about. I was worried the lightning might have changed you. Somehow rewired your brain so that you no longer believed in . . . you know." Her attention was far away.

"I still believe. Is something wrong?"

"Yes. No," she said, her startling eyes fluttering in distress. Her tentative smile only added to the picture of confusion, then she spoke in a nervous burst. "Sorry. I'm tired. I'd rather be sleeping, but, because we have special guests from the burned churches and temple, Mother wants me to sing *Ave Maria*. She says I can do that in my sleep. See! I'm rambling. How are you . . . really?"

"Okay, considering," he replied then dropped his voice. "Flash is miserable without you around, and I feel the same, if not worse." He fought the urge to scratch. How much should he tell her about the idol and Shade's dead ringer?

"That's kind of you to say. I . . . wondered, since you didn't mention it Friday."

Scooter instantly felt stupid and gypped. "Oh, I mistakenly assumed you'd gotten enough kisses from Flash," he joked, and she laughed delightfully. Had she expected to be kissed? He boldly swept up her hand, like a character in a book, and kissed it. "I beg your pardon."

"You are forgiven. I guess we needed blackberry bushes," she said and blushed. He almost kissed her right then and there, but this wasn't the place. "Tell Flash I feel let down."

Scooter thought he understood. "I think he knows. We're close now," he said, holding up crossed fingers. "I'm chasing birds in my dreams, and he has a preference for smart redheads who don't mind him howling at sing-alongs."

"Oh, how I have missed you!" She hugged him genuinely. Never had anything felt so wonderful, leaving his ears ringing. Her hug rendered him almost speechless. Then he felt a weight in his pocket and remembered.

"I believe this is yours," he said, handing her a silver and opal cross pendant.

Her glow transformed. "You found it! Oh, thank you!" She leapt into his arms and kissed him resoundingly. His ears rang, and he might as well have been hit by lightning again.

"Where was it?" Kristie finally released him to ask. "Mother, he found Grandma's pendant!" She held it aloft. Mother watched, her arms crossed, as Kristie looped her current silver chain necklace through, immediately wearing the cross. With a sound of relief, she said, "I feel better. Thank you."

"I found it yesterday near the boat, where it had been washed ashore. I tried to tell you, but Nurse Gabby refused to put the calls through."

"Look at me? What do you see?" Kristie asked earnestly.

Put on the spot, he wondered if this was a trick question, so he stalled for time, even as he looked at her outfit and jewelry. Had he missed something obvious and important? How much trouble would it cause if he were completely honest? He recalled being honest recently with Marcus and Judge Grandpa.

"C'mon, what do you see?" Kristie cajoled.

He felt people listening. He made sure his eyes never left hers. "Kristie Candel, age fifteen, charming daughter of the spiritual leaders of Gunstock," he began, and she groaned, "also the next American Idol sensation, and most importantly, a dear friend of mine and Flash the Wonder Dog. This amazing young lady boldly saved our lives."

By her expression, he was afraid he had missed the mark. She looked ready to cry, then she sort of laughed at herself and growled at the same time. "Life is so unfair."

Scooter stood confused. What was he supposed to be looking for?

"How's my aura?" she finally asked.

Scooter really felt foolish.

"I had the oddest encounter with a doctor. Dr. West seemed to look right into me and know what I was thinking. He asked me about Shade and claimed to believe in the undead. Of course, as far as the hospital is concerned, there isn't any Dr. West. He doesn't exist." She shivered. "For a moment, I wondered if I had been bitten, because my neck hurt a lot. But I rubbed on it and prayed, and it's much better. Am I paranoid? Or crazy? What does my aura tell you?"

Kristie looked different, even the air around her had changed, but he couldn't rule out the lightning affect or even her anger. His own aura looked different in the mirror and when he held up his hands. "Lightning changed all of us. None of us look the same, but the black spiky spots are gone." He looked around, not seeing anybody who might have been influenced by the vampire. There were a lot of visitors, making it more difficult.

"Good. Well, you know if I start acting crazy, do something," Kristie said.

"Oh. Define that for me, please. It might be helpful later," he said, having just mistaken her previous suggestion. "I would hate to offend you, if you dyed your hair pink and got your nose pierced, along with the tattoo: Jesus Rides a Harley."

She giggled, taking some time to recover. He was pleased to see her laugh. "Oh, I don't know. If I give up singing. If I hurt somebody intentionally. That kind of crazy."

"Okay," he replied. The bites' itching was maddening.

"You know, I couldn't help but think I was glad you were chasing birds in your dreams instead of vampire bats. I'm flustrated that nobody believes us. I don't know about you, but I have never lied to my parents. They make me so angry sometimes I can barely see straight. Only you, Russell, and Mr. Chandler believe me, and that's one of the reasons I miss y'all. It's like y'all are the only ones who understand about the world. None of my brothers or sisters believe me, especially Mary, the little witch. I slept awful, which is why I look like this."

"I think you're beautiful," he managed to say without stuttering. He had practiced, waiting for an honest moment.

She was thoughtful as she took his hand and squeezed affectionately. "Flatterer. You make this hard."

"Well, the last time I saw you, you were unconscious."

Kristie laughed, clamping her hands over her mouth. "Ha! Compared to then, I'm sure to look better. Well, I know I'll sing better now, too. Thanks to you."

He liked the feeling of being her inspiration. Scooter still silently debated about whether to tell her about the floating corpse and the Gibbering Darkness idol. She would find out sooner or later. Telling her about it now would make her no safer and most likely ruin her desire to sing. "I also tried to see you Friday, and well, Nurse Gabby kept emphasizing family."

"You are church family," Kristie said, although her eyes and smile told him far more.

"I tried that. She added the word immediate."

"Mother," she growled, stepping back. It was like the sunny skies had just been consumed by thunderstorms, her mood matching the weather. "I can't believe she's doing this! It isn't your fault. And it isn't Russell's, either. Even so . . ."

"Doing what?"

"Um. Mother thinks you and Russell are bad influences. You've been keeping me out late, overnight sometimes, and I come home injured, so . . ." Her voice caught.

Scooter waited, dreading her words. When things got rolling bad, sometimes they kept going downhill.

She wiped the tears, then gathered herself angrily. "Mother has forbidden me from seeing y'all, except at church functions and the like. She doesn't want me to be any part of those vampire hunters. No bicycling. No boating. No fishing. Too tomboyish."

No! Scooter almost screamed. "The world certainly feels unfair today," he managed, tightlipped. He wanted to lash out and break something, or rant, but there were important things to say first.

"Good morning," Russell said, joining them. "Or is it?"

"Buddy! You're here! They let you out? Or did you escape?" Scooter asked.

"Good to see you, too," Kristie said. She embraced Russell.

"They can't find anything wrong with me. Well, nothing n-new anyway. Have you noticed all the new people here?"

Honestly, Scooter hadn't. Kristie nodded. "We extended

an invitation to those at Temple Bat Yam and Hail Mary Church of Grace. We're going to help fundraise."

"What's wrong? Did somebody die?" Russell asked.

When Kristie couldn't respond, Scooter mentioned the ban. "We keep getting Kristie in trouble, so we're only allowed to see her at church functions."

Russell shook his head, disgusted. "Well, we have been judged and found wanting. What are we going to do?"

They all heard a denial, loud and abrupt. The rest of the crowd hushed.

"Well, I don't believe it! Not Herb! He was all talk," Mrs. Hernandez said, raising her accented voice as loud as when she was calling at the county fair.

"Yep, a big hat with no cattle," her husband chuckled. She subtly elbowed Ramon of Martinez Lawn and Landscaping.

"All talk?" Ms. Emmitt snapped. "That so? They found guns, a Minuteman uniform and the white cowl of a dragon. He was out at the Pickup Ranch cheering when the Gunn boys nearly hung Marcus Chandler!" The librarian had been vexed at Scooter before. She had sounded sweet compared to now in her righteous indignation. She always defended Marcus as if he were family. "Seems to me this goes a long way into explaining what happened to Marcus Chandler, the Hail Mary Church and Temple Bat Yam."

"But Herb swears on the holy *Bible* that he isn't involved with the Minutemen or, God-forbid, the KKK. He says someone planted everything," Carlson's best friend spoke up for him. Aaron Nathans credibility was limited to zip codes, postal rates and routes.

Scooter did a double take. Had he heard right? The gas station owner was part of the Klu Klux Klan? The prejudice group that believed in white supremacy? He recalled that Mr. Martin had also been associated with the Minutemen and hate crimes, as well as drugs. Right now, illegal immigration was a hot issue. Judge Grandpa said everyone seemed to need somebody to hate to unify people.

If they knew about vampires, would people of varied backgrounds and beliefs unify? Scooter figured that was impossible, but what a worthy crusade.

"Who would want to set him up?"

"Why Marcus Chandler, of course. He's a director and writer. He could figure it out." The postman was known for serving beer and Twinkies to the extra-terrestials that landed in his back yard. It kept them from mutilating his cows. He had showed many the burn marks that were most likely the black scars of barbecuing while inebriated. An inability to BBQ could be embarrassing to a native Texan.

"Be realistic. There's been nothing but trouble since Chandler came back from Hollywood!" Mr. Peters proclaimed, stepping into the argument. "Last night, I had an uninvited midnight visitor who looked just like Chandler, all dressed in black, seeming even darker because he's dead-fish pale. He warned me to leave town or else."

"Talk some sense," Ms. Emmitt pleaded.

"Sad, isn't it? We should all be tolerant of each other. After all, we are all God's children. Today, the adults are acting like brats," came a voice close behind Scooter and Kristie.

Startling them, BJ had stolen upon them unnoticed. Byron Jefferson looked hearty in his bull-riding Sunday best—austere black pants and a buttoned down shirt so white it blazed incandescent below a silly bow tie.

"You're looking mighty fine today, Mr. Mochrie," Kristie drawled.

"Thank you, Ms. Candel. My body is a gift from God. I should take care of it," BJ replied.

Scooter studied the older boy. He admitted he had envied BJ and his good looks until CJ had aired the truth about the abuse at home. He recalled the elder Mochrie boy's vacant stare from the time he had been possessed by Shade. Now BJ seemed fiery, with a zealot's air.

"Hello, BJ. Has CJ come home yet?" Kristie asked.

"Nope. I wish y'all had hog-tied him and dragged his butt from that hunk of rock. He's deserting his family and his responsibilities."

"Last time, when y'all ran away from home, y'all ran into a vampire," Kristie persisted.

BJ sniffed in disdain. "Y'all have been deceived by an agent of the Lord of Lies, as was I. There is no such thing as vampires."

Scooter glanced at Kristie, just as she looked at him. Even Russell seemed to share the same thought. This was not the Byron Jefferson Mochrie they had known.

"Well, don't look at me like I got horns. I'm ashamed at how I was tempted," he spoke bluntly. "It opened my eyes. Changed me. I suggest y'all examine yourself, fall upon your knees and pray for forgiveness and guidance. I did."

Scooter couldn't help but hear a lie, because BJ had always been fibbing. "We didn't bring CJ back because it would have taken beating him into submission. BJ, CJ is afraid of you."

"CJ is scared of me? I knew he was mad, but I didn't know he was scared. That's never happened before." BJ sounded quite puzzled. "Why?"

"He said he didn't want to end up like you."

"Which means what?" BJ asked, steeling himself. "Go on. He's called me lots of names. I doubt any of them are new."

Scooter paused to scratch and stopped. "He didn't want to end up a hypocrite. He thinks you are living a lie—pretending to be someone you're not."

BJ stood so still it was eerie, as if the words had frozen him. "I don't know what to say."

Scooter felt anger even before Pearl Mochrie joined their

conversation. BJ's mom was a stern woman, her face a perpetual frown and her eyes expressing disapproval. Always willing to speak her mind, she often wrangled with fellow parishioners and neighbors. "Have y'all seen my boy? Y'all trucked with him."

"I saw him two days ago on Fisherman's Island. He said he was camping out," Scooter replied.

"Camping out?! Lying has always been his favorite vice!" Mrs. Mochrie snapped. Scooter could envision her with a raised switch in hand.

The hiss of brakes working to slow a big vehicle turned everyone's attention to the circular driveway. A faded black sedan with darkly tinted windows stopped in the shade of the covered entryway. The driver's door opened, but before the chauffeur could reach the rear passenger door, it swung wide.

Scooter was as shocked as everyone when Marcus Chandler climbed out of the back seat. He wore a white suit and a wide-brimmed field hat to protect him from the cloud-defused sunlight.

The congregation milled, a little subdued and stunned. No one could remember the last time Marcus Chandler had come to town. The 'local vampire' walked in broad daylight.

"That's him," Peters simmered.

Scooter thought some of the women would faint.

As Marcus strolled up the walk, the sun peeked out. A ray of hazy sunshine beamed down on him as a spotlight. He seemed to have expected it, smiling broadly and tipping his hat even. Scooter thought he couldn't have plotted it better, with all the extra people in attendance. He wanted to be seen in a 'new' light.

When he noticed them, he smiled more broadly and strode forward, cane briskly tapping. He seemed oblivious to everyone's stare. In Hollywood, he would have learned to handle it.

"Welcome, Mr. Chandler. This is an unexpected pleasure," Kristie said, beaming and stepping in like angels do.

"You picked a good day. Kristie is singing *Ave Maria*."

"That sounds fantastic. I am glad to be here."

Scooter studied his mentor. He looked calm, but his eyes revealed he was struggling. The sun was getting to him.

"Did y'all feel that?" Kristie lifted her umbrella to protect them, especially Marcus.

"Welcome, Marcus," Judge Grandpa said, joining them. He was quick on the uptake. "Let's go inside before it rains."

Almost as quickly, Reverend Candel arrived to greet Scooter's writing mentor. Peters stood still, white-lipped angry and narrow eyed. He started to approach Sheriff Knight, who simply gestured to settle down. They must have talked about Marcus before.

Around them, emotions shifted in mixed ways, some frowning, while some were shocked. Scooter was gratified to see just as many accepted Marcus Chandler's presence.

Moments later, the bell tolled, calling everyone inside. Kristie's father signaled to her, and she rushed inside.

Scooter realized he hadn't told her what had been found on the island yesterday. It was probably just as well. He took his friend's hand, then his grandmother's, and got in line to go inside.

He glanced over to BJ. He seemed haunted, as if he had seen a specter of the Grim Reaper. BJ's skin gleamed gray and waxy, with his face set in a determined grimace. BJ met Scooter's gaze, then he smiled through a horrible rictus. "Free at last."

His aura was gone in a flash. With an unexpected suddenness, BJ clutched his chest and keeled over atop a pew.

FIFTEEN

LIFE SAVERS

Russell rushed to BJ's side, checking his pulse and breathing. "He's in cardiac arrest. Scooter, help me!" He tossed a face shield to him. Scooter caught it, bewildered for a moment, before he tore it open and set it across BJ's mouth.

"Check to make sure you can read the writing. If it's not face up, flip it. Somebody, Mr. Nathans, get the AED at the VFW," Russell ordered him. The postman raced off.

Russell watched as Scooter breathed through the mask into BJ's mouth. He was doing it right, holding the nose and C-clamping the jaw and mask. BJ's chest rose, then fell. After a second breath, the lungs remained still. The heart stayed quiet.

Russell pulled off BJ's bow tie, opened his shirt, and found 'the landmarks' of the chest to place his hands over the heart. With a loud cough to cover the cracking of bones, he pressed on BJ. He felt the heart resist, when he compressed it fifteen times.

"No breathing. No pulse. I think BJ wants to stay dead."

"But would he? We can't stop," Russell said. He feared BJ would return as a vampire, the mental image haunting him. They worked for a full minute, when they checked again.

Byron Jefferson Mochrie remained dead.

Every second counted, so they were aware of time slipping away. The urgency sapped Russell's strength, and he had only been working a short while. The minutes stretched longer, but Russell just kept at it. Help should show up soon.

What seemed an exhausting hour later was only ten minutes when he heard bustling behind him. Big Bruce stepped in with the AED. While Scooter gave two more breaths, they hooked up the Automated Electronic Defibrillator.

It took over. *"Analyzing. Keep clear of the patient."*

While waiting, Bruce hooked up the oxygen to the mask.

"Shock advised," the machine said.

Bruce had them back up, then he hit the yellow lightning bolt button.

"Shocking."

BJ lurched once. "Analyzing," the AED continued.

Nobody in the church seemed to move, collective breaths held, hoping. Praying.

"A second shock is advised. Stand clear."

Bruce hit the button again.

Watching BJ thrash made Russell wonder about the lightning strike that had hit them. Had they danced like that? It disturbed him, but at least he didn't feel helpless. He had done his best to give BJ a chance.

"No pulse. Discontinue use. Shutting down."

Russell watched, finding out more about emergency care. Conchita stepped in with a large carrying case. Using a long syringe, Bruce injected medicine designed to jump start the heart.

BJ remained lifeless.

Russell looked at Scooter. His friend seemed in shock. Russell also felt numb. He knew that CPR only worked one time out of four, but that was better than nothing. That meant 25% who were dead had a chance to live.

Bruce and Conchita wheeled BJ into the ambulance. They assisted Pearl inside so she could sit beside her son. On her way, she cursed Mr. C, blaming him for all to hear.

They sadly watched the ambulance drive off.

"He spoke to me the moment before he died," Scooter said.

"Who? BJ? What did he say?"

"I'm free," Scooter said. He appeared beaten.

"Whatever that means," Russell said. He remembered what CJ had said about BJ being possessed. Had BJ killed himself to escape? He exchanged looks with Scooter. He could almost read his friends mind, wondering if BJ would stay dead.

The shocking suddenness of the incident turned the church service into a session of prayer and mourning. Russell had trouble sitting still. He itched all over, feeling as if bugs were chewing on him. Scooter acted just as antsy. It was embarrassing to be twitching when everyone else sat still in serious prayer.

Rev. Candel talked about the brevity of life. How we never know how many pages the book of our lives contains. We were the main characters in our own stories, but sometimes we had to step up to be one of the Creator's main characters in moments of need and service. We should also expect, because we are human, to fail sometimes.

Russell found it little solace. He had done all he could, and it still wasn't enough, depressing him. He should stick with motors and electronics.

Afterward, Rev. Candel reminded everybody of the town hall meeting at the VFW, fifteen minutes after the service. A prayer vigil would follow.

Russell overheard numerous people claiming that Mr. C's appearance led to BJ's heart attack. They had felt their own hearts flutter. He tried to steer Scooter away from them.

"Mr. Chandler, I want to have words with you!" Hank Peters growled. All morning, the clean-cut rancher had grumbled about Friday night.

"Yes, sir," Mr. C said as he turned to face him.

"You look at me like you never stormed onto my ranch to threaten me," Peters snapped, staring the man down.

Slumping, Mr. C appeared fatigued. "Sir?"

"Then you're denying it?"

"I haven't set foot on your ranch since I was ten, when you didn't own it," Mr. C replied.

"You said, if I didn't stop my subversive activities — subversive . . . who uses words like that except writers or actors anyway—that I would lose everything."

Mr. C spread his arms. "I have no idea what you're talking about. Honestly, I don't have the energy to harass you."

"It was you! There's no mistake," Peters snarled. "Be warned: I have posted extra no trespassing signs and have my shotgun next to the door." He left in a huff.

Russell could feel the sullen mood beginning to turn angry. Another kid had died. The wrong attention was on Mr. C. He sensed his visit worked against him. If BJ hadn't collapsed, Russell thought Mr. C would have won over all but the prejudiced.

"Well everybody, Marcus' big Sunday adventure is over. I have extended myself and am weary. I think it's time to head home," Mr. C said. He genteelly thanked many people, taking their hand in both of his. They walked him to his big car, which waited in the shade. Ms. Emmitt's brother was his driver and opened the door.

On the way back inside, they walked by the kitchen. "Psst! Get in here!" Kristie sussurated and crooked a finger for them to come in.

Russell looked around, elbowed Scooter, and then darted through the door into the kitchen. He let his best friend by.

"Hey, you guys were great. You did the best anyone could expect. Even the machine didn't revive him," Kristie told them. "You're my heroes."

"Failing ones," Russell said. He had trained so he wouldn't feel hopeless. This wasn't much better.

"Even superheroes fail," Kristie said. "And y'all are just heroes, not supermen. Y'all gave him a chance. Y'all delayed death. Wow. I have a reward for y'all."

She set a bag in Russell's hand. Things inside sloshed.

"The sealed ceramic jars contain holy water. Protect it when you add them to your vampire hunting gear," she said.

"Thanks. Is that all right with your dad?" Russell asked.

"I don't know. I prayed on it and felt good about removing them. I told him I knocked over the basin. It might keep y'all alive sometime. I know y'all face darkness, and I'm afraid I won't be there, so this will have to do in my stead," she said. From out of her purse she handed them two small porcelain, cork-stoppered jars. "This is the real reward. It's Granny's June's 'Bite Mending' ointment. Try it. I brought four jars for a friend, but I can tell y'all need it. Y'all are as twitchy as five year olds. Did the chiggers getcha?"

"Yep," Russell said, exchanging looks with his best friend. "Thanks," he said at the same time as Scooter.

"It's good stuff. I mix it with the holy water, but water works, too. Mom has also used olive oil."

"Are you coming to the meeting?" Scooter asked.

"No. I'm scheduled to sing at the assisted living home, Green Acres," Kristie said.

"Listen, before you go," Scooter began urgently. "There are things you must know about yesterday."

Russell already knew about the body and idol. Just watching Scooter describe it almost made him ill.

For the most part, Scooter spared her. "In the water, they found the body of a man they believe to be Lucius Shade."

"How can that be?" Kristie asked.

"It's not," Scooter said.

"I agree, but they believe it is," Russell added. "The dental work matches the bite marks. Plus, his name is similar to Lucius Shade."

"So they believe they caught the ringmaster," Scooter said.

"Remember that stick pin? It was drugged. They found traces in Kellen and me. Now they think we hallucinated the whole thing," Russell groaned.

"Is this related in any way to what happened to BJ? I kept thinking about what CJ said . . . ." Kristie wrung her hands.

"I think it does," Scooter said.

"What are we going to do?" she asked.

"Kristie!" called her mother.

"I've got to go. If she sees us, she won't let me see you at church, either," Kristie whispered. She embraced Russell, pecking him on the cheek. "Farewell, my heroes. I'll text message y'all when I get another phone."

The serious, full on kiss she gave Scooter left him dazzled.

"Let's see if this stuff works. I'm itching so bad I can't stand still," Russell said. He didn't want to be scratching all during the VFW meeting.

In the men's restroom, he sat on the bench. He was quite surprised to find that most of his chigger bites were gone, leaving only about a dozen. Now they looked more like fire ant bites. He smelled mint, then put a little ointment on his finger to dab a sore. The whitehead hurt and wobbled.

"I smell aloe, eucalyptus, and peppermint. How's it feel?"

"Soothing," Russell said. As he smeared his bites, he counted them. "I have thirteen sores. Was Flash bitten?"

Scooter shook his head. "You want to know something creepy. I have thirteen, too. What did they say at the hospital?"

"They said they were chigger bites. That's not what worried them."

"Did BJ have any bites?' Scooter asked.

"I didn't see any. He had other problems."

"I can't get it out of my head what he said. CJ said that BJ wasn't acting like himself. Could that have killed him?"

"I don't know what to think. Even about this. Do you want to see something weird?" Russell asked. He walked over to the hot air hand dryer on the wall. He reached out, sensing, but not touching the machine. He felt a static shock, then the dryer died. The light bulb burst.

Darkness sprang. He stood stunned, feeling pounced upon.

"Did you do that?" Scooter squeaked. He clicked a penlight on a key chain, shining a light.

"Yeah. The bulb was by accident. Sorry."

"Well, it would be cooler if you could get the light to come back on." Scooter propped open the door. He stood back and breathed a sigh of relief in the sunlight.

Using his lightning gift, Russell got the hand dryer to work. "The same happened on a bunch of the medical equipment. It's one of the reasons it took so long for them to test me. The doctor's think the ringing in my ears is Tinnitus, but they can't explain why I blow fuses in electronics. I think I hear electricity flowing."

"I'm not bringing my Gameboy around you."

"Good thinking" Russell replied. Fortunately, he had

gotten his to work again. He could play it with medical gloves.

"Do you think it was the lightning?"

"I guess so. What else could it be?" he asked. He glanced at his watch. "Hey, we better hurry. The meeting should start soon."

"It's probably just more bad news," Scooter said.

Russell didn't like being part of it. Why couldn't they save BJ? Who was next to die?

SIXTEEN

THE INTERLOPER

Back home after the meeting, Scooter checked on the bites. The town gathering had been hot and lacking any new information. People still joked about the Vampire Hunters. Fortunately, none of those found in the graves were from Gunstock. Agent Pryde showed up, causing a stir. Russell created an even bigger splash when he repaired the air conditioning. For months, it had defied fixing.

And yet, BJ's death overshadowed everything. It had happened right before their eyes. Russell had tried his best, but BJ had wanted to die. Scooter wondered if he had resisted returning to the living. He hoped BJ didn't come back as undead.

While dabbing on more Granny June's bug bite ointment, the one on his wrist erupted. A small red spider crawled out of the pus pocket. Scooter swatted it, but it scuttled away. The one on his shoulder popped, releasing another arachnid. A leg bite exploded, oozing white ichor.

Awakening with a shout, Scooter bolted upright. He leapt out of bed, searching for spiders and finding none.

He looked around, disoriented before remembering that he was in the Jaystone's house. The brand new superhero images Scooter had temporarily posted on the walls and door did little to bolster his courage. The crosses helped more than the images of Spiderman, Superman, or the Silver Surfer.

In the bathroom, he examined the bites and applied ointment. The sores looked the same, but he couldn't stop thinking about it.

Unless he thought about Kristie. She dominated his wonderings, including his concerns for her safety. Her grounding, BJ's death, his arachnid nightmare, and knowing vampires walked the night made it impossible to sleep.

Over the bellowing chorus of frogs, the wind chimes sounded discordant, harshly counting the number of bodies he had seen in the crude graves, plus one for BJ. That made twelve kids that had died since late May.

Until today, he had been as sure as certain could be that Shade had been destroyed. He rubbed his neck again, just to be sure the scar was gone.

Scooter had written about his first visit to the Pickup Ranch, meeting Shade, and everything else in *The Vampire Hunters Club*. Only those involved had read it. Judge Grandpa had described it as a highly effective, atmospheric, and disturbing yarn. Marcus said it flowed, keeping things simple while being riveting and thought-provoking.

Eyes closed, Flash whimpered and woofed softly.

"Just a bad dream, boy," Scooter said, commiserating as he patted his dog. His fingers played along the dog's blest collar.

In Scooter's weary state, his body was in hyperdrive with senses on maximum. He could smell and hear things he'd never noticed before. The frogs and crickets sounded as if they were trying to loudly out perform each other.

Unable to endure the wind chimes any longer, Scooter struggled out of bed. The breeze wasn't the only thing that stank. He found some old socks under the bed, and all his shoes smelled rank. He gathered them up, waking up Flash.

His golden dog struggled to his paws wrapped in medicated socks and trotted gingerly into the living room. At the backyard screen door, his best friend woofed and cocked his head, whining softly.

Scooter strained his senses. He heard something scurrying across the ground. He clutched the cross on his amulet, then he went to the window, expecting the worst.

He saw the glow of life around a creature bumbling across the yard and relaxed. "It's just an armadillo."

When Scooter pushed the screen door open, Flash snapped, bite-grabbing his shirt. Then Scooter smelled it. He hastily shut the door. A skunk meandered across the porch.

"Thanks," he said and hugged his super dog. While he waited, he went to the kitchen. He gave his best friend three doggie cookies as a reward.

Looking perkier, the golden Lab checked the back yard, giving him a tail-wagging all clear. The night air smelled of newly mown grass, decomposing leaves, and duck poop with a hint of passing skunk. Flash rushed to water the trees leading to the lake.

Scooter took two steps and got snagged by a spider web strong enough to slow a low-flying jet. It was tough and springy, letting him back out and draw away. He ducked and grabbed a broom to clear a path. Even so, two spiders dropped on him.

In the distance, he could see lightning cavort among black clouds. He felt like he wore a fur coat and wool cap. Was he crazy? Or was he sensing what Flash felt? They had been together since Flash's birth. The pup's mom had died while giving him life. He had been runty, not expected to live. Scooter had immediately loved the little guy.

The nearby frogs and crickets hushed, leaving a distant

throbbing of the night's lake song. Flash growled, throaty and angrily protective. Scooter's hackles rose as he tensed. The air grew cooler with a chilling wind. The darkness grew thicker and opaque, the stars disappearing behind clouds.

Nobody was along the lakefront beach or the dock. The breeze ruffled the water, rocked the pier, and made the wind socks flap madly. Leaves and pine nettles tumbled by.

A vampire was here! Was it Ripley? Shade? BJ?

"I know you're out there," Scooter whispered. At his words, the darkness remained still. He could barely breathe, and he wanted to run, but he couldn't outrace a vampire. In the background, he heard drumming, then he realized his heart pounded hard and fast against his chest.

Flash growled again.

"That's enough of that," came a voice. Scooter saw the man's life light before he stepped out from behind two trees and a bush along the fence of Siete Hombres. Mr. Little, the white-clad reporter, was a pain in the neck.

Scooter took a deep breath and sighed. It was obvious that he had assumed wrong when he had felt somebody but hadn't seen any life light.

"Why are you snooping around here?"

"For a story. For glory. What else is there? Are you going to beat me with that broom?"

Scooter felt sheepish. He hadn't realized he was holding it like a weapon. "Of course not."

Little popped a piece of gum into his mouth, then he folded the foil wrapper into the shape of a cross. "I hear you spend time with Marcus Chandler at the Pickup Ranch. How's the local celebrity involved in this?"

Flash growled in a low tone reserved for vampires. Little was another kind of bloodsucker.

Turning to go back inside, Scooter said, "I don't do interviews before sunrise."

"I read your manuscript: *The Vampire Hunters Club*."

Scooter stopped, hooked. How had he gotten his hands on a copy? "So? That's fiction."

"Is it?"

"Why? Do you want to send it to the *National Inquirer*? They already came by."

"Cute, kid. I think you have a future as a storyteller. You write a hundred times better than I did at your age. Come on, tell me a story about Friday at the island. Or Saturday, I heard you found the body. Was it really Lucius Shade, the vampire?"

"Talk to the sheriff's department. I wrote a report."

"I figured you might've remembered something new."

Instead of coming inside, Flash darted off.

Scooter thought about it. He wasn't sure what to say about today. He also heard Judge Grandpa trying to sneak up. "Mr. Little, I'm too tired and too worried about my friends to tell stories, but, if you need something to do, look up a Mr. Ripley, a reporter for the *L.A. Times*. He has an interesting story to tell. I wonder why it hasn't been printed yet," Scooter said, setting his own hook.

"Mr. James Little!" Judge Grandpa said. He didn't look like a kindly Santa Claus tonight. "What are you doing here at this time of night? On private property?!"

"I was meeting with your grandson about current events. There's something odd going on here, and it isn't just the Gunns, Martin, Carlson, or the concern over illegals and Minutemen. People are hiding secrets. I can smell a succulent story. So, what about being struck by lightning?"

"I'm a writer and an illustrator. I get struck by inspiration all the time," Scooter replied.

"Go away, Mr. Little. You have the count of ten to be out of my sight. One." Grandpa said, opening his phone.

"Hey, what's that smell?" the reporter gasped.

Flash barked. Little screamed. The stench of an alarmed skunk wafted pungently through the night air.

The last they heard was Jimmy B. Little cursing.

"That should take care of him for a while. I just hope we don't have to wash Flash," his grandfather chuckled. They slipped inside ahead of the rain.

Scooter closed his eyes. Flash felt joyous, running around. He had a feeling his dog was chasing Little off the property. "I think he spooked the skunk into spraying Little."

"Then we owe him a special treat," Judge Grandpa said. "Let's get some rest. Morning will come soon enough."

SEVENTEEN

A WAY OUT

On her way out, Kristie slammed the door. The impact shook the back wall and porch, causing the stack of boxes to tumble. When they hit the ground, rubber duckies escaped. The Downwater ducks for the fundraiser bounced and scattered in every direction like kids deserting a disaster.

Just a few minutes ago, the toilet had clogged and overflowed. Because she was the oldest, she had the privilege of fixing it.

"Oh Cinderella, come mop the floor. Do the laundry, Cindy. How about picking up those ducks for us? You're such a big help. What would we do without you?"

Like a javelin, she hurled the mop across the yard, barely missing the laundry hanging on the line. If she had dumped the clean clothes, she wouldn't have been able to withhold a primal scream.

Mother was having one of those painful mornings. Kristie saw it in her eyes and by the way she uncomfortably shifted every few minutes. That didn't keep her from complaining about Russell and Scooter. Mary had found her copy of *The Vampire Hunters Club*. Mother had shredded it into pieces.

Even after Russell and Scooter had saved Kellen and tried to revive BJ, Mother still described them as troublemakers. Kristie had missed Scooter over the previous six weeks, and now she longed to spend more time with him. She hoped he thought of something because she couldn't. Mother shared stubborn traits with a mule.

On her way to the garage, rain drops splattered Kristie. Wanting time by herself, she stormed to the garage to organize things. If one of the kids came out for help, she would give them a task. Donations already piled up. If she separated and labeled them as they arrived, it didn't seem like such a overwhelming task.

She pondered BJ's life, death, and the funeral, and she wept. Life could be short. Vampires made it shorter. She didn't know how, but she knew they were somehow to blame. Where was CJ?

The family tabby limped up to her. Kristie rubbed on Chester. She had once tried to paint stripes on him, having named him after the Chesire cat in *Alice and Wonderland*. While she stroked his fur, she could sense the cat's arthritis. When she finished, Chester darted off, then looked back gratefully.

Her hands felt stiff. When she stretched them she got spiky twinges. For a while her fingers were reluctant to do what she wanted, especially write. On her notepad, her scrawl looked childish.

She stuck stickers on lawnmowers, chest of drawers, vacuum cleaners, and such, while composing a price list. She moved small things, thinking about calling her brother to help with the big rocker and the dining table, but she preferred the peace and quiet.

For a silly moment, she could picture the mice, raccoons, and armadillos gathering around to listen to her. They would probably wait until the song was done, then applaud and ask her to gather nuts for them, pull some weeds, or smuggle them a few tomatoes.

Some people wondered aloud how, at the tender age of fifteen, she could sing about heartbreak and suffering. Sometimes it seemed like that's all she encountered. Last night, Mrs. Warner had died. She had been a wonderful voice teacher, but cancer had taken her abruptly.

This morning, just before dawn, she had awakened, dreaming she had sung at a hundred funerals. She worried about Russell and Scooter with a vampire prowling Gunstock. Would it seek revenge? Would she be singing at their funerals next?

It was spitting rain when Mrs. Ringly drove up in her old, blue car. The big Cadillac was almost completely packed with clothing and knickknacks. Two bicycles perched on the rack attached to the rear bumper.

As she was rolling a girl's Schwinn bicycle, Kristie watched a swallow slam into the rear window of the Caddy. The bird landed in a heap at her feet.

She set down the bicycle and picked up the swallow. It only had one eye, which explained its flying difficulties. When Kristie first picked it up, she thought it was dead, but she felt some of its pain. Its little feathery breast rose and fell. The bird was still alive!

The bird stood up, shook itself, flapped its wings once, and then with a chirp, flew away.

"You have a healing touch," Mrs. Ringly said.

The entire time Kristie helped unload the donations, she kept thinking about Chester, the bird, and the times she had laid her hands on Scooter and Kellen.

It gave her an idea that might lead her to freedom. Mother could be a mom, and Kristie could pursue her dreams of singing to heal others.

EIGHTEEN

UNLIKE OLD TIMES

Scooter tried to wake up, excited about getting out on the lake. He had been in a daze, feeling sluggish and sad since BJ's funeral. Sleep remained elusive. Nightmares of spiders eating on him and the Mochrie brothers dying haunted him nightly.

He was less excited about the ungodly hour—the dark of the early morning. Russell agreed it was necessary because they were out of bait. The fish weren't biting lures, so they had to harvest night crawlers.

The friends sat on their life jackets while they paddled east over the wide-open waters. Tawakoni reflected the stars, creating a twinkling sea that led to a sky broken by the shadow of land.

Scooter looked over their supplies. It included fishing equipment, weather gear, their bucket of fireworks paraphernalia, Russell's backpack, his own duffel bag, and two red and white Coleman coolers.

Russell had chosen a canoe, Scooter realized, because he didn't want a motorized boat. He reminded himself to be careful of letting him touch anything electronic.

Feeling sticky, Scooter paused in paddling to adjust his shirt. He stopped scratching after one stroke. "How are your bites?"

"I was doing fine, getting a decent night sleep, until last night. I'm out of ointment."

"Already?"

"There's more of me to cover. I need to get more from Kristie. I feel chewed on, and it's not even hot yet."

"You can use some of mine."

"Thanks. Did your grandfather want you coming out today? Dad didn't. He was digging in like a mule."

"Neither did Judge Grandpa. He's worried about predators. I said, why? The Gunns are in jail. It doesn't look like we have to testify. Lucius Shade is dead. What should I be worried about?"

Russell laughed nervously. "You really said that?"

Scooter was a little sheepish. "Well, mostly. He asked me if I was going looking for trouble. I said never. I think BJ dropping dead really spooked him. It did me. I keep hearing what BJ said about being free." He resumed paddling.

"I have news about Lewis Shaddock. He drowned, apparently without a struggle. His bite matches the marks on the dead kids."

"They told him to just walk into the lake," Scooter thought aloud. "He would obey. We would have to do the same." He rubbed the phantom pain in his neck. "My marks are smooth. That's why I still think Shade is gone. "

"The authorities believe they have an open and shut case with a fresh corpse, the dental records, more bodies, and of course, the poison on the stick pin which just happens to be a hallucinogenic. Isn't this all kind of neat? Yep. Now they're looking into whether there are other cultists. That's why my dad hesitated. I said that if I had to die, I want to go fishing. I promised to stay away from Shade's Island. What did Mr. C say about the cultists?"

"Not much. Just a bunch of crazies, who believe his movie is true. He recalled that Micah was involved and phoned him. When Micah called back, he was cut off, or the call was dropped, but not before he warned us that 'they' were on the way."

"That sucks. Why didn't you tell me at the funeral?" Russell asked. Of late, he was easily offended and slighted.

"Sorry. I figured after Ripley and the island, you were on high alert already. I don't know who *they* are. Why lose more sleep? Perhaps they can travel through shadows, and they were already here. Do you want to go back home?"

"Hell no. Staying at home doesn't mean we're safe. No place is safe," Russell snapped, then breathed deeply to relax. He kept paddling. "Have you heard that another person filed a complaint about Mr. C threatening them?"

"No. Why won't people leave him alone?"

"Mr. Chung said he and his wife were harassed Tuesday night. Dad said the report read a lot like Peters' and Ringly's."

"This doesn't make sense. Why is somebody pretending to be Marcus?"

Russell shrugged. "Maybe to piss off everyone. Are you going out to the Pickup Ranch later today?"

"Don't worry. Flash is with me. That's almost as good as a guardian angel, Judge Grandpa says."

Flash licked Scooter along the side of his face.

"Smile, you two!" Russell said as he held up his phone. It flashed. Russell grinned, then showed off the phone's screen. "It takes photos!"

Scooter was surprised. "You didn't overload it."

"I've been practicing. If I hold back, I'm less likely to zap anything. I'm better when I'm not all itchy." He handed it over for Scooter to check out.

On the phone's screen, he looked grim. Flash was overjoyed. "I wish Kristie were here."

"Yeah, I can tell. I sent her a text message. No word back."

"Next time we face a vampire, you can take his photo."

"That's exactly what I was thinking," Russell snorted. He put down the phone, scratched, and returned to paddling.

"Judge Grandpa suggested I use my imagination to figure out how to see Kristie again. He said I should look at her mother as the problem to solve in the story, but that I should look for some way to change her mind."

"Have you thought of anything yet?" Russell asked.

Scooter shook his head and stared morosely about.

To the south, they could see the dark expansive of dam. Red lamps highlighted its presence to promote safety. They passed Heron's Point.

"Hey, that's where you sank," Russell said.

While fishing in waders, Scooter had stepped into a deeper channel before the rise of the point. Russell remembered because he had helped free him. They continued to stroke beyond the Sabine River mouth, Tawakoni Dam, and the TU Electric hydroelectric plant.

"We need Kristie if we're going to hunt vampires."

"Marcus said he didn't want to be a vampire hunter. He would defend himself, but he wouldn't try righting all the wrongs in the world. He's too old to go looking for trouble."

"I just planned to be ready. I'm not looking for trouble."

"Uh-huh." Scooter wasn't so sure. Lately, Russell had been behaving aggressively. "He hoped that vampires were similar to people with different outlooks. He even wondered if there were such a thing as vampiric policemen or detectives. He decided there would almost certainly be cliques, because they were once human. Look at what Shade wanted. A movie of his life. If nothing else, the vampires would disagree on how to handle their cattle."

"Meaning us? Hmm. Come to think of it, to live long years in secret, they need to quietly bump us off one at a

time, making each one seem like an accident. I'm starting
to think you should stay away from Mr. C. He's snake-bit."

"Russell! He's my friend. If something were to happen
to him, and I wasn't there to help, I would feel awful. He's
been such a big help to us. You can count his timely rescues."

"He's also the focal point of trouble. Some people now
blame him for BJ's death. It could get ugly."

"I don't even like leaving him alone with Redgraves.
He might develop a messiah complex and try to murder
him."

"You're getting paranoid."

"I feel justified. We're here. Look," Scooter pointed out.
Along the shore, he could make out five figures. Russell
aimed the spotlight on them. The painted, cardboard aliens
appeared rain-droopy on their stands. They were burnt here
and there from previous barrages.

They landed, armed themselves, and hiked a little into
shore, past the figures to the worm farm. It sat in a lowlands
in a dry creek below the Spooky Tree.

"One of us should keep watch," Scooter said. Flash
barked.

"I will. I brought a surprise," Russell said.

Scooter nodded, then set down the halogen light,
selecting a lamp mode so he could see. It lit up the giant
oak, a sprawling tree given character by lightning. The great
tree was missing about half its upper trunk and branches.
Much of the rest was blackened. Near it, Scooter found the
half-buried rebar. As he'd been shown, he wired the twenty
metal spikes together, looping through the top. Neither of
them had believed this worked until Judge Grandpa
showed them. Ever since, they harvested worms this way.

It hadn't seemed like a big deal, before vampires stalked
the night. Scooter suffered worry-visions that BJ would
suddenly spring out of the darkness. He grabbed a mallet,

then repeatedly tapped a stake. In bunches, worms oozed out of the ground.

Flash barked and dashed to the canoe. Scooter followed closely, stumbling over a rock and falling onto his hands and knees. He barely got there in time to see the raccoons abandon ship and lumber off.

"Good dog!" Scooter said.

Big and looking mean, Russell held .38 in hand. It was the same one they practiced with when they visited Russell's father at the shooting range. Scooter was shocked.

"Don't look at me that way. Your grandfather knows and Dad's been giving me shooting lessons, as well as my own gun. I have a special license. I finished the course last week."

Scooter wasn't sure what to say. "That's why you've been so busy! You're taking two classes. I just figured you didn't want to help with the house." He was disappointed and worried to find his bud with a gun, even a legal one.

"Ha! I help you all the time."

"Why didn't you tell me? "

"I wanted to surprise you with my amazing marksmanship. I was going to tell you last Friday, but I know Kristie doesn't like guns. After what happened with the Gunn brothers, Dad doesn't want me to be defenseless. I don't want to be helpless, either." Russell Knight looked far from weak, meek, and stuttering, now bigger and holding a gun. His best bud looked mean as the Incredible Bulk. That bothered him, because Russell wasn't nasty-natured.

"It's a huge responsibility."

"I know, it scares me."

"It scares me more," Scooter replied. Just because Russell had learned how to use a gun safely didn't mean he wanted it on the canoe. It wouldn't save him from dying like BJ, either.

In a tense silence, they returned to hunt more worms. Scooter banged on the metal spikes, making the night crawlers escape the trembling ground. As he scooped them up, the worms made him think of people. "You know this kind of reminds me of what's happening in Gunstock. What if a vampire has set up several posts to shake out the weirdoes in Rains County? That could be why it seems like lunatics are running loose."

Russell shivered. "How many vampires do you think there are?"

"One is too many," Scooter said. He didn't want to think any more about it. He could stay at home and live in fear, or go fishing. They had plenty of crawlers to tempt fish.

Back in the canoe, it only took minutes to paddle near the marina, close to the fallen oak and a sunken house boat. Wisps of fog blurred shapes and diffused their lights. They wouldn't need them much longer, as dawn gained color. They baited a half-dozen hooks with crawlers dipped in a special 'Sheriff Sauce', cast for sand bass, and watched the sunrise.

"Do you think the marina is haunted?" Scooter asked. He recalled that old man Creech had been a bit of a fishmonger. His marina was shut down since he had died. As rumor had it, Creech had seen a ghost for a week before he died, having been entangled in fishing line and drowned.

Russell shook his head.

"Hey, you claimed you had new vampire hunting tools to show me," Scooter said.

His bud unzipped the bag. Scooter could see various stakes, a claw-hammer, mallet, and flares. In a smaller box, he showed off a pair of silver crosses. He had packed flashlights and headlamps in one padded bag. The small holy water ceramic jars sat with a case of nightvision goggles.

"What's this?" Scooter asked, pointing to a hard metal egg.

"It's a smoke grenade. There's another one that's a flash grenade. They're legal. They don't explode, but they can start fires. Think of them as serious fireworks."

They were pleasantly interrupted by twitching Deco rods and bouncing bobbers. The fish went into a frenzy, biting all at once. Poles bent and rods and reels rattled. Scooter wrestled in a two-foot long carp. Russell dragged in several eating-size sand bass. When a pole leapt from the boat, Flash snagged the Quantum Energy rod with his teeth, keeping it in the boat.

He forgot all about vampires and BJ's death. In a little over an hour, they caught and stowed their limit.

The sun no longer seemed an enemy, as it had in summers before with its unmerciful heat. Its light made them feel almost safe, warming their backs as they paddled westward.

They planned to get in a little pyrotechnic cannon and bow shooting practice before going home. Scooter wanted a weapon to defend himself. It seemed a wooden shaft fired from a distance might work like a stake.

The recent rains meant they could safely shoot bottle rockets without setting fire to the sodden grassland or dripping trees. Scooter set up apples and two watermelons from the garden. They reset some of the plastic 2-liter bottles filled with sand and stood up their cardboard vampires and aliens.

About forty feet from shore, they dropped anchor. Each pulled out a PVC bazooka from the old, charred, five-gallon paint bucket. The two white tubes of plastic were an inch in diameter and three feet long with blackened nozzles. Unlike real life armaments, the PVC bazooka's rear opening had to be capped. Otherwise the rockets lacked thrust.

Russell got hot and sweaty and pulled off his shirt. When he turned around, Scooter noticed his bud's back and neck. Pimples covered his shoulder blades and gathered along his neck, but worse, he had been tearing at the bites. Some were scraped raw, looking bruised, too. He gave Russell his jar.

"You need this,"Scooter said. He pulled up his shirt and turned around. "How's my back?"

"Sunburned and peeling, white boy," Russell replied. He dabbed on medicine, set up another volley, and they let loose.

After going through nearly a gross of bottle rockets, modern times caught up with them. Russell opened his backpack, pulling out the .38.

"Heroes don't use guns," Scooter muttered. He unloaded his bow from its case, then he bent the graphite to string it. In a way, he felt like Russell. Since Shade, he didn't like going fishing without it. At least his frog-gigging had improved.

"Heroes use guns in the real world!" Russell said offended. "What do you suggest? Tasers? Nightsticks? Bows?"

"It doesn't accidentally go off and blow a hole in something. I have to work to pull the string, although I have poked myself with an arrow. Can I shoot first?" he asked. Russell nodded. Scooter concentrated and fired, missing all the targets but hitting a willow. "Just don't call me Treekiller."

Raising his gun, Russell sighted. In rapid succession, his buddy squeezed off a round of shots. Plastic bottles went flying. An apple shattered, and a watermelon exploded, spewing pink flesh and seeds. It made Scooter a little queasy.

Russell was getting scarier by the minute.

NINETEEN

THE SHOOTERS

They paddled back to shore and picked up their trash. Scooter called for Flash, several times. His reply came as a distant bark somewhere beyond the fences.

"He wants us to come see something," Scooter said. Grabbing his bow and quiver, he expected that he was going off on an adventure. They could be dangerous.

Russell packed his gun and carried the vampire hunting tools on his back. Now that he was bigger, the Incredible Bulk toted them easily.

Scooter resumed calling for his dog. Flash's return barks sounded about the same distance away. "Pick up the pace. Flash is chasing something."

Out of the trees, they encountered a leafy green and thorny wall of blackberry bushes. They had been picking here before, but had stayed away from the power plant.

Several trails twisted through the mass of thorns and berries, but somehow Scooter chose the right one, despite Russell's doubts.

They came out of the brush to a fence running along a wide open river embankment. Through a large hole in the chain link, they found Flash tracks, following them down the sloping concrete wall. Muddy streaks like sliding footprints smeared the man-made banks of the river.

Russell peered through his binoculars. "Yep, he's

chasing somebody toward the power plant. You know, it could be CJ! Do you think he knows about his brother?"

With the flooding rains, mudslides and algae had created a treacherous slope. They descended with unsteady care to navigate the slimed concrete. Just as Scooter was about to say, 'watch out, it's slippery', his feet bolted out from under him, heading for the sky. Head below heels, he fell down, knocking the wind out of him. Like a natural water slide, he sped down the green stretch of algae to the base of the dam. He plunged into knee high muck with a splat.

He was taking deep breaths, making sure everything worked right as Russell assisted him to his feet.

They dashed for the power plant, a brick building with large second floor windows squatting along the river. Lines ran from it to the fenced-in electrical towers, then out to the county.

Flash waited for them. When they were close, the golden Lab sprinted up another slippery slope of concrete. Scooter put on a burst of speed, chasing him to an asphalt parking lot. His muddy running shoes squished with every step.

"That's my dog," Scooter told the guard as he ran by and out the gate. Still in pursuit, Flash raced up the drive. Across the street there was a Supreme Crafts boat manufacturing plant. Even at a distance, the stench of burnt plastics and poisonous chemicals hung in the air. The fire had reached the road, blackening the grass that led to Creech's Marina and out to the county roads. He remembered they had been afraid it would reach the power plant.

Scooter waited for his best bud at the **Keep Out, Rains County Sheriff Department** tape. It surrounded the entrance to the offices within a cube of aluminum storefront framing glass. Behind it, a huge metal silo sliced down the middle, then set flat on its side, stretched out to cover the manufacturing floor. Flash pranced eagerly outside the front's double doors.

"CJ! It's just us! We want to help. There's another vampire on the prowl. We think you were right, and that it got BJ," Scooter called out. He looked at Russell and shrugged. "Let's explore."

"Who is looking for trouble now?"

The storefront windows and doors were charred as if smoke had poured out around the edges. Finger marks were smeared through the blackening, giving the impression the door had been recently opened. They checked it, finding the door unlocked.

"Flash, stay here. If somebody comes out, bark and howl," Scooter said. "We're going to scout first."

They slowly walked the perimeter, along the burnt fences. The fire had escaped into the grass and trees, creating a wildfire. The blackened weeds crunched eerily under his feet. Many of the metal corrugated outbuildings were burnt husks. A fenced storage area holding hulls was full of partly melted boats. Explosions had blown out windows.

"There is suspicion that the fire is arson. Some of the executives were under scrutiny. Agent Pryde was originally directing an undercover investigation into the employment of illegal immigrants."

"Hey! There!" Scooter pointed. He had seen the flash of a face, certain it was CJ. Had he been carrying a handgun?

"We can't just leave him. I'm going to call Dad. They'll want to know we've seen somebody inside the crime scene," Russell said. He dialed county dispatch.

They were told to stay out, but they pushed the door open.

"CJ! It's us, we want to help!" Russell said.

"Yuk. Disgusting," Scooter said. The lobby had been

blackened and ravaged by fire. A boat in the lobby was warped and distorted, contributing to the pall of burnt plastic. Water dripped from the open-air stairs and down from the balcony and the second floor.

They searched the offices downstairs, finding mostly dark-screened computers. Scooter saw two rats, but no sign of CJ. He wasn't worried about sneaking around, since his shoes were noisy. Up on the second floor, they discovered the ceiling had burned away, leaving it wide open to the interior of the factory.

Kablam! Blam! Inside the metal building, the gunfire sounded like artillery shells being launched. Heart in his throat and stumbling, Scooter dove under a table. He bumped his shin and head, but he hadn't been hit. Now he knew CJ had a gun and knew how to use it. He checked on Flash, finding him frightened but unharmed. "Russell? Are you okay?"

"Yep."

Several slugs came through the wall just above Russell. He crawled over to the window that opened onto the floor. Popping up, he fired, just about deafening and blinding Scooter.

"I heard him curse. I think I got him," Russell said.

A machine gun blasted away. Slugs tore through the walls, sending drywall confetti flying and poking holes in Russell's defense. He rolled across the room to the hallway. "I'm calling dispatch for help."

A bow wasn't any help against a semiautomatic. Bullets sprayed throughout the room, tearing up what was already burnt. A slug came through the table, lodging in the floor.

He and Flash bolted. He stumbled, having to put down a hand. A slug whizzed past his ear. He tumbled through the doorway. He could hardly hear over his heart, and Flash's anxious panting.

"They're coming!" Russell said. He dug a grenade out of his bag, then tossed it back into the room. As it bounced, smoke poured out, providing cover. The place remained quiet, except for the squeaks and rattles of wind shifting metal.

The wait seemed timelessly long. When they heard a squad car, Russell phoned again.

The deputies announced themselves, then burst in armed. Deputies Don and Ross searched the area, while the other team of Al and Lewis found them. They escorted them outside.

None of the deputies ever found CJ, but they did find bloodstains.

"Do you think whatever got BJ, got CJ?" Russell asked.

Scooter found an empty can of Skoal. "I'm afraid so." First, BJ acted unusual, then he died. Now, CJ was shooting at them. Would he die next?

And what about Russell and Kristie?

Scooter thought about the way Russell had changed. He didn't listen to rock 'n roll anymore, nor the Grateful Dead. He didn't obsess about driving. Instead, he had spent his time learning to use a gun and save people's lives.

Was this really Russell? Or had he been touched by a vampire?

TWENTY

BREAKING AWAY

Sitting in the shade and drinking only water, Garrett hated life. It sucked. But he could only think it. He couldn't scream the truth, or worse, even stop from living a lie.

Everyone believed he was so polite and wonderful. They wanted to know what had turned on the light. He loathed being nice to everyone. There were some real idiots and goof balls involved in the forest crew. All of them loved nature.

Just a bystander, he was compelled to say the right drivel, to go stomping through the woods, and maintain the trails through the state park. He and a dozen other deliriously thrilled-to-be-outside inmates had just repaired a bridge at Purtis Creek State Park. They whistled while they worked! Garrett had never met so many good old boys who loved to get their hands calloused. He was a mess. His arms were leaden. His back ached, and he couldn't straighten it.

Each day, he followed Tai's commands, but he slowly chipped away at them. He pretended to break them through imaginings—puffing on cigarettes and guzzling beer. Somewhere, he had heard that everything you wanted to accomplish began with a thought.

This time he was able to imagine Racquel sitting next to him. To beat the heat, she sipped a frozen margarita. She laughed, asking which sweat more, him or his beer bottle. Taking her hand, he drew her close to kiss her.

He smiled. This was the first time in almost a week he had been able to hold a thought of Racquel. Was *Chaquita* going stir crazy, too? He could barely think of shooting Sheriff Knight when he used to dream of it every night.

Because of what he was doing, his heart pounded constantly, like he was running a marathon. Last night he had awakened in a cold sweat from dreams of trying to escape the straight jacket of a suit and a noose-tight tie.

Today, he would try again to counter his programming. Like a virus, he stuffed a candy wrapper in his pocket. When the group stopped to plant some trees, he tried littering. As always, he felt the undeniable urge to pick it up. It was so obvious that the nature freaks would play a game, dropping trash, knowing he would pick it up immediately. That's what gave him the idea.

Even if he did have to pick it up afterward, it was defying the vampire's will. Yesterday he had been able to drop it a second time. For a long while, he stared at the Snickers wrapper in his hand. A gust from the brewing storm blew the packaging away. Closing his eyes, he imagined walking away.

When he opened his eyes, the wrapper was gone! He looked for the paper, but he didn't see it. Tai's command compelled him to search. He didn't find it, although he picked up a McDonald's cup, two beer cans and an empty pack of Camels. He kept it and breathed deeply.

Garrett's smile broadened. The crack was there. He would keep working at it. Through determination, he would eventually be free.

TWENTY-ONE

STORY TELLING

Friday evening, shortly before sunset, Scooter bicycled with Flash to the Pickup Ranch. The sun shone golden off the undersides of the fleet of clouds.

While the dogs dashed off to play, Scooter weaved through the scattering chickens along the way. Except for a little soft clucking, the place was quiet enough he could hear the hum of gnat clouds. At least the buzzing mosquitoes left him alone. He thought he heard whimpering.

Rushing forward, he worried about Marcus. "Flash, here boy!" His golden friend flashed to his side.

Scooter yanked open the barn door, hearing puppies crying. He wasn't surprised to find them prodding their mother. Dead, she would never feed them again. He just stood there, heartsick and saddened.

Smelling Flash, the puppies yapped excitedly. His dog sniffed and shuffled among them to reassure them. They responded with playful and hungry nips.

Scooter found a cardboard box and threw in straw and a tattered old blanket before putting it in the wheel barrow. The puppies yipped and howled in protest as he trundled them to the back door of the house. He propped it open and carried the box into the kitchen.

He found an eye dropper in the utensil drawer. Scooter

fed milk to the cute little buggers. The ones that weren't eating were sniffing around him, scampering over him, or gnawing on him between happy licks.

The sound of car brakes interrupted his fun.

"Mr. Chandler? It's me, James Dandy with Kellen Redgraves," came the call from the front door.

Scooter's mood crashed. He wandered with a puppy in his hands to the front door. When Flash followed, all the puppies stumbled along like a parade of bumblers. It seemed an omen that the mother dog had died, as if she had known the Intruder's return was too much to endure.

"You must be Jonathan Keyshawn," the dowdy man said, then Mr. James Dandy introduced himself. The roly-poly social worker looked familiar. Something about his manner caused Scooter to squirm. The man took his elbow when they shook hands and seemed to offer condolences without saying much except with sympathetic body language. He dressed in drab brown and tans, making him look more indoor pale.

Scooter tried not to immediately dislike him. After all, he was trying to help a troubled kid, not ruin Scooter's day. Mr. Dandy's aura seemed tainted. "Do I know you?"

"I worked at the Rolling Green Funeral Home in Greenville," Dandy replied. "I wanted to help people, like Kellen, before it was too late."

The Intruder didn't really look happy, but he looked less haunted than before. Instead of darting about, his pink eyes were almost steady. His arms were wrapped in bandages.

Scooter wasn't sure what to make of him and swallowed his rising jealousy. It was difficult, but he didn't have a monopoly on Marcus' writing advice or his time. Besides, his mentor had asked him to give the Intruder a second chance. Scooter reasoned a vampire-tainted looking aura could occur due to spending too long in Shade's ruined lair, or something far more sinister.

The Intruder sneezed, probably awakening Marcus. "I'm allergic to dogs!" He scratched.

"What a surprise! Cats too, I'll bet." Then the ranch is a wonderful place to be, Scooter almost snapped. "Then you may want to stay out of the kitchen."

"Scooter! Mr. Dandy! I'm sorry. I overslept. Hello, Kellen. Are you ready to write?" Marcus asked as he limped into the room. In jeans and a sky blue shirt, he looked tousled, stiff, and barely awake.

"Yes! It's gotta be better than sitting in a boring room with four blank walls. I felt like I was going to be stuck in *The Cube*. People watching me around the clock. All that time, I was thinking of a horror flick screenplay kind of based on me. What if someone is trying to eliminate my family line?"

Scooter thought there might be sound reasons behind that.

"Excellent! Start with a what if question. It's normal for writers to use familiar places for settings and known people for characters. I wrote about my brother," Marcus said.

Scooter recalled seeing photographs of a sibling. He wondered what had happened to him.

"I was sorry to hear about BJ," Marcus said.

"What happened?" the Intruder asked.

"He died. I think vampires caused him to have a heart attack. Some people, the dumb ones, blame Marcus," Scooter replied.

"Y'all and vampires," the Intruder moaned.

"I was proud of you and Russell, and your heroic attempt to revive BJ. I wrote about it in my journal," Marcus said. He paced and stretched. "Scooter is learning to write screenplays, since it's the same format as crafting comic books, but instead of one hundred and twenty pages, you're dealing with twenty to thirty. How is issue two coming along?"

"Fine," Scooter replied. He didn't want to talk about it. He could feel his creative river threatening to dry up.

The Intruder would be here for two hours, which was bound to inch forward in the way of Einstein's Theory of Relativity and time-warping—when you're confined with someone who grates across every fiber of your being.

Because of the Intruder's recent suicide attempt, Mr. Dandy stayed.

"Well, I need some coffee," Marcus said. He started for the kitchen, but the Intruder protested. He sulked and slumped in the seldom used living room.

"Why do I have puppies in my kitchen?" Marcus asked kindly. He rubbed on them. Even Mr. Dandy joined them.

"The mother died. I'm feeding them," Scooter replied.

"Oh, no," Marcus said. "You've done the smart thing. Even so, they may not survive."

"I know, but that's true about everything. Sometimes, it just needs a chance. I'll do what I can to help with them."

"You'll have to spend more time over here."

"I will . . . if I can. I can ride over. It's not far, but I'll have to get an okay from my grandfather," Scooter said.

"Come sit with us when you're done feeding them," Marcus said.

Scooter milked his time for everything it was worth, forcing Marcus to come get him. He didn't really want to leave the rambunctious pups, but he was here to learn.

"This is not a writing class, but more of a writing forum—an exchange of ideas, inspiration, imagination, perspiration, and constructive criticism," Marcus began. "You see, Kellen, I had lost my passion for creating. Scooter rejuvenated it by asking questions. He reminded me of the excitement, adventure, and the opportunity to literarily play God."

"Kind of like *Finding Forrester*?" the Intruder scratched.

"Do you relate everything to movies?"

"Sure. Why not? At least with movies, you can turn them off when they get bad. Or put them on pause and come back later when you're ready. Life just keeps broadcasting the bad news, kind of like Headline News: News 24-7. Mine's the Redgraves News: bad news and nothing but bad news 24-365."

"Perhaps you could write about your life, except fictionalize it. Give it good writing and snappy storytelling."

"Ha! A good movie has nothing to do with good writing. Dudes, babes, some action, lots of special effects, and we're golden. Bad Luck Is My Middle Name," the Intruder interrupted. His hands shaped a marquee. He seemed to be thinking about who might play him in his biopic.

Marcus paced like a defense lawyer. "Kellen, after an idea flares, it's all about good storytelling and writing. It gives the director, actors, costume-makers, and set-makers something to work from. Universal themes are a must because they strike strong cords within many people. Rarely does a good movie come from a lousy script. For one thing, a bad script rarely gets the green light. Scooter, what's a writer's job?"

"To create memorable characters and stress them."

"He's paraphrasing, Gary Trudeau, the *Doonesbury* creator. I had him watch an interview. You should, too."

"Why stress? Wait, I know. It makes it more interesting?" the Intruder asked. He scratched his bandages.

"Exactly. And just as important, we pressure them because people don't reveal their true character under normal conditions," Marcus said. Scooter wondered if he was thinking of people's reactions to the children's death. "Only when put to a crucial test do we discover a character's true mettle. The plot is a succession of events that tear away our daily mask. It is man's, or woman's, will pitted against adversity and adversaries, whether it's social mores, the law, love, or the elements."

Scooter couldn't help but think of Kristie. During the crisis at Fisherman's Island, she had proved her mettle.

"Another important aspect is the 'or else' alternative. What happens if the problem isn't solved?" Marcus continued. "The alternative lends suspense to the story. The viewers want to know what's at stake. Does this make sense?"

"Yeah, I think so," the Intruder replied. His eyes might be spinning along with the wheels in his mind.

"Remember, good endings are more successful than sad."

"But *Braveheart* and *Gladiator* won Oscars."

"And for every one of those, there are many incarnations of *Star Wars, Cinderella,* and *Rocky*. To get a happy ending know how to get your main character out of a dire situation and have them grow through triumph or failure."

"You've been working on a couple of stories. How did you start? At the beginning?" the Intruder asked Scooter.

He backed up, watching the boy scratch. It was almost as if it jumped to him. Scooter started itching all over again. It made it hard to remember what they were talking about, especially since he was missing Kristie. "I tried to begin at the start, and it didn't work very well. People don't want a boring beginning. I'm trying to engage and rivet the audience."

"It's called a hook," Marcus said.

"So, what did you do?" the Intruder asked.

"Well, I thought it out, including character briefs. But I didn't start my book there. I made sure I had some of the elements I needed set in my mind first. What kind of characters were needed? Who has the most at stake? What happens at the end. Marcus has a list."

"Huh? The end? You know it already?" the Intruder said.

"The list of ingredients to 'cook up' a good story helped him decide what kind of story he has, although you really don't know until you're done. Is it about a character? An event? Or a mystery to solve? If you know that, it will help you begin and end your story."

Scooter figured they were giving him too much information, but Marcus liked to do it because you never knew what was going to stick. "You probably have your idea. Do you have your characters? Write a couple paragraphs about them. Why are they important to the story?"

"I never thought of doing that. Doesn't that happen while writing?" the Intruder asked.

"When authors are learning about characters, it clutters up your story. I usually throw away the first chapters."

"I have all these ideas spinning in my head. I hear voices of characters? Do you?" the Intruder asked.

"Are you talking about the loud screaming ones, or the soft ones?" Marcus asked.

Scooter knew what they were talking about: your characters coming alive. His rarely screamed at him. Did hearing voices make them writers?

"Is that all right with you, Scooter? You seem distracted."

"I can't shake the feeling that something is going wrong."

The Intruder guffawed. "Already you're picking up on my vibe! Maybe you should just call me *The Cooler*!"

"Let's do an exercise," Marcus suggested. "For a screenplay, we need a setting, here, a character, Kellen, and a conflict or a problem to solve. In your story, Kellen, what's the challenge?"

The Intruder sat and thought a long time.

"Keep thinking. Each hero has strengths and weaknesses. How are yours involved in this challenge? This problem to solve? Now, if you were in control of the story, what would you do to get where you wanted your character to go?"

"I've started some scribbles. I'm going to write more on those," the Intruder said. He gathered up a spiral note book and lumbered outside onto the screened porch.

"I'm off to Nirvana," Scooter said, faking a smile. Just being around the Intruder made him itch. But what Marcus had said set him to thinking. His challenge was to see more of Kristie and to earn Mrs. Candel's trust. He noticed the bulletin from church. A green leaflet announced events. He read through the list, wondering if Kristie would be involved.

He suddenly knew what to do. Mrs. Candel might be convinced he was a good influence, if they spent time together without one of them ending up in the hospital.

At the computer, he typed away, pretending to go to these events and be helpful, getting to see Kristie. Mrs. Candel was impressed and willing to let them go to the county fair.

While Marcus showed the Intruder how to set up his screen, and how to use the Word program, Scooter mustered the courage to call Mrs. Candel and volunteer to help pick up donations. She thanked him and told him nine o'clock.

Scooter returned to writing, putting in his CD to work

on *The Vampire Hunters Club.* Concentrating was difficult, because the Intruder grew restless and scratched relentlessly. "I feel like I've got bugs crawling all over me."

"Do you have bug bites?"

"How did you know?" the Intruder asked.

"Russell and I have them, too, from the island. Here." He handed him a travel jar of Granny June's bug bite miracle healing ointment. He could use this as an excuse to get more.

"It helps?" the Intruder asked. Scooter nodded. "I'll try it. Sometimes I feel like I'm in *ED TV*, except it's Kellen TV. They keep doing things to me just to see how I'll react. Hey, we're bored with this. Let's try this! I'm tired of sitting. I'm going to ask Marcus to take me on a tour of the grounds."

Scooter was pleased to see him go. He no longer itched. After ensuring they had left the house, Scooter crept to the closet with the cabinets. In two of the drawers were loads of boxes with black and white and sepia-toned photographs of the Chandler family. He picked through them, searching for a story, including more about his mentor's brother.

A box of newspaper clippings and releases contained several astounding articles from the local paper. A huge headline screamed MIRACLE! ETHEL ALIVE! As a child, Marcus had climbed inside a drain to help a toddler.

GUNSTOCK THUNDERSTICKS WIN DISTRICT. Scooter didn't know Marcus played baseball. In the war, he had received a Purple Heart and silver star. Scooter had no idea he had served in the military. He suspected Judge Grandpa had been referring to this.

He decided to make Marcus some kind of hero or magician. Superman had started on a farm. Perhaps his pallor could be a sign of his powers manifesting, like in *X-Men*. Or a mask of honor, like the ritual markings of shaman.

When Scooter heard them on the porch, he put things

back the way they had been. He shut the closet before heading into the kitchen. He was thirsty for lemonade.

Scooter soon found it impossible to work with the Intruder, who breathed noisily, so he went on break. He sat on the porch and imagined seeing Kristie—what he might say, and what other events he might get involved in besides the rummage sale and the Downwater Duckies fundraiser.

He had the feeling of being watched, so he looked closer at the shadows. In the stable's shadow, he thought he saw eyes, but it was just May Bell, the horse. The second time, it was a nameless tom cat prowling through. Before he went inside, he spotted what he thought was an opossum, until its eyes seem to grow larger and angrier. He had the sense he should already be dead, then the eyes disappeared.

Flash never barked, playing with Beauty. Unsure it even happened, Scooter went back inside.

Almost a hour later, Scooter stiffly climbed out of the chair. His timing was good as the Intruder returned from a break outside. Mr. Dandy entered holding his belly and disappeared into the bathroom. The Intruder's face was waxy.

"Are you feeling okay?"

"I finally don't feel like I'm beating eaten alive. Thanks for that stuff. Can I get some?"

"Call Kristie. She gave it to me."

"I'll call her mother. It's great not to itch," the Intruder sighed.

Scooter noticed his bloodied and torn pants along one knee. "What happened?"

"Is that where you scraped yourself jumping over the fence?" Mr. Dandy asked, leaving the restroom.

"Yep. I'm a mess. I should clean up," the Intruder said.

The dogs barking got Scooter's attention. It sounded as if Flash had found a dead critter. He hurried outside, beelining to his dog by climbing over a fence into a grazing pasture. It started to rain, again.

He was surprised to find the goat dead. Billy Gee's throat had been slit. Blood saturated his white coat and darkly stained the dirt. Looking closer, he noticed that the goat's back legs had been slashed to hobble him. He recalled something he had read about serial killers in a book called *The Mindhunter*. As youths, murderers liked to torture animals.

The Intruder had been bloodied.

Scooter wondered how to tell Marcus. He probably wouldn't believe him. Why didn't Mr. Dandy say something?

TWENTY-TWO

RUMMAGING AROUND

Scooter burnt off his pent-up eagerness by bicycling into Gunstock to the Candels. Today he got to see Kristie!

Flash kept pace, loping along easily like the DC superhero speedster. They took the shortest route along an oiled, gravel-dirt road and cut through a shady copse of cottonwoods into a wide-open neighborhood of trailers and ranch-style homes.

Leaving the grassy fields behind, he cruised by the small community park to coast into the small town of Gunstock. He passed a 7-Eleven and a Whataburger, then he turned down Austin St, just before the Community Church and the VFW, to reach a sprawling one-story house of white-painted brick. The walls were covered with a wealth of ivy. He didn't know if it looked like a minister's house or not.

The Candel's home sat only a block away from the church. He used to think it held the same reverent atmosphere.

Knowing Kristie had ruined his mental image and stereotyping of the minister's family. There wasn't any disharmony in the manicured grounds, nor the garden beds of roses, indian hats, and snapdragons. The flowers flourished in a dazzling spectrum of colors that celebrated life and welcomed visitors. The statuary stood in greeting, a white host of cherubs and protective guardian angels.

Scooter was disappointed to see that the place had been invaded by a cluster of youthful volunteers gathered around a green pickup. Two of the garage doors were open with donated clothes, knickknacks, furnishings, and durable goods sprawling out onto the asphalt.

He set his bike against a tree, then went to join the group. The lawn felt lush under his sneakers and had been edged along the driveway. A faded green Chevy one-ton truck stood next to a '50's yellow-cabbed flat bed parked in front of the three-car garage. He was surprised by the number of girls huddling around the back of the Chevy. Eve and Hope were very pretty and popular, but not as smart as Kristie.

Scooter suppressed a groan. He had assumed there would only be a few workers, enabling him to spend lots of time with Kristie. It was going to be a long afternoon.

"Nick, where did you say you're from? You don't sound like you're from here," he heard Hope ask. Russell said the blond beauty had the most inviting smile he had ever seen.

"I'm from Gunbarrel City, over along Cedar Creek Lake. I haven't been there long. I moved from California, near Anaheim," Nick replied. By the way the girls were clustered, he guessed Nick was handsome. Good for him.

"No. I didn't play football," Nick continued. "I prefer rugby. I like a good scrum now and again."

Scooter spotted Kristie inside the garage, taking notes as she fussed through an area of excess furniture, dusty lamps, and old vacuum cleaners. In here, the donations were well-organized. Kristie stopped to lean on a rack of hanging clothes. Despite looking a little stiff and weary, she hummed a happy song.

"Good afternoon. I'm looking for a songbird," he said,

having thought about what to say to her. Hello seemed to understate the occasion. "Do you know where I can find one?"

"Scooter! Flash!" Kristie celebrated, embracing him. It was too brief, as she spent more time hugging the lucky dog. "I'm so glad y'all are here. This is a great idea and a big help! We were praying for help." She groaned as she knuckled her back. "I feel like I'm fifty. Y'all don't know how really glad I am to see y'all."

"I know about being glad to see someone," Scooter said. Flash barked.

"I have worried about you. Are you all right? I really miss my phone," she laughed.

He stopped his hands in mid-scratch. "I'm okay, thanks to Granny June's bug bite miracle cure. But, I'm just about out and could use more. I gave some to Kellen."

"I'll get you some. We keep lots because chiggers like Mary. Have you been busy working on your grandparents' place?" she asked.

"Most of the time. I've also been taking care of puppies at the Pickup Ranch. They're cocker spaniel-retriever mutts, I think, abandoned at the gate. They are adorable, almost as cute as Flash," Scooter said, patting his ear-to-ear grinning friend.

"I'll bet they're cute. I wish I could see them."

"I've been plotting out ways to see you."

"Really? What do you have in mind?" she asked, leaning forward and very curious.

"Well, I talked to Judge Grandpa. He told me to use my imagination. Then last night, Marcus was talking to Redgraves about putting together stories. He mentioned character motivation, challenges, and goals, which started me thinking about your mother."

"You talked to your grandfather and Marcus about me?" She now seemed amused.

"Of course. Well, I figure your mom is loving and caring, as well as overprotective. We have unintentionally stayed out late, and you've come home the worse for wear."

"Uh-huh." She frowned, now worried about him.

"So I decided convincing your mother to let me see more of you as my challenge. I'm the protagonist with a goal of seeing more of Kristie Candel. Your mother is the antagonist and the obstacle. If we can only be together at church-related functions, I need to get involved more with the activities. Show her we can have fun together without a catastrophe."

"That sounds like a good strategy."

"I was thinking about it when I saw the church program on Marcus' table. Everybody always wants moving help."

"What else were you thinking of?"

"I know you're doing the Downwater Duckies fundraising for the YWCA. What work do you do that I can volunteer for?"

"I also do meals on wheels. That probably wouldn't work. What else? I read aloud at the library. Want to join me?"

"That's an idea."

"I got your thank you card. How is Russ? He felt odd the last two times I saw him, especially at the funeral. Do you think anything is wrong? Does he feel like he let down BJ?" Kristie rubbed her hands as if she were working out cramps.

He gently took one and began to massage it. "Some. We went fishing yesterday. We caught a boat load of sand bass. He's doing all right," he said. He didn't want to tell her about Russell's gun. Or that CJ had shot at them.

"Have you noticed how big he's getting?" Kristie asked.

"Yeah. I think of him as the Incredible Bulk," he replied. She giggled. "All that weight training. Surviving the vampire changed him. I know I look at things differently."

"Do you look at me differently?" she asked.

"Oh, yes." Scooter nodded, smiling. He swallowed then said, "You're even cooler than I imagined."

"That's sweet. I know what kind of imagination you have," Kristie said. He thought he'd said something wonderful. Why wasn't she smiling? Then she did, and he recalled seeing that look before, when she wanted a kiss for helping him escape the blackberry bushes' thorns.

Flash barked, warning them.

"Company," Scooter said.

Kristie had him move a box. Then she pointed out two chairs in need of relocating.

Moments later, Mrs. Candel walked in. "Well, hello Jonathan. Good to see you already working."

"Yes, ma'am. It'll be good practice for moving my grandpa and grandma into their new house."

"That's a good way to look at it," Mrs. Candel said with a bedazzling smile. Scooter had never seen her this spry and ramrod straight. "What a wonderful turnout. So many young people. I'm impressed. Kristie, have you met Nick Sloan?"

"Yes, Mother, I did."

"Oh, before I forget. Russell and I caught a boatload of sand bass," Scooter said. He pulled the bundle from his backpack, then unwrapped the newspaper to show off the iced fish filets.

"That's wonderful! Dinner tonight! We might have a fish fry! Thank you," Mrs. Candel drawled.

When her mother went back inside, Kristie whirled on him, looking petulant and hurt. "You brought my mother fish, but you didn't bring me anything to read."

"No. I brought you a drawing," he said, handing her a poster tube. She unrolled the sheet of paper. He had been inspired by comic superheroines, Storm and Siren. Among the storm clouds and lighting bolts, Kristie flew in the light of a gloryhole. She was singing, her music notes allowing her to fly above the lake. Down below, a young woman piloted a boat over the waves.

"This is fantastic!" she said, smooching him on the cheek.

He loved being fantastic and an inspiration. Before he could tell her about his plans, she disappeared inside.

"Hey, buddy, are you all right?" Russell asked.

"Most definitely. Where did you come from?"

"My mom dropped me off."

"Cool! I'm surprised you're here."

"I thought you might hurt your back, so I got my ambulance time rescheduled. I told them I probably would see more action hanging with y'all."

"I want your opinion on something, okay? Watch Kristie for a while, then tell me what you think. She seems to be moving like something is wrong," he said, then explained about her feeling old and weary.

"How's her aura?" Russell asked.

"I'm not sure, because of the lightning, but I think fine. Just tell me what you think about her demeanor, posture, and grace. She used to glide. Now she seems clumsy."

"What do you think is up?"

"I have my suspicions," Scooter replied. Hearing footsteps, he held up a finger.

"Hey, dudes. What's up? I'm Nick Sloan," the new boy said. He stood tall, tanned, and handsome with sun-bleached blond hair, piercing blue eyes, and a carefree look. When he shook hands with Russell, they squeezed each other in a battle of grips. "Glad to have some muscle along."

"Russell and Scooter are vampire hunters," Eve said, her voice full of scorn.

"That's sic. What was he like?" Sloan asked, dead earnest.

Russell stammered. The girls were shocked. Scooter just knew he was going to make a fool of himself, but instead of being smart and keeping his mouth shut, he described Shade and Ripley.

"You're lucky to have all your pints. Back home, they call those darkwalkers. I worked for a county morgue, and they talked about them. The term vampire is usually reserved for a big corporate executive, you know, like the Enron guys, movie moguls, or your best friend hitting on your girl."

Scooter couldn't believe he was having this conversation. Nobody had ever casually talked with him about vampires. Eve and Hope were agape, caught off guard and looking silly.

"Thanks for the warning. I'll keep my rosary handy." Nick crossed himself.

Kristie returned with yellow-brown ceramic jars. "Here it is. The stuff's a little dry. Add water or olive oil to make paste."

"Thanks," Scooter said. Sweating made him a little itchy.

Mrs. Candel split them up, driving the pickup with the girls. Scooter, Russell, Flash, and the Gomez brothers got stuck on the back of the flatbed while Nick drove. Kristie sat in the navigator's chair.

Standing on the flatbed, hanging onto the straps as they slowly rumbled down the weed-lined back roads, Scooter wasn't having much fun listening to Nick and Kristie banter. At first it had been all right, because the California boy just talked about himself. He sure enjoyed rugby, planning on going to Australia to play. His dad had been a plumber and carpenter, but now he was minister over in Gunbarrel. Blah. Blah. When Uncle Thomas had needed them, they had come running. After all, they were family. He started singing the old song, *We Are Family,* and Kristie joined in.

That was when they began to exchange stories about having spiritual leaders for parents. Scooter could sort of relate, since his grandfather was a judge. Russell could sympathize as well. They shared stories about the stress of being a moral role model. Kristie sang, *Kiss the Girl* from Disney's *The Little Mermaid.*

"Hey, play some Salsa! Did you know, that in some religions, kissing is a sin?" Julio Gomez asked. He wore a Texas Rangers cap backwards and enough aftershave to fumigate a small house. For a long time, Russell hadn't gotten along with the brothers, but they had given up hassling him about being a half-breed. One day, they said, everybody would be related to somebody from Mexico.

"So is dancing," brother Juan added, then adjusted his red do-rag. The two boys were wiry, rawboned, and of Hispanic descent, part of the Gomez brood of nine. Scooter didn't think he'd even seen one alone. Juan and Julio were the second and third eldest. They were American born, their parents legal immigrants. They supported the cause by selling and wearing t-shirts that had Old Glory on the front and the Mexican flag on the back.

"And card playing," Julio said, touching a deck in his pocket. "*Dios.* Why isn't it something like eating spinach? And why does pitching manure make you mature?"

Scooter choked a laugh, liking it.

"How long have you been working on that?" Juan asked with a huge, crooked grin.

"How about spanking? Thou shall not spank your child," Julio said. The brothers agreed and high-fived each other.

"Mama, we didn't mean no harm by it," Julio whimpered.

"We really are sorry. It was an accident."

Julio grew serious. "It's on account of original sin. So it's really not my fault. I'm trying to get better. Fifty Hail Marys."

"I blame it on Papa. Tia Maria credits guardian angels with keeping him alive. I figure I'd give them something to do."

Nick and Kristie's laughter interrupted them. They were singing *Don't Let Your Babies Grow-up to Be Cowboys.*

"How come Nick gets to sit with the girl?" Julio asked.

"Because he can drive without running over mailboxes," his brother replied.

"Soon, I'll have my license," Russell said with an eager glint in his eyes. Scooter's imagination ran wild. He could see his best buddy armed, mobile, and dangerous.

"Hey, I wanna ask you vampire hunters a question. Did you really see a walking dead guy on Fisherman's Island?" Juan asked.

"We saw Lucius Shade. He's inhuman," Scooter replied.

"Well, me and Julio saw something inhuman, a ghost, last week over at Creech's Marina. Scared the piss out of me," Juan continued.

"I spilled my Bud we left so fast," Julio admitted.

By road, the boat factory sat only a few minutes away. When Scooter thought about it, it wasn't too far from Fisherman's Island, perhaps fifteen minutes by a fast bass boat. But then, so were a lot of places on Lake Tawakoni.

"You don't believe us, do you? Well, we're going fishing tonight. Come with us! We could use a duo of brave vampire hunters," Juan said.

Scooter wasn't sure if he was serious or mocking them.

Eating dust, they bounced along behind the green pickup turning into Mayor Jones' driveway. The silver-haired and former beauty queen, Mrs. Tanya, was Texas hospitable with iced tea and donuts. The teens devoured them like popcorn, now smiling at work. Scooter mentioned she should be on a postage stamp to commemorate gentility.

Nick showed them how to lower the entire flat bed and set up a ramp to move the olive-green washer and dryer. Scooter was impressed with the way Russell and Nick manhandled the washing machine. He had a feeling they were showing off, but then Russell was infatuated with Hope. Scooter helped with the dryer.

At least he got to watch Kristie. When her mother was occupied, Kristie winked at him or threw him a wild smile.

To the Knights, the Cauthons, and the Gonzalezes, then beyond, a pattern developed. Mrs. Candel led the way like a major at the head of a convoy, pulling in first but leaving space for Nick to park near the garage.

They were thirsty when they arrived at Ms. Emmitt's. The librarian was ready, coming out to meet them, serving lemonade while they unloaded her shed.

Scooter handled the old camping equipment including a pair of tents, which he had his eye on. The rest of the boys dealt with the big stuff, including a portable generator — portable if you were Goliath—and a sleeper sofa. Scooter felt impotent. The long-limbed Gomezes were wiry, but it was Russell and Nick who moved the old, stout refrigerator. They grunted, grimaced, and grinned a lot.

In gratitude, Ms. Emmitt sent them off with still-warm chocolate chip and peanut butter cookies.

Figuring they had enough room for one more stop, they pulled into the Brownstones. They had a ton of furniture, much of it antique, including heavy oak and cherry bedroom sets and a mammoth entertainment cabinet.

Scooter was helping Julio with one of the heavy, oak chest of drawers when he stumbled. His foot stuttered down a step onto the porch. He lurched, blinked, and then caught himself, thinking 'klutz'.

But the chest shifted, smacking the side of his face. Scooter slipped again, dropping to his knees, and losing a sense of everything but crushing weight.

TWENTY-THREE

STRANGE ATTITUDES

"How do you feel?" Kristie asked.

Scooter just stared at her. He knew her, yes. Where was he? Why was he sitting on the ground?

Looking around, he tried to digest what he saw. It looked like somebody was moving in or moving out. There were other kids, including Russell, who stepped close.

"Do you know what happened?"

Scooter took a moment, gazing about. It was coming to him. He noticed he didn't see light coming from anybody. He doubted their auras were gone, but he no longer saw them. He gently touched his face, finding it tender along his left brow and cheek. His ear felt swollen. "I caught a chest of drawers in the face."

"I'm sorry," Juan said. "When you slipped, I slipped, too."

Russell asked him about the day, the place, and his dog's name. He knew them all, so Russell pronounced him okay. "Tell me if you feel dizzy or get nauseous."

Mrs. Candel handed him a cold pack. "Why don't you rest, and I'll stay with you while the others finish up. Go on! Pack it up, and we'll go home for lunch. There's watermelon and chili in the crock-pot."

Scooter sat and observed, Flash leaning on him, while his friends unpacked, rearranged, and then loaded the wealth of furniture donated by the Brownstones. Scooter felt a little left out and disconnected. He said nothing as Mrs. Candel gave directions. Between the Gomezes, Russell, and Sloan, the moving was in good hands. The Incredible Bulk was amazing, and the kid from California matched him in feats of strength.

Scooter missed seeing everybody's life lights. They now seemed somewhat two-dimensional, or at least missing an important ingredient to round them out.

When they were securing things, Kristie checked on him. She ran her hands along the sides of his face, staring into his eyes. "How are you feeling?" he asked, preemptively.

"Dog tired. You think getting hit by lightning would give you a boost in energy, like a jump start."

"Barry Allen got struck by lightning to become the Flash."

"So you named your dog after him. Here," she said, giving him a shoulder rub.

Her touch felt wonderful, healing, and he began to see more clearly. Thinking came a bit easier, but he still didn't see auras. "Thanks. What did you do?"

"Nothing," she said and shrugged.

He wanted to ask her about her apparent fragility. Her mother moved more youthfully than her eldest daughter. Something was wrong here.

"Jonathan, can you walk?" Mrs. Candel called.

"Yes, ma'am, I'm feeling better," Scooter said.

On the way back, he rode inside with Mrs. Candel, moving Hope over with Kristie. Mrs. Candel wanted to see how he was before putting him on the back of a truck. They mostly talked about his grandparents' rebuilding project, while he thought about what Kristie was doing to herself.

"So what do you think about this Lewis Shaddock being caught?" Mother Candel asked, ambushing him.

"I'm glad he's no longer a danger. There's no telling how many kids he hurt," Scooter evaded.

"He's not the monster that . . . hurt you?"

"No, but it could be a brother," Scooter replied. He didn't really want to talk vampires or religion with Mrs. Candel.

"What do you think happened to Lucius Shade?"

Scooter thought long and hard about what to say. "The light of day. He was a creature of darkness. I don't know who Lewis Shaddock is, but he scared me half to death when I bumped into him." He flashed back and squirmed.

"I'm sorry. It's just that Kristie has crazy ideas about vampires, and you write about them," her mother said.

"I think Kristie is one of the most levelheaded people I have ever met. I think you should be proud. She saved my life, Russell's, Racquel's, Garrett Brashear's, and the Mochrie brothers, as well as Flash."

"I am proud of her, but she takes your wild stories too seriously. I like my stories more down to earth or spiritual in nature. Now, please stop passing on your wild ideas to my daughter. Otherwise, she will have to stop talking to you."

Nothing else needed to be said.

After lunch, Scooter intended to talk to Kristie about it, but she snuck up behind and gave him a neck rub. He fell asleep next to a snoring Flash.

"Hey, are you coming along?" Russell asked.

Scooter sat up, feeling much better. The brief nap had cleared his head. He still couldn't see life light around anybody, but he hopped to his feet with barely a wobble. "I'm ready." To show them, he walked a row of bricks with his arms outstretched, then balanced on one foot and touched his nose.

Russell pronounced him fit.

"You didn't have to do that," Scooter told Kristie. He believed that she took on too much.

"Of course I did. I'll be better soon, you'll see. I just need a nap," Kristie said. She curled up in the cab of the truck.

Scooter scrambled onto the flatbed, hanging onto a rail. Russell helped him up just as Nick shifted into first gear.

The Gomezes had a challenge. Which of them could endure having the most Warhead candies in their mouths at once. On five lemon sours, Juan clutched his throat as his face puckered and almost fell off the truck. Russell snagged him.

They slowly rolled along the wall of half-buried trucks and past the entrance of the Pickup Ranch.

"That is a creepy place," Juan said.

Scooter remained quiet, listening to Kristie sleep. She was still catnapping when they stopped at Hank Peters ranch house.

Scooter didn't think of the man as a giving person. He had always seemed bitter and judgmental.

Tanned and smiling, Peters strolled bandy-legged out to greet them. His hat, hair, and shirt shone a gleaming white, creating a halo. Even Mrs. Candel seemed caught off guard by a hug from the codger. Scooter spent a lot of time watching, careful to carry only light stuff. Peters wasn't himself, chatting with Kristie's mom about how he only worked legal immigrants.

After they had moved everything, Peters offered them a reward, passing around a bowl of Tootsie Pops. The rancher thanked them profusely for helping him clear out his attic and garage, giving Sloan a golf club set and Russell a weight set. Scooter was certain he must be dreaming. This didn't make sense.

"You boys tell Mr. Chandler, no hard feelings. Live and let live, I say," Peters told them.

Scooter was speechless, so he just nodded. He couldn't see any auras, but the look in Peters' eyes reminded him of BJ.

The trucks rolled on. Along the way, Scooter smelled cigarette smoke. When Nick offered, Scooter declined.

Russell explained about emphysema until Nick hollered, "Enough!" Scooter was glad to see Kristie seemed immune to his brawn, his charming smile, and the cigarettes.

At the Hernandez's homestead, Scooter's expectations weren't met. The yard and gardens were lush and immaculate. The landscaping made the eye wander like a masterpiece, but the air of calm had worked magic on the testy Ramon. The husband and wife gave Scooter a note of apology to take to Marcus, along with some 'killer' homemade salsa.

"Is something killer truly a peace offering?" Russell asked.

Scooter wondered what was going on.

Aaron Nathans seemed to have changed overnight. The postman had lost weight, and he seemed to be abnormally hyper, willing to help them. The man Scooter knew would have just sat back, saying he got his workout at the post office.

"I'm starting over, yes I am. Getting healthy," he pointed to a stationary bicycle and treadmill. Beaming with joy, he guided them to a closet where he unloaded boxes of Twinkies on them.

"Where's the beer?" Julio asked.

"I gave it to Alvin," Nathans replied.

Scooter was even more flabbergasted by the eccentric

postman giving up his home-brewing and beer-making equipment. He was shocked when Nathan apologized.

"I'm sorry I doubted y'all. I should know better. I haven't seen vampires in my back yard, but I have seen aliens. Perhaps that's it. Tell Mr. Chandler to live long and prosper." His smile didn't reach his eyes.

If the eyes were windows to the soul, the postman was screaming.

At the Mochrie place, Pearl frowned, grim as ever. "You, two! I hear y'all saw CJ again?"

By Kristie's expression, she wondered why she hadn't been told.

"We're not a hundred percent sure. I only saw him through binoculars," Russell said.

Scooter bit his lip. He didn't know how much she knew.

Pearl gripped Scooter's shoulder with her bony hand, hurting him. "Did he really shoot at you?"

"We aren't sure it was CJ," Scooter said.

"CJ wouldn't shoot anybody," Kristie said.

Scooter thought about how BJ, Peters, Chung, and Nathans had all acted strangely. Even Russell's current bulking up and using a gun seemed suspicious.

"If it was CJ, he knows about BJ. I was hoping he would come back home," Russell said.

"No. I'm afraid he's gone. If it hadn't been for Marcus Chandler moving back from California, this never would have happened. Damn the man. If he is indeed a man," she ranted on. The shrewish woman flushed, looking a little panicked. Her eyes started to roll.

He and Russell helped her sit.

Kristie came and sat with her. Scooter watched in amazement as Mrs. Mochrie rapidly improved. Soon, Pearl was just as cantankerous as ever. Kristie rapidly faded.

As she swooned, Scooter caught her. She looked dizzy, when she boldly kissed him.

Mrs. Candel cleared her throat. "Kristie!"

"Thanks, I feel better," Kristie said. She didn't walk that steadily, even after her mother took her by the arm.

On the way back, even with the windows up, you could hear Kristie and her mother arguing.

TWENTY-FOUR

DEATH AND DEPARTURE

Due to Scooter's headache, Judge Grandpa taxied him by boat to Pickup Ranch's dock. His grandfather planned to fish nearby while Scooter fed the puppies. The jog into the house was hot. Flash panted, overheated in his fur coat. Sweat soaked Scooter to the bone, but then he would have looked about the same after a lazy walk. Just breathing made him perspire.

He itched again, too. This batch of Granny June's wasn't working. That made him think about Kristie, depressing him.

The kitchen was hot, so the puppies appreciated ice water and the box fan cranked on high. He fed them two at a time. After Goldie dipped herself and stood in front of the wind machine, other pups joined the dunking and blowing fun. He carried them outside, letting them loose in the grass under a pair of large cottonwoods. Flash and Beauty helped wear them out. Grabbing his drawing pad, he sketched them, bestowing them with names: Goldie, Starr, Speedy, Ace, and Happy.

They eventually fell asleep, even in mid stride. He carried them inside to their box home in the kitchen.

He left a note about the weird day and odd people, really wanting to talk to Marcus about Kristie's kiss. He checked his watch. He met Judge Grandpa in twenty minutes. Going to the closet in Nirvana, he explored the photos in the chest of drawers. He set his watch on five minutes. Otherwise, he would get absorbed in the mystery of Chandler's history. Without Marcus, life would be different in Gunstock, almost like *It's a Wonderful Life.*

When he finished putting everything back, he discovered the Intruder standing in the doorway. His arms were no longer covered in bandages. He blew his nose, sneezed, then he snorted loudly into another tissue. "Damn dogs. Can't they stay outside?"

"I'm leaving."

"Oh, well, I wanted to ask you . . . uh, a writing question. Is it hard? The writing?"

"Getting good at it is hard, just like learning to play an instrument or sport can be hard and yet fun. I miss it when I'm not doing it, and I think about doing it when I'm not. You need to find out if you have one story to tell or a truckload."

"Then why do you need the photos of Mr. Chandler?"

Scooter was a bit angry at first, then he shrugged. "It's a surprise for Marcus. I'm going to do a comic book history of him with photos. I scan them, print them, bring them back, and use them in a copy of *The Incredible Mr. C.*"

"I like the sound of it," he said, looking sheepish. "I thought you were just fingering them to sell on eBay. Everybody's trying to make a buck."

Scooter remained silent, holding his tongue. When the Intruder scratched, Scooter itched. He wanted to be gone.

"Hey, can I ask you another writing question?" the Intruder asked. His rheumy eyes seemed distracted. "The whole plotting it out stuff. Got any other exercises I can do while I wait?"

Scooter couldn't believe he was giving advice about writing. "This is from something I read about writing by Well's Root. He taught a UCLA screenplay class."

"Screenplays. I like it! Roll, baby!"

Scooter was unamused. "Right. Anyway, there's the hero and the river. In the first act—the beginning—put your hero in a frail skiff on a hazardous river. Using both a hero and heroine might work better, since this way they can argue and interact in a more personal confrontation than with nature. For some reason, they're trying to get farther down the river. Make it urgent. Give them a time limit with little or no margin of error to reach their goal. Failure should have dire ramifications."

"Like in *Rooster Cogburn*? Or *The African Queen*?"

Scooter nodded. His grandparents liked those old movies. "Let's say they're delivering medicine downstream to help the sick. Once you launch into the river, there is no turning back. Maybe people will start dying in three days. Use your imagination."

"*Balto!*"

Scooter took a deep, balancing breath. "The river curves sharply, just like the storyline, so your audience can't see what is coming. We don't want things to become predictable and lose suspense. The rocks and white water are everywhere. Maybe the river has become unexpectedly flooded by rain."

"Can we have bandits? Or hostile natives?"

"Sure. But safe passage is impossible. Pain and death are imminent."

"I can tell you have been talking to Mr. Chandler."

"At the beginning of the third act, there is a class five rapid—a crisis that appears insurmountable. To make matters worse, our hero admits he can't swim. Notice we withheld this piece of information."

"Uh-huh."

"Good evening, everyone," Marcus said. Looking freshly awake, he walked in. "The other thing you need to set up is what Wells Root called the invisible lifeline. The hidden clue. A surprise piece of evidence."

"The other half of the ticket, like in *The Last Action Hero*?"

"Yes. Just make sure you plant the seed early, whether it's the glass slipper in *Cinderella* or the exploding CO_2 canisters in *Jaws*. Don't make it a sudden, gee whiz where did that come from saving grace," Marcus said. "Don't let the power of God Almighty wipe out your villain. They did that in Greek tragedies, so it's really old hat. Make the hero do the work, and when it seems appropriate, give him a lucky break."

Scooter checked the time. "I've got to go. Judge Grandpa should be waiting. We want to get home before it storms."

"Gone so soon?"

"I've been here for two hours taking care of the puppies. Here are some sketches," he said, showing off. He let them look while he packed up.

"They look great! Thanks for taking care of them."

"It's fun," Scooter replied. What he didn't say was he could use some fun right now, since he was forbidden from seeing Kristie. Russell carried a gun, making him seem dangerous. He had nightmares about spiders and the Gibbering Darkness. Thanks to the Intruder, he had difficulty enjoying Marcus' company. "See ya."

Judge Grandpa wouldn't like the 'woe is me' attitude.

Running to the dock might help. When he called to Flash to follow him, his best friend barked from the field. Both he and Beauty refused to heel. Scooter felt sadness. Shortly, he found out why. Flash and Beauty sat dejected around a horse, looking forlornly back and forth between the collapsed animal and Scooter. He rushed in and checked to see if it was alive. Thankfully the horse still breathed. He used his cell phone. "Marcus! May Bell has collapsed."

A moment later, his mentor burst out of the house. He

ran and actually leapt over the fence. Breathless, he knelt near May Bell.

"Oh, May B! May B! What's wrong with you, girl?" he asked, cradling the beloved horse's head. He stroked her forehead. "I know you're old, is it just time?" One handed, he operated his cell phone, then tossed it to Scooter. "Talk to Dr. Daniels. Tell him sweet May B is in a bad way. See if he'll come out right now!"

After the vet promised to come immediately, Scooter placed a second call. He couldn't reach Judge Grandpa, but unless something was wrong, he would be at the dock early. That was just the way his grandfather had been raised.

During the excitement, the skies had darkened with storm clouds. They looked like brutes bruised from battering. Lightning appeared to crack livid fractures in clouds.

"Marcus, I hate to leave, but I can't reach Grandpa on his phone. He's supposed to be at the dock waiting for me."

"I understand. Beauty and Kellen can wait with me."

Scooter didn't trust the Intruder. He realized he was beginning to suspect just about everybody.

"Call us from there, okay?" his mentor asked.

Scooter took off running, racing out to the dock.

Less than a hundred feet from the Pickup Ranch dock, Flash skidded to a stop, causing Scooter to stumble over him and fall on his knees. The golden Lab growled low and throaty, interrupting his complaint.

Scooter thought it was odd, but he smelled Judge Grandpa. Flash knew he was there, too. "Let's get a little closer." He wished he had a flashlight.

Lightning illuminated the evening. In a flash, he could see the dock, empty except for Grandpa's Four Winns bow rider. Scooter didn't see his grandpa anywhere. "Grandpa?!"

Lightning flickered, giving off echoing booms. The air tautened, raising the hair on the back of his neck and arms. Looking wired, Flash's fur stood like porcupine quills.

Peering closer, Scooter saw somebody settled in the front seat of the Four Winns. Why would he be sitting in the dark? He knew Judge Grandpa carried a book light everywhere so he could read any time or place.

When Scooter set foot on the dock, his dog grabbed his pant leg, holding him back. He almost fell again, putting his hands on a post to remain afoot. "Easy, boy." While he backed up, he exposed his amulet, taking the cross out from underneath his shirt. BJ had worn a crucifix, and it hadn't kept him alive. Scooter still carried another in his hand, keeping it outstretched as he walked onto the pier to flip a switch.

Nothing happened. Gathered under the roof, darkness hung heavy and thick like oily smoke clinging to the water.

He reached for his cell phone, planning to dial 911.

"No need for that. There is no danger. Your grandfather is simply asleep," a disturbing voice said. Scooter felt needled a hundred times over. The yellow dock lights came on, flooding the area with light. It gave a sense of false safety, even as Scooter's eyes adjusted.

He didn't see anyone, but something oozed from one of the shadows on the far side of the boat. A creature of darkness coalesced into a mockery of life wearing a dark suit and fedora with a feather. Scooter knew there was nothing alive underneath the hat and jacket, although its eyes belied the truth.

"Stay, boy! I know it's a vampire, but it's not attacking yet, so let's not provoke it," Scooter said. Flash felt prickly under his hand. "Mr. Ripley," he managed without stammering. "Have you harmed my grandfather?"

"No. I suggested he sleep."

Scooter wasn't sure what to do. Was he in the power of the vampire? He finally hit dial on his cell phone. He heard Marcus say hello and clicked to speaker mode. His next words rasped out. "Did you feast on him, Mr. Ripley?"

"No."

"Is Judge Grandpa asleep so you can tell me something in private?" he asked hopefully, even as he dreaded the answer.

"I wanted Marcus Chandler to know I am leaving. Thanks to your cell phone, I believe he knows. Another item of interest for you: I am not your problem. Farewell, Mr. Chandler. I am an admirer, but my hands are tied."

"Wait?! Who is our problem? Is Shade really dead? You don't sound like his friend," Scooter blurted.

Ripley stared at him—through him to inside him.

"Who is Lewis Shaddock? Did he really kill those kids?" Scooter asked. In a moment, Ripley would be gone and answers would disappear with it. Who was threatening people while pretending to be Marcus? Where was CJ? Had BJ been enthralled? Who was killing the kids?

"Wait! A moment, please," he begged. "You hated Shade, didn't you? You're glad he's destroyed."

Ripley paused, its stare boring a hole through him. It suddenly blinked in rapid succession. Scooter's life flickered across his mind's eye. He should have let it go.

Flash gently nipped his hand. "Ouch! That hurt! Thanks."

The jacketed vampire turned away.

Scooter couldn't leave well enough alone. "Now, because Shade is dust, you're just leaving. You don't care that he is the reason so many people are screwed up. If Shade were here, you would try to stop it. Well, Shade might be gone, but this chaos is its legacy. You said so yourself."

"I have done what I came to do and more than allowed."

Scooter thought that an odd statement, then he jumped to a conclusion. "You influenced Marcus' neighbors. Peters, Chung and Nathans? How long will it last?"

Ripley remained preternaturally still.

Scooter persisted. "What about the Cult of the Vampire? Are you their inspiration?" He felt reckless, perhaps because Marcus was listening. If the vampire wanted to kill him, he doubted he could stop it, but he wasn't going to just let it walk away and leave his town in a mess.

The living shadow called Ripley brooded and fired up a cigar. The match light only touched its eyes as black as basalt. "I have nothing to do with it. If you want to solve one of your mysteries, go to Mr. Short's mother's house in two nights. You should do something soon about the Curse of Thirteen, or you won't be drawing or writing any more stories."

"What is the Curse of Thirteen?!"

The cloud of burnt tobacco swelled, surrounding the figure as a shroud. Lost in the smoke, the undead one seemed to fade to nothing. The smoke drifted down the shoreline, sweeping across the sand and grass to disappear, clearing away the sense of spiky wrongness.

"Did you hear that?" Scooter asked into the phone.

"Yes, I did, you crazy boy. Are you all right?"

"Yes, the vampire's gone, as far as I can tell. You heard it claim it wasn't its fault. That sounded human enough. I'm going to check on Grandpa. I'll call you back."

He rushed onto the dock and to his beloved grandfather. Flash beat him there, licking him awake. Grandpa blinked, confused for a moment, then he smiled, rubbing on Flash. "Oh my. I must've fallen asleep. Are you ready to go?"

"Yes, sir," Scooter said hoarsely, then hugged his grandpa, lifting him up out of the chair. Right now, he forgot about Kristie, BJ, and the Curse of Thirteen. He was grateful that his grandfather lived.

TWENTY-FIVE

THE MARINA GHOST

All through the next day, while working on the lake house, Scooter fretted over what to do. Ripley had left. Shade was dead, but another vampire stalked Gunstock.

He had called Kristie, but Mary said she couldn't come to the phone. If he wrote her a letter about Ripley leaving, it would be read. So might an e-mail. He was tempted to sneak over and toss pebbles at her window.

He scratched. His bites burned. He would like to ask for a different batch of Granny June's homemade ointment. His skin seemed softer and began to yellow around the whitehead. An angry red circle surrounded it.

How far might Kristie go for somebody? He was afraid she might accept too great a challenge and die.

Scooter would like to confide in her about his best bud and this morning's phone call. It kept replaying in his head. "Hello, Scooter. This is Dr. Daniels. Remember that pill you left with me? It's a steroid, trenbolone, used to improve muscle mass in cattle. I destroyed it. Do you have any idea whose it is?"

Scooter wondered how to discuss the revelation with his best bud. So now he knew Russell was willing to undergo a chemical transformation to become the Incredible Bulk.

His grandparents were out at a fundraising dinner,

leaving him at home. Scooter grabbed his folder and sketch pad, then he climbed to the top of the Jaystone's sun deck over the dock to watch the sunset and work on *The Incredible Mr. C.*

It was getting harder to see when he heard the angry growl of a motor. The ATV stopped, its rider unlocking and opening the chain link gates. The three wheeler swung wide, then parked near the back deck.

The broad-shouldered man in a helmet and armor seemed huge, even after Scooter realized it was Russell. He had always been tall, getting it from his father's side, but now he was wearing his dad's gear. What was he going to say?

For a moment, he could only think to hide. Russell knocked on the door and waited. Flash finally barked, letting him know they were out on the dock. Scooter waved. "Great. Now what?"

Flash grabbed a fishing pole, offering it to him.

"Okay. Fine," Scooter replied. Russell spoke more freely while around water, especially fishing.

The Incredible Bulk clamored up the stairs, making the dock shake. Flash greeted him with exuberance given only to best friends. "Hey, are you catching anything?"

"Uh, not yet. I haven't started. I've been sketching," Scooter said, slapping at a mosquito. "If you're here to stay, good, but put on some bug spray. The mosquitos are out in full force."

"I think they would die biting me. My sores look worse, and they're starting to hurt again. This batch of Granny June's isn't doing it."

Scooter tossed his best bud the can of repellant. "Well, you don't want bites on top of bites. You're bigger now, so there's more to eat."

"You're funny. At least Mrs. Candel being furious at you hasn't killed your sense of humor."

"I chopped wood earlier. That helped. Grandma Mae's mad, and Judge Grandpa thinks it's tragic that a public kiss is making a scandal while kids are still dying."

"I say let things cool off. Kristie's probably stuck at home, grounded."

"Did you notice what I was talking about? How she moves like she's fifty?" Scooter asked.

"Yep." Russell nodded.

"She can't keep healing people," Scooter moaned, worried. "Hey, do you hear that?" he asked and turned around to face the lake.

"Well, if you trust vampires, it isn't Ripley. Any more thoughts on the Curse of Thirteen? Do you realize twelve kids have died?"

"I'm worried because we have thirteen sores."

"*Buenos noches!*" the driver of the bass boat called. A sleek and low-riding craft idled up, gliding through the water.

Only because of Flash, Scooter could see two tanned boys without shirts. Scooter smelled Julio's potent aftershave. "It's the Gomezes."

"Nice boat," Russell whistled. Red and gold, it was a Nitro 400 Bassmaster with an Evinrude 200. It could race from spot to spot, almost flying, and still ease into the shallows.

"Jose' is making good money playing clubs in Dallas. When he has time, he likes to come out here and relax. We watch it for him while he's gone, making sure everything's in good working order, and that he has fish to eat. How's the fishing here?" Juan asked. He adjusted his Ranger's cap.

"We haven't started yet. How about you?"

"We caught our limit. We'll be glad to take you. The fish were biting like crazy," Julio said.

"Biting like crazy?" Russell asked, perking up.

"Julio was fishing with three lines and moving so quickly you'd think that he was stuck in fast-forward," Juan joked.

"Where?"

"Near Creech's Marina. They might still be biting. I think you don't believe us," Julio said. He opened the live well and a large cooler. Whitefish, sand bass, and sunfish, along with a few crappie, flopped in both containers.

"Wow!" Scooter wished he could see auras so he could tell if the boys were possessed. His fears were unfounded, he realized, when he saw them in the yellow illumination of the dock's light bulbs. They looked happy, their eyes a little bright, but otherwise normal.

Russell withdrew a silver cross from his backpack and tossed it to Juan.

He caught it, then returned it. "I have one." Juan lifted up his shirt to show off the crucifix tattooed on his chest. "I'm covered. A Warhead sour, anyone?"

Flash wasn't disturbed. He hopped into the boat.

"Let's go," Russell said, eagerly.

"What about vampires?" Scooter asked.

"I am not going to hide inside. I'm going fishing."

"Let's do it!" Scooter said. It gave him an excuse to have fun with Russell, but not feel pressured to address the steroid issue. He left a note, letting the Incredible Bulk pack.

The symphony of crickets, cicadas, and frogs sounded loud as though they were giving them a heroes' sendoff. With Juan at the helm, the Nitro 400 swiftly carried them onto the lake.

"This really is a nice boat," Russell continued on. He set his hands on the outboard. "It runs so smoothly."

"We got beer from Mexico and Texas," Julio hoisted a Corona in one hand. "Plus, Pearl, and Lone Star. Want one?"

"We also have chips and salsa so hot it will make your tongue sweat. You'll have to drink beer!" Juan added.

"Got anything else? Last time I drank alcohol I saw a vampire," Scooter replied. Russell choked back a laugh with a cough. They smiled, then unleashed their most skeptical expressions on each other. Flash snorted, then sneezed in disbelief, making them laugh uproariously.

"What are you three on? It's better than beer! Gimme some!" Julio begged.

"They're not like us, Julio. They don't need liquid courage!"

"What?" Russell asked.

"Want to see the dead walk?" Juan continued.

"I already have. Once was too much," Scooter said.

"Is that what this is about? Ghosts? I want to fish," Russell said.

"On the other hand, the ghost could be CJ. It's close to the boat factory. He might be trying to scare people away," Scooter said.

"*Tu no comprende, mi amigo.* I told you, it's old man Creech! He drowned and bloated up like a puffer fish. The ghost kid did it. I've seen him. Julio thinks he saw a ghost cat," Juan finished doubtfully.

"Its wailing creeps me out. Of course, you two have seen vampires, so you might not be bothered by ghosts," Julio said. He took another swig of beer.

"Have you tried talking to it?" Scooter asked.

Juan and Julio looked astonished. "Why would we do that?"

"To see if it's friendly," Russell added.

"Are they ever?" Juan asked.

"Well, not all vampires attacked us. One claimed to be a reporter," Scooter said.

"Big surprise there," Juan chuckled.

"Why don't you come along?" Julio asked.

Scooter looked at Russell. After all, they had seen vampires—believed in the impossible. With that in mind, there might be ghosts. All Scooter really wanted to do was toss some worms and catch a whole bunch of fish.

And yet, nobody had believed them about vampires. "You aren't exactly damsels in distress."

"They're scared. I told you ghosts were scarier than vampires," Julio said.

Scooter burst out laughing. Russell joined him, and they collapsed upon the seats with Flash barking.

The Gomezes didn't know what to make of them. "Come see. You be the judge," Julio said.

"If this is some kind of joke," Russell growled.

"That's why we want you along. Come prove to us it's not what we think it is. You've seen unnatural things. You might be able to see something that we don't," Julio continued.

Past the dam and eastward, they came around the point and into sight of the spooky marina. Scooter had been skeptical until then. He couldn't see the shoreline, and the trio of buildings making up Creech's Marina seemed to be floating atop a pulsating, green cloud. It slowly swelled to consume more of the lake, hiding the shallow water. The docks and pier were concealed too, their piles standing like lonely sentries.

"It wasn't like this when we left," Julio said.

Scooter pointed. "The lights are coming from the windows of the old bait and tackle shop." He sneezed harshly, catching the odd scent. He couldn't identify the weird stink among the skunk, mice droppings, and pungent dead armadillo. Flash picked up on a high whine from somewhere behind the dock. Scooter listened for it, hearing what could have been a motor.

A weighty something crashed out of sight. A cloud of debris roiled upward. Several chunks disappeared in the fog and landed in the water with crisp splashes. Scooter could feel the sound rush across the waves. "Wow," he said, not sure where he had felt that before.

A hideous caterwauling echoed off the buildings and the shores of the inlet. In a flash of black, a winged creature flew from the mariner's store to the boat warehouse.

"Did you see that?" Russell asked.

Scooter was skeptical. Through Flash, he smelled chemicals. The fog reminded him of dry ice mist.

"I think that was the cat," Juan said.

"No, that was the boy," Julio argued.

"Hey, come out! We mean you no harm!" Russell called out.

So far, his best bud had bought into it hook and line. Scooter thought it appeared real enough, making it easy to assume, but he had Flash's nose on his side. He wasn't sure what the glimpse of white might be, but he doubted it would withstand direct light.

Juan and Julio were great actors, mostly hanging back. The fog cloud swallowed the bow of the bass boat.

"I'm getting out the spotlight," Scooter said, reaching for his bag.

"Good idea," Russell said.

Flash barked at the pale phantoms rippling through the fog as they dashed to the store after the cat. The caterwauling started again, followed by the weird muffled moaning of an older man.

"Doesn't sound particularly friendly to me," Julio said.

Scooter got out the halogen ray-beam, but dropped it when the door of the store came crashing open. Fishing poles tumbled out, then a sail unraveled, rolling out toward them like a silken carpet. A white skeletal face appeared in the doorway, then it flew toward them.

Scooter was stunned when Russell whipped out his gun.

"Hey!" Julio shouted.

"Stop! It's a prank! A hoax!" Scooter said, touching his shoulder. "Relax, there's no ghost."

"What do you mean?!" Russell asked. His gun was still raised. His knuckles were strained white.

"I don't want you to hurt anyone!" Scooter replied. They really needed to talk, but now wasn't the place or time. Nobody else needed to know. Scooter was certain he could talk reason into his best bud, especially after this.

"Wow! Man, Juan, we did a much better job than we thought. He was about to blow holes in Javier. Russ, kick back and sip a cool one. It's all good and just for fun! Javier will be the next David Copperfield!" he said and applauded.

Back at the marina, Javier thanked him.

Russell was livid, his teeth grinding. He could have bitten through a fistful of nails.

"Uh, you see, Javier brought home a truckload of dry ice. It's only good for a couple of days. We thought it would be fun to create a spooky place, since Maria is reading a scary story about a ghost," Julio chattered on.

"You were going to bring her out and do this to her?!" Russell snarled. He sputtered, spitting mad. "It's not funny! There are dangerous lunatics out here without you making up this crap just to scare the piss out of somebody!"

The brothers were slack-jawed and now covered with spittle. Scooter knew and understood why Russell reacted this way. He might have, even without the steroids.

"Hey, we were just trying to have a little fun. Maria is always trying to show us how brave she is. Tougher than us, she says. We thought scaring her would shut her up for a while. Sorry. We didn't know you were so uptight," Juan replied. He burped then grinned.

Scooter thought Russell was going to shoot him.

TWENTY-SIX

ADDICTIVE SECRETS

"I would understand if you hit him. Just don't shoot him," Scooter said.

Russell's eyes were wild, his face livid, the flush creeping down his neck. "I wouldn't, but I would like to," he said, lowering his gun.

"Would you like to see it dance across the water? You could shoot at that. Keep your eyes on it," Julio said. This time he openly used a remote control. The window popped open and a tattered, white sheet seemed to fly across the surface as it rolled along on a wire.

"You were right about Scooby-Doo!" Russell snarled. "What did you say this was for again?"

"Scaring the piss out of our sister, Maria. We took Ana snipe hunting, but she warned Maria about that," Julio bemoaned. The brothers exchanged pitiful looks of longing, as if they had been denied a basic sibling pleasure.

"Thanks for letting us test it on you. I would just love to show Eve how brave I am," Juan said, shifting into muscle building poses.

"I hadn't thought about shooting, though. I could bring my shotgun and fill it full of blanks. I've got some fireworks we could use," Julio mused aloud.

"Guys, I don't think this is a good idea," Scooter said.

"We thought you liked fireworks," Julio said.

"Idiots! Wake up before you blow yourselves up! There's flammable gasoline, oil, and other chemicals spilled around here! Man, oh man, oh man, I can't believe I almost shot Javier! People will think I'm even crazier if word gets out that we were out ghost hunting! They'll call us the Fool Hunters," Russell groaned, then he leaned into Juan. "What if Maria has a heart attack? I almost had one."

"Relax," Julio said. "You're all jumpy."

"How about relaxing by flying on our favorite rope swings? It's close," Scooter suggested. Flash yipped his yes.

"Yeah! We can turn on boat lights. We got a spotlight for frog giggin'. Yee-haw!" Juan yelled.

They cruised for a few minutes. Russell radiated angry heat, but the wind cooled him down a little. Scooter hoped a swim in the lake would bring back the real Russell.

Juan slowed as they neared a jutting point. It stuck out around a shallow cove crowned by poplars, oaks, and twisted mesquite trees. A pair of oaks leaned over the water, making great spots to tie rope swings. Juan steered them into one of the common landing spots where the land dropped off steeply. The other side was renowned as Lovers Beach. It was concealed from view by the trees and the lay of the land.

Ears aloft, Flash jumped into the water. After setting up lights, the boys stripped down to their shorts.

"Scooter, what are all those ugly red and white bumps? They're gross," Julio said, backing up.

"Bug bites," Scooter replied. They looked worse.

"From Fisherman's Island. I think they're spider bites," Russell said. No longer scared of the height, Russell scaled higher than ever up the wooden footholds nailed into the swing tree.

Scooter watched as his buddy grabbed the rope with a

stick and drew it to him. He checked it for fraying, then he swung like Tarzan out over the water. "Yee-haw!"

He didn't create steam when he hit, but the splash was huge. He was smiling when he surfaced and swam back.

For the next hour, they dove, jumped, and swung out, splashing and having a blast. The Gomezes finally hemmed, hawed and guffawed through an apology.

Russell mellowed, almost coming back to his old self, but Scooter had seen his bud pull the gun on a skeleton when they could have just boated away. He agonized over how to help.

While Julio and Juan went exploring to see who might be lip wrestling on the beach, Scooter rested on a flat rock.

He decided now might be a good time, especially after seeing Russell furious. Scooter didn't want to confront him. But what else were friends for if they didn't tell you your fly was open? Or you had something stuck in your teeth? Was this any different than if Russell had decided to dodge cars to improve his quickness?

"Nowhere feels safe, does it?" Russell said. "Not home. Not the lake. Not since I first met Mr. Lucius Shade. Before that, I thought I had been powerless when dealing with Racquel. It was nothing compared to the helplessness I suffered, thanks to Shade. You know, I just stood there and watched as he was going to kill you and 'transform' Racquel. Because of vampires, the night will never feel safe again. Even during the day, I'm concerned about their servants."

Scooter understood. His friend had been terrified by Shade. Fear could change you but rarely for the better. He had to find courage now, when he might lose his best bud. "Is that why you carry a gun?"

Russell nodded. "Yep. That and the Gunn brothers' kin. You know, you're safer staying away from the Pickup Ranch."

Scooter knew that Russell didn't dislike his mentor, but out there, odd and harrowing things happened. "You think it's a vortex of strange events."

"I think you're spending too much time there."

He could say there were puppies to feed, but it would sound like an excuse. "Then we need to fish and bicycle more. You're in classes all the time, or working out, or shooting. If I wasn't with Marcus, Judge Grandpa would have me work until ten o'clock each night," Scooter moaned.

Russell's laughter made him feel better. "Fishing is about the only relaxing thing I do any more."

"You need to kick back more. You almost shot Javier," Scooter said. "When I get frightened, it's easy to over react. I understand not wanting to be caught unaware or be enthralled again. I hated being a puppet. I don't want to play the victim again and just count on luck and the grace of Kristie to survive."

"Amen to that," Russell replied. He stared up at the stars.

Scooter almost couldn't say it. He stammered, so Russell gave him a wondering look. He watched his best bud closely as he said, "But I don't think steroids are the answer."

"What are you t-talking about?" Russell asked guardedly. His eyes flashed as if the fuse of his temper had just been lit.

"You're bigger, stronger, and faster in six weeks."

"I've been taking a vitamin supplement."

"Please don't get mad at me. I am your friend, and I'm trying to help. Wait, listen to me before you ad lib. In fact, don't say anything at all. Let me make a fool of myself," he said, taking a deep breath before plunging on. "At the island, in the shack, I found a pill. I picked it up, thinking it might be Redgraves, or maybe even CJ's. I took it to the hospital."

Russell paled.

"But I forgot about it until we took Flash to Dr. Daniels. He checked on the pill. It's a steroid, a growth hormone called trenbolone, used in cattle. I think it's yours."

"Hey . . . ."

"But then, I could be wrong, too. I'm just assuming. If I am, I apologize. I was looking out for your best interest, and my own, too, as I don't want to lose my best buddy. I have been wrong a lot lately. But I didn't want to remain quiet, just in case you had put yourself in danger because you wanted to be bigger, stronger, and heroic. You enjoyed having Eve and Hope eyeballing you."

Russell grabbed Scooter, shaking him. "Why are you mad at me? I didn't try to get Kristie in trouble any more than you!"

"I haven't told anybody, but it would explain why you're on the way to becoming the Incredible Bulk without the benefit of gamma rays," Scooter said lightly. "Your father mentioned you had some strange tests after the lightning strike."

"Yep. I did."

"Were your hormones up? Russell, steroids can have horrible side effects. You become a science experiment like the guy in *The Fly*. You lose your hair. Grow breasts. Sprout hair in weird places. Shrink your balls. Die young."

Russell just stared at him. At least he was listening.

"Are you trying to get yourself before the vampires? For a little while, I wondered who you were and what had happened to the easy-going Russell I knew, then Dr. Daniels called. Now, I know it's not vampires. It's drugs," Scooter said. "We survived because of our brains, and because we helped each other, not our brawn. Believing each other is important to combating vampires. I'm sure of it."

"I'm not possessed, Scooter. I know you can't see my aura, but I'm not. I just don't want to be impotent—there's a big word—or desperate. I'm still the same old Russell but without the stutter. We were lucky last time, and we could use some brawn."

"Then you don't deny it?"

Russell threw up his hands. "Why are you doing this?"

"I don't want to turn you in or get you in trouble. I just want you to stop. You can learn paramedic stuff and save lives without turning into a body builder. You got them from Mr. Martin, didn't you?"

Obviously frustrated, Russell clenched his fists. His frown was grim, tight against his teeth.

"Please don't hit me with your juiced up punch."

Russell relaxed with a great effort. "Scooter, I wouldn't do that."

"Good. You have this new look in your eye, a mean one, that worries me. Russell, what's going on? I know you're taking first aid classes, a gun-touting certification course, and hanging out at the garage learning about cars. What's going on?"

"Nothing."

"I know life is short, but this is ridiculous. Do the steroids help you get more done? Give you energy? Allow you to be two places at once? Dr. Daniels said it was popular to take this with amphetamines."

Looking grim, Russell opened up. "I don't feel like such a weakling. After the Gunns and Shade, I just felt like I had to do something! Now I can protect us from the Gunn brothers or anyone like them. I'm not helpless any more. I'm not a victim."

"Your strength won't help you against vampires. They're supernaturally strong. I worry you'll become a shoot first, ask questions later, kind of guy. Have you noticed that you have a short fuse?"

"If you're my friend, you won't tell anybody. Let me deal with it."

"What am I supposed to tell them if you drop dead while catching the Tawakoni monster catfish? Sorry, he wanted to look like a baseball player? Or how about, he wasn't able to cast far enough so he started pumping iron and chemicals. Yes, Sheriff Knight, I saw him cast so far yesterday that the worm burst into flames from the velocity of the hook's return into this atmosphere."

Russell hopped to his feet, mad at him. "Enough! I don't have to listen to this." He shoved Scooter hard.

He landed with a splash. "You almost pushed me across the lake!" he yelled. Scooter swam to shore. "Well, that was fun," Scooter told Flash.

Scooter waited for quite a while, but his bud didn't return. Neither had the Gomezes. He sent Flash after Russell. The dog came back quickly.

It was dark so he just felt along behind his best friend, weaving to avoid bushes and stones that shifted underfoot.

Shortly, he saw a light across the trees and a faint, flickering glow. He heard music and singing. It sounded familiar, like an angel.

"I like to fly like an eagle, to the sea. Fly like an eagle let my spirit carry me . . . "

Kristie! He would recognize her voice anywhere.

He also heard Russell coming to meet him. "Come on, let's go."

"Do you hear her? That's Kristie's singing. Let's go say hi," Scooter suggested. He started to step past, eager to see her.

"You aren't supposed to be around each other."

"But she's out. She must be feeling better. This is kismet!" Scooter said. He felt a rush, and his palms perspired. He figured he looked a mess, but she had seen him at his worst.

"Didn't you just throw doing the right thing in my face?"

"Yes." Scooter felt a little sheepish, and yet he wondered what she was doing out here. His curiosity dragged him along. Who could she be with? He listened carefully, hearing a second voice. She had brothers. But if it wasn't . . . . He was angry that he couldn't enjoy time with such a fantastic girl.

"Come on," Russell said, picking him up around the waist. "I don't want to see you get in more trouble. Juan. Julio. Let's go! I haven't caught any fish yet."

"Did you see them kiss?" Juan asked.

Who was Kristie with? Scooter's desire surged into an unquenchable thirst to know.

"No," Juan replied. "Did you? Did I miss something?"

"They're singing," Russell said.

"Who?" Scooter wanted to know.

"By the look on your face, I think you understand about addiction. If you want me to get off the stuff, you're going to have to relax about Kristie. Now come on."

Scooter reluctantly let himself be led away. He better understood wanting to shoot somebody.

TWENTY-SEVEN

INTO THE CULT HOUSE

The next day, Garrett eased his stolen black Jimmy into the Terrell Wal-Mart. He looked for another auto, just in case the authorities were seeking this one.

This morning, at the Rusk-Palestine State Park, he had finally broken free of the Tai impersonator's commands by hacking down a willow sapling. He pretended it was Scootboy, the Superzero. He even managed to hide a handful of fast food trash in a clump of weeds. Fighting to stifle a laugh, he waited for the right opportunity to escape.

The chance popped up so suddenly he almost missed it. A blue-haired granny had collapsed nearby. When everyone responded, he slipped into a faded yellow Volkswagen Bug loaded with junk like a home boy was moving out and moving on.

Some of the clothing fit, a faded shirt promoting Black Sabbath and a pair of baggy jeans. At a Palestine Food Lion Store, he had stolen this battered black GMC Jimmy and ridden the speed limit out of town to Terrell.

When he cruised past a rust-orange van that looked like a metal box on wheels, Garrett did a doubletake. A darkness surrounded it, feeling of pain. He smiled, then parked nearby.

The van sat locked, but he put a sweatshirt over the window, then elbow-bashed it. Unlocking it, he jumped inside. The air within smelled sharp with a tang of old blood. A swift search uncovered some unusual gear, along with rope, wire, and duct tape. A kit full of sharp implements sported blood stains. The shotgun and AK 47 semiautomatic under the rear bench seat gleamed, looking ready for danger. Not surprisingly, the serial numbers had been filed down. He couldn't find any ammo.

Darkness must have guided him to the Murdermobile.

Without a second thought, Garrett hot-wired it. The only worry nagging him was if it had any outstanding tickets. He doubted the Murdermobile would be reported stolen.

He was just backing out when he had to hit the brakes. A man and a woman crept past, wearing long sleeves, pants, and big hats, along with glacier glasses to protect them from the sun. He noticed their shadows were ill-defined, as if they weren't all there. Vampire-kissed thralls. He chuckled: it takes one to know one.

Perhaps they could lead him to a vampire.

Impatient—knowing that any moment the owner could return—Garrett waited for the pair to stick their bags in the enclosed bed of a bright red Dodge Ram truck, then drive away. He let them gain distance, traveling north on State Route 34 toward West Tawakoni.

He paid little attention to the gently rolling grasslands, the antique shops, or Ma & Pa run gas stations. Cottonwoods, poplars, and oak trees huddled about houses, streams, ponds, and lakes. Otherwise, the heat killed them. The blue sky soared cloudless from the morning horizon to the west, but it looked flat, hazy with humidity and big city pollution blown in from Dallas.

Mostly, he wondered about Racquel. He missed her caresses and her smiles.

The blazing red pickup cruised past the old Pilot Point graveyard. Garrett remembered having explored this area.

As far as he could recall, there were old houses and several trailers. When the truck turned at the worn Highland Estates sign, Garrett kept going, past the planned community that never happened. There wasn't another road out, except a dirt trail, but it would do.

He slowed and turned onto the wide trail that came in a back way. He parked the van just out of sight of the road. With the boxy AK-47 in hand and a few explosive surprises in his pockets, he felt armed and ready. If he shot somebody, the van owner would get blamed.

A little ahead, a tan trailer home was dark except for dogs locked on the outer balcony. Garrett heard one whimpering.

A wild laugh escaped from him. He must be getting near.

Around a corner, he spotted the red pickup. The Dodge truck backed out of the driveway, parking off to the side. A large black motor vehicle rolled from the dark insides of a metal garage. He peered more closely. With tinted windows but no chrome, the 2005 Thunderbird blended into the night.

Certain he didn't want to be seen, he slid behind a tree. The Thunderbird turned the opposite direction, leaving its lights off until almost out of sight.

The Master had left his lair. Garrett's timing fell perfectly. He tucked the gun in his waistband, then drew a machete. He strolled up the driveway to investigate.

The garage door had closed behind the Thunderbird. The threefold door had been dented, just one of the many signs of house abuse. Even in the full darkness, he could tell the wide one-story home for the wayward had seen better days. Its white paint was gray, as if all the life had been leeched from it. No lights were on, but all of the windows and doors stood wide open to let in the sweet darkness. Like a messy glue job, spider webs appeared to hold the place together. Tangles of shoulder-high weeds and ivy clutched at the siding, ready to drag the building underground.

He took the driveway because the walkway was tracked and matted with overgrown weeds. A pair of motorcycles stood hidden in the tall grass.

Stealing in like death's hounds, a trio of silent, black dogs rushed out to attack him. He crouched and stared down the two Dobermans, but one kept coming. He backhanded the beast, sending the other two cowering, their short tails tucked between their legs. They knew the look of a vampire. Garrett imitated unlife. After all, he was just a kiss away.

He sweet-talked the dogs. He had always had a way with females. He was sure they would protect him now. With a pat on the head, he encouraged them to lead him inside. They took him around back to the patio.

A wickedly crafted scarecrow wearing a witch's hat had rotten eggshell eyes. They followed his every move. Garrett scrutinized the weird guardian. The barnyard mannequin carried a pitchfork hidden within its broom. Its dry, brown apple smile seemed to say he meant to use the sharp, three-pronged tool as a nasty surprise when he pulled out your guts.

Peeved at himself for a split second of fear, Garrett snatched the pitchfork from the shell of clothes and ascended the steps. Strange bells rang softly, joined by chanting.

A frightening mask confronted him. It jutted out, a guardian of the back door. The mask's three bug-eyes glared. It demanded payment, so Garrett cut himself and ran it along the dark sentinel's long tongue. The spiders on the webs blocking the rear entrance blew aside, letting him enter. The air was almost chewable with the smell of cough medicine. Meth maker, Meth maker, make me a batch, he thought crazily.

The chanting came from elsewhere, but the living room was occupied with someone alive. He stank of tequila and sat quietly in the darkness.

Pitchfork in hand, Garrett said nothing. He let his eyes adjust to the inner darkness. A latino *hombre* remained motionless and staring, his eyes wide with shock. He had been bitten and drained, left to recover on his own.

The thrall's feet rested on the coffee table. A newspaper had sloughed off onto the floor. The *Dark City Times*, Garrett read, All the Night Community News Fit to Print.

He peeked into the kitchen, then listened down the hall where several voices chanted. The air hung heavy and chilling. The walls radiated the cold of a freezer. He sensed hate and loathing for life, disdain and superiority, all tanged with the stench of urine. He fought temptation to join in and searched the place.

A quick skim of the articles told him the *Dark City Times* was a paper for vampires. Scissors held down a pile that had been cut. Clippings lined the mantle of the cold, brick fireplace. Mice looked up at him memorizing his face to tell their master.

From the *Dallas Morning News* to the *Ft. Worth Star-Telegram* and all the way to the *New York Times* and *L.A. Times*, the articles were about Gunstock, Texas, starting back in April. The earliest dates covered pretty Peggy Jones' disappearance, Debbie and Misty's deaths, and carried through into the Gunn's trial and finding Shaddock's floating corpse. Among the many were the arrests of Herb Carlson, Al Ringly, Ben Martin, Ramon Martinez, Dat Chung, and Hank Peters.

He found articles about the principal's son, the

renowned Garrett Brashear, his arraignment, and sentencing to the state vacation home for the mental. Was this all the work of vampires? Then he saw a *Dark City Times* article that confirmed his fears. Tai was dead, killed in Texas.

"What are you doing?"

Garrett calmly turned. He had never heard her coming,.

She was a slip of a girl and barely breathed. Her black hair was lank, and her dark eyes languid, surrounded by circles. From her ears, nose, and black lips, silver studs and spikes protruded. He thought snakes writhed up her swanlike throat, until he realized they were slithering tattoos.

She snapped her hands to reveal fingernails akin to claws. "Are you deaf? Or just dumb?"

"This is my lucky evening," he said with a smile. "I am Garrett Candace. I have been orphaned, but I'm checking into being a vampire."

The thrall blinked, surprised. "You are bold. You are here to continue your service?"

"I want more information on the Night Community."

She pondered his request. All the while, her fingernails clacked against each other. "Who was your master?"

"Tai Candace. I've been bitten twice."

After more thought, a nail running along her jaw, she pointed to the coffee table. "There is an orientation book. You may take it. Just know, if you fail to return it, we will find it and you."

Garrett flipped it open, checking the contents, then coolly tucked it under his arm. "I'll be in contact."

The dogs escorted him to the end of the driveway. In the darkness of the walk, he started reading about the community of vampires and orientation for Newblood. Knowledge was power. Some called it dirt. He would use it to rise above the grave.

TWENTY-EIGHT

THE STAKE OUT

Steering his ATV, Russell ripped along a straightaway of the back roads. He loved being bigger and stronger, able to better control the all terrain vehicle. But now somebody knew his secret. For a moment, he had the wild urge to whip the ATV around and spill his passengers, ending his problem.

Flash and Scooter would tumble out at high speed, never able to tell anyone that he popped Mexican beans—trenbolone—and Greenies to get stronger and faster. Professional baseball players and other athletes had used them.

He shouldn't have come along on this wild goose chase. Russell felt a wild surge of euphoria and power. He immediately geared down and stopped.

"Why are you driving like a maniac?! This isn't the Texas 500!" Scooter shouted. "We want to make it to Mother Short's place in one piece."

Russell tried to shake off the crazy urge. He hopped off and stretched, then scratched the itches driving him insane. Just concentrating on not thinking about them was tiring.

They hadn't told anybody what they were doing. He wasn't so sure they should be following a vampire's advice, and yet Scooter was determined to discover who was pretending to be Mr. C. "This is a dumb idea, trusting Ripley's advice."

"I don't trust him, but sitting at home isn't going to solve anything," Scooter snapped.

"We're vampire hunting."

"We might be," Scooter replied solemnly. "I know you're pissed off at me, but thanks for coming. Just slow down. We're not in any hurry, are we?"

Russell climbed back on, fired it up, then he gently kicked the ATV into gear. They had found out that old Mrs. Short had just moved into an assisted-living place on the edge of town. Mr. Short, the plant manager of the power company, was going to get her place ready for sale.

Mother Short's place sat close to the creek, so Russell picked a little knoll with several trees for their stakeout. "This isn't public knowledge, but Nathans, Ringly, and Chung were also staked out."

"You're kidding? And the officers didn't see anything?"

"That's why it's hard to believe them. Since we don't have fancy cars with video cameras yet, I brought ours."

"Vampires don't show up on film."

"I know, but common criminals and thugs do," Russell said. He caught himself, starting to talk like his father.

He parked on the back side of the hill, then removed his helmet and his dad's riding armor. With spy and vampire hunting gear in hand and on his broad back, he easily led his bud up the rise to a small gathering of cottonwoods.

"It's like following Paul Bunyan," Scooter joked.

Russell whirled about on him. "Are you going to bug me about it? I don't keep mentioning that kissing Kristie got you in trouble."

Scooter winced. "No, but then kissing Kristie is healthy. Steroids are not. It might kill you."

"Kissing Kristie might get you killed, too, if she'd had a shotgun in hand. I saw that look in Ma Candel's eyes.

"Ah, but it's worth dying for," Scooter laughed.

Russell grunted. Comparing the two was pointless.

Down closer to the creek, a home of pale blue, white trim, and gray river rock walls sprawled within a fenced-in yard full of white fuzz from big cottonwoods. In the driveway, a U-Haul trailer was hooked to a white one-ton Ford. Mr. Short worked at rearranging the garage and occasionally loaded boxes into the rented moving van.

Russell arranged a video camera on a tripod. While the light was good, he filmed the surrounding area, including the county vehicle and Deputy Ross.

Scooter unpacked their fireworks gear. They planned to use it as a surprise and lighting. Two mortars aimed toward the front of the house. Shells might reach about halfway up the walk.

An elm tree was a perfect hiding place with a wide V between branches, allowing them both to sit. Scooter sketched, while Russell studied emergency care medicine until it was almost too dark.

He checked his cross pendant to ensure it hung on his chain. Out of his vampire hunting bag, he withdrew his gun. He had almost killed Javier Gomez. Russell checked the safety and returned it, then he drew out a pair of nightvision goggles.

"Russell Knight stars in *Armed and Dangerous*."

"You sound like Redgraves," Russell snapped.

"Ouch. You win. Where did you get cool nightvision peepers?" Scooter asked.

Feeling ashamed, Russell almost stammered. "I borrowed them from Dad. It's an obsolete Army Surplus model."

"Are you juiced tonight?" Scooter asked.

Russell sulked. He was feeling strong tonight. "Shut up. We're on a stake out."

"I thought we were going to blind and film whatever comes our way. Are you planning on tackling it?"

"Shut up!" Russell snapped. He gently shoved Scooter.

"Hey!" He fell backwards, arms flailing. One crashed on a branch, slowing him. Upside down, he swung from his knees. "Help!" He grabbed the branch, but he couldn't pull himself up.

"Swing down," Russell said. He dropped down to catch him. "Okay."

"You pushed me. You'll let me fall."

"No, I won't."

"Do you see my point, yet?"

"Drop, or I will let you fall and hurt yourself!"

"Here I come!" Scooter said. He flipped over and let loose.

Russell made sure he landed all right.

"Put me down! You might crush me like an eggshell," Scooter cried. He hopped back, then he paused. "Hey, I hear something. Maybe a car." Scooter tilted his head.

"I hear you scratching." Russell said, still irritated. "I see something coming up the road. It doesn't have any lights on." He climbed into the tree and lifted the binocular strap off a branch. He was pleased they hadn't broken when he'd poked Scooter.

Russell peered through. The Thunderbird seemed to have been formed out of darkness, making it almost invisible.

All of a sudden, blindness struck, a white-green brilliance washing over him. He snatched off his glasses. "Damn! He turned them on." After rubbing his eyes, he hit the record button.

Through spotted vision, Russell watched the black Thunderbird pull behind the deputy's patrol car and kill its lights. Rifle in hand, Ross hauled himself out of the county Explorer. He flipped his spotlight on.

"Relax, I mean you no harm," Scooter whispered. Russell didn't hear anything, but Deputy Ross lowered his light and rifle, then approached the car. A few moments later, he tipped his hat and ambled back to his auto.

"FBI?" Russell whispered.

Scooter shook his head. "I don't think so. Call your dad right now. I don't have a signal."

"Zip here," Russell said.

The only lights shone from the corners of the house and the front porch. One by one, they went dark.

"How did he do that?" Russell wondered.

"I think he shot 'em out," Scooter said, cocking his head.

"What makes you say that?"

"There were several forceful coughs, one for each light, then I heard the breaking of glass."

The Thunderbird's driver door swung open. Black on white, a man climbed out and stood tall, much like Mr. C. He wore a high-collared cloak and dark knee-high boots. By wearing gloves, only his face was stark, so pale it seemed like a phosphorescent mask. His eyes radiated a reddish hue in an unnerving, catlike way.

"You won't believe how much he looks like Mr. C."

With a cool breeze, the temperature seemed to drop. Russell wouldn't have been surprised to see his breath. The night stranger stood for a moment, sniffing the air before heading to the front door.

"Does Flash smell anything?" Russell whispered. He handed his best bud the nightvision goggles.

After studying the visitor, Scooter said, "You're right. He looks amazingly like Marcus, but more . . . theatrical. Flash smells a smokiness and . . . a urine, old-blood kind of stench. Ready with the fireworks and camera."

Knocking on the door sounded loud. The hard raps echoed in the unearthly quiet. His hand gripped his cross.

"*Open up! Now!*"The night stranger pounded on the door, causing the air to shake.

Short's dog whined.

Russell opened his book. Scooter flipped open his sketch pad. The night stranger had given a powerful command. If there had been any doubt, there wasn't any now. Fireworks wouldn't help them against a vampire. "Go call. I'm gonna get the plate number," Russell said. He palmed a jar of holy water.

"That's dangerous. Not long ago, you were scared to help Kristie escape from the Gunns."

Russell shrugged. That was then. This was now. "I was stuttering then, too."

The stranger repeated his command. Out at the car, the deputy opened his door.

"At least we know Deputy Ross is alive," Russell said.

"Remember, there's still a driver in the car," Scooter whispered. He crouched, looking to make a break for it.

Before they could go their separate ways, the house door opened. Light spilled out across the front lawn. The night stranger stretched tall, dark, and long across the grass as if a giant shadow lurked inside the shell of a man's clothes.

"Purvis Short, leave town, or . . . "

"Now listen here, Chandler!" Short snapped. They heard the shotgun cock, a deadly metallic click.

"You will regret the rest of your days. I promise it."

"Threaten me, will you. Put down that gun! Stay back!"

The shotgun blast roared, riveting everyone's attention. Russell held his breath, even as Scooter gasped.

They were both still standing.

Russell didn't know what to think. He drew his weapon. He gave Scooter a gentle push. "Go call my dad."

"Man, my ears are ringing. I can barely hear. Poor Flash," Scooter groaned.

The golden dog whined, then growled and turned.

"Drop your weapons. I never miss from five feet." The figure with a silenced and blackened .45 was almost invisible. He wore a hooded charcoal-colored shirt. Gloves hid his hands and dark paint concealed his face.

"What the . . . I shot you!" Short exclaimed.

Russell glanced over. The fake Mr. C opened his jacket with one hand. He drew and aimed his pistol. Why did a vampire need a gun?

"Destroy the video camera," the gunman demanded.

Russell grabbed the camera. He didn't want to do this, but he felt the compelling power of the gunman's voice. Why didn't his cross work? Why did the vampire carry a gun? He was confused.

"You're not a vampire!" Scooter accused.

"Not yet. But I will soon!" the gunman replied. "We aren't allowed to harm Short, but . . . the idol needs to be fed! Mr. Chandler, I got some nosy kids!"

Armed and dangerous, the pretender turned his attention on them. "Take them to the car," the fake Mr. C croaked.

Short took the opportunity to slam the door. Russell hoped he called his dad or anybody at the county building.

The best buds exchanged looks. Russell had the fiery urge to explode into violent action, wanting to go for it. He had a feeling Scooter wanted them to wait.

Their assailant gestured with his weapon. "Get moving. *Smash the camera and get in the car.*"

Russell hesitated, so the gunman hit him atop the head, staggering him. With a dying flare of light, darkness caved in. Gravity seized him. Scooter slowed his plunge, helping him to the ground and talking with him, asking questions he didn't understand.

"Take it easy, boy!" Scooter pleaded.

"Get mov . . . ." With a crack, the gunman collapsed partly on Russell. A softball-sized rock landed nearby.

"Ah, I may not be able to hurl a fastball anymore, but my aim is still impeccable," Jimmy B. Little said as he hustled up to them. "I hate to be part of the story, but you're kids. Run boys! My car is over there!"

Scooter ignited the lighter, touching flame to the tubes. "Let there be light." He helped Russell to his feet.

"Hurry!" Little said. He gave them a hand, then returned to grab the camera.

"Stop!" the fake Mr. C raced toward them.

The rockets launched, leaving sparkling trails.

"Get down!" Scooter dropped down, taking Russell with him, just as the gun blast fired.

Russell still felt dizzy, stumbling as if the earth quaked. Bullets whistled overhead, all around, ripping leaves, destroying branches, and lodging in tree trunks.

The rockets exploded. Red stars shot across the sky, erupting into white sparks. They descended to create a weeping willow. Illuminating everything below in a garish red light, a flare floated from a parachute.

The car's engine roared and revved, then the Thunderbird raced off.

"Good riddance," Scooter said.

"This will make a great story!"

"Uh, thanks for helping us," Scooter said.

"Just remember this when I'm asking questions."

Russell wanted to snarl. They had needed rescuing. He had done nothing but get whacked on the head. He regained his gun from the down assailant, curbing the urge to kick him.

TWENTY-NINE

THE CULT OF THE VAMPIRE

Russell's dad happily speculated with Scooter while he drove them to the county jail. Dad was as proud as a peacock over his theories being proven correct. Just this morning, Agent Pryde and the FBI had raided a house, arresting five cultists.

According to Dad, there was no such thing as supernatural monsters. People were bad enough, taking weirdness to extremes. Vampirism was just another disease for the sick of mind.

It was dangerous to jump to conclusions. Who would have thought that James B. Little would rescue them? Needing to be rescued made Russell furious, wanting to punch somebody or break something. He had been no help against the cultist. A reporter wearing white had snuck up on all of them.

Worse, any moment, Russell irrationally worried that his friend would blurt out his steroid use. If only Mexican Beans stopped his itching.

"You don't think you'll see this Mr. Shade, do you?"

"No," Scooter replied. He kept scratching and looking over at Russell, as if he were expecting him to add his voice to his best friend's protest. "I expect to see thralls."

"Isn't that what you call the agents of the vampires?"

Scooter nodded. This conversation had happened before.

"Boys, if you hadn't passed those tests with flying colors, I would be worried."

"Imagination is revered, but as much persecuted as rewarded, Judge Grandpa says."

"I'm beginning to wonder if you two are fifteen."

"We aged a lot last month," Russell murmured.

"Yeah, well, it can happen quickly. I vividly recall watching Uncle Warren get shot when they tried to rob my father's grocery store."

His dad was still telling the story when they pulled into the parking lot of the county building. The structure was functional and geometric, a two-story rectangle made of brick, as solid and practical as the people who worked within.

When he was a kid, Russell had enjoyed coming to the county sheriff's station. It seemed abuzz with excitement and mystery, probably because of the stories his father told, or the unreality of law enforcement on TV. Now it seemed less glamorous. Places like this were necessary because of the staggering number of 'antisocial' people.

Russell felt uncomfortable walking inside. He must be suffering guilt, never having broken the law before. Even when he rationalized it, he didn't like the thought of having to explain to his dad. He hadn't seen a vampire and didn't know the feeling of being absolutely and completely helpless.

Due to the capture of the cultists, security had been increased. If there were vampire worshippers still loose, such fanatics might try to free their fellow lunatics.

In the viewing room, Agent Pryde stood and greeted them. "Welcome, gentlemen? Where's Flash?"

The wonder dog had won over another fan.

"It's a federal building," his dad said.

"I didn't expect that to stop him," the agent replied. She smiled, obviously pleased about the arrests.

"What can you tell us about the cult?" Russell asked.

"Same as I reported in the news. They were working out of a place near the middle school. We found a Gibbering Darkness idol—a new one, I believe, since it seems less disgusting and nauseating—five cult members, various psychedelic drugs, and a large number of weapons, especially ritualistic and bloodletting knives. Are you ready?" she asked.

Russell nodded. Scooter shrugged. He claimed that last time, when they had to identify the Gunns in the lineup, they had known they were on the other side of the glass.

The first group was a half-dozen rough-looking females. Russell hadn't seen any of them, but he knew which two had to be the vampiric thralls.

One was tall, bony, and shaven bald. The other was short with dyed blue hair, dark eyes, and black lips. He could see their veins and arteries in their transparent flesh, as if they never saw the light, or might be allergic to it. Their teeth had been filed to look like vampires. Even so, it was their eyes that gave them away. They reminded him of Garrett and BJ after encountering Tai.

Garrett had claimed the same. Where was he?

"I've never seen any of them before," Scooter said, agreeing with Russell.

After the women were herded out, a lineup of men shuffled in. It included a couple of latinos, three good old boys, as well as a Big D city slicker. Although he had never seen them before, Russell thought he knew the two cultists.

The pair might have been weathered and leather-vested bikers, except they appeared to never have seen the sun. Their tattoos looked fresh on their fleshly parchment. Like fish from deep under, their skin gleamed a slick, underbelly-white. The veins in their eyes were engorged with a bloodied gaze.

"Any of them look familiar?"

None of them looked like the false Mr. C. "Just the guy who got the drop on us last night," Russell said. He pointed to the gunman with the vulpine face and beak nose.

Russell wasn't looking at him, so when the city slicker slammed into the glass, shaking the transparent wall, he jumped. The safety glass cracked and protruded toward them.

A blur, the maniac pounded on the cracked safety glass. The impacts sent the fracture spidering out, blood splattering from his mashed hands. "Keyshawn! Knight! You so-called vampire hunters. Yes, I feel you there! I sense the shadows in you!" he laughed, then drove a gory fist through the safety glass. "They are eating you from inside."

Even as Dad and Agent Pryde drew weapons, the damaged chunk gave way. The half-smashed cultist tumbled into the chamber. Blood poured from his flattened nose and swollen mouth, even as he continued to chuckle.

Russell jumped back, wishing he was armed.

"Stop! Or I will shoot! Hands over your head! Now!" Dad ordered. His voice was powerful and commanding, but it must have fallen short of the demands of darkness.

The blood-smeared madman crawled to his knees. "I am just a messenger. You have been touched by *The Curse of Thirteen!*" the cultist said as he staggered to his feet.

"Stop! Stand still!" Agent Pryde commanded.

Carrying a shield, Deputy Ross darted in, swinging a truncheon. The cultist caught it, yanking it free. He smashed it against the deputy's shield. "Chandler will get his way. He has defeated death. What makes you think you have a chance?!"

He shoved the deputy aside, then he lurched toward them. Russell heard his dad pull the trigger. The firearm's blast thundered in the room. The bloodied madman stumbled a step before collapsing.

Agent Pryde moved in, ready in case he was playing opossum. The cultist was a grisly sight. Besides the broken facial bones and open wounds, his mouth and teeth seemed to be collapsing. The decay continued to eat away the rest of the madman, quickly leaving a bloody bag of bones.

"Son, you all right?" Dad asked, hugging Russell.

"I wanted to shoot him."

"So did I, but I waited. I'm both sorry and relieved he died," Dad admitted. "What I saw in that cult house was horrible. Well, we have more answers to questions now."

Russell simply nodded. He fought the urgent and swelling urge to claw his bites.

"Think there's any reason to worry about *The Curse of Thirteen?*" Dad asked.

When Russell looked at his fingers, he saw blood. Along his left arm, where he had scratched, he had dislodged a flap of skin. It oozed blood and yellow pus. The skin looked mushy, like rotting melon. "Yes, I think we should see a doctor."

THIRTY

TOO HOT FOR A HOUSEWARMING PARTY

On Saturday, a dull clank awakened Scooter from a nightmare of Kristie as an emaciated skeleton. He was fuzzy headed and confused in the gray predawn.

He caught himself scratching vigorously and stopped. His bites bothered him again, since he'd been rubbing them in his sleep. What the doctor's had prescribed gave little relief.

When there was a second clank, he realized it was the sound of the lid closing on one of the grills. Judge Grandpa was mesquite smoking the baby back ribs.

Through his dog, Scooter smelled breakfast, buttery flapjacks and maple syrup. Usually Scooter would be smacking his lips. This morning, he could hardly rise out of bed.

For two days and nights he had been worrying about the bites, all thirteen, like the curse. When he wasn't, he thought about Kristie and worried about the vampires' plots and machinations. Or Russell on steroids and carrying a gun. No surprise, he had done little creatively.

He had spent the last two nights on the Internet, checking for anything about the Curse of Thirteen. According to his e-mail, Marcus had never heard of it.

Despite his gloominess, Scooter had high hopes for today. They were christening the house. It wasn't a church function, but Kristie might make it.

Excited by the possibility, he washed, studying his sores in the bright bathroom lights. They looked horrible, white-headed swelling with red streaks shooting out. The surrounding skin was jaundiced, but the dermatologist couldn't see him for a couple of days.

With very little appetite, he stumbled down for breakfast. Grandma Mae was serving on the front porch.

While he was picking at his blueberry pancakes, the sheriff's car parked next to the steps. Russell climbed out, scratching and looking a little under the weather, although he was smiling.

"Bruce called this morning. I passed my written EMT exam. Now, if I was eighteen, I could get certified. I'll have to settle for the knowledge, Dad says."

"Excellent! We have many accomplishments to celebrate," Grandpa exclaimed. "Much to be thankful for, I'm sure. Boys, when you get a chance, please set up the games."

"I will be more thankful when I don't itch," Scooter moaned quietly. "I'm surprised they let you out of the hospital."

"They're clueless."

"So am I," Scooter said. He entered the storage shed, digging around for the badminton racquets, the croquet set, and the inflatable pool.

"Did you hear Mr. Peters was arrested yesterday for holding illegals and forcing them to work? Nobody would have known, but they escaped."

Scooter should have been surprised, but he wasn't. Mr. Peters had favored lynching Marcus, before Ripley changed his mind.

"He's also a Minuteman. Before the summer started, his arrest would have been a major topic. Now it's a ripple in a wavy pond," Russell continued.

"With all the reporters around, I guess they were going to find some kind of story. Look at Little. He tailed us. But Carlson and Martin were Minutemen and now, Mr. Peters," Scooter said.

"They all blame Marcus for setting them up."

"The pretender did. We heard him."

"They heard Marcus." Russell stretched, then scratched. "Today should be peaceful, unless you believe Racquel. She's coming. She believes Garrett will be here."

"Garrett. Really? What do you think?"

"I don't take her seriously. Scooter, uh," he paused, his voice dropping low. "I wanted to thank you for not telling anybody about, well, you know."

Scooter nodded. "I couldn't just stay quiet, like I didn't care. If you have to carry a weapon to feel safe, or take martial arts classes, do that. But . . . ." He paused, daring to ask the next question. "What are you going to do?"

"I'm not sure yet. I can't think straight. My brain seems stuffed, and I don't know about you, but my bites are driving me bonkers. I now have twenty-six!"

"What?" Scooter stammered.

"So much for the Curse of Thirteen!" Russell said. He turned around and lifted up his back. It was peppered with bandaged sores. The red streaks connected them.

"It could be a reaction to the steroids."

"They should have helped me get rid of them," Russell groused.

Scooter didn't know what to say or do.

Shortly, a delivery van from the Furniture Barn lumbered down the grass-gravel driveway that stretched from the gate of Siete Hombres to the peninsula point. They carefully circled and parked next to the porch.

With a little finagling, they situated the rear of the truck so the ramp would bridge the gap between the bumper and the concrete front porch, making it easier to unload. An Office Depot van rumbled in right after.

Grandma served up coffee, ham, and biscuits to the drivers. Before they finished chowing, a Sears truck tailed by a van from the church pulled in next to the other trucks.

"It's a military furniture assault organized by Grandma," Judge Grandpa said.

On cue, the volunteer movers arrived. Grandpa had said you never knew how many true friends you had until you asked people to help you move.

Several professors from the nearby community college, where Grandpa sometimes taught and lectured, added to the churchgoers at the party. Most of the people from the court house and all the off-duty deputies attended. Big Bruce was off ambulance duty and ready to help if anyone got hurt.

Grandma Mae acted like a major directing her troops. Using her feather duster as a pointer, she motioned the volunteer movers into the correct rooms. She complained more about her knees than the moving. That meant they were doing an excellent job.

Grandpa tried to stay out of the way, except to supervise his office. Grandma sent him back to the grill under Rev. Candel's watchful eye.

He drafted Scooter. Handling the grill was searing work. His sores distracted him, and he burnt himself twice. He loaded a squirt bottle with ice and doused himself and the grill. Even so, his bites hurt as if hornets had just stung him.

"Good morning, boys. Y'all did a fantastic job on the place," Racquel interrupted. Her tone and friendly demeanor caught Scooter off guard. Dark-haired, black-eyed, tanned, beautiful, and smiling, this wasn't the Racquel he knew. She carried herself differently.

"T-thank you," he stammered.

Racquel chuckled good-naturedly. "You and Russell do rub off on each other. Try to pick up his good habits and not the bad. And please, don't cook like him. He would burn the ribs. Hey, do I see Garrett over there?" She took a few steps in that direction. "Ah, just wishful thinking."

"I'm glad to see you here. Russell was concerned that you might go away."

"Oh, no. I'm not going anywhere. I have big plans for this school year. As long as I pass my mental exams," she replied, her smile faltering. "But I'm sure I will. The dark is past, and there is partly cloudy sunshine ahead. There's a line from a song that the future is so bright I gotta wear shades. I prefer it to a hat." She put on her sunglasses and sashayed away.

"Your sister isn't herself," Scooter said.

"That's good."

"That's what Pearl Mochrie thought."

If looks could kill, Scooter would be dead.

Rev. Candel blessed the event, saying a prayer on the front porch among the flowers. Afterward, seeing the question in Scooter's eyes, the reverend smiled kindly and told him that Kristie and the family had driven into Dallas. Scooter's hopes were crushed.

"They are the ones missing out," Kristie's father said. "Even among tragedies, we must find reasons to celebrate life over death. Let's have a good time. We are overdue."

Amazingly enough, the moving happened much faster than the cooking. About eleven, when the mercury topped 100 degrees, the trucks were empty and all the furniture, including a new fridge, deep freezer, and washer and dryer, sat in place, hooked up and running.

Twice, Scooter thought he saw Garrett.

After moving the trucks, Russell's mom directed them

to assemble the EZ-Up shades and arrange the folding chairs around the tables.

Checkerboards were brought out, despite the threatening weather of black clouds. Horseshoes clanged into play. Bubbles, badminton birdies, and footballs filled the air.

Between badminton games, Flash gently took his hand and guided him through the woods along the shore. Russell followed closely. The golden Lab stopped behind a cluster of trees near the dock. They could barely see the big, dark green outboard of a small boat parked on the far side. It sat low, so he figured it was a bass boat.

Dangling her feet, Racquel sat on the edge of the dock. She stared out over the water, pretending to be idle while she secretly spoke with a mystery visitor. A large gray floppy hat was on her right, blending in with the planks.

With the music, games, and the happy conversations, Scooter could hardly hear what was being said. It grew worse when somebody turned up the music and a handful of kids danced in the bed of the pickup trucks.

One at a time, Scooter, Russell, and Flash darted to the overturned canoe about ten feet away from the h-shaped dock. From there, Garrett's voice carried more clearly.

"You have to believe me, *Chaquita*. The vampires are here." The slight wind seemed to make his voice warble with an otherworldly compelling.

Because of the celebration, Scooter couldn't hear Racquel at all.

"Yes. A friend of Tai's. Lucius Shade is here to make everybody suffer for killing her."

Shade! Scooter almost cried. The hot day seemed to change to winter, his sweat cold with dread as his worst nightmare was affirmed. And yet, Ripley had acted like Shade was dead and gone. Garrett must be mistaken.

"You have to get away from your family before it's too late. Come on, we'll live together forever as master and mistress of our own fates."

She replied, then Garrett's voice sounded strangled. "What do you mean you have to get in shape for cheer leading tryouts this year? What's come over you? Why do you want to be Homecoming Queen?!"

His jaw hitting the top of the canoe, Russell was just as astounded as Scooter.

"Did you hear that?" Garrett asked.

Scooter could feel him looking around. Hunched together, they flattened on the ground. He ground his teeth to keep from itching.

Garrett snapped his fingers. "I know what's happened to you. Shade tried to make me into somebody I'm not, but I didn't fail Tai, and I'm stronger than Shade thinks. I broke free from what he compelled me to be. Could you really see me becoming a health idiot and hugging trees? That's what happened to you. You're enthralled. The real Racquel doesn't care about cheer leading or any of that juvenile high school bull . . . did you hear that?"

"We should get your father," Scooter said. He thought about sending Flash, but Russell dialed his cell phone.

"You're coming with me!" Garrett snarled. He seized Racquel by the wrist. She teetered then fought back, never crying for help.

Russell charged. Flash bolted after him, bounding onto the dock. Scooter lagged, less gung ho, looking over to the party.

Nobody had noticed yet. They clustered around the back of the sheriff's pickup, getting a look at tonight's fireworks. Scooter yelled at them, but nobody heard.

Garrett hauled Racquel into the boat, then he turned to face Russell. Flash hit the black-clad boy first, staggering him, but he managed to stay on the boat. He unsheathed a knife just as Russell tackled him, sending them into the water.

Scooter raced up the dock and grabbed an oar.

The sound of a rock striking one of the dock's pilings caught his attention. Wood shards flew as he heard a crack that sounded like a shot.

He dove behind the cover of the storage box at the front of the boat slip. A second shot hit the roof. A third bullet severed one of the cables holding Grandpa's Four Winns bow rider. The boat slipped loose of its harness, cantering to one side and striking the storage chest and a piling.

The impact felt like an earthquake, throwing Scooter onto his back. He had to concentrate to hear Garrett cursing Russell. They thrashed in the water, oblivious to the gunfire.

Scooter dialed the house. "Grandpa! It's Jonathan! Somebody is shooting out at the dock and nobody . . . ."

Shots pinged metallically when they struck the parked cars. Glass shattered. Someone yelled in pain.

The gunfire became a barrage, as if the shooter, upon finding the range, had switched to automatic. Bullets screamed by, then they ripped across Sheriff Knight's truck.

An explosion shook the pickup's bed. Smoke billowed out as the fireworks sparked, then erupted. Saturn missiles screamed as Roman Candles spat fiery balls. Mortar shells shattered, sending bombs whizzing everywhere. They let loose with air-quaking booms that deafened Scooter.

One bounced off the house and exploded into a fiery sphere. Sparks fell like rain, while others zipped and spat dangerous fireworks' flak. The roof started to smolder. A burning branch fell into the bed of a big blue pickup truck. It flared aflame.

"Russell!" Racquel screamed.

Scooter couldn't stand by any longer. He crawled to

the side of the dock and hung upside down, peering under. Racquel had jumped out of the boat, now wading toward her brother. Russell floated face down.

Scooter flopped off the dock into the water. Trudging through the clinging muck, he waded to Racquel, helping her haul Russell back toward the dock.

Ahead of them, Garrett crawled into the green Lowe bass boat. The huge outboard roared angrily. The boat leapt away from the dock.

Scooter knew Garrett would run them over. "Look out!"

Racquel stood defiantly in the way. "He still loves me. He won't hurt me!"

"Come on! Hurry!" Scooter implored.

She looked at him coldly. "I don't care if I die."

A bullet whistled by Scooter's ear to kick up water. Two more sprayed near Racquel. Scooter thanked God that the shooter was a poor marksman.

The bass boat almost ran over them. Garrett plucked Racquel from the water. She dragged Russell and Scooter along before she finally let go. Garrett tossed her into the craft, then, the boat surged ahead. Scooter lunged aside, hauling Russell with him to avoid the churning propeller blades.

Bullets yipped and splashed around them as he struggled for the dock. Debris flew as more shots chewed at sideboards. Scooter ducked underneath, dragging Russell with him. Gunfire came from both directions now, Sheriff Knight returning fire. Russell's father paused and reached out a hand to Scooter, drawing them next to him in the protective lee of the dock.

Scooter checked Russell's condition. "He's unconscious but breathing."

The sheriff's gun blasted twice, then Scooter heard a gasp and groan. He glanced back. Clutching himself, Russell's father dropped to his knees into the water.

Suddenly, another firearm resounded off to his right. Scooter heard a pained yell from across the lake.

"I got him!" Deputy Ross Hoss shouted.

Big Bruce and Russell's mom raced into the lake to help Russell's father. He favored his left leg. Even so, he waved the paramedic over toward them. Bruce stepped in, taking over from Scooter. He watchd as the paramedic conducted an assessment. "Do you know if he's taking any medication?" the big man asked.

"I think so," Scooter stammered, hating to be put in this position. "I know he's taking stuff for the bug bites."

Sheriff Knight knelt nearby. "How is he?"

"He sustained a blow to the head. We won't know more until we perform a CT scan at the hospital."

"I was only grazed. Send two ambulances. One here and one over there," Sheriff Knight ordered.

Bruce bandaged Russell's father's leg while Scooter and Flash kept an eye on his son.

Scooter was glad to see everybody else was unharmed. Several volunteer firefighters had hauled out a ladder and were watering down the roof. They couldn't extinguish the pick up, so they just backed everything far away.

"Sheriff Knight," came the radio call. "Call Pearl."

Scooter realized that CJ must have been shot.

THIRTY-ONE

SWAN SONG

Typical of Texas in the summertime, the air hung moist and oppressive. Black anvil clouds weighed upon the mourners, much like the relentless bad news. The wind tasted of rain. It created stickiness, making Scooter itch and twitch, but he wasn't the only one. There were numerous complaints about the bugs. With all the itching, he wondered if no-see-ums were jumping from one person to another.

Wearing a suit and tie made matters worse. Judge Grandpa was a stickler, not for appearance sake, but to details. The thought you put into dressing for the occasion showed your respect and affected how others first saw you. Scooter usually didn't care, but Mrs. Candel would certainly be here at the funeral. Kristie might attend, too. Knowing this, Grandma had put two yellow roses in his lapel.

He hadn't seen Kristie since the donations pick up, but he couldn't stop thinking about her. He felt out of place, excited with everyone else sad.

"Such a tragedy, dying so young," Pearl's sister bemoaned.

"Awful. Simply awful," Ms. Emmitt agreed.

Scooter heard someone blame Marcus, and he took offense. But when he saw Kristie, he forgot everything else, his attention seized by her beauty. She looked stunning in a black dress of mourning. With her hair up and back, her beauty seemed older, perhaps because of her grieving expression.

"Scooter, great to see you. How are you?" Kristie asked. Just talking to her smoothed the rough edges around him.

"I can't believe CJ died. I wish I had done something different back when we were on the island."

She nodded, commiserating. "We can't change the past. We can only move forward with wisdom gained from that experience. At least, that's what my father says. Listen Scooter, y'all would've had to tackle, bind, and gag CJ to get him into the boat. I can't see y'all doing that. How is Russell?"

"Doing all right in the hospital," Scooter said, even as he scratched. "Too bad the lightning didn't make us super-fast so we could run on water and dodge bullets."

"Y'all were incredible. You did your best. What do you think came over CJ?" Kristie asked. She kept glancing around, as if she wondered who might be watching.

"I can only guess. BJ claimed he was free just before he died. CJ said BJ had been possessed, then he disappeared and began shooting at people. Garrett said he had broken free of a vampire, he thought was Shade."

"I don't believe it. I believe you," she whispered.

"Garrett thought Racquel was possessed. So do I, because she was acting opposite of the way she usually is. Just like CJ and BJ. Kristie, we may not have long. So, for you," he said, taking the rose from his lapel and offering it to her. Her frown transformed into a smile.

"How sweet. Bless you," she replied, bringing the yellow rose to her nose. She breathed deeply and beamed, bringing a touch of sunshine to the stormy skies. Despite her pleasure, he thought Kristie was going to cry.

"You're welcome. It adds color to this gray day, just as

you add color to my world," he said, surprising himself. He hadn't meant to say that. It was a line he'd taken from his writings.

"First, I have something important to ask you, but I have to go sing. Find me after the service." She bit her lip to keep from saying more, then she was gone.

Including the itching and scratching, the feeling of deja vu haunted the rest of the day. Although there was intense sadness and weeping, the emotion seemed eerily subdued and resigned. Just another funeral in a long line of saying good-bye to a dead child, totaling thirteen for the summer.

CJ rested in an open casket. Far different than the last time Scooter had seen him, serenity graced CJ's expression.

Looking down at his lifeless body caused Scooter to squirm. The whole experience seemed surreal and morbid. Only the good died young, some said. If that were true, Scooter worried about Kristie.

All his concerns were blown away by Kristie's angelic voice. She sounded clearer, more divine than ever before, but instead of uplifting, her sadness resonated with the crowd. He had never heard her so melancholy.

Because Scooter was listening closely to people grump about the biting flies, Kristie startled him when she touched him. She took his arm and guided him away from the others.

"You sounded amazing," he said.

"Thanks. Scooter, I'm afraid."

"That makes two of us," he said, gently taking her hand. "Russell, well, he's not afraid anymore."

"What do you mean?" she asked, withdrawing her hand.

"He's ready to fight back. He's learned to wrestle. He knows first aid. He carries a gun and knows how to use it. Worse, he's ready to use it," Scooter said, then he gave her a brief summary of the fake ghost at the marina.

Kristie looked at him a long time, as if she were trying to memorize his face. "This town is cursed, Scooter."

"It's starting to feel that way."

"There's a madness about this place. It's starting to infect me. I have to get away."

Scooter couldn't believe his ears. He hoped he had misheard. "W-what do you mean?"

"I'm leaving town, soon. I don't want to be buried like CJ and BJ," she replied, grimly earnest.

Scooter's world tilted askew as if the earth were moving underfoot. Had he heard correctly? "You're leaving? Running away?"

"If we stay here, we'll die. Come with us."

"Us? Who? Where?" he stammered, feeling lost and confused.

"Orlando. I have an aunt who lives near there."

"Florida?! What about your mother? Your family?"

"Mom is doing wonderfully." Kristie's smiled seemed forced.

Now that he looked beyond being thrilled to see her, Scooter realized she didn't look like the vibrant, effervescent girl he knew and loved.

"I think the only way to survive is to be elsewhere. They won't hunt us there. Come with me and live."

Scooter struggled with words. Was this the Kristie he knew and loved? Had the vampire gotten her, too? "I can't run away and leave my grandparents. Who is driving?"

"Nick is taking off, too. He's going to Miami. He'll drop me off in Orlando."

Scooter thought he had seen this coming. Even so, he still felt blind-sided. "Of course he is."

"Come with us. I know Russell won't, but I was hoping you would, at least for the ride to Orlando. Come live. Let this settle down."

He should go along to protect her. Yes, he was crazy. She shouldn't go at all. This not only felt wrong, but it defied logic. Had a vampire emboldened her? Or had life and near death?

"Your mother will be thrilled that she banned us from seeing each other, so you can run off with Nick Sloan." Scooter was saddened by the choice, feeling ill at the thought. How could he choose? His grandparents would be heartbroken if he left. And yet, he couldn't imagine letting Kristie leave alone.

"Nick is not a bad influence. He's liberating. We're going to chase our destinies. I've had enough of being a surrogate mom. If I stay here, one of two things will happen. I will live the rest of my life taking care of things for my mother, or the vampires will get me. I think you can save me from the undead, but I don't think you can save me from my mother."

"Listen to you. Running away is not the answer. It wasn't for CJ."

Her face flushed, as her lips compressed to a white line. "Scooter, you don't understand!" she snapped, then she lowered her voice. "My mother is driving me crazy. She is running my life, following me around, and giving me orders. I don't have time to think. I can't do anything I want! That's not living. Can you tell that Mother's not sick anymore?"

Scooter nodded. "So you have been taking on her ills."

"You are perceptive, Scooter. That is why you're special to me. Taking on her disease is my price for freedom. I still get the shakes, but given time and the Almighty willing, it will heal," she said. Now that Kristie had healed her mom, Mother Candel could take care of the kids.

"Don't go. It feels wrong. You can always run away later, but you can't always come back."

"Come with me to Orlando. We're leaving Tuesday morning. Think about it." She kissed him on the lips and left, leaving him confused, ecstatic, helpless, and overwrought about what to do next.

He was supposed to have a great imagination. What could he do?

THIRTY-TWO

BLAME GAME

After CJ's funeral and Kristie's earthshaking invitation, Scooter sat on the dock at the lake house. He placed his hands on his stomach, feeling physically and emotionally ill.

Should he stay?

Should he go?

He studied his sores, poking at them. He might not be strong enough to go, he finally admitted. Collapsing on Kristie would burden her. And yet, he felt he must go, just to protect her. When he thought about it further, she took care of herself just fine, but he didn't trust Nick Sloan.

Right now, this was about Kristie. She was leaving, with him, or without him. He was thrilled that she wanted him to come along.

If he went with Kristie, he left Judge Grandpa, Grandma Mae, Russell and Marcus, among many others, to the vampires. He wished he could split himself in twain and be in two places at once.

Last time Shade had been impatient and direct in threatening them. This time, the vampire was sneaky and subtle, emotionally and psychologically destroying the town. As he pondered it, he reached a certainty. People weren't acting like themselves. He had tried to tell Kristie. CJ had talked about it. Garrett had mentioned it, too. The vampires weren't harvesting bodies, but they turned flesh against their hosts, making them act counter to their nature. BJ, CJ, Racquel, and Garrett were victims. Were Kristie and Russell? Was he the only one left uninfluenced?

He didn't know how long he had been staring at the water, when Flash barked a warning. He pointed up the peninsula to the gravel and grass driveway.

The vehicle seemed to sound louder and move faster than Judge Grandpa would drive. Fear crept up on Scooter, making him worry who it might be. He left the dock, rushing for the huge oak tree among the willows. He hid behind it, yanking Flash next to him.

The battered blue pickup truck looked like something the Gunns would drive. It sped closer, bumping over the uneven rolls in the ground, swerved, then screeched to a stop just short of the front porch.

Ms. Emmitt threw open the door and slipped out. "Good afternoon, Scooter."

"H-hello. I'm . . . surprised to see you," Scooter stammered. She was almost the last person that he expected to see.

"I can tell. Are you feeling all right?"

He swallowed. "Not really. Who taught you to drive?"

"What's wrong with my driving?"

"How would I know?" Scooter managed.

"Good!" she said with a cheery smile. With a sweeping gesture, she motioned toward the truck. "Now get in."

Scooter was suspicious again. Vampires could impersonate people, except it was daylight. But what if Ms. Emmitt was enthralled? "Why?"

"Marcus hasn't heard from you since the shooting," she said. "Talking to him might help. He would understand why you feel down about CJ and BJ."

"Why?"

"Has Marcus ever told you about his brother?"

"No," Scooter replied.

"I'm not surprised. Marvin died when he was young. Marcus blames himself. I suspect the town did the same," she said with powerful disgust.

Scooter was intrigued. "How did Marvin die?"

"I think I'll leave the choice of telling you to Marcus. I just wanted you to know you aren't the only one who has felt guilty about someone dying. You tried to save BJ and I heard CJ had a chance and a choice. Listen, you can herd lambs to water, but you can't make them drink. People can be like sheep at times. When you try to guide in one direction, they get skittish and jump off a cliff."

Flash was already in the bed of the pickup, leaning over the side, tongue hanging out, ready for the cooling wind.

Well, he had wanted to talk to Marcus about Kristie and the Curse of Thirteen.

He called and Judge Grandpa gave him permission to go. Scooter grabbed his satchel, then he climbed inside the cab. As soon as he buckled up, Ms. Emmitt threw the truck into reverse. The clutch popped. The pickup lurched backward, throwing him forward. He heard Flash's nails scrabbling for a grip. Scooter sensed his panic.

Like she was driving for the NASCAR Truck Series, Ms. Emmitt rolled to a stop, then she smoothly shifted into first, gunning it. Earth and grass went flying as the tires took hold, catapulting them ahead. In moments, they were doing forty, then she shifted into third. The trees blurred as she put it into fourth. The roses flashed by.

He never would have imagined that Ms. Emmitt drove like a bat out of hell. "You know there's a gate ahead."

"I left it open."

The truck shot out the gateway and roared onto the road, careening right and speeding past the scattered one-story houses along the road. Two intersections later, she blew past a deputy's patrol car. She waved gaily.

"Um," Scooter began, unsure of what to say.

"Allen is such a nice boy. Did you know I taught him how to read? They would have just passed him through, letting him graduate illiterate, if I hadn't gotten hold of him. Showed him there was more to life than a pigskin. Now I have to help kids see there's an exciting life away from video games."

"You drive like a gamer."

Ms. Emmitt cackled. Driving as if she were drag-racing against the rays of the setting sun, she floored it, grinding the pedal through the carpet to the metal. Before he could catch his breath, they were speeding ninety down a back road.

Ms. Emmitt swerved with aplomb around the chuck holes, laughing as she pointed out which ones had sent hubcaps flying in the past.

Faster and faster, the needle dancing, the speedometer registered one hundred oh five. The fence post nearly blended together. The tall green grass appeared to meld into a long green wall.

"Is something wrong?" she asked archly, taking her eyes off the road. That almost made Scooter panic, as they began to drift. She deftly corrected their rocketing trajectory, keeping them on the road. "You aren't scared, are you?"

"No, ma'am," Scooter managed without stuttering.

"Good, I expected nothing less from a vampire slayer."

"You believe me?" he asked, then he scratched.

"To be honest, on your own, not even with Russell and Kristie, who I don't think would ever lie. When you have young eyes, though, you don't see the complete picture, layers and such. Heck, by the time you have enough experience to see, you need glasses. But Marcus, I believe him. Yes I do. And I don't think of you, or Flash, as bald-faced liars."

"It's just," Scooter began, licking his lips. "I didn't expect you to drive like . . . this."

"Ha! And how did you expect me to drive? Like a librarian? How are they supposed to drive? Hmm? Sounds to me like you were stereotyping me. Well, at least you don't profile me because of my teasin', pleasin' tan."

"Huh?' Scooter asked, then he realized she was talking about her skin color. He joined her chuckling. "No, I just figured . . . I don't know, that librarians who enforced quiet in the library wouldn't drive like Han Solo meets Dale Earnhardt!"

She cackled like a wicked witch, even as she downshifted to squeal around a corner, heading down Tawakoni Dam road.

Flash stretched his head around the corner of the cab where his ears flew in the wind. He barked joyously. He could have been pretending to run as fast as his namesake.

"Now, would you feel differently if you knew my two brothers were dirt track racers, who taught me how to drive?"

"I guess that would change my expectations. How many times have you been pulled over for speeding?"

"Zero."

"None?!" He hesitated in calling her a liar.

"You have to choose your moments. Knowing when to do something is just as important as knowing what to do. You know how to give CPR, right?"

"Only because I've been helping Russell."

"But you know enough to only do it when the person's heart has stopped. Otherwise, you break bones and make matters worse. And in a story, you don't give out information before it's time, do you?"

Scooter gave that some serious consideration, or as much as he could when he felt he was hurtling through life. Judge Grandpa had said it wasn't always what you did, but when you did it that could make a difference.

How could this relate to vampires? And Kristie? He even had second thoughts about keeping Russell's secret. He hoped his buddy would change his mind. They might just discover the truth while he was in the hospital.

He hoped they figured out a way to stop the painful itching. The sores were getting worse.

Could he string Kristie along, making her think it over a few more days?

"You're a little young to be carrying the weight of the world," she said. She vigorously scratched her forearm.

"I'm sure not Atlas."

"He carried the weight of the universe, but back then, the world was their universe."

The truck raced up to the Pickup Ranch's hubcap archway and the metal gate. Scooter swore they were going to crash, but she downshifted expertly, then braked to a stop.

His heart beating wildly, Scooter volunteered to open the gate. He threw the door wide and leapt out. The chrome bumper was less than a gnat's width from the metal partition.

Ms. Emmitt drove much more sedately on the gravel. "You have to be careful on loose rock. It's tricky stuff."

As they reached the bottom of the first hill, the sun seemed to set, then rise as they crested the next knoll, only to disappear like a fireball snuffed by the water. The clouds billowed, the day steaming. Scooter noticed a dust cloud drifting away from the driveway.

Ms. Emmitt stopped near Mr. Dandy's car. Was the Intruder here?

Pretending to be Superdog, Flash leapt out of the back and flew to greet Beauty. They cavorted in an excited circle, glad to see each other instead of chasing their own tails.

Despite having been in the house many times, Scooter always flashed back to the first time he saw the place—how the white paint seemed to glow and the shade appeared darker and deeper, like holes falling away to an abyss. The shadows appeared to writhe, ready to come alive. He shook it off and knocked on the door frame.

"Well hallo, Ophelia!" Marcus strolled down the front walk and opened the front gate for her. "And Scooter. What a pleasant surprise. It seems like my evening for visitors. Come in, please."

"Good evening. No mobs?"

"It's been quiet. Why?"

"There were angry people at the funeral, some blaming you," she began, then went on to explain about the accusations. Scooter recalled it, but he had been thinking so much about Kristie, he had forgotten about it.

"They say it's the Curse of Chandler. Thirteen kids have died. I'm worried, Marcus. I was having tea and pie at Joe's and Carlson's brother, Earl, and a handful of Peters kin are stirring up each other. They left before I did."

Scooter now knew why she drove like a maniac.

"Thank you for coming out to warn me."

"Strange things are happening all over," Ms. Emmitt said. "Herb Carlson's escape bothers me."

"What?" Scooter stammered.

"Herb Carlson is gone from jail," Agent Pryde said, coming outside to join them. "And so are Martin, Peters, and Nathans."

"This means there are others who think like him," Ms. Emmitt said.

"You sound suspicious. Are you saying that people are

killing kids in order to place the blame on Mr. Chandler?"

"No, I am not saying that. What I am saying is, it wouldn't be the first time this town has blamed Marcus for something that wasn't his fault. He's actually a local hero, but then, people have short memories, and they don't read."

"I've almost finished the book you gave me on the history of Rains County," Scooter said. Marcus' father was mentioned in this area's history.

"The first vampire came here because of me," Marcus moaned. "Perhaps I should just move away."

"You have a right to live here. You were born here. People are alive today because of you!" Ms. Emmitt exclaimed.

"That was then. Now my leaving might save lives," he replied. Scooter couldn't breathe. He had just heard those words from Kristie. Was everybody crazy?

"Mr. Chandler, please think over my proposal. Deputies are posted nearby. Good night," Agent Pryde said. They wordlessly watched her get in the car and drive off.

"Let's start over. Good to see you, Ophelia," Marcus said, hugging her. He moved to Scooter and gave him a gentle embrace. "And you as well, my friend. Writing always cheers me up."

"You are writing again?" Ms. Emmitt asked.

"Scooter inspired me," Marcus replied with a smile. "Thanks for bringing him out. I was starting to worry."

"He blames himself for what happened to CJ. I thought you might be able to relate and lift his spirits."

"Perhaps. Come inside," Marcus said.

"Thanks, but I have to go see Momma," Ms. Emmitt said as she scratched. Scooter must have given her a suspicious look, because she said, "The skeeters are sure awful this year!"

"Goodnight, then. Give her my best wishes."

As Scooter entered, he checked the crosses to make sure they were all intact. "What kind of proposal did Agent Pryde make?"

"If I told you, I might have to silence you forever," Marcus replied. "Sorry. I was joking. She suggested assigning me an officer to help around the place. I'm not sure having an FBI agent here would be conducive to creativity. Plus, I doubt he would be of any help against a vampire."

Scooter nodded. Agents wouldn't be properly armed, but they might deter a mob.

Following Marcus down the hall, he asked the question that had been bothering him. "Why did Ms. Emmitt think you could relate to me feeling guilty about CJ's death?"

Marcus avoided answering by asking a question. "Why do you feel responsible for CJ's death?"

"We should have hauled him from the island in chains if we had to."

"I see," Marcus said thoughtfully. "To answer your question, Ms. Emmitt was referring to my brother. Marvin the Magnificent. He was healthy and vibrant, unlike me. Anyway, when we were young, one of our chores was to chop wood for the stove. One evening, while I was splitting rounds, the head of the axe came off, flew back, and killed him, dead on the spot. If I had cut the wood earlier, like I was supposed to, while Marvin was doing his chores, it would have never happened. If . . ." his voice choked.

"If I had checked the axe first, made sure the head wasn't loose, it wouldn't have happened. But I was mad over not being able to go to the sock hop in town. I never have forgiven myself. Probably never will. All it took was a moment of inattention—a moment of sullen, angry self-absorption—and my brother, my best friend, was dead. You remind me a lot of Marvin. He absolutely loved to draw, and he was a far better story teller than I will ever be. I think you will be, too."

Scooter didn't know what to say.

"Sometimes I feel his ghost around here. That's why too much quiet, I've come to realize, is bad for me."

"I'm sorry. I would have liked to have met Marvin."

"The more I consider it, Marvin wouldn't have wanted me to suffer. He would have said that he was sitting too close.

"What I'm trying to say is that CJ made a decision not to come. Whether rightly or wrongly, that's up to him. You made a lot of the right choices. The authorities encounter people all the time that won't leave when a hurricane is coming. That's their decision."

Scooter thought about it.

"Hey, if it isn't Butch. Where's the Sundance Kid?" the Intruder asked as he ambled into the room. He scratched himself. "Lemonade, anyone? I made a fresh batch."

Scooter nodded. The tart drink helped with the heat. With the Intruder here, he didn't feel like he could talk to Marcus about all the insanity.

"I brought this along, today's *USA Today*. Mr. Dandy thought you might like to see it. He said they printed one of your short stories," the Intruder said.

Scooter's mentor snatched the paper. After a moment, he slammed the paper together. "I've never sent a copy of that to anybody. How did they get a copy?"

"It could have been stolen," Scooter said.

"That's true," Marcus mused.

"I saw Scooter going through your old stuff. I thought he was going to sell it on E-bay. He said he was using it for a story," the Intruder said.

"Scooter, is that true, that you've been going through my old stuff? I went looking in there yesterday and couldn't find one of my favorite photos."

"The one with Marvin?" Scooter asked.

Marcus nodded. He turned the paper so Scooter could see. It was the missing photo. The short-story had been titled *Marvin and Me*. "What kind of story, Scooter?"

"A comic book," Scooter stammered, then he explained about his writing Marcus' story, part true and part fictional. His mentor looked skeptical. That really hurt.

"You don't believe me, do you?!" Scooter snapped. "You think I did this. What for? Money?"

"Easy, Scooter, easy. I concur. Please bring back the photos and clippings. And I would love to see your book about me. Were you planning it for publication?"

"No, I'm making it as a thank you present for helping me become a better storyteller. It was supposed to be a surprise," Scooter said. With that he got up and headed out the door. "I'll bring it by tomorrow."

"Scooter, you don't have to go."

Without turning back, he walked the road toward the front gate. Flash joined him. He didn't see any reason to ask Marcus about Kristie.

He scratched and despaired. With all that had happened, he felt like he had lost just about everything. Kristie was leaving town with Nick Sloan, and he either lost her, or left his grandparents. Marcus thought he was a thief and profiteer. He even wondered if the Incredible Bulk was still his best bud.

Scooter called Judge Grandpa for a ride, then he lovingly patted Flash. As long as Scooter had his dog alongside, he was never alone.

THIRTY-THREE

TAKING BLAME

Suspicion reigned where trust once held sway sounded like a good line for a story. Too bad it was realistic instead of fiction, Scooter thought as he rode his bike through the blazing sunshine. He crested the second hill and down the gravel driveway to Marcus' house. Flash loped alongside, his long pink tongue lolling.

Scooter planned on leaving *The Incredible Mr. C* and taking care of the puppies. He was saddened by Marcus' accusation. But he had larger problems. He hadn't slept all night, between painful itching and wondering how to convince Kristie to stay. He needed her help to find the cause of all the tragedies.

With that in mind, he had come to a decision late last night and stuffed his blue backpack with clothes and a sketch pad. He would ride with Kristie to Orlando, then get a bus ticket back. He had checked prices and availability on the net.

What he had in his old, faded green backpack would prove he was telling Marcus the truth, at least about why he had been going through the dresser drawers. But it wouldn't exonerate him of sending in the short story. How could he prove his innocence? He could show him his meager account balance.

Did he want to come back here if Marcus didn't believe

him? Marcus didn't even accuse the Intruder. Each time it crossed his mind, it made Scooter angrier.

It was the Intruder's fault. Even the bite sores could be traced back to him. He scratched viciously, tearing skin. The dermatologist had an emergency and put off seeing him until tomorrow. He wanted to scream in frustration.

If not for Redgraves, Marcus wouldn't have accused him. Kristie wouldn't be leaving with Nick Sloan.

Barking let them know Beauty heard them. She bolted down the steps and raced toward them.

The dusty ride left Scooter thirsty and lightheaded. The day was already a scorcher, inflaming his sores. He had finished his bottle of water. Ice-cold lemonade sounded good. He hoped the puppies were staying cool.

Usually by now, they would be howling the injustice of being left alone. The farm seemed dead quiet.

"Starr? Ace? Goldie? Curly? Yeller?" Scooter called to them. No puppies burst upon him. In the tense quiet his ears rang. He pushed the barn door open. He called again, missing their yapping and bounding to greet him.

Four of the five were sprawled around. He didn't see Starr. Goldie slept in the linens in the box with the stuffed animals and ticking clock. Curly, Yeller, and Ace slumbered next to the water bowl. As soon as he touched them, he knew something was wrong.

He carefully picked them up, first Goldie, then Curly and on, finding all four dead. He leaned back against the wall and wept. Life was inhumanely unfair. Where was Starr? Calling her name repeatedly, Scooter gently set the pups aside and hunted for the missing puppy. "Flash! Beauty! Find Starr!"

Noses down, they sniffed along, poking here and there. They barked, but there was no puppy yelp reply.

Just being in the barn, he felt like he was taking a sweat

shower. Perspiration stung his eyes. His clothing hung on him like wet rags, irritating his bite sores. A spider dropped on him, and he killed it.

Flash slurped from the water bowl. Beauty nudged him out of the way and finished it. They begged for more.

Outside felt blistering hot, and yet still cooler because he was wet and in the shade with a breeze wafting by. Shadows crossed the yard and driveway as two buzzards winged overhead, then wheeled back, circling them. Scooter and his dog detectives searched everywhere for Starr.

Finally, his throat dry and raw from calling out her name, Scooter went inside for a water break, taking the dogs with him. He flipped on the fans to roar and blow. He added ice to both dog's water bowls. Flash seemed to look up, chin dripping, and plead with him to rest for a while.

Scooter found a pitcher of lemonade in the refrigerator. While he wrote a note to Marcus about the pups, he drank down the sour pink treat. It tasted sweeter than usual.

He returned the newspaper clippings and photographs to the bottom drawer, putting them underneath some old yellowed folders. Underneath it all, he slipped in his half-finished *The Incredible Mr. C.* This way, the Intruder wouldn't hide them, then claim Scooter had never brought them.

On second thought, he added a postscript to his note, mentioning that he would be gone for several days, driving with a friend to Orlando to visit relatives. He hoped Marcus didn't think he was running away.

He found two shoe boxes and placed the dead puppies within. After grabbing the shovel, he trudged out to the place they had buried Billy Gee. Digging was hot work, even in the shade. He perspired profusely, melting away, his skin feeling soft and gooey.

By the time the graves were dug, he felt dizzy and

thirsty again. He figured he sweated so much he leaked lemonade. In the shade of the oak tree, he rested and drank more water before he returned to say a few words over the grave.

On the ride home, his stomach began to churn. He stopped and threw up. His bite sores felt afire, hot nails driven into his flesh. All he wanted to do was get home. "Flash, make sure I don't hit anything."

The golden Lab perked up. He wasn't a pointer, but he guided him along the oil-gravel road toward Siete Hombres.

TH I R T Y-F OUR

EARLY DEPART URE

At two o'clock in the morning, Kristie awakened, jarred by her wristwatch alarm. She turned it off, then she said a lengthy prayer of thanks for the quiet house.

Feeling fifty and moving stiffly, she struggled into her traveling clothes. She removed her note from under the pillow and left it on top. She hoped Scooter would be there waiting for her, along with Nick. Aunt Lucille, here we come!

Dressed for the road in jeans and a black, sleeveless shift, she only hesitated for a moment, then quietly stole away from the house into the fog. When she looked back, the mists had swallowed her home like a forgotten memory.

She drew out her cross and kissed it. Mother was healthy, thank the Almighty. Now Mom could do what she was supposed to do—raise her kids. Kristie's gift was singing. She needed to utilize it. What was wrong with wanting to teach the world to sing in perfect harmony?

The fog swirled coolly as she crept down the driveway. Her imagination jumped to Garrett. He was still loose, and who knew what other freaks, even if the cultists had been caught.

At the end of the driveway, she retrieved her backpack and handbag from the bushes. She assumed Scooter would be here. He cared for her deeply. She could tell by how he listened to her, the way he smiled, and what he didn't say.

Yet, Scooter wasn't here. It worried her that she hadn't heard from him. Could she really do this alone?

A figure stepped out of the fog, startling her. Smoke gathered around the slender young man as Nick exhaled. "Good morning. Nice to have a fog to cover our departure. Are you ready for adventure?"

He gave her a brief hug, and Kristie touched him with her cross, just to make sure he wasn't a vampire. He chuckled, removing his necklace from under his shirt. "I got one on, too. It's always smart to have a knowledgeable guide."

She noticed his cross was cracked. "What happened to it?"

He looked surprised. "I don't know. I'll have it fixed in Florida. I hope it isn't a bad omen."

Kristie shivered. Should she stay? If she didn't leave now, she might be stuck home for a long time.

Nick offered to carry her bags, but Kristie toted them to his yellow mustang. The trunk was open.

She looked around. Where was Scooter?

"By tomorrow night, we will be in Florida. What are you looking for?"

"I was thinking how futile it was to try to commit anything to memory in the fog."

"You'll be back. We need to get going before somebody discovers you're gone."

Kristie agreed. She slowly climbed into the Mustang, praying Scooter would show up at the last minute.

But he was a no-show, disappointing her. Had she assumed wrong that he cared for her? She couldn't wait any longer, hearing a clock ticking in her head. By sunrise, they needed to be far away. Nobody would know where she was except for Scooter. With all her heart, she hoped he was well.

She buckled up and settled in. "Let's go," she announced.

"Sunshine State, here we come!" Nick laughed. He popped the clutch and drove off.

Kristie wanted to cry. With the fog, there wasn't anything to see, except for mailboxes, signs, and telephone poles. Stop signs seemed to be everywhere.

Each time they stopped, she thought about getting out. She had to get away from Mother and Gunstock. It was now or never. She ignored the signs. After all, they were man-made.

To be honest, she was scared that if she stayed in Gunstock, others would discover she could heal people. The injured and sick would come to her, pleading, and she doubted that she could say no to people she knew and loved, and the people they knew and loved.

Closing her eyes, she placed her bruised hands on herself and let the lightning work through her body, healing her mother's illness. She drifted for a while.

A mechanical sound, a shudder, and a profanity brought her attention back to the car. The headlights slashed across the fog as the mustang headed off the road. It dove hood-first into a ditch, then careened into a muddy corn field.

THIRTY-FIVE

AN ILLCONFRONTATION

Curled up in bed, Scooter awakened, scratching and thinking he should be someplace important. He didn't remember getting in bed. Or getting home, either. "Thanks, Flash," he muttered. He couldn't think straight, but he sensed Flash was just as sickly.

It seemed drafty, even under the covers. He was bitterly cold, instead of July hot. If he was this sick, he was no good to Kristie. He had to call her. Rubbing his eyes did little to improve his blurred sight.

The itching drove him to lunacy. He wanted to tear off his skin. The sores had flattened and spread out to the edges of the Band Aids. Even as he watched, the wounds grew larger, as if he were being eaten alive.

Somewhere, almost like in a different world, the doorbell rang. He paid no attention to it until his grandpa spoke more loudly. "Why yes, Jonathan is here, but he's in bed running a fever."

"Are you certain?"

"Absolutely. I just looked in on him. Why?"

"There was only a note on Kristie's pillow."

"A note? I don't understand."

Scooter couldn't think straight. What day was it?

"Kristie is gone. Her note said she left with Scooter."

"She ran away?" Grandma Mae asked.

"Not with Jonathan she hasn't. He's been here all night.

We found him on the floor and had to help him to bed. I'm beginning to wonder if he has the West Nile virus," Grandpa said. "The mosquitos have everybody scratching."

How long had he been out? Scooter groggily thought his way through the conversation. Oh, please, God, no! He had slept all night, and Kristie had left without him! She was alone, angry at him, sure he didn't care for her, and on the road with Nick Sloan.

"Well, she's gone. I want to talk to him."

"I understand. Have a cup of coffee. I'll go see him, and we'll go from there."

Scooter glanced over to Flash who looked at him with a despondent gaze of utter worthlessness. "That's okay. You don't need to come along."

Standing up was difficult, his knees wobbling. Without the railing, he would have fallen downstairs. He was dizzy, clumsy, and his stomach hurt, but he made it to the living room. "I'm here, Grandpa."

"Well, there he is. Doesn't look so sick to me," Mrs. Candel said. She looked healthy, standing ramrod straight.

"Jonathan, how do you feel?" Grandpa asked.

"Like I should carry around an airsick bag."

"Then I will get you one," Grandma rushed off, rattling in the kitchen after a paper bag.

"Scooter, tell me right now: where has Kristie gone?" Mrs. Candel demanded. "Why did she think she was leaving with you?"

"At the funeral she asked me to ride with her to Orlando." Scooter doubted he could explain the depths of his depression. Even heartsick seemed inadequate, worse than any bug he had ever suffered.

"I didn't have any trouble with my Kristie until she started spending time with you."

"What?" Scooter asked. He had hardly seen Kristie.

Because of Nick Sloan, she was on her way out of danger, on her way to a big city with bright lights. In Orlando, she could pursue her Disney dreams.

"If you hadn't asked her to join the Graveyard Armadillos this never would have happened."

"But I didn't . . . ." Scooter started. He hadn't asked Kristie, although he had been pleased to see her.

"Once she got a taste of causing trouble, she couldn't resist!"

"Nancy when you said you wanted to talk with Jonathan, I didn't know you intended to yell at him," Grandpa said, coming to stand beside him.

"Your grandson has turned my daughter against me. She won't do anything around the house. She stays out late. When I won't let her go out, she sneaks out to see Jonathan. More than once she was hurt around you!" Mrs. Candel jabbed a finger at Scooter.

He couldn't stand for it, so he sat. For a moment, he thought he was going to upchuck. His belly churned, as if he had swallowed a whole bottle of jalapeno peppers hidden in five-alarm chili.

"Nancy, easy. Get a grip on yourself. Can't you see Jonathan doesn't feel well."

"Of course not. He's having to face the consequences of his poor decisions."

Scooter's fury burned through his fever, and he jumped to his feet. This was not his fault. He almost fell over, but grabbed a chair. "Is that what she told you?"

"No. She lies to me. Whenever she's in trouble, she's with you. You're bad for her."

"I'm bad for her? I'm bad for her! First, it was Kellen Redgraves. Well, he's a pleasure to be around. He lost stuff, and he broke stuff, and he complained, and he dawdled, and we ended up getting stuck in a thunderstorm. Kristie told me you had Redgraves come along. If it had just gone as planned, the three of us, we would have been back in plenty of time. But you know what's best . . . ."

"Jonathan, perhaps now isn't the time," Grandpa began.

Scooter couldn't care less. Kristie was lost to him. "Mrs. Candel, I don't know what Kristie told you, but the funeral was the first time I've seen Kristie since helping pick up donations for the rummage sale. Hey, that's where she met Nick Sloan. And a couple nights back, when I was out fishing and rope swinging with Russell, we heard Kristie singing with Nick Sloan on the beach."

"Well Nick is a fine . . . ."

Scooter had heard more than he could stomach. "If you're looking for Kristie, she left town with Nick Sloan. That's what she told me. You were feeling good, and you could finally be a mom, and she could go off and sing for Disney. Did you know that Nick wants to be a singer?"

"Now listen here . . ."

"Are you feeling good, Mrs. C? You look the best I have ever seen you. Standing straight. Walking briskly. Full of vim and vigor."

"Why yes. It's a miracle!"

"Yes, it is. You know, I thought Kristie was a miracle, too. Not only is she wonderful, but she saved my life. She talked about running away once to chase her singing dreams, but she couldn't leave you sick at home with the children. She's thoughtful, and she wouldn't do that to you, except she's solved that."

"What do you mean?" Mrs. Candel looked stricken. Perhaps she was starting to get a clue.

"Have you noticed she's been coughing? Not standing up very straight? That the light bothers her a little? That she moves slower? Her hands shake."

"Yes. If she'd get more sleep . . . ."

"When the lightning struck us, it transformed us. It made Kristie an empathic healer. She showed me she can heal. She had helped me heal my aches, just as she helped Mrs. Mochrie. "

"You're crazier than a loon." Mrs. Candel shifted uncomfortably.

"Well, you aren't sick anymore, thanks to Kristie. She has taken on your disease. I couldn't talk her out of going. Does she have an aunt near Orlando? Lucy?"

Mrs. Candel stammered, beginning to believe.

"Why didn't you tell somebody?" Grandpa asked.

"Because nobody believes me about anything anymore! Mrs. Candel doesn't believe me now. Well, you have your health, but you don't have your daughter. And I'm heartsick to say, neither do I. I love her very much, but I never would have asked her to desert her family."

"Oh, Lord. Kristie couldn't have left at a worse time. The Gunns have escaped," Mrs. Candel wrung her hands.

"Heavens, no," Grandpa said. "How?"

"I don't really know. During transit was all Sheriff Knight would say."

Scooter couldn't believe it. What if they ran into each other? A spasm caused him to double over. His stomach heaved. He fought it, struggling to make it to the kitchen sink. He puked his guts out, until there was nothing but dry heaves and bile.

"You are hotter than a stove!" Grandma Mae exclaimed.

"I'll get the car. We're going to emergency."

Over the pounding in his head, Scooter could hear Flash spitting up. He had vaguely thought it odd that his best friend hadn't come downstairs to defend him. Now he understood. He felt doubly ill because Flash suffered, too.

"Flash's badly sick."

"Now come on, Jonathan, please. Let's get in the car. Dear, he's getting confused," Grandma said.

"Grandpa, please! Check on, Flash! He's sick! Take him to Dr. Daniels."

"Jonathan . . . ."

Scooter yanked away, almost falling down. "Why won't anybody believe me?! Why won't you at least check on Flash to see if he's sick! If he wasn't, he would be right here with me."

Grandpa briefly pondered it. "Scooter, if you'll get in the car, I'll go check on Flash."

Almost spent, Scooter leaned on Grandma as she led him to the car. He slumped into the back seat, but he wouldn't move his dangling feet until he heard, "Go on, Mae. I'm taking Flash to Dr. Daniels."

As grandmother's car pulled away, all Scooter could think of was hurry.

THIRTYSIX

DOG DAY AFTERNOON

In the back seat, Russell stroked Flash, trying to console Scooter's best friend. The dog's nose was as hot and dry as West Texas during an August drought. His eyes were glazed. The fur around his mouth was lathered and matted. His breath came in ragged gasps with long dead spaces between.

It was fortunate Mama had driven him over to tell Scooter about the outbreak, having seen the hospital packed. The judge had been alone, having trouble moving the half-dead dog. Russell had carried him to the car. Despite the judge's speedy driving, the ride seemed unbearably long.

Scooter's grandfather got off the phone with the vet. "Dr. Daniels will meet us there."

"Here that, boy? Hang in there! You have to be strong for Scooter," Russell said.

"He doesn't sound good," Judge Keyshawn said. He slow-ran a stoplight and roll-paused a stop sign. "I'll pay the fine. I was very glad to see you walk in, Russell. I'm not sure I could have handled Flash."

"You're welcome. They got test results back this morning. They think my bites were caused by brown recluse spiders. Their venom is rapidly destroying my skin."

"That could be why he's so sick. We found him on the floor last night and had to help him to bed."

Russell continued to wonder what anybody could do about the Curse of the Thirteen. While the medical professions believed the outbreak was caused by mosquitos, Russell knew better. It came from Shade's shack.

When they pulled in, Russell didn't see Dr. Daniels' dark green Suburban with his name and number on the side.

"I'll see if he's here," Scooter's grandfather said. He strode more briskly than Russell had ever seen him walk.

The lights were on, so there was hope, but Russell feared it was going to be too late. Even worse, he had a sense that if Flash died, Scooter would die with him.

He couldn't let that happen. Scooter hadn't told anyone about his steroid use, just further proof they were best friends. How did that almost get lost? Flash must live.

He tried Kristie's cell phone. Her voice mail replied.

Unable to sit, Russell hopped out of the car. He left the door open and paced. All his training hadn't really prepared him for this. He threw his arms up in frustration.

Just as suddenly, his prayers were answered. He squinted to be sure. Across the street, Kristie sat on the bench in front of Al's Auto Repair. Even from a distance, she appeared tired and exasperated. Nick Sloan's bright yellow mustang sat inside the garage on the rack.

Judge Keyshawn returned more slowly, limping a little. His frown told the truth before he spoke. "He's not here yet."

Russell knew exactly what he had to do. "Judge, I'll be right back. Flash! You hang in there," he said, petting the golden dog. "Kristie's coming."

"Russell? Where are you going?" the judge called.

"I'll be right back!" he yelled, before he crossed the street.

Kristie didn't see him, until he reached the gasoline pumps. She crossed her arms and glared. "Are you here to try to talk me out of leaving?" she snapped rudely.

"Out of what?" he asked. Had she said leaving?

Kristie startled, then resettled. She studied him, her gaze narrowing when she asked. "Scooter didn't tell you?"

"He's sick. They took him to ER."

"Emergency? Why? What's wrong?" she asked. She seemed unsure and suspicious.

"It could be the bites. D-did you say leaving?"

"I'm going to Orlando and the Magic Kingdom."

"You're leaving right now?"

"We tried to leave earlier. Nick's car snapped a tie rod and sent us spinning into a corn field."

"You can't leave now!"

"Can't? I can't?"she growled. "I can't stand my mother any longer. She's running and ruining my life."

"You s-sound more and more like Racquel."

"Hey!" Kristie replied, acting slapped.

That's not what he had meant to say, even if it was true. Like Scooter had said, he was letting his anger best him. "Kristie, I'm at Dr. Daniels with Flash."

"The vet's?" Kristie asked. She glanced across the street. "That's the judge's car. What's wrong with Flash?"

"We don't know. Dr. Daniels isn't here yet. I'm afraid that if Flash dies, Scooter will die with him."

"This sounds like a load of bull," Sloan said. He seemed to be working on standing tall. "Kristie, the car will be ready shortly, then we're out of here."

Russell clenched his fist. He wanted to smack Sloan.

"Oh my God, is that Mother's car?" she asked, hushed and horrified. "Thank Heavens, no."

"Kristie, Flash is deathly ill. It's easy enough to see for yourself and say good-bye. We may not have long. We're across the street," Russell said.

She didn't budge. Russell couldn't believe how she had changed. It infuriated him. "You know, Scooter risked his neck to save you from the Gunns. You rescued us from Shade. Back then, you thought we were worth saving, even risking your life and your reputation. Has that much changed?"

"Russell! He's here!" Judge Keyshawn yelled. He pointed to Dr. Daniel's Suburban as it pulled into the driveway. The brake lights flared, then the veterinarian hopped out.

Kristie just sat there. "If Mother finds me, she'll never let me leave the house again."

Russell wanted to shake some sense into her.

"Get out of here, Russ," Sloan said.

"Or what? You'll make me?" Russell said. He had never been good with words. Scooter might have talked Kristie into helping, for old times sake. All he had done was get mad, making her angry, too. "Kristie, I'm going back to tell Flash that you left him to die without saying good-bye."

He sprinted back to help Dr. Daniels with Flash. The old vet readied a gurney, and they rolled the limp golden dog up the ramp. "Rest easy, you mangy hound. I'll help you. Any ideas?" the vet asked them.

"Jonathan said the puppies at the Pickup Ranch died," Grandpa said.

"From what?" Dr. Daniels asked.

"He didn't say."

"It could be an illness. May Bell died, but I don't have the lab work back yet. There may not be anything we can do."

Russell was stunned. He was going to lose his two best friends. When Dr. Daniels asked for help, he did his best rigging up an IV for Flash.

Starting to cry, Russell rushed out. If it wasn't too late, he would haul her stubborn butt over here right now.

He rushed outside, still hoping. He didn't see Sloan's yellow mustang at the automotive garage. Kristie was gone.

THIRTY-SEVEN

HEALING TOUCH

Kristie watched Russell race across the street to the vet's offices. He helped Dr. Daniels load a limp Flash onto a rolling cart. Neither lightning nor a vampire had ever laid the wonder dog so low.

"The car's ready," Nick told her. He smiled warmly, earlier frustration at being delayed gone. "Let's go before your mother shows up."

"Why would she show up here?"

"I don't know. I'm just anxious. If you get caught, my parents might not let me go."

"I didn't think about that. I'm sorry."

"Well, we should have been gone hours ago. Are you sure you really want to go?"

"Why?" Kristie asked.

"Because you're sitting here out front."

"I just needed some fresh air," she replied. The smell of gasoline and grease turned her stomach. She had been ready to go ever since she sensed that Manny and Bart had lung cancer. Both had wives and kids. She wasn't sure why they were scratching themselves all the time. Perhaps it was a manly act.

She bit her lip, caught between staying and going. They had already been stuck here beyond their planned departure. "Can you wait a little while?"

Nick shrugged and said, "Sure. I'm in no hurry. We

could leave tomorrow, if you really wanted. Just be mindful of the weather. I just saw that they're still expecting severe storms. It could make driving tough."

"I'm sorry to make you wait, but I must see what's happening to Flash."

"If you go over there, it might be difficult for us to leave."

"I am not with you. I've been trying to hitch a ride."

Startled at first, Nick smiled slyly. "They might believe you. I appreciate that, except I really want to help."

"Have you ever had a favorite pet?"

He nodded. Something in his eyes and expression changed, softening him. "Yeah, I did. Biz, short for busy. An amazing dachshund. He died a couple of years ago."

"Would you be leaving now if he was still here, in Gunstock, but dying?"

Nick shook himself, as if trying to shed a chill. "No, of course not. Kristie, I understand. I admit it would be nice to have your company on the long drive, but you gotta do what you gotta do. I was just trying to help with that."

She threw her arms around him, then kissed him on the cheek. "You are wonderful."

"Just remember, I have dreams to chase, and they're not happening here in Gunstock. You have dreams to chase and some divine path, too. You have to decide where you might find it."

Kristie thought furiously, aching to go—as she might never, ever, have another chance—but unwilling to leave Flash. She thought back to what Russell had said. Scooter hadn't met her because he was in the emergency room. He hadn't abandoned her. Had she been so self-absorbed that she missed him being ill? She had been distracted by CJ's death and her decision to leave. "Can you give me thirty minutes? Maybe even an hour?"

"Sure. I'll be over at Joe's Java."

"Thanks for understanding."

Kristie rushed across the street. Her worries drove her fear that she was too late. She charged up the front steps. If she healed Flash, who and what would be next? And yet, if Flash died, and she could have saved him, she would never forgive herself. If Scooter died, too, as Russell warned, she wouldn't want to live.

She yanked open the door, finding Russell in the lobby. "Where's Flash?"

His smile and seeing his confidence in her changed the way Kristie felt. She was no longer weary and worn. She followed him down the hall into a treatment room.

Seeing Flash immediately sobered her. The beloved dog looked lifeless. "Hello, Dr. D. Hey, Flash. You look a little under the weather."

The golden Labrador barely reacted, except for a few thumps of his tail. Kristie gathered him into her arms and opened herself as she had with her mother. When she connected, information came pouring in, so she had a sense of how and where somebody hurt. At first, there was just a growing heat, maybe an exchange of energy, then her stomach boiled and her bowels churned. Dizziness crept into her thoughts and threatened to run wild. Flash was very sick.

Unfortunately, she wasn't strong enough to heal him.

"What is she doing, Russell?" Dr. Daniels asked, then his old, gravely voice changed, softening with wonder. He sounded young again. "I remember a time when I saw something like this is New Orleans as a child."

"It comes from . . . being a minister's d-daughter."

How nice that Russell kept the lightning secret. Kristie began to hurt, making it difficult to talk. "Come on, Flash. Stay here! I'll help with the pain. We'll figure out what's wrong," she cajoled. She had been sick before, but this was worse than Montezuma's revenge, throwing up from her heels, and a urinary infection to boot. She forced her shaky voice to be calm, knowing it had soothing powers. "It's all right, Flash. I'm here now. You're going to be just fine soon."

Wonder dog whined and managed three good tail waps.

"Good, boy. From what Scooter has told me, he's with you, linked in some way, so there's three of us working here." Kristie closed her eyes and shuddered.

"Are you sure you're up to this?" Russell asked. He put a hand on her shoulder.

"No," she said with a shrug. It didn't matter whether she was up to it or not. Flash needed her. You didn't desert such loyalty and call yourself a human being, let alone a child of the Almighty. Her dreams didn't include Flash dying.

She also realized this might be why Scooter hadn't mentioned he was sick. She had been ranting about everybody wanting a part of her.

"Miss Candel, I don't know what you're doing but don't endanger yourself," Dr. Daniels told her. The vet put his fingers on her wrist. "Your pulse is racing."

"Flash is being chased . . . by death," Kristie said, through clenched teeth. She sounded like Scooter. Perhaps he was here. "We're trying to outrun it. So, it's my decision to make, but thank you for your concern," she said through clenched teeth. She wanted to scream, letting the pain burst free, but she didn't. Having visited the terminally ill, she had seen how long life could hold off death, especially with hope.

His transformation was amazing over the next few minutes. Flash's eyes brightened, and his hair shone brightly. He nuzzled her with a cold nose, telling her to stop, then broke contact.

Kristie wanted to puke. "He ate or drank something that made him sick," she said as her knees buckled. She might have hit her face going down.

THIRTYEIGHT

THE RACE AGAINST TIME

Scooter awakened sluggishly, slogging through the murk between sleep and a shred of alertness. Resting on a cold and hard floor left him wondering. Where was he?

He had been sick. Grandma Mae had taken him to the hospital. In fact, he still wore a flimsy gown. Bandages covered his body.

Sitting up, he felt a little dizzy. He had been drugged. Along with Garrett and vampires, the Gunns were loose. Had he dreamt that? Could they have kidnapped him?

The feel of immensity and the sound of dripping made him think of a cavern. The chilling breeze smelled earthy with a rotting and burnt stench. Underneath his hands, the ground felt like a bare floor of polished concrete.

Lightning flashed, and he discovered his pillow was a pile of his clothes. Dressing helped him feel less exposed.

Last he could remember, Mrs. Candel had been chewing him out for turning Kristie into a bad girl.

Flash! His best friend had been sick, too. Scooter closed his eyes and tried to find his furry companion. He grew concerned when he couldn't locate him. Had Flash died? Nausea welled within him at just the thought, too horrible to stomach. He reminded himself not to jump to conclusions. After all, he had lost his ability to see life lights. Could the same have happened to his rapport with Flash?

He prayed that was why he couldn't sense his dog.

A harsh spotlight cut the air, blinding him. Lifting his hand, he protected his eyes.

"Jonathan 'Scooter' Keyshawn, you are quite a survivor. You look good for someone who should have died in a heap of flesh from the Curse of the Thirteen," the hard-edged voice said. It sounded nothing like the Gunns. "What did you do?"

That voice! Shade? His heart skipped an awkward beat, and he couldn't breathe. Or another vampire? The one that haunted Gunstock?

Lightning flashed, but it failed to touch the vampire, except for its eyes. Bitter, cold and red, growing larger like a bloodstain. They promised bloodshed. "Ah, I see. June. No. Yes. That would do it. But," he chuckled harshly, then hysterically. "Nobody realizes how, so you and many others will die. Can you feel death coming?"

Eaten alive, Scooter could feel it. He glanced down at his wounds. The gray-white patches of skin spread larger as more flesh died.

"Give them credit at the hospital. They tried to save you, and succeeded, from poisoning."

Poisoning? Scooter was confounded, then he recalled Flash feeling like he had drunk bad water.

"I'd say you have a top flight guardian angel. Shall we put her to work?"

"You said I was cursed and poisoned?" Scooter continued to work it out. He wasn't all here, between the drugs and the jittery sensation of hordes of ants nibbling.

"Cursed, you are. I protected my old resting shack with a nasty spell. It starts out looking like chiggers, then it converges, turning into what looks like fire ant bites, before resembling brown recluse wounds. The antitoxin will actually speed up the flesh breaking down into sludge."

The vampire thought he should be dead, and yet it saw that he was still alive. Something had slowed the curse. But what? The miracle bug bite ointment seemed to have worked at first. "How's my dog?"

"I have no idea. Jonathan, listen to me. *Attend me.*"

Scooter was riveted, but he had something important to ask. He would not go quietly. "Did you kill my dog?"

"No, but don't trust me. I would kill you, if it suited me. Instead, I brought you here to offer you a once in a lifetime opportunity."

"To do what? You kidnapped me! Where am I?"

"*Stop yammering and listen.*"

Scooter's lips locked. His tongue felt flattened, and he had lost his will to voice. His ears strained as if they were growing.

"How would you like to record the nature of humanity in action?"

"Who are you? How did I get here?" Scooter asked.

"You know who I am. I ask the questions. You answer them."

Scooter's entire body shook, but he didn't believe it. He recalled the tall, long-limbed, almost spidery figure with dead-pale skin, lank, bowl-cut black hair, and eyes darker than coals, until they gleamed red-hot with bloodlust. The cruelly bent face would be emotionless, like wax, until it flashed its deadly incisors. Scooter had watched Lucius Shade crumble to dust. "You're a vampire, but you're not Shade."

"I should expect such disrespect since you assumed children could destroy me. *Hit yourself.*"

Scooter smacked himself.

"*Again. Harder.*"

Unable to control his body, Scooter clenched his fist and punched harder, hurting both his jaw and his hand.

"Throw yourself on the floor."

Scooter jumped up and landed a belly flop on the floor, leaving him with a crushing pain. "You may be a vampire, but if you're Shade, the light changed you," he gasped.

"It has made me more patient. I was going to let the curse kill you, but I have a use for you."

Scooter dreaded the possibilities.

"Yes, even a writer and artist can be useful. They can portray beauty and truth through stories. I want you to write about the trial of Marcus Chandler."

"Who is holding this trial?"

"Some concerned citizens of Gunstock."

"This sounds like some kind of vigilante committee," Scooter said. The vampire remained quietly poised. "Who's defending Marcus?"

"Nobody. He has the freedom to speak for himself. If a man speaks the truth, no one need defend him."

Scooter had been told many court systems thought differently. Some people, despite telling the truth, weren't believable. Politicians, lawyers and lobbyists spun and danced convincingly.

"I think they said the same thing in the Salem witch trials." He knew his arguments fell on uncaring ears, but he couldn't help it. He refused to face death in the same manner as last time. He would be braver, even if he seemed flippant. He had lived longer than expected. The last time he had been at a vampire's mercy, he had been sure that pain and death were imminent.

"I can offer proof that Marcus is a good man. A kind and caring human being. History would be different if he had never been born in Gunstock."

"If you fail to prove him innocent, you will share his painful fate."

Scooter stopped, his breath and heartbeat skipping. He

had to think about that consequence. There were bound to be things he didn't know about Marcus. But he refused to leave his mentor defenseless, or in the proverbial lurch, alone. Judge Grandpa would have urged him to defend Marcus, and to inform the authorities.

"You won't be able to tell anybody," it said.

"I know. Won't the Curse of Thirteen kill me anyway?"

"Yes, if I do not dispel it."

Scooter suspected he was dead already, not quite a dead man walking. That was one description of vampires. "I want to see him."

The light went out. Scooter waited in the darkness. A stone-cold clasp took his warm, flesh and blood hand, guiding him along. The stink of machine oil and burnt plastics was cut by the breeze of lilies on a grave. Up metal stairs, he was drawn along a hallway. The vampire opened a door, then pushed him in. *"Say nothing."*

Through a window into a lit conference room, Scooter saw Misters Carlson, Nathans, Martin and Peters playing poker. The authorities were ill-equipped to deal with vampires who wanted to free inmates.

"His accusers, judges, and jury. These men have proof that Marcus has framed them. He retaliated for them getting conned by the Gunns into lynching him."

Conned? Right. Marcus had not threatened them. It wasn't in his nature. For revenge, he would have just killed them in a movie manuscript.

Scooter noticed a black box the size of a bowling ball. Dark beyond belief, it seemed to absorb light, graying the area around it. Its shadow seemed to jump and dance as the men played cards and spoke nastily about Marcus.

The vampire guided him into another room adjacent to the first. Through the open door, he saw Marcus blindfolded. They hadn't beaten him. *"You may whisper."*

"Yes, I'll defend him."

"Excellent. That will add spice to the legend."

Legend? Scooter didn't understand.

"Even in reality we find stories worth handing down. The story of Lucius Shade shall be one," it said, always mindful of its place in history.

The vampire hauled him off again, back downstairs into what must be the immense interior of the burnt and abandoned manufacturing plant. Scooter smelled fiberglass. The interior arched upward, like the belly of an aluminum beast. Was he in the Supreme Boat factory?

The vampire uttered strange words that stung Scooter, making his sores flare. With a talon, it scooped a gooey hunk of flesh out of his shoulder, showing it to Scooter. "I have accelerated your curse. You have one hour before the trial."

"One hour!" Scooter exclaimed. He couldn't run there and back. He might be able to hitchhike. Once he got home, he could grab his bicycle. That might work, except he was weak, losing skin and muscles mass. His ribs ached from hitting the concrete floor.

Out of the darkness blazed a pair of black eyes lined in red, angry and demanding. "You *will tell nobody where you have been. What you are doing. Why or where you are going. If you try, you will suffer the unspeakable—the pain will be unbearable*," the vampire commanded. "Anything else you can do. Be creative. Be adventuresome. Break the law."

"Why are you doing this?"

"You have sixty minutes to return," it said, pushing him out the door into the night.

Scooter turned around to examine the charred boat factory. Yellow crime scene tape fluttered in the wind. This wasn't too far from the ranch, except he was on foot.

He gathered himself. Well, it was his choice. He'd rather die on the move, trying to help Marcus, than sitting around waiting to turn into a heap of jelly. Of course, he hadn't realized he was without transportation. He better start thinking creatively.

The bugs had gathered en force tonight. The mosquitos who bit him simply died, still stuck in his skin. The crickets seemed to be shouting at him to hurry.

How was he going to get to the Pickup Ranch? He didn't have a cell phone, or even a bicycle. Just his feet. Normally, they might work, but he had little or nothing left.

To the northwest, lightning flashed, brightening the dark sky but making the black thunder clouds shimmer with a sickly green tinge.

Creech's Marina wasn't too far away. On the other hand, he might have a better chance of thumbing a ride out at the highway. Ramp Road led to an intersection with a blinking yellow caution signal.

He jogged toward the road, then stopped when he heard growling. A second snarl made him change his mind. Ahead, there were at least two dogs that sounded feral. The bushes thrashed near the road. Two black dogs burst out.

Scooter turned and sprinted. He raced back to the boat factory, the black hounds nipping at his heels. At first, his running was more like a lurch, but fear pushed him faster. He was gasping by the time he reached the fences. He climbed up and over them, pulling his legs up just high enough above the snarling dogs.

Continuing to climb, he reached the top and hopped over onto a heap of scrap topped by a roof. It didn't break under his landing, but it did tip. He hit the ground rolling out of the way of the crashing piling.

When he could breath again, he sat up and stared at the dogs. They were searching for a way to get in. If he left by the other side, far way from the dogs, he could make it to Creech's Marina. There might be somebody seeking shelter from the storm.

He could hear the clock ticking as he crossed the yard. Out a gate, he headed down a gravel road toward the marina. He heard the dogs, spurring him on.

The headwind from the lake worked him harder. Splattering drops of rain fell, wet harbingers of the coming downpour. Tiring quickly, he sweated like he was trying to lose fifteen pounds an hour. Each breath stabbed through him, but he couldn't stop. There wasn't time to rest.

He reached Creech's Marina faster than expected, seeing it through the trees. At first, he thought he was seeing things, but now he felt certain that lights danced across the three buildings. The wavering light playing across the mist looked somewhat familiar. The Gomezes were crazy.

He hoped to bum a ride to the Pickup Ranch. There was a bicycle in the barn that he could use. Staying close to the trees, he crept closer. If he popped out, he might frighten everyone. Those in the boat might jet off, leaving him high and dry.

"Get the hell out of here, ghosts!" Juan commanded. Scooter imagined him holding some object, perhaps an orb or a copper Atlantian power wand.

With a shrill squeal, the ghostly light fled into the trees.

"It's gone now! Why Liz, you're shaking. Here, take my hand. I think it's safe, but don't stray too far," Juan said. "We found this magical pendant that repels the haunting spirit."

"I didn't want to come here, but the lightning . . . I heard about kids who were hit on Lake Tawakoni."

Scooter peeked. Julio steered them in. Juan handed the girl something. While she studied it, he tied up.

"Let's bring in the beer, chips, and salsa. It will help us

ride out the weather," Juan said. He lit up a cigarette. "I think there's candles in the glove box."

"What I really need is something to keep away the bugs. I'm itchy," a girl said. Scooter didn't think he would be able to convince them to leave, since they were out partying. They might give him a cell phone to call somebody who cared, but he couldn't tell anybody what was going on or why.

He would have to steal their boat.

Using flashlights, the Gomez brothers and the two girls crept across the pier to the bait and tackle shop. They listened for a while, whispering all the time, then Julio opened the door. Scooter waited for the skeleton to come springing out to scare everybody.

"*Muy bueno.* This place will give us protection. I brought a radio. We can dance and listen to the weather reports."

Scooter slipped around the corner, darting stealthily for their Nitro 400 Bassmaster. Hoping no one came out, he dashed past the open door. He couldn't believe his luck. He couldn't believe he was doing this. He hated stealing, but the clock was ticking.

He quickly unwrapped the lines from the grommet, slid into the Gomez's boat, set their gear on the dock, and then cast off. Finding an oar, he weakly paddled away, his ribs grinding and complaining with every stroke.

"Did you hear something?" Juan asked.

"That's not funny," a girl said.

Noises carried easily over the water. Scooter wanted to get as far away as he could before starting the engine. In the natural quiet of the bug-noisy lake, it would be blaring.

"Hey! These aren't twist offs! I'm going to get an opener."

Desperate now, Scooter dropped the paddle and reached for the ignition.

"Wait. I'll take care of that."

"Gawd! You did that with your teeth?!"

Scooter kept paddling, working his way around a bend. The land would block some of the noise. When the engine roared distantly, they wouldn't investigate. He flipped the choke, then turned the ignition. The outboard roared to life, thrumming to go.

Then it sputtered and died.

In the distance, he heard, "Did you hear that?"

"Sounded like a boat. I hope they don't come here!"

Two more tries, then the engine roared to life. He grabbed the wheel and throttle, giving it more gas for speed. The boat lunged out of the water, skipping across the surface as though it had been launched by a slingshot.

Well, now the boys had an excuse to hang out with the girls. He would apologize later, if there was a later. He was headed into the teeth of the storm.

THIRTYNINE

INTRUDERS

The boat trip to the Pickup Ranch was a dark blur with jagged lightning and intermittent crashes of thunder. Between his eyes watering and the wind-blown spray, Scooter could barely see. He might not have seen anything, except the sky slowly transformed into an odd green. This eerie brightening highlighted a sky full of bold, black, cumulus building cloud cannons ready to bombard land and water.

Having too much to think about made it difficult to focus. He must find proof that would exonerate Marcus.

But other thoughts and worries kept intruding. Where was Kristie? How was she? Did she live?

Gritting his teeth, Scooter tried not to scratch. It wouldn't do any good. All of this might be pointless, except it mattered to him. He glanced at the clock in the dash and wondered if it was accurate. If so, he had thirty-five minutes left.

He cruised into the dock a little too swiftly. His landing rocked the piles and planks and sheared off the light on the bow. If he lived, he would pay for that. He hastily tied up, then paused for a moment, looking at Marcus' Stingray. It was bigger with a deeper V-hull. It could handle the stormy waves more easily. He flipped the switch, pulled the cord, and set the winch to lowering. The boat would be down when he returned.

He was getting tired of running. He never thought he would say that, but then, usually he was with Flash. Just the draft alone was enough to always get him home.

Lightning washed the ranch white, the ponds glaring brightly. Tightfisted clouds bludgeoned each other and battered their way across the sky. He could feel a wind picking up, the trees thrashing as leaves and nettles were torn away.

At the ranch house, Scooter noticed that more lights were on than usual. Why? Marcus wasn't home. The front porch lamps were hazy through the screen, but cast long shadows that clawed through the trees and across the front walk to darken a car. The red eye of a blinking alarm on the state vehicle seemed an ill omen, especially since he recognized Mr. James Dandy's car and license plate.

What was he doing here? Scooter couldn't think straight. Too often he drifted off into what he planned to say or foolishly wishing he had telepathic powers. He couldn't even use the phone at the house. Huffing and puffing, he jogged up the steps. The moths swarmed the screen door, scattering when he yanked it open.

The slamming of the flimsy door against the frame rattled discordantly, as if he had broken something, but it didn't bother Mr. Dandy. He slept on the outdoor couch.

"Kellen? Are you here?" Scooter asked, leaning inside the front door. He still blamed him for many of his problems.

Scooter checked Mr. Dandy to ensure he was alive, especially since he looked waxy. He breathed shallowly but slept heavily, so Scooter continued his quest to Nirvana.

"Kellen?" he called again as he approached the writing room. A chair rolled, and its wheels squeaked. He thought he heard faint music. Trying to be ready for anything, he turned the corner into Nirvana.

Eyes closed, the Intruder rocked in a chair while listening through head phones. Next to him sat a frosty mug of root beer and a slice of pound cake sitting atop scribbled notes.

The sight made Scooter livid. Marcus was imprisoned, on trial, and under the threat of death, and here the Intruder sat dancing in his chair. Scooter barely restrained from smashing his face to a pulp.

Startled, the Intruder sensed him. He pulled out his ear pieces. "Hey, man, you're noisy enough to wake the comatose. Are you all right? You look like an extra in *Dawn of the Dead*."

"Why is Mr. Dandy asleep?"

"It's a secret. Is Marcus with you? I have something very important to show him." He held up his video camera. "Where's Marcus? He's been gone a long time." The Intruder had a strange look in his eyes.

Scooter didn't have time for the Intruder's prattling. He went to the dresser to get the files of newspaper clippings and photographs, plus the unfinished book *The Incredible Mr. C*. He grabbed Marcus' day pack and put everything inside.

"Going to steal some more personal effects to sell?" The Intruder put a hand on his shoulder. "I'm not letting you take anything else without Marcus' permission."

Scooter slapped the hands away. "Don't touch me! You intentionally lied to Marcus. You know I'm creating a comic book of him. You wanted him to distrust me. You also got us in trouble with Kristie's mother too."

He didn't even mention poisoning the puppies. If he got started, he would do something he might regret later.

"I've never seen your book about Marcus."

"I didn't make it for you. He can show it to you, if he wants." Scooter looked over at the clock. Less than twenty-five minutes. He stalked past the Intruder like he wasn't there.

"Don't ignore me!" he screamed as he slammed into Scooter. They landed against a folding chair that bit into his back before crumpling. "Don't blame me. It's not my fault!"

"You always say it's not your fault. Face it! Because of you, Mrs. Candel wouldn't let me see Kristie. Now she's left town! You murdered the puppies, May Bell, Billy Gee, and poisoned Flash!" Scooter raged. He struck out, elbowing the bigger kid in the nose, then kneeing him in the gut.

Scooter mustn't let himself get sidetracked. Snatching up Marcus' day pack, he staggered toward the door.

"Take it back! I didn't do any of those things!"

He saw the Intruder charging. Throwing a chair into his way slowed his enemy, but Redgraves still grabbed him, dragging him down. "I can prove it!"

His head hit. Scooter heard bells and drums exploding with thunder, flashing lights, and shooting stars that seemed to rip the fabric of reality. He kicked out, catching the Intruder, then he followed his rush of blind anger. Scooter struck repeatedly. His hands hurt, so he grabbed a stone carving of a bear.

Suddenly, he heard a bark. Somebody grabbed his arm in a strong grip. "Scooter! Easy!"

He turned to look at Russell. Flash barked happily and jumped into his arms. "Flash?! Russell! Flash, you're alive!" His golden Lab slobbered him with joyful kisses. Scooter couldn't help but laugh and rolled off the Intruder. Fatigue and violence faded as he felt hope renewed. His friends were alive and well! He should have felt his best friend coming, but he had lost himself to his fierce anger and the ringing in his ears. Scooter squeezed his dog and never, ever, wanted to let go. "What are you doing here?"

"Looking for you. Flash led me here," Russell replied. "What are you doing?"

"Beating the snot out of me," the Intruder moaned as he hauled himself to stand. Once afoot, he leaned on the table. "I didn't know a little guy could hit so hard. The way you jumped me was like something out of *Karate Kid*."

Russell eyed Scooter warily. "And you were talking to me about my temper? What's your excuse?"

"Redgraves poisoned and murdered the puppies. He tried to do the same to Flash and I . . ."

"I did not!"

"How do you know Flash was poisoned?" Russell asked.

"I felt it," Scooter replied. "I don't have time to explain all this. I don't even have time to make the Intruder pay."

"Who? An intruder? Where?" Redgraves asked.

"I have to leave. Now. I'm on a tight clock."

"Leave? For where? Have you looked outside? A tornado hit Fate just a few minutes ago. The prevailing winds are bringing the front this direction," Russell said.

"There's no way I'm staying here with Redgraves. If he's here, the tornado will hit here," Scooter retorted, then headed for the door.

"Stop! You're acting crazy!"

"The same has been said of you, and it makes you angry."

"That's true. Why can't you tell me where you're going? We may be dying from this curse."

Now that he really looked at Russell, his best bud appeared awful. Large bandages covered his sores, most of his arms wrapped. "Did the hospital give you treatment for brown recluse bites?" He nodded.

"Me, too. I feel worse, but what else is new?" the Intruder said.

"The Curse of Thirteen is quickly killing us. I have less than an hour. The flesh will entropy and slide off our bones," Scooter said. He showed him a patch of gelatin-like flesh. A puss pocket flared and oozed. He didn't have time for this, but he didn't want Russell to die.

"Oh, my God. We're dying? I should have kept taking steroids. My sores got worse after I quit," Russell bemoaned.

"After the first batch of Granny June's, mine flared up," Scooter said. He flashed back to the vampire reading his eyes. What had it seen? What had it said? June?

"Yeah, the one mixed up by Kristie worked better. She has a healing touch," Russell replied.

Scooter realized something. "She used holy water! Let's try that?!"

"I'll try anything," the Intruder said, scratching.

Russell popped the stopper of the ceramic jar and poured drops of holy water onto Scooter's swollen wrist. The wound ruptured, puffed a wretched smoke, then sank like a fleshy crater. The fierce itching was gone. He wanted to dance.

"Marcus has some of that. I was here when Kristie delivered it," the Intruder said, heading to the bathroom. He returned with a ceramic container.

"Take off your bandages," Russell said.

The Intruder unwound the bandages to expose himself. "Scooter, I know who poisoned your doggie," the Intruder sneezed. "It's why I drugged Mr. Dandy."

"You drugged Mr. Dandy?" Scooter asked.

"I caught him on videotape poisoning the lemonade in the refrigerator with antifreeze coolant. I've tried to tell somebody, but nobody will listen," the Intruder said. Scooter thought that sounded familiar. "I got sleeping pills out of Marcus' medicine cabinet and ground them up, putting them in Mr. Dandy's coffee."

Scooter didn't know what to believe.

"I thought I saw him kill Billy Gee, but I wasn't sure. So I tried to follow him around with the video camera. I got lucky and accidentally left it running on the kitchen table. That's how I taped him," the Intruder said as he removed the medical tape and gauze.

"You got lucky?" Scooter tried to scoff, but he couldn't. The holy water worked a miracle. Russell stretched out his arm. Scooter poured a little onto his wounds, popping one sore after another.

Because of the stink, they moved to the porch and listened to Kellen tell his tale about Mr. Dandy killing Billy Gee, and poisoning May Bell and the dogs. "So I think my luck has changed. I've caught a murderer. Man, that lightning hitting me might be the best thing that ever happened to me."

Russell was giddy, almost giggling. He rubbed his hands up his arms and down his legs. "The Curse is gone! Yee-haw!"

The three of them high-fived. Scooter felt wonderful with the maddening itching gone, but the clock kept ticking. "Bye!"

"Where are you going?" Russell demanded.

No words would come out of Scooter's mouth. When he could finally put air to the sounds, he stuttered as Russell had often stammered speaking English. When the chest discomfort became intolerable, he finally gave up. "I'm tongue-tied."

"Been there, stammered that. Worse, thanks to Mister S-shade I've been lock-jawed. Is . . . it?"

"Sounds like BS to me," Redgraves said.

Scooter growled.

"I know you wouldn't lay into Kellen unless you were almost out of your mind. How can I help?" Russell asked.

Scooter seethed. "I don't know."

"Take a moment and think."

"I don't have time to think!" Scooter screamed. "I don't have minute! Why am I standing here!" He kicked Mr. Dandy, again and again. "That's for my dog! And the puppies!"

"Stop! Think! That's what they teach us when in an emergency situation. Breathe. Count to ten. Think about what's going on, and what you should do."

"There's a bicycle in the barn. I'll ride to the dock."

"I'll take you. I drove my ATV. You came by boat?"

"I stole it. Does that tell you anything?" Scooter snapped.

"I'm not letting you leave until you tell me about Marcus," the Intruder demanded.

"Call the sheriff. I'm sorry I accused you. I was wrong," Scooter said.

"I said, you're not going anywhere until you tell me about Marcus!" he persisted.

"Think *Lost Boys* meets to *Kill a Mockingbird*."

"What's the second movie? What are you talking about?" the Intruder asked, following them to the ATV. "Don't tell me I can't handle the truth. This isn't *A Few Good Men*."

"This isn't a movie! This is life and death!" Scooter roared. He hopped onto the back of Russell's ATV. His buddy stood so he could sit, throttled it, then kicked it into gear. With a jerk, they rode the gravel road to the dock.

The strong wind kept pushing them right. Russell had to fight to keep them straight. Flash looped alongside, ears flying like the wings on the Thunder God Thor's helmet.

"Flash looks great!"

"Between Dr. Daniels and Kristie, he's made a remarkable recovery."

Scooter rejoiced. It was unbelievably good news. "Kristie?! How is she?"

"Resting in the hospital. I think she's pretending to sleep so she doesn't have to face her mother, but Flash wouldn't have made it without her."

The golden Labrador barked agreement.

As nasty as the sky looked, Scooter wasn't as worried. Flash alive and Kristie still home! The Vampire Hunters were all together, at least in spirit. Her holy water had cleansed him, and he no longer felt chewed alive.

The lake was choppy with small whitecaps. To the north, the storm obliterated his view of the trees. The nearby cottonwoods flailed in the gusty winds.

"It's horrible boating weather. You'll need a storm spotter," Russell said upon cutting the engine. He braked at the foot of the dock.

Scooter patted him on the back. "I wish you could go, too. But I can't let you."

"I suspected as much. Hey, I recognize that Nitro 400." Russell whistled.

"Uh, yeah. They think it's stolen," Scooter replied embarrassed. "They were scaring and romancing some girls, so I boat-jacked it. Now I'm taking Marcus' boat. When the weather improves, will you return the Nitro 440?"

"Great. They'll be pissed off."

"Tell them I jumped in just before a ghost took off with it. I wrestled it away, and you are returning it."

Russell roared with laughter. "I can't wait to see their faces, but I want to be watching when you tell them."

Scooter found the spare key in a hidden box with a combination matching his mentor's initials. "If something happens, and we don't go fishing again, well, get off steroids."

"I promise," Russell said. "Let Flash stay with me. He

can find you wherever you go."

Scooter didn't want to let his best friend go, but he did when the golden Lab chuffed, then licked him before backing away. "You like the idea?"

Flash barked three times.

"I should know better than to doubt you." He embraced his dog. He held back tears, knowing he might not see him again. "I guess we should think of it as Hide and Seek. Leaving was difficult, but time dwindled. He hugged his dog, again, then jumped into the boat.

"Good luck," Russell said. He handed him his waterproof bow case and quiver.

"You brought this?"

"I thought we were dying. I'd rather go out as vampire hunters. You won't take me along, and I need Flash. You might need it to protect yourself."

"Thanks," Scooter said, taking the bow and quiver. He had less than twenty minutes. If he pulled ashore as close as he could to the boat factory, he could make it.

In reverse, Scooter steered out of the dock slip and glided into the rough waters of Tawakoni. White caps marched southeast, the direction he was headed. He opened up the throttle and hung on as the Stingray 220L bounced across the breakers ahead of a storm of funnel clouds.

FORTY

DEADLINE RACING

Scooter steered southerly down the lake, riding the stern wind. He slowed a little, timing the waves. The Stingray 220 skipped across the crests. With a deeper v-hull, Marcus' boat handled better than the Nitro in the rough water.

Over his shoulder, Scooter studied the sky. It looked darkest westward, like a wall of black rain.

During a flash of lightning, he thought he saw something huge and black behind him. He kept glancing bow to stern, so when the sheet of brightness vividly lit the night, he saw the waterspout. The spinning cone of water stretched from the lake into the low-dipping clouds. It looked to be headed for Marcus' house.

Maybe the Intruder's luck hadn't changed.

In a flash of lightning, he saw a white hull and ragged canopy, despite the boat keeping its lights off. He had no idea of its size, but by its whine, it sounded large with twin engines. The lack of lights told him the water craft wasn't law enforcement. Raiders attacked under cover of darkness.

Scooter already drove fast, but now he shoved the throttle most of the way forward. The tachometer's needle leapt from green through yellow into orange, skirting the red line of RPMs. Adjusting the trim on the outdrive made little difference, as the Stingray banged and skipped across the waves. There was no point in looking for debris, but if he hit a floating log, it would be a spectacular crash ending to his personal story.

All he had to do was stay ahead, but, he could see they swiftly sliced into his lead, convincing him it was a bigger boat. He estimated that the mystery craft would catch him before he reached the far shore, east of the dam.

A flash flared from his pursuers. His windshield shattered. Too late, he ducked. They were shooting at him! Another window spewed safety glass. He could hear bullets slam into the fiberglass hull. A slug hit too close in the driver's seat where he crouched.

One-handed, he donned a life vest. Who could it be? Cultists? He assumed vampires wouldn't be shooting at him. Had they been on their way to the Pickup Ranch when they spotted Marcus' boat?

"Why did everything come down to the last few minutes in movies?" Scooter had asked Marcus. It isn't considered drama without urgency. Stress changed people.

Coming up on his left, he recognized Heron Point, where he had almost drowned. The deep spot he had fallen into was a channel before rising to the point.

With the torrential rains, the lake was full, the point underwater. He was alone and light. With luck, speed, and waves, he might slide through while the others got stuck.

He steered to cut the corner and braced himself for a crash. Marcus' boat sliced close to shore, churning up a little mud, spewing a brown wake. The engine slowed as the prop spun through soggy muck. A clank shuddered the hull, then a squeal made Scooter wince.

Without a dreaded clunk, Marcus' boat cut through the shallows. The water smoothed, this immediate area protected by the land. He backed off the throttle. The RPM needle dropped out of the red danger zone.

He watched the dark vessel swerve after him, arrowing for his stern and close to shore. A moment later, the chase boat stopped fast.

"It worked!" Scooter's own cries of victory still filled the air when the Stingray's motor stopped, then started again. He cut back on the throttle. The illuminated gas gauge read empty. How could that be?

The engine coughed twice. He steered closer toward the shore, hoping the prevailing wind and waves would carry him to land. Although the white caps were gone, the breeze was stiff. He smelled gas. When he checked the back of the boat, the fuel stench gagged him. One of their bullets had punctured the tank. He hoped they didn't shoot anymore. If they hit metal, there could be fire and explosions.

Scooter lowered the trolling motor and let the small propeller work along with his paddling and the wind. He braced the little motor to remain engaged, the prop turning.

Curses and cussing followed the rolls of grumbling thunder across the lake. The profanity sounded familiar.

The side windshield shattered. Then Scooter heard the report. Fearing he only had moments left, he prepared to abandon ship, packing a floating flashlight and a flare gun. He pulled off his shoes, shirt, and pants, then packed the stuff inside the waterproof bags, sticking them in Marcus' pack. Swimming would be slow. He wasn't going to make it.

Unless the waterspout helped him. It swung wide around the point, but the spinning vortex of water swept toward them. If he was lucky, it would push him ashore.

A metallic ping and a roaring whoosh announced a flaring of flames. The gasoline ignited, trailing out into the water behind the boat and leaping upon the craft like fiery buccaneers intent on razing.

Scooter dove off the boat. Before he hit the water, the Stingray exploded. Hot flames seared his back, throwing him farther away.

Moments passed before he got his bearings. He found a floating cushion. After snuffing its flames, he wrapped his backpack around it and set his bow case on it. Now ready, he side-stroked like a lifeguard, dragging the cushion along.

The thunder boomed louder, rippling across the water. Rain fell sporadically, then harder as the wind picked up. The sound of a distant cheer was not music to his ears. The gunman's boat motor turned over, then roared to full power. After several seconds, it died again. The howling moan of a distance freight train thundered closer.

The gunmen's boat engine restarted, and it carved toward the burning patch of water, searching for him. They reached the flames just ahead of the water spout, but it came rushing in, forcing them to turn away. It swept up Marcus' burning hull, snuffing it and tossing it away.

The winds surged, howling as the elemental taskmasters whipped and drove the water aground, taking Scooter with it. His vest saved him, and he hung onto the cushion until his butt slammed into the mud near their shooting targets. The aliens had fallen into the water, some swept away. Scooter found his footing, then dry land. After pulling on his pants and shoes, he took off. The deadline had to be imminent.

A searchlight found him just as he darted into the woods. Gunfire ripped through leaves and struck tree trunks. He dove, rolled, prayed, and kept on sprinting.

Risking it, he turned on a flashlight and found the gap in the fence. It had been repaired. He despaired, wanting to scream. He would never make it through the dark woods.

The searchlight swept across the trees. Scooter felt trapped and hopeless. Except, Russell had left him armed. He opened his bow case and quickly reassembled it. He found a less wet area and tried to keep the string dry and protect the shaft's fletchings. The sweeping light enabled him to find the flare gun, helped him ready the bow, and arrow-in on the target.

He aimed, breathed to relax, then fired repeatedly at the light. He hit it on the third try, killing the light. They returned fire, bullets stripping the trees. Before they returned fire, Scooter fired the flare gun.

The missile rocketed away, leaving a smoky trail. All the practice shooting fireworks paid off. The flare found the boat, skipping off the windshield and exploding above his head.

Scooter looked away just before it glared brightly. He watched the woods light up, giving him a good idea where to go. He gathered up the backpack and bow, then ran.

Any minute, Marcus' trial would begin. How long would it take to convict him without witnesses? A nanosecond? Scooter felt like a failure, knowing better late than never meant death this time.

The flare's light cast shadows and helped him speedily navigate through the rain-blurred woods. He used the rubberized flashlight to knock away branches, wishing he had a machete for the blackberry bushes and its thorns. Hitting a soft spot, he slogged through boggy muck.

He fell when he stumbled into the drainage ditch next to the road. The water swept him a few feet before he dragged himself onto the far side and the road. He followed his nose toward the stench and the Supreme Boat factory.

Reaching the front doors, he yanked on one, then the other, angry and frustrated to find them locked. "I'm here! I'm here!" No lights were on. Had the trial started?

The shotgun blast was over his head, ricocheting off the wall. Debris pelted him. "Gotcha! Now, don't move!" one of the gunmen drawled.

The warning stopped him cold. Hands up, Scooter turned around to face the cultists.

FORTY-ONE

JUDGE, JURY AND EXECUTIONERS

Lightning bolted too close overhead. The fulgent blast glared sharply off the double barrel shotgun and illuminated the rain. The fast crack of thunder assaulted the building, rattling large windows, aluminum frames, and the corrugated metal walls of the burnt out factory.

His hair raised, Scooter felt the shock down to his bones. He knew this indescribable and unforgettable feeling. "We have to get inside, now!"

"Why are you runnin' here? Where's that Hollywood murderer?" the cowboy spat a wad of chew. "A Gunn always pays his debts."

Scooter was shocked to see the Gunn brothers. "Inside!" He thought furiously. His skin vibrated, flesh and blood instinctively knowing it must escape. But Jake Gunn would shoot him in the back, then let loose an uproarious laugh or yee-haw! If Scooter led them on, the vampire who claimed to be Lucius Shade might deal with them. "He's hiding inside, protected from the storm and lightning."

The wind began to keen around the fence and through the fire-ravaged building.

"Why here? I don't trust you. You're tricky!" Jake said.

"Check out your brother," Scooter said. Even wet, under hats, and in the Gunn boys' beards, the static stiffened hair.

"I'm tired of being wet." Unleashing his sawed-off .12-

gauge shotgun, Jack blasted the lock, leaving a shredded metal gap. With his manure-kickin' boots, he stomped open the door. "You first," he ordered, gun-gesturing ahead.

Scooter rushed inside, glad to be out of the weather. Of course, being in a metal building with lots of glass didn't exactly sound safe. The three-story storefront lobby reeked of melted fiberglass and burnt plastic. Ahead of the Gunns, he wandered between the sodden couches and charred chairs. Water dripped from the balcony of the second floor and down the open air stairs. The walls of blackened windows hummed eerily like the coming of tree-toppling winds.

"This place stinks of burnt wire. Why's he hidin' here?" Jake snarled. "Hey! I see smoke. This place is still on fire!"

A cloud drifted in from the dark hall of offices to choke the lobby. It stank of burnt rubber, tobacco, and lilies, then the temperature plunged, making it feel like the water should freeze. Shade had never radiated such cold hate.

The Gunns' weapons suddenly disappeared.

"Stand still. Stand quietly!"

Scooter tried to resist, but his body seemed to slam on the brakes. His heart thudded heavily at the abrupt stop. Sores dotted their faces much like chicken pox marks.

The vampire loomed larger than life. Dominating eyes appeared to blot out the known world. The harsh stare sharpened to dissect Scooter of knowledge and secrets. "You, like most writers, are late, missing the deadline. Fatally so in this case, even though you discovered the cure for the Curse of Thirteen. Good for Russell and Kellen. Regardless, a deal was a deal. You shall die with Chandler."

Scooter had known this might happen. He feared this less than living the rest of his life with relentless regret.

The undead monster looked to the Gunn brothers. "I freed you. You are here because I wish it. *Guard this place.*

Shoot without asking questions. Have fun and don't let yourself be taken alive."

The expression in the Gunns' eyes shimmered with thankful awe, as if they had just been given a zealot's blessing to slaughter every man, woman, and child. Cheering the decision, the wind howled through the wall of windows, leaving the lobby vibrating. The waterspout had passed, so this must be another wave of the storm's wrath.

"Scooter, it is a pity the world will never get to read your writing. You showed promise. Oh yes, you may speak."

The invisible glue on his lips disappeared. "I have the proof I mentioned."

The vampire's stare made him feel tiny, and yet, it wasn't Shade. It didn't smell like it, and the eyes were commanding, but they were inexplicably dissimilar. The Lucius Shade he had known had been indifferent to humans. This vampire had feelings and hated.

"The jury has already decided guilty on all charges. Marcus Chandler has a reserved seat in the electric chair."

"What?" Scooter stammered, infuriated. Was all his rushing around for nothing? "I want to appeal."

"Denied."

Scooter struggled with every ounce of energy, but his best attempt was pitiful and pointless, like pounding his head against a wall to get rid of a headache.

If the weather kept degrading, it might get them before the vampire. The sheet metal walls shook continuously now, even as the wind increased to a ghoulish-peel.

A force of nature, the vampire cared less. The second Shade, as Scooter had begun to think of him, even Shade II, took him to the conference room without a ceiling. He had been here before, looking for CJ. The bullet holes in the walls, table, and floor were reminders.

From above, a spotlight suddenly shone on Marcus. His mentor sat bound to a chair. They had rigged together a metal helmet contraption with electrical wires and strapped it to his head. Cables stretched back to a large cabinet of portable power generations. Four of the gas-powered engines roared, barely discernible within the storm's fury.

"You can't do this!" Scooter shouted.

"*Hold your tongue.* I will call back the jury to witness the consequences of their decision."

Scooter knew if this happened—white men murdering a famous black—parts of Texas might burn. The news would spread like wildfire, and the Cult of the Vampires would be known better than the Branch Davidians of Waco infamy.

"Scooter," Marcus began. "I'm sorry you have to watch me die and feel like you have failed, because you haven't. I apologize for accusing you of stealing my work. I don't know what I was thinking. You offered me friendship and inspired me."

Scooter almost felt released. He had needed to hear that.

"How touching. We would not want Scooter to die of guilt. That would take too long," Shade II said.

Would it hurt? Scooter wondered what it felt like to die. He hoped Flash wouldn't die of loneliness. Maybe Kristie would sing a song about him. His parents would wonder what went wrong. His grandparents would blame themselves.

"Then who will write this story? You? You're not Ripley," Marcus said. "If you're anything, you're an actor."

"*Silence,*" Shade II commanded. "Scooter agreed to die defending you."

Why was this happening? Was it still all about Lucius Shade? Assumptions were well and good for hypothesizing, but Scooter needed to let them go when he was proven wrong and find the truth. Would it set him free?

The vampire forced Scooter to march to the adjacent projectionist booth. He could barely see through a couple of undamaged spots on the booth's Plexiglas window. Shade II transformed into Marcus' evil twin, then got nose-to-nose close. *"Stay here. Remain quiet. Watch closely. Remember vividly."*

Scooter's vision grew sharper and focused. Time might have slowed due to his attention. By name, the vampire summoned the local Marcus-haters to reconvene.

Peters, Carlson, Nathans and the muscular Martin were all white men. Where were Chung and Hernandez? They hated Chandler, too. Why weren't they freed from jail? Scooter knew it was even more important that he speak up. Marcus was an important element in several of their histories. They were a fidgety foursome, scratching and frowning. Under Scooter's scrutiny, he noticed they were covered with sores. They would die, too.

"You are here to witness justice. You have proven that Marcus Chandler has set you up, ruining your reputations and your lives," the vampire said. "Who will pull the switch?"

The rancher, the P.E. instructor, and the grocer exchanged glances, appearing eager. The postman seemed content to watch, so he broke three cigarettes and let them 'draw straws'. Peters drew the short one. "He's all yours, Hank."

"Wait, a moment. *Stay here.*" Shade II stepped into the darkness. By the change in the atmosphere, Scooter sensed the vampire had left. Now he had a chance to talk. He feared he was going to fail again, until he sensed a newfound strength.

Flash! Pure joy! Tail chasing excitement.

Scooter cleared his throat, coughed, and then spat out a wad of phlegm. "Don't you love this weather? A good-day-to-die kind of weather. I get the feeling that any minute this building will just fly away."

"Who said that?" Carlson asked.

The storm gusted. The entire place squealed and struggled as if trying to escape the bindings of its beams and rivets.

"Mr. Carlson, your parents will be disappointed to the depths of their very souls," Scooter talked it up. "If you murder Chandler, Ethel won't forgive you."

"What are you talking about?" Carlson snarled.

They couldn't see Scooter. No door led into their room.

"When Ethel was three and you were five, she fell down a drain. The firemen and deputies were too big to fit inside, so they lowered a rope. She was too scared to help herself, so a nine-year-old volunteered to be lowered."

"What does that have to do with anything?"

"I recall that as well," Marcus said, giving the date. "The nice fireman was Bubba Earl. Ethel was so cute. She wouldn't come along until I promised I was taking her back to Sherbert, her older brother, Herbert."

Herb Carlson stood stunned.

"Who are you?! Show yourself!" Peters declared, looking around. "You sound like that idiot Keyshawn boy."

Scooter wished he could hand them the articles over the wall, but speaking was an incredible strain. "I have newspaper clippings inside my backpack in a waterproof container that tell the truth of history, like Zito Peters."

The rancher stopped cold.

"He was a fantastic baseball player on the team that won the Texas state title. Marcus was a teammate. Zito is quoted as saying he was the best teammate ever. He threatened an obnoxious reporter with a bat if he kept calling him boy."

"You are just full of crap!"

Scooter refused to stop, although he knew they didn't want to hear the truth. "Mr. Nathans. Your father was thrown by a horse before you were born."

"Yeah, I remember my momma telling me about that. Some stranger found him and ran to the nearest phone."

"That was Marcus out bicycling at night. If you will just look in my backpack, you'll see the newspaper articles." Scooter feared Shade II would be back any minute.

Carlson's eyes were deep, turned inward and trying to remember. "Where are you?"

"Behind the glass in a projectionist room."

Moments later, the hefty Carlson opened the door. "What's wrong with you?" he asked. Nathans followed closely, coming right up next to Scooter.

"I'm paralyzed."

"I don't believe it," Nathans snorted. The postman gave Scooter a push, sending him to the floor. He fell hard on his elbow and jaw. The impact compounded the pain in his ribs, making it harder to breathe. For a moment, Scooter feared he couldn't speak with a broken jaw.

"I think he's having a seizure."

"Aw. Ow! Do you pick on handicaps, too? Look inside the backpack," Scooter finally groaned.

Nathans grabbed the pack. He pawed through, finding the waterproof tube and opening it. "Ha! A bunch of yellowed clippings from the local rag and the Dallas and Ft. Worth papers. Check out the date." He paused. "I don't believe it!"

Carlson gasped.

Scooter couldn't see. They had left him on the ground.

"Uncle Zito was my favorite. He taught me how to hit and catch," Peters moaned.

Gunshots blasted from the front of the building, echoing

down the hall. Returned fire answered, tearing into the metal side walls and sounding like a hail storm.

"Bring the pack. I got him." Carlson finally hauled Scooter like a sack of potatoes. They set him next to the table where his backpack's contents lie scattered, including the flashlight and blue-gray Nokia phone. They could call for help.

"Tell us about this man, Shade?" Peters asked.

Scooter knew he would lose them by telling the truth. The word vampire would undermine his proof. "Well, for starter's, he's got the Gunns guarding this place for him."

The men looked at each other. Nathans muttered.

"The monster you're following kidnapped the Mochrie boys and kills kids for fun. I don't know what to call . . . him, but if you take a photo, well, the truth will be shown," Scooter continued.

"You're crazy!" Peters told everybody.

"Does it work?" Nathans asked, holding up the picture phone. He took an electronic photo of Scooter. "Ayep. You ain't a vampire. Hee-hee."

A barrage of gunfire raged, then it suddenly died down. A single shot led to a longer silence.

The smoke whirled cold and black to coalesce into the form of Shade II. "Jonathan, your dog is causing problems for my wolf hounds. I . . . ."

With a glaring flash, Nathans snapped a photo.

"Put that down!" Shade II snarled.

"There's nothing! A vampire!" Nathans dropped the phone. The other men released the articles as if they were hot.

"We may have rushed to j-judgment," Peters stammered.

"You have already reached a decision," Shade II snapped. It reached back into the shadow and withdrew an intensely black box and set it on the table. The vampire might as well have created a hole in the wooden table top. When the undead monster opened the small chest, it seemed to reach into the underworld.

Shade II withdrew a horrific and unforgettable statuette. The Gibbering Darkness idol seemed alien to life. A nasty twist of queasiness and slick greasiness overwhelmed Scooter and dropped him to his knees.

The vampire arranged the sickening sculpture in Marcus' lap. "This needs charging."

With his wrists clamped down, Marcus had no choice. He twisted and heaved, trying to bounce it from his lap.

"I will plant it as your grave marker and reminder. Henry Peters, are you ready to enact justice?" Shade II asked.

"Like I said, I do believe I have changed my mind about doing this, at least right now," the rancher replied.

"What are you babbling about? You swore this is the man who threatened you and set you up to go to prison. Who linked you to the Minutemen and, far worse, arranged for you to be connected with hate crimes you didn't commit. The proof was buried under this Hollywood star's barn."

That must have been the clincher for these men to convict Marcus, Scooter figured.

"Hands in the air, everybody. I would like to see how this plays out, but a tornado is about to hit," Agent Pryde said. She was torn, wet, and dirty, having already been in one gun fight and unhappy about being shot. She bled from her shoulder, the jacket and shirt bloodied.

"Are the Gunns dead?" Shade II asked.

"It depends on how fast the paramedics arrive."

"Then the clock is ticking," the vampire smiled, pleased.

"You must be Lucius Shade," Agent Pryde said.

"So nice of you to come to my anonymous phone call.

Drop your weapon," the vampire commanded.

As Agent Pryde watched, astonished at her actions, she released her FBI regulation piece. The .48 Glock clattered to the floor.

"Leave it," the vampire replied. "It is time to do what you came here to do, Henry Peters. *Throw the switch."*

The rancher struggled, his body shaking. Peters didn't know Marcus, but there was doubt in the man's eyes.

"Shade will blast Agent Pryde with Jake's shotgun, then he'll shoot you with hers," Scooter shouted. This was a sham. "Nobody will ever know the vampire was here! Y'all will either be dead, or taking the fall for killing an FBI agent."

"*Be quiet and stoic, Jonathan. Flip the switch, Henry!"*

Peters' twitching hand inched closer, making him appear eighty and enfeebled. He screamed in anguish, then his fingers darted to flip the death switch.

FORTY-TWO

A BRASH DEMAND

Like a torrent of Fourth of July fireworks, sparks cascaded down, spilling over the electric chair, Marcus, and everyone nearby. The lights flickered, then died, even as the last of the fire danced across the floor, fleeing the darkness.

The lack of light empowered the vampire. One moment they were inside the storm-wracked factory, the next they plunged into a giant, yawning maw, completely swallowed by terrifying darkness.

"Now, *come out, wherever you are,*" the vampire compelled. A soul couldn't miss, let alone ignore, such cajoling evil.

"Not quite a secret is it?" Scooter gasped, breaking through the command of silence. If he was a character in some grand story—which he wasn't, but who really knew when your story might turn into The Big Story—he preferred to die true to himself, rather than voiceless in word and deed.

"Who said I wanted this unknown?" Shade II replied.

The air fizzed painfully, carbonated with tiny needles and violently shaken. Just when Scooter thought he would break under the agony, the feeling of open space returned. Above he heard flapping. By a flash of lightning, he saw that the vampire had transformed into a large, bat-like beast similar to the one that had chased Marcus' boat weeks ago.

Peters and the rest of the men said nothing. Held helpless, they were reduced to watching and sweating. Reeking fear oozed out their pores and sores, unable to escape through screaming or running legs.

"Hey! L-let g-go of me!" Russell yelled. He must have used his lightning gift to disrupt the electricity.

With a concussive wind-blast that knocked him flat, the large, winged beast landed atop the conference table. *"Tell me what you have done, Russell Knight."* The darkness swarmed with black, viciously biting no-see-ums of rage.

"I s-shorted out your portable generators."

Scooter believed that Flash still led the wolves on a merry chase. That's how Russell had snuck inside after the gunfight!

"Go fix it so the electricity flows!"

"I don't even know how I broke it."

After a moment of consternation, Shade II forced Russell to admit his lightning-struck ability. "And you, Jonathan?"

"What's your name? It isn't S-shade," Scooter managed.

It laughed, sounding cold and detached, barely a semblance of forgotten humanity. The vampire's eyes told the angry truth. "Have no doubt, I am Lucius Shade."

"You are not the Lucius Shade that wanted a movie made of his life, unless you had . . . some kind of epiphany."

The vampire stared hatefully. "Epiphany? What an interesting word, but it has divine origins. What makes you so bold? You believe you have already died and in a sense been reborn. I see you are disappointed you didn't face death more courageously last time. Well, then let me tell you I am pleased to give you another chance."

A flashlight beam came down the hall and into the conference room. Mr. Short walked in, looking wooden.

"Fix the flow of electricity to the chair."

Short trundled off.

Shade II stared at Russell, then hissed. "I see that Kristie is still in town!"

A light dawning, Scooter realized that the vampire had been manipulating all of them—the whole town—including Kristie. Sloan was a thrall. "Was Redgraves spying for you?"

"No, but it amuses me that you thought so. You almost killed him. You could blame the Curse of Thirteen, but I know better. If Knight hadn't arrived in the proverbial nick of time, you would have blood on your hands."

Scooter began to deny it, then thought better. It would have been an accident, manslaughter, but it was possible.

The lights came on, bringing back the expansiveness of the factory. It trembled as though the howling thing outside attempted to rip it from the ground.

"I sense . . . another," the vampire said.

"Where is Tai!" Garrett Brashear strolled to where they could see him. The former leader of the Graveyard Armadillos stretched tall to match the vampire eye-to-eye. There was an odd wrongness about him, as if he were sick, or perhaps just ill-defined.

"You are arrogant and brash. I am right here," the wolfen Shade II said. Its entire body morphed, leaving the exotic and beautifully cruel Tai. Its clothing had changed to a Catwoman suit, a dark leather outfit clinging to its harrowingly curved figure.

Garrett locked glares with the supernatural beauty. Scooter could feel the sweltering waves of hate.

"Who are you?! *Tell me!*" Garrett demanded.

Tai Shade II casually waved him away, her finger nails more like claws. "You are an insolent pup, thinking of yourself as two-thirds vampire."

"You are no Tai! You look like her, but your mannerisms are wrong. Tai and Shade were destroyed by the sunlight. Don't deny it! I read about it in the *Dark City Times*."

While twirling the ring of keys, the vampire changed into Marcus. "You know the truth of who I am."

"You are a liar!"

Shade II left the pale face behind, assuming an East Asian guise and nobody familiar. "Kristie Candel killed my mentor's mistress. You see, Tai enjoyed pretending to be my mentor, Lucius Shade Sr. She was his greatest fan and pursued this idea of a movie for his life. "

"So Tai, looking like your father, died?" Scooter said. He didn't know vampires had kids. None of them were going to have offspring if the factory blew away.

"He was my mentor. A vampire hunter got him last year. Should I just kill you for the joy in your voice?" Shade Jr. asked.

"Why did you offer Kristie a chance to be a vampire, Dr. West?" Russell asked.

"By law, vampire slayers are always offered the chance to be transformed before they are killed," it said.

Scooter wasn't sure what they were jabbering about. It wasn't going to matter in a moment. The weather ripped the earth apart while they yakked. A jet-loud roar assaulted the metal building, causing it to quake.

Sections of it were bashed in as though something was hammering away. A windy hand tore away some of the arcing metal roof, opening the factory floor to the black sky. Scooter was closer to a tornado than he had been in nightmares.

The floor collapsed, falling away and taking part of the walls. Scooter tumbled with it all. He crashed softly atop carpet rolls that were beginning to truck across the floor toward the gap. He hit the floor and they ran over him. Debris and metal flak flew wildly, a piece slicing through his arm. Unattached seats and aluminum windshield frames flew past.

He crawled behind a workbench, but it scooted and almost turned over. Scooter found a bolted eye-hook in the concrete and tied himself down with a rubber water hose. The wind seized him, trying to tear him away. With the squeezing and the speed of the wind, he could hardly breathe.

A boat hull crushed Ringly, then tumbled on to hit Carlson. Screaming, Peters flew off like a kite.

What seemed to last hours, lasted perhaps a horrible, desperate minute of barely hanging on as pallets, windshields and hulls whirled into the sky.

Nature's fury finally veered away. The twister took more, the metal building unraveling. Scooter couldn't believe he was still alive. He thanked his guardian angel.

The tornado's glancing blow didn't seem to bother Shade Jr. or Garrett. On what was left of the second floor office, both looked unharmed. "See. I withstand the storm. I am worthy!" Brashear proclaimed. He lashed out with a whip to snag Shade Jr.. The Asian vampire sneered, even as its clothing and flesh sizzled. The interwoven crosses left welts everywhere it touched the vampire. Despite the agony, it broke free, snapping the whip.

Garrett yanked out a taser, jabbing it into the vampire's neck, jolting it. "I want to see more pain because you have shown me how to feed on it. Yes, I can feel the Gibbering Darkness. That's how I found you."

He zapped the vampire again, leaving its body quivering. Shade Jr.'s face registered less pain, although its limbs spasmed, giving false breath to the beast's heaving chest. "You are unworthy."

Scooter was almost able to think now. He tasted blood, not really feeling his nose but knowing it bled.

He hurried across the floor and grabbed a set of keys that the Shade Jr. lost. Hurrying his clumsy feet, he climbed up to second floor and the electric chair. Excited and scared, knowing every moment lost was life-or-death precious, Scooter tried to unlatch the headpiece. His jittering left scratches on the metal and scraped Marcus.

"Easy and steady, Scooter. We survived a tornado. There's hope. There's time. Count to three. Breathe."

Scooter finally slid the key into the lock, grateful and wary of snapping it. Garrett continued to rant, giving Scooter more time. He slowly turned the key. With an audible click, he freed the straps to pull off the headgear.

"Easy. Breathe. The hero shouldn't hyperventilate and pass out at the end of the story." Marcus forced a smile.

Scooter removed the neck cuff, then he began unlocking the restraints, starting with his wrists.

Short marched back into the room. "Master, I found some batteries. They're reconnected. The power is hot to the chair."

Shade Jr. seemed revived, straightening with resolve. "Good work, Purvis. Laugh all you want, child." The vampire seized Garrett's arm and snapped it like a twig. His flailing knocked the ring of keys from Scooter's grasp.

Out of nowhere, the Intruder was there, doing what he did best by getting in the way. "This is for cursing me!" He shattered a ceramic container on Shade Jr.'s left shoulder. The undead flesh slagged, turning into blood-glazed clay oozing out of shape down the side of his body. The vampire lashed out and knocked Redgraves backwards onto the floor.

Scooter tried to ignore the dizzying stench, finally opening the last lock. "Come on!"

"I can't! My legs are numb!" Marcus said.

Scooter couldn't lift him alone. "Russell!"

"You are too much trouble!" Shade Jr. said. His hands extended into claws, his fangs into wolfen canines.

A dog without fear, Flash slammed into the vampire. Shade Jr. crushed Russell and Scooter atop Marcus, trapping them against the electric chair.

The undead monster instinctively reached for the dog's throat, finding the cross-studded collar. It screamed in agony.

Garrett yelled in triumph. He seized the headpiece and shoved it onto the head of the vampire. "They will reward me for this. Flip *the switch, Short!*" he shouted.

"Get off!" Scooter screamed, having trouble breathing. Russell tried to push up, crushing him. Eyes bulging, the undead monster writhed, trying to let go of Flash. Its claw was welded fast, while its right arm was half-melted.

Scooter grabbed the collar's buckle and tried to free Flash. His fingers fumbled.

Shade Jr. kicked Russell, dislodging him and knocking Scooter away, too.

Lightning struck the building. It ran along the cable to the chair. It coursed through the vampire, leaping from undead flesh to skin and bone, attacking, Garrett, Flash, and Marcus. His mentor jerked. Scooter barely saw it, overwhelmed by intense pain.

FORTY-THREE

THE DARK AUTHORITY

Russell heard the lightning too late. When the electricity hit the metal helmet, the surge seized the vampire and shook him. Like a boneless rag, Shade Jr. flopped about with his remaining hand welded to Flash's collar.

The golden dog shook violently. Then he bolted loose. He crumpled at the feet of Scooter, who pitched onto the floor.

Garrett flew off, crashing through the window of the projectionist booth. Smoke trailed him, fading as though his spirit left his abused body behind.

"I . . . w-will . . . not d-die," stammered the vampire. Shade Jr. had disappeared, replaced by a silver-haired, Asian female. Like her insides were seeping out, worms rippled through her skin. Hate shone crisp and bright from her fully black eyes. The killer helmet seemed to get larger, sinking down over her face, partly covering one eye, easing the dominant gaze.

Russell didn't know what to think. How many sheaths of skin could a vampire shed?

"You all shall die to soothe my agony," the thing said. The vampire tugged at the helmet, finding it welded fast.

His gun and newfound strength were worthless against such a monster.

The vampire ripped the metal helmet loose from its head. "Now you die."

A second time, lightning struck.

The vampire screamed in pain as she seemed to contract, pinched from within. The current cast horrible changes in her flesh, from warts to boils to pimply eruptions that seemed to skitter with spiders. Balling up, springing and thrashing, the vampire warped into ferocious animals—a coyote, a huge black bat, and even a hog-sized rat. She twisted through an incomplete change, part man and half animal.

The lightning passed, leaving a spasming corpse. Russell gave it a wide-berth to check on his friends. Mr. C wasn't breathing, pulseless, he was dead.

"We have to try and revive him, like we did BJ," Scooter croaked, rolling onto his side.

"Hey, you're alive and awake!" Russell exclaimed. He smiled, thrilled beyond expressing.

"Shade Jr. said I had a hardworking guardian angel. I must have something important to do," he coughed.

"You look like death warmed over," Russell said. Scooter's hair stood out like a porcupine's back. His friend was beaten and battered, his face bloodless.

"It takes one to know one," Scooter replied, crawling over to help. He passed close to the twitching vampire. "Is it dead?"

"How would I know? Kellen, watch him," Russell said. He pulled a face shield from his pocket, dropped the plastic breathing sheet over Mr. C's face, and gave two breaths. Last time he had tried this, it hadn't worked on BJ.

He forced himself to exhale calmly, praying for spontaneous breathing. After repositioning to clear an airway, he repeated the process, watching for the chest to rise. Mr. C. remained lifeless.

"I'm going to do CPR." Russell positioned his hands, then began compressions, catching the heart between the backbone and the ribs, manually pumping the organ.

"Go for it," Scooter said. "I'll be there in a moment to help." He began crawling.

"Oh, God, no. No!" Redgraves moaned.

Russell paused to check for a pulse and glanced up.

Throwing off the execution helmet, Shade Jr. staggered unsteadily to his feet, then with a shake, he transformed himself into Mr. C. When he leered, the left side of his face drooped. "You are very disrespectful." He slapped Redgraves. The blow sent him flying into a beam, where he fell unmoving.

"Leave us in peace!" Scooter yelled.

"I can't. Tai was an amazing vampire. She must not be forgotten. Because of what has happened in Gunstock, and will happen, neither my mentor, nor Tai, will ever be lost to time, immortal in legend and recalled in whispers this land is accursed."

Russell didn't know what to do.

He heard the twang of bow as Scooter fired an arrow. The shaft pierced undead flesh, but Shade Jr. snagged it, stopping it short of its heart. Scooter readied another arrow.

A new voice halted the vampire in its tracks.

"Lucius, junior. *Stop!* The boy is right. Enough is enough," proclaimed another vampire.

"You stay out of this, Shiv. It isn't . . ."

"In my jurisdiction? You know it is. *Russell Knight, go ahead with what you're doing.*"

Russell checked Mr. C, then repeated the CPR process. Bow and arrow still in hand, Scooter staggered to his side.

"Stay out of my way!" Shade Jr. commanded.

Clad in a bowler and a midnight-black, leather trenchcoat, the swarthy vampire called Shiv commanded attention. Russell could barely resist, except he had been told to continue with saving Mr. C.

"I take my job dead seriously. The Night Community is worried," Shiv said.

Shade Jr. spat an expletive and transformed back to a distorted version of his mentor.

"I agree, but for different reasons. Just a few minutes ago, I found James B. Little shooting your tale. I took this from him," Shiv replied. He held up a digital video camera.

Russell listened for heartbeats. Regardless of how much he compressed it, Mr. C's muscle pump remained lifeless.

Taking care of the airway, Scooter exhaled into his mentor's lungs. Mr. C's chest rose while Russell felt for pulse. When he sensed nothing, they repeated their lifesaving procedures.

"You must realize that there has been too much publicity. Knowledge of our existence can be deadly," Shiv said. With the volume loud, he replayed a minute of Peters backing out and Shade forcing him to do his bidding. "That undermines your case, and what we are trying to accomplish."

"Tai deserves more than the butt of a joke because a bunch of kids got lucky! This town must remember Lucius and Tai. People will talk about why this is such a Godforsaken place," Shade Jr. ranted, then unleashed a burst of profanity.

"You and Ripley have operated counter to the Community's wishes, galvanizing the people in opposite directions. We want them unified in their disbelief of vampires and their hatred of their own kind. You know this. Now, did you make the offer to Kristie Candel?"

"Yes."

"You have done what you were required to do. Leave peacefully. Let the Cult of the Vampire take the heat. It is easier for people to believe," Shiv said.

"You don't want anybody to know real vampires were ever here, do you?" Scooter said "Your cultists have been arrested and jailed." He had to pause to give breaths. "And they'll catch the ones you controlled."

Shade Jr. smirked lopsidedly. "I never compelled them. I simply fanned the flames of hate already in their hearts."

Russell counted and pumped. Mr. C remained dead-still.

"Let me finish it!" Shade Jr. demanded.

"Your time here is done. This county and everything within a twenty mile radius is now off limits to vampires. Remain at your immortal peril," Shiv said, handing Shade Jr. a sheet of paper. A moment later, the writ flashed into fire and disintegrated. "I have completed my task. Think, Lucius. You are acting like an avenging human. You are supposed to be beyond love and hate. Even so, whatever else you do is on your head."

"Are you a cop?" Scooter asked.

"No, but I suggest you both change occupations. Something other than being vampire hunters," Shiv said.

"Consider it done," Scooter replied.

"Breathe and switch," Russell said. His arms felt weak and heavy. It seemed as though he had been futilely pouring his life and energy into Mr. C. He would stay dead like BJ, and Russell Knight would fail again.

"Come on, Marcus. You told Kellen I resparked your creativity. How about your heart?" Scooter said. He laid his hands over his mentor's heart and compressed flesh and bone.

"More firmly," Russell said. He glanced around at the vampires. "They're gone."

"So is Marcus. I want him back!" Scooter pumped.

Nothing happened for a few minutes, but they kept Mr. C oxygenated. They changed positions again, and Russell continued to work. He felt Mr. C shudder, gasp, and lurch. Another breath led to coughing.

Scooter cheered.

Russell felt awe and relief. "Help me roll him. He may

puke when his body reboots." With Scooter's help, Russell maneuvered him onto his side. Mr. C heaved, but he didn't upchuck.

"Thank you, Russell! If you hadn't learned this, Marcus would be dead. See, we can bring the dead back to life! Hey, you know, I don't feel so . . . ." Scooter fell over.

Russell caught him. He wasn't certain that Scooter was all right, but his best friend breathed.

Flash left and returned with help, including the paramedics and Dad. Russell didn't feel like explaining it all, so he pretended to be in shock. That was easy.

FORTY-FOUR

CURSED REMAINS

At full lope, Scooter chased a bicycle along the back roads. The oil-gravel surface was hot under paw and stinky in his nostrils, but it was balanced out by the aromas of the lake.

Opening his eyes changed everything. Scooter was back from playing dog, and Kristie stood at his hospital bed side. She leaned on the rail, her hazel-green eyes radiant. Her pleasure at seeing him seemed almost too good to be true. He had never expected to see her again.

"Hello, sleepyhead. It's wonderful to see your eyes."

"Hey, hi, Kristie," he cleared his throat. "I would think this was Heaven, except I hurt." Body parts throbbed and ached as if all that dream play had worn on him. If only. He recalled wrestling with his body to get it to disobey Shade Jr. and the mad scramble to free Marcus. "I can't thank you enough for saving my dog. I'm sorry I missed you that morning."

Talking exhausted Scooter, making him wonder how he would have felt had she not been near. If it had been anybody else, he probably would have gone back to sleep. "By saving Flash, I think you saved me again. I owe you my life twice. I wonder what the record is?"

She blushed. "Wonder dog needed me. I couldn't just leave him. But I wasn't at the factory. Everybody else was."

"But Flash was there. He brought Russell . . . and Kellen to me. Who would have believed Kellen as a hero?" Scooter couldn't remember much except the Intruder had interrupted the vampire's plans. Little had been there, too. He had been wrong about them. "Russell saved Marcus, didn't he?"

Kristie patted his hand in a motherly way, comforting him. "You and Russell saved him. Y'all broke a bunch of ribs and cracked his sternum, but Marcus is alive. He'll be sore for a while." She stretched, seeming a little pained.

"You helped him. Are you strong enough?"

"I only assisted a little. Not enough that anyone would really notice, unless they were observant like you. Most people's attention is on what happened at the boat factory and the outbreak."

Scooter was confused. "Outbreak? Is Russell all right?"

"He's okay, except for worrying about you. Kellen's in the hospital, a room down and over. He seems like a different person. The black cloud is gone."

"Good," Scooter said. He had thought Kellen a thrall, but he was just another victim. He owed him more than just an apology. The Intruder was no more. "Did you mention an outbreak?"

"Do you remember y'all's chiggers?" she asked. He nodded. "They turned into spider bites . . . ."

"Then our flesh began to decompose. Holy water took care of that."

"Y'all's. This hospital is overrun with patients in various stages," she continued. "Nobody has died yet, but it's been close. There isn't enough holy water, and some people refuse it on religious grounds. The doctors think it might be some kind of bird flu."

Scooter mulled over what she had said. More than Russell and Redgraves suffered along with him. Had other people been out to the island?

Kristie kept updating him. "Not many people survived the other night. Agent Pryde shot and killed the Gunn brothers. Her partner died from his wounds. Hank Peters, Aaron Nathans, Herb Carlson, and Mr. Martin all died in the storm."

Scooter felt sick. He disliked the men for what they had done, but he hadn't wanted them to die. It seemed a waste.

"Agent Pryde has a concussion and remembers very little. Mr. Short seems to be in shock. He won't say anything."

How convenient, Scooter almost said, but then that would sound cynical. Seven people had died. Others would be scarred by the events, especially the outbreak. He wondered what to do.

First he had to say the words that wanted to leap out. "Kristie, I'm sorry I couldn't meet you. I was going to talk you out of leaving, and then if I failed, leave with you. I was so sick that I didn't even know it was morning."

"It's all right. I was really disappointed, too. Crushed, kind of, but I didn't want to believe it." Kristie said. "Then Russell told me about you and Flash. I was afraid something worse had happened. I wanted to wait, but I was afraid. In the end, though, I couldn't desert Flash, or you."

"I thank my guardian angel and you. What happened to James Dandy?"

"He's in custody."

"I hope they castrate him!" Scooter spat.

She waited for him to settle down. "Garrett is still missing," she said uneasily. Kristie had good reason to be worried, as did anyone associated with the Graveyard Armadillos. "But at least Racquel showed up. She's here, too, but she's unaffected by the sores, at least so far. Deputy Ross found her wandering in a daze."

Scooter tried to wrap his thinking around what he recalled, and what she told him. "How long have I been out?"

"Three days. I'm here to nurse you to health. I think you and Russell and Flash, even Marcus have a great deal to be thankful for. People lost lives and homes to the tornadoes. Thirteen twisters hit in the county."

Vampires and tornados are both destructive storms, Scooter silently concluded. "We have to do something about the Curse of Thirteen. I thought it just plagued those of us on the island. I figured you healed it, but you said it's affecting the whole town. Are you better?"

"I'm much stronger, and I would be fine if I didn't add to my burdens. They are my choice. Sometimes, I almost feel like my old self. Except," she giggled, hiding her smile. "I eat more than my brothers, combined. I know, what a problem to have."

She twirled her auburn hair around a finger. "Of course, Mother's mad at me for healing her and making myself sick, and crazy, too, she claims. She won't let me help her anymore. In fact, she made me put it back."

"Some parents are hard to please."

They shared a laugh.

"I kept a little of her illness, but I think I'll heal it soon. If I catch people early enough, especially with this outbreak, all I need to give is a boost to their immune system by taking on a little. I break out, but I pour holy water on them, and the sores disappear."

Scooter disliked the idea of what she was doing.

"I still have more than enough energy to take on your aches and pains."

"Thanks, but having you smiling and nearby is healing enough. I would prefer that to feeling good and having you feel like me."

"You know, I can handle your pain. I have a high tolerance. I don't need coddling," she replied.

He grinned. "I have no doubts."

"I wish Mother did."

Even with greater concerns, he couldn't resist asking a question. "Does Mom hate me?"

"She was glad you were honest with her."

"Oh, I'll bet," Scooter said sarcastically.

"I'm sure not at the time, but when she learned the truth, she changed her mind. She was driving me away."

"Well, Shade Jr. might have given you the nudge. He was angry you had stayed in town. He said he had even offered you a chance to become a vampire as Dr. West."

Kristie remembered. "He was very interested in vampires, and he wasn't listed on the staff. That was Lucius Shade's son?"

"Apprentice or heir, I don't know. I'm certain it wanted to split us up to make us vulnerable. It almost worked. Then there's still this Curse of Thirteen to take care of."

"How?" she asked.

"I don't know. I'm thinking."

"Well, whatever happens, Mother and I are communicating better. Did I tell you we have a new dog? She loves the puppy, Starr."

Despite all the bad news, Scooter almost jumped out of bed. "Starr?! She's alive! All right!" he said, relieved. Since Flash hadn't been affected by the curse, he doubted animals would suffer. But what to do about the people?

He thought frantically, pitching ideas to Kristie. They wondered if the island might be a central point. "I think we should burn the shack," he finally said, getting ready to get out of bed. "It should be done as soon as possible."

"Kristie, is he awake?" Mrs. Candel said, peeking in. She looked a little older, less radiant, but she glided compared to her previously stilted limp. "How are you feeling?"

"Better with Kristie here."

"I understand. Scooter, I don't have to eat my words very often, but please forgive me for the things I said earlier. I was just being a concerned mother. Now I realize that you are her friend and a true friend to our family. Please forgive me."

"Apology accepted," Scooter said. He understood about second chances.

"Now then, I expect you to respect and take care of my daughter, as best friends do."

"I promise. I think Kristie is amazing and a boon to all people," Scooter said, repeating what Marcus had once said.

"She is that. It's not lightly that I allow her to help you heal, but it's her choice. Just as it's mine to refuse. May I caution you to be careful what pains you give her. "

"I understand," Scooter said, holding her gaze. She was talking about his powerful feelings for her.

"I almost despaired when I thought she had run away, and I know better. I should have faith. Sometimes our perspective and perception finds trouble when there is none." Scooter knew better than to hold onto his assumptions. Who would believe a vampire had saved them? Or a reporter? Or Kellen Redgraves as a hero? That vampires hung onto the human quality of wanting to be immortal.

He had figured that when Shade Jr. left, that everything was done, but the story wasn't over. The Curse of Thirteen was causing pain and threatened to kill people. He had a feeling people might have already died if not for Kristie's intervention.

Nurse Gabby came to get Mrs. Candel. Last rites were needed for a friend of hers.

Scooter waited until Kristie's mother left, then they called Russell. He agreed that they must visit Shade's Island and end the curse.

FORTY-FIVE

CLEANSING THE RUINS

Scooter was shocked to see Russell *and* his father. They looked grim, but the sheriff said little on the drive to the lake. He hardly grunted when Kristie and Kellen joined them.

"My son has pleaded with me to do this. I don't see much sense in it, but the shack has been condemned and taken off restricted status, so why not," Russell's father said.

Meaning it was no longer a crime scene, Scooter realized. He understood this went against Sheriff Knight's grain, but with the county being quarantined, he seemed willing to grasp at straws. Scooter would love to sink Shade's Island, but they would have to settle for burning the tainted remnants of the vampire's legacy.

Black clouds hovered over the lake, but they convinced Russell's dad to go on. Standing on the shore, they had agreed it was worth the risk. Even Sheriff Knight mentioned the strangeness in the air. He captained the county's boat, a Patriot with a hard top.

On the way, they saw hundreds of dead fish, increasing numbers as they boated closer. Schools of them seemed to have croaked around the fog-covered island, making them nervous. The curse was affecting everybody and everything, Scooter realized. If they didn't do something, they were probably going to die, too.

Mosquitoes swarmed at the edge of the fog, causing them to back track. After splashing on repellant, they returned. Sheriff Knight steered the boat into the bug-infested fog. Like a billowing veil, the mists blurred the imagination-reality line. The damaged dock and ruined shack wafted in and out of the hazy shroud, disappearing and reappearing.

Something splattered Scooter.

"It's raining. That figures," Russell said.

"That's fine. It will limit secondary fires," Sheriff Knight replied.

"It'll also dampen the awful smoke," Scooter said. He squashed a mosquito on his arm. Despite the repellant, the bugs continued to harass them, but they retreated for cover from the rain. "And drive away the mosquitos."

"Nice of you to look for a silver lining," Kristie said.

"Since your mother is letting you boat with us, then there is a bright side to all of this," Scooter replied. He was hopeful, where not long ago he had despaired. He had thought Flash was dead and Kristie long gone.

"Do you really think this will work to stop the outbreak?" Kellen asked.

Scooter nodded. "I think so, but I have been wrong a lot recently. If nothing else, it does fit the unity of our story, coming around full circle."

"What do you mean?" Sheriff Knight asked.

"Well, things started going wrong here first, although they never really stopped going wrong. Shade Jr. has been working its compellings since shortly after Tai's destruction. It put together all that bogus evidence, like Shaddock's body, the Minutemen uniforms, and who knows what else," Scooter replied. "Besides, outbreaks can't be stopped until the source is realized and neutralized."

"I still can't believe this about Shade's name," Kristie said.

"Name and death. Junior wanted revenge by helping us destroy ourselves, by making us untrue to who and what we are. Shade Jr. also hoped, I think, that by making Marcus' death a spectacle, it might be made into a popular book, and then a movie. The one called Shiv warned against publicity."

"In my opinion," Russell said. "True unity and justice would be if I could cast lightning bolts out of my hands to blast the shack to pieces. Didn't you tell me that in stories lightning symbolizes purification?"

"Yup. It's a type of fire." Scooter smiled.

Sheriff Knight grunted. "I know you told me this cult is a sham, so vampires can keep the truth secret from the public, but I find that hard to swallow."

"You're letting us prove ourselves. That will have to do," Scooter said.

Russell's father rolled up his sleeve, showing them a familiar looking sore. "Your mother has them, too, thirteen like just about everybody else, including your Grandmother Mae."

Scooter almost panicked. He looked to his best buddy. This had better work. Kristie couldn't save everybody.

Getting close to shore, Scooter jumped out, helping to ease the boat onto the muddy soil. Hot water seeped into his shoe, making him jump back. The lake teemed with green wigglers, looking like worms with teeth. "Stay out of the water," he warned and pointed.

Flash stood as a sentry, watchful and silent, while they unloaded the gasoline cans. With low whines, his dog hesitantly led them toward the shack.

It called to mind the blackened bones of some half-dead beast that stubbornly refused to die. The air seemed heavy and oppressive as they approached the darkly hunching ruins. Then it changed. A headwind kicked up, whirling about and blasting them with sand. The ground seemed softer underfoot, turning into quicksand. Scooter found the going difficult, sinking with the weight of the fuel can. Russell helped him, staggering closer.

"This is crazy," Sheriff Knight said. He gritted his teeth.

"Yep," Russell replied.

"It knows we're going to burn it. Be careful," Scooter replied. His old wounds burned. When he looked at his wrist, he saw the sores had returned. "Russell, it's back."

"Then this is the place!"

"Go ahead," Scooter told his buddy.

Russell staggered ahead and yanked the cap off the plastic gasoline container. He liberally splashed the fuel over the ruins. Sheriff Knight emptied the second can of fuel. Kellen couldn't make it, suddenly sitting down.

"Hurry up! Light it!" Scooter said. He backed up, feeling the ruin's dark anger.

Russell used his lighter, but it just clicked. They tried matches, but the rain snuffed them.

Despite the torrential downpour, a horde of horseflies descended upon them. The big, nasty flies swept through, harrying them. The bites were blindingly painful, forcing them to flee back to the boat. They shoved off and raced away from shore, staying ahead of the cloud of vicious flies.

"What do we do now?" Kristie asked.

"Fireworks still work in the rain," Scooter said. "I wish I had brought a rocket or two. We could launch from here."

"You're in luck," Russell said. He reached under the seat, pulling out his bag of vampire tools. "I brought some, just in case, but I didn't bring a tube."

"I don't want to go back into those flies," Kellen said.

Scooter had an idea. "I brought my bow. We can attach one to it. I may not be able to hit a small target, but I can hit the broad side of a barn."

They gathered under the canopy to duct tape the Shooting Stars Rockets to several of his arrows. Russell lit a punk stick, which burned in the rain.

At the edge of the bug cloud, about a hundred feet out, Scooter readied his bow. He notched the special arrow, then nodded for Russell to ignite the fuse. When the rocket sparked, Scooter let fly.

The smoking arrow arched out, falling short and off target. They eased closer, exposing them to the flies. They bit and clogged up their ears and noses, even getting in their mouths. Just as he was bit in the neck, Scooter fired again, overshooting this time.

"Scooter, you can do it," Kristie said, blessing him. While they bit her, she protected him.

He breathed to relax, then unleashed a third arrow. Even before it arrived, it exploded. It was still burning when it stuck in the side of the shack. The flames rippled like wildfire to billow out across the ruins. With a great huff, it erupted into a towering inferno. The conflagration roiled upward, creating a pillar of fire that spewed a dark cloud.

They retreated to watch it burn. Scooter checked his arms, finding the sores still there. Hopeful, they watched it burn. The flames lingered, and the ruins burned a long time, as if they had a will and refused to die.

It finally disgorged a huge cloud of black smoke, like a final breath. Scooter suddenly felt relief, the painful itching and burning fading away.

"They're gone!" Sheriff Knight celebrated. He hugged them, each and every one. "It's a miracle! You were right. I'm sorry I didn't believe you."

Scooter saw Russell smile larger than he had ever seen his buddy smile before. Right then, he believed everything would be all right.

Sheriff Knight called the hospital and dispatcher. Everywhere, people were getting better.

The rain eventually stopped, and when the cloud disbursed, they returned to shore. The ground felt firmer, and the air seemed lighter. They poked around and found a charred Gibbering Darkness idol. Kristie poured holy water on it, shattering it into a million pieces.

"That should do it," Russell said.

Kristie prayed and poured more blest water over the blackened ground. The gloom faded, and the sun seemed to shine brighter. The birds flocked to the island.

"Amazing. I still can't believe it," Sheriff Knight said, running his hands over his arms, feeling the healed skin.

"We felt the same way when we learned the truth about vampires," Russell said.

"I didn't think you were lying, but after nearly forty years, I was sure that vampires were just monsters from scary stories. It's hard to change my beliefs, even after seeing the truth."

"That's the way the bloodsuckers want it," Scooter said. From what he had seen, people really didn't want to know the truth. They were comfortable with their assumptions and half-truths. But finding the truth was worth it, although he felt as much burdened as free.

"Well, I know not to trust my eyes," Russell said. "But the sores are gone. So we either did something right, or it's a strange coincidence."

"Whatever y'all did, it was the right thing, and you did it when nobody believed in you but yourselves," the sheriff said, hugging his son again. "That's a sign of greatness."

"It's wonderful to be believed," Kristie said.

Scooter called Marcus to tell him the news and put him on speaker phone so everybody could hear. He sounded exhausted but cheerful. "I knew you must have done something. Suddenly, everybody is doing better. Patients they thought were going to die have miraculously recovered. Oh, and Micah called to apologize. I get the feeling he contacted some kind of vampiric authority. Maybe it's over."

"I hope so, but I don't want to assume anything," Scooter replied. He would live today and find out, cherishing every moment. He promised to actively write his own story, despite others' disbelief in what he knew was true, and make every breath worth while.

The Vampire Hunters
Chapter One
The Initiation

"Can't be much farther," Scooter Keyshawn panted as he and his young golden Labrador charged through the darkening woods, racing the rapidly setting sun. The redheaded boy gasped, his breath short, his heart hammering loudly in his ears. His eyes stung from the sweat that dripped down his face.

What would happen when darkness descended? He wondered. His canine companion, Flash, whined in response, as though he'd heard Scooter's thoughts.

Scooter put on a burst of speed. His gaze flicked about as he searched the woods. Flash had no trouble keeping up, loping alongside Scooter. Except for their crashing strides echoing in the silence, the air was unnaturally still, the twilight eerily calm. Even the crickets and frogs were silent, the woods absent their lullabies.

A faint mist gathered near the small stream to their left, threatening to obscure part of the darkening woods. Scooter knew the fog could get thicker than smoke from a chili cook-off. If that happened, he might get confused, unable to find his way back to the abandoned house where he'd left his bicycle.

Scooter shivered. He'd better slow down. He certainly didn't want to get lost out here in the woods.

He paused and wiped the sweat from his brow. He was thoroughly soaked, the humidity suffocating. The evening air draped itself about him like a wet blanket.

Beyond the forest and above the lake, the setting sun sat teasingly upon the flat Texas horizon. The high cirrus clouds were crimson stains smeared against the golden twilight. The waning light was low-angled and weak, barely touching the shadow filled forest. Any moment now, the sun would disappear, plunging the woods into darkness.

"Come on!" Scooter encouraged Flash, then started running again. The Lab needed no encouragement; the pure joy of running radiated from his sparkling eyes. His ears flapped like wings, and his flailing tongue seemed to reach all the way to his lively tail.

Despite the ninety plus heat, fear chilled Scooter to the bone. Where were they? What would they do to him? Again, Scooter cursed the flat tire he'd had to fix in front of the old Pilot Point Cemetery. His new-found friends would be mad with him for being late.

Getting into the Graveyard Armadillos meant a lot to him. Heck, until two months ago, the only friend he'd ever had, besides Flash, was Russell Knight, the sheriff's son. Then he'd met Garrett Brashear and the rest of the Armadillos. Today at lunch, Garrett told Scooter that if he wanted to join the Armadillos, he should meet them outside the fence on the woods' side of the Pickup Ranch.

Scooter hoped that Jo wouldn't call him a "wimp" - afraid of fun and scared of adventure. Cause it just wasn't true! It wasn't! He'd show her! Show them! Tonight was the first night of summer! The first evening of three months free of school! Free of time constraints! Full of long days and total freedom!

At last, off to his right, Scooter saw a trio of white buildings beyond a cluster of tall mesquite and oak trees. The ranch was quiet, unearthly still even for sunset, as if holding its breath, waiting for something strange to happen.

In many ways the old place looked the same as other Texas farms - mostly used for livestock with a huge garden along the side and a modest sized chicken coop out back.

In other ways, the Chandler's Pickup Ranch was very different. A line of pickup trucks spread out from the driveway, as though it might be a metal picket fence. It halfway surrounded a barn and a single story house. The back acres ended in water; the grazing field sloped along the backside of Lake Tawakoni's earthen dam.

A moat and a metal castle wall, Scooter thought. He studied the line of trucks buried nose first and hood deep in the dirt. Most were in good condition as though repainted before being buried. All their windows were intact, and their rear bumpers were shiny. The oldest models started at the road with the newer makes farther away from the driveway.

Why would anyone do that? Scooter wondered. A Texas sized picket fence? A historical museum of pickups? He'd always heard the Chandler folks were peculiar. Some people were glad they had died. Well, most of them were dead, he thought.

The barn to his left was being repainted; it had been all red once, faded and peeling, but now bone white swathes covered it. Against the pink sky, a star shaped weather vane stood starkly atop the rusted corrugated metal roof. The hayloft door slowly swung back and forth as if moved by an invisible hand.

A gentle lake breeze brushed Scooter; he smelled hay, dung, and freshly mown grass.

A pigpen was on the left side of the barn, and a horse corral surrounded the back of the building. Strangely enough, Scooter didn't see any livestock. Where were all the animals?

As though compelled, Scooter's gaze was drawn to the house. The place caught the last light of day and appeared to radiate an odd, hypnotizing glow. The shadows seemed darker than normal. Cave dark. Tomb dark. The strange sight mesmerized Scooter.

He was still running, but he felt as though he weren't moving. Yet, the house continued to grow larger and larger, looming and distorted; the details becoming sharply defined as it magnified. He had never before experienced such a weird feeling.

The house was painted off-white with green trim and shutters. The massive chimney stretched into the twilight like a blunt finger - pointing out that this was someplace special. Across the front of the house was a covered porch where the waning light failed to reach. The shadows seemed strangely opaque and foreboding.

He saw something move, at least he thought he did. The dark swaths seemed to writhe as though striving to break free. Scooter sensed the shadows were waiting for something. Waiting for darkness. Waiting for release. Waiting for a victim to come near. Too near. Scooter grew closer . . . and closer. He told himself he should cut back on his favorite comic book, SPAWN. His imagination was getting the best of him, again.

Scooter and Flash suddenly burst out of the woods and into the row of pickups. Scooter immediately slid to a stop. "Oh -."

"Quiet!" someone shushed and grabbed Scooter, pulling him to the ground behind a blue '74 Ford pickup. The hands shifted quickly, one clamping across Scooter's mouth. He smelled garlic.

Flash barked, ready to defend Scooter. A familiar voice off to their right spoke the Lab's name. Flash grew quiet.

"You're late, Scoot boy," came a voice from behind him, "And you brought your big ugly mutt!" There was a heavy sigh, "Not a good way to start . . . if you still want to join the Graveyard Armadillos."

"We do! I do!" Scooter mumbled. "And so does Flash."

"No dogs allowed," the handsome, dark-haired boy snapped, implying a double meaning as he released Scooter.

Flash stiffened, glanced up, then cocked his head as if understanding. With a highly insulted look, the Labrador took a couple of steps forward. Now Flash began gagging, then suddenly threw up on Garrett's boots.

Garrett didn't step back in time, getting the toes of his boots sullied. "Hey! Damn your mutt!" Garrett reared back preparing to kick Flash.

The Lab looked up with shining eyes and an expression of wonderment - an angelic face of innocence.

"Don't kick my dog!" Scooter said forcefully.

"Shut up!" Garrett snapped. "You still want to join the Graveyard Armadillos, don't you?"

Scooter nodded.

"Then listen up and keep your mutt away from me. Tonight's your initiation, and you'll do exactly what I tell you to do or you're gone!"

Flash chuffed; then with tail and nose in the air, the Lab returned to Scooter's side. "He's not a mutt, and I will." Scooter leaned down to the Lab and whispered, "Always a comedian, aren't you?" Flash grinned.

"Don't be a smart ass, or you'll be out on your butt," Garrett said. "Hey, I'm talking to you, you know."

Scooter nodded to the older boy.

With piercing blue eyes, a charming smile and the looks of a movie star, Garrett was the heart-throb of Tawakoni High; and he reveled in it. He was as proud as a strutting peacock. Despite the heat, Garrett wore a dark leather jacket without breaking a sweat. "Listen up. We need to get in gear. That movie guy ought to be coming soon."

"I'm tired of waiting," Scooter heard someone drawl, then noticed BJ Mochrie. Below his black cowboy hat, he was scowling. As far as anyone could remember, Byron Jefferson Mochrie had always worn a look of barely restrained impatience. It went along with his arrogant walk that proclaimed he wasn't afraid of anything. With his curly, white blond hair, green-blue eyes, and the build of a rodeo champion, BJ drew lots of attention from girls, although none of them seemed to stay around for long.

With BJ and Garrett were the other members of the Graveyard Armadillos; BJ's twin and bespectacled brother, DJ; the stout tomboy Jo Gunn; skinny Russell Knight and his coldly beautiful sister, Racquel, who had a crush on Garrett; and redheaded Kristine Candel, the minister's pretty daughter.

They all nodded at Scooter. Russell smiled, looking as though he wanted to wave but unsure if it was cool. Scooter shot Russell a look that said, "You didn't mention Kristie was a member!" Scooter tried not to stare but wasn't succeeding; Kristie was very, very cute.

Flash went over to Russell, was petted for a moment, then moved to Kristie, settling in her lap as if it were his new home.

Kristie smiled warmly as though she'd read Scooter's thoughts and patted Flash. The Labrador's eyes rolled back, as his tongue lolled lazily.

Scooter smiled back at Kristie, his flush hidden in the twilight. Never in his wildest dreams would he have imagined that the minister's daughter would be part of this group.

She'd changed a lot in the past year, no longer gangly, but tall and pretty - on the verge of being beautiful. In some ways, she reminded Scooter of himself, tall and trim with auburn hair. Beyond that, the similarities ended. She was pretty and looked composed. He was awkwardly gangly and felt very out of place.

"Ouch!" Scooter slapped at his neck. "Damn mosquitoes!"

"Here!" Kristie tossed him a plastic bottle. "It keeps the 'skeeters at bay." Her voice was lilting, reminding him of the times he'd heard her singing in the church choir.

"Really?" Scooter asked. Kristie nodded, so he applied some to his exposed skin.

Scooter found himself wishing she'd offer to help, and that thought surprised him. Embarrassed, he avoided eye contact and stared at the others. They were all dressed in dark clothing and, to his surprise, wearing homemade necklaces of garlic. Each absently clutched a crucifix as though it were a life preserver they might need at a moment's notice. What was going on here? Certainly not a prayer session.

"This is gonna be great! We're gonna prove there's a vampire in Gunstock!" CJ announced. BJ's nearly identical twin wore thick glasses and a cowboy hat similar to his brother's. Calvin Jefferson was a little taller, but the main difference between the brothers was their expressions. CJ's face projected so much innocence that no one could possibly believe he'd ever done anything wrong - was even capable of doing wrong.

"A vampire?" Scooter wondered dumbly. What was he

missing? Oh, that explained the garlic and crucifixes. But he didn't believe in vampires. They were a myth or characters in a fictional tale.

"Yep, a vampire," Jo Gunn began. "We're gonna make the TV big time!" Her already wide face stretched with a crooked, toothy smile. Her brown cowboy hat pulled down tight, its shadow all but hid her doubled chin. Jo was thick everywhere, through the face, neck and shoulders with legs the size of tree trunks.

"You . . .see, S . . Scooter," Russell Knight began, stuttering as usual. "Garrett believes . . .that the moviemaker, Marcus Chandler, isn't sick like the paper says, but actually a v . . .vam . . .vampire."

Russell was tall, dark-haired, tanned and as skinny as a tent pole. His expression and gray eyes were placid and unreadable. Russell was half Hispanic and rarely showed any emotion, especially his frustration over stuttering. He compensated by singing - which never led to stuttering - or humming Grateful Dead songs. He wore a t-shirt with a skull on the back and dancing skeletons on the front.

"He came back last month to kill his parents," Garrett explained, "and now that they're dead, he's hungry again. Ready to prey on someone else."

"I guess that line of metal didn't protect them like they thought," BJ chuckled giving reason to the strange museum of pickups.

"That's why people have been disappearing," Garrett continued.

"By revealing Chandler's a vampire, we'll show everybody we're not kids anymore," Racquel said bitterly. "We're adults."

Other than their coloring, Racquel and Russell looked very little alike, Scooter thought. Racquel was a blossoming beauty with nearly flawless features and cold, uncaring eyes the color of obsidian.

"Soon, Chaquita," Garrett looked at her, then Scooter. "This is gonna be fun - and memorable." With a wicked smile, Garrett pulled out a Polaroid and handed it to Scooter.

Made uneasy by Garrett's expression, Scooter licked his lips as he accepted the camera. "What do you want me to do?"

"When he comes out for his evening walk, you'll be hiding nearby, ready to snap some pictures. Vampires can't be photographed, so when the picture's blank, except for the background, we'll know he's truly one of the legion of undead."

"How can you be so sure he'll come out now?" Jo asked.

"He always comes out after the sun sets," Garrett replied.

"H . . . how do you . . . know?" Russell asked.

"Been watching him," Garrett replied. "There's something very, very strange about him. I've seen his picture. He's one weird looking dude! Never seen a white African American."

CJ said, "This Chandler fella looks like he's been bleached!"

"Yeah," Garrett continued. "His face is pasty white, almost colorless. His eyes are red, sorta like a rabid wolf's. Boy howdy, he is ugly! The kicker is he can't stand the daylight. It blisters and burns his skin. What did I tell ya? He's a vampire. Why else would he look like that and make movies about the living dead?" Garrett asked. "He knows all about being one with the darkness. It's a perfect cover!"

"Maybe he's related to Michael Jackson," BJ snickered.

Scooter didn't believe any of this and was fairly sure none of them did, either.

"P . . . paper says he's an anemic albino and has vitiligo," Russell responded. "Don't ask me to s . . . spell it.

"What's that?" Jo asked.

"A lie to cover up the fact that he's a vampire," Garrett persisted.

"Maybe he has AIDS," CJ suggested.

EXCERPTS FROM VEGAS VAMPIRES

CHAPTER ONE

With a flick of her glow-in-the dark fingernails, Heather Winslow dealt a ghostly playing card, spinning out luck. It sliced through the twilight of the casino, leaving an evanescent trail as fleeting as good fortune. What appeared to be fortuitous, in the form of a ten of clubs, settled on the velvet table in front of chair seven. The black-light bumper brightened the card's greenish radiance.

"Ha! Beat that w-witch!" the drunk customer slurred triumphantly. The portly brute pointed at his radiant cards, then he rudely exhaled smoke in her face. "I would like to see this chick's bust."

Dick 'the Dude' was typical of the nastiest guests, blaming, cursing and blowing smoke. She thought of him as a brute. He had doubled down on a pair of aces. Making a big deal over digging out black chips from his hunting vest, he bet his entire stash. The $500 cheques sat atop the illuminated betting circle in two tall stacks like World Trade Center's Twin Towers. The ten had given him twenty-one, a nice second hand to go along with his first, a twenty.

Heather glared, wishing looks could kill. Or better, she thought, her look could make him lose it all. She was silently thankful for her good luck and prayed her fortune continued its winning ways. Beating rude customers was the best way for a dealer to shed them. The Suits were renowned for reading minds and ignoring improprieties when big money played.

She shifted uncomfortably, feeling pricked as though the entire casino were sharply watching her. Large bets summoned scrutiny from the Eye in the Sky. Security cameras and black lights hung concealed within the heavily brocaded awning overhead, giving the Twilight Paradise Tahoe gambling floor an intimate feel.

Because she was pretty—some had proclaimed beautiful to flatter her—guys had always 'checked out' Heather Winslow. Most assumed she was a typical, blue-eyed, blond and tanned Californian. She was actually from northern Nevada. Having grown up in a resort town, she was accustomed to eyeballing, especially when she was doing her best Barbie imitation. Along with the glow-in-the-dark effects, make-up was a great disguise. Hardly anyone recognized her away from the casino. It was safer that way. She had been blamed, angrily cursed and threatened often in the five months since she began working at the Twilight Paradise.

"Her luck'll change. You'll see. Nobody wins all the time," the obnoxious brute proclaimed.

"If you're really interested in winning, maybe you should try table hopping," she suggested, hoping he might take the hint.

"Why the hell for?" the rude brute stammered. As if he were inhaling it, Dick drank deeply of a beer. It was a chaser to the shot of Wild Turkey that had fortified this gamble and steadied his hand. Ten out of ten casinos would recommend such an action.

"A Michigan State study revealed that by playing two losing games there is a ratcheting effect that enables players to win."

"So what are you trying to say?"

"They did this despite playing in two games where the odds were stacked against them. They dubbed it Parrondo's Paradox."

"Sounds like BS," Dick, the tasteless brute, burped.

Ignoring him, she checked with the distinguished gentleman sitting in the seven spot. She spared a smile for Mr. P, a self-proclaimed admirer and glutton for punishment. On more than one occasion, she had delicately informed him she was absolutely—wholeheartedly, body and soul—in love with Skyler Everhart, and not looking for a sugar daddy.

Mr. P laid his hand flat, standing pat. He looked at her for a long second, then he smiled as if he knew what she had for a hand.

"I suggest you do as your friend advised. It is foolish to tempt fate and risky to flirt with Lady Luck."

"Why's that?"

"The beauteous Heather of Tahoe is the queen of blackjack here, at the Twilight Paradise, and perhaps all of Nevada. Dare I say, the world. She has the good fortune of three, a very lucky number."

"You'll make me blush," she replied. By his comments, she knew he had been talking to her sister. Who else knew about the luck of three? Amber's tongue wagged when she had been imbibing. She seemed to have the uncanny knack of saying something inappropriate, or being at the wrong place at a bad time.

She flipped over her hole card, then gave herself the two of hearts to go along with the three of diamonds and two of clubs. She dealt another two, the spade, her hand adding up to nine.

"Come on ten spot!"

If she drew a ten, she would have to stand. Dick would win both hands. She inwardly groaned. That would encourage the insufferable brute to stay longer. Just lose and go home, Heather wished. She played another two, giving her all four suits and the unimpressive total of eleven. With a face card or any ten, she would beat him twice over.

"Aw, for Christ's sake. No ten. No ten!" the brute chanted.

"I sense something familiar happening," Mr. P said dryly.

Heather paused, letting a little drama build while she glanced up. The crowd was large for late October, with the tourist season long over and locals' summer waning. She was pleased to find security guards close by, watching along with the Suits.

Her brutish player should have been eighty-sixed long ago, but he had already lost thirty grand. The pit bosses' bonuses were calculated from the table winnings, encouraging them to catch cheaters, bring out new cards, and switch dealers whenever there was a run on the House. Harry Coxswain loved having Heather deal in his pit.

She didn't get a ten spot with her sixth card, dealing a three.

"Fourteen! Ha! Bust baby!"

With the stakes high, the tension was almost unbearable. Heather gave herself another card—the ace of hearts. She cleared her throat, finding it a little difficult to breathe. The ace of diamonds made eight cards and sixteen. She wasn't allowed to stand on sixteen, only seventeen and higher.

Her current situation was a perfect example for her dissertation. After getting her degrees, she had taken a year off from the University of Nevada-Reno to get an idea for an organizational behavior study. Did the customers' blaming affect the dealers? If casinos, like the Paradise, focused on making the employees feel like winners, did they win more? Her long term plan was to eventually work in career counseling, which meant she had to get her doctorate. Even having a masters meant little when trying to get a job or hang your own shingle. She wanted to apply Dr. Carl Rogers methods and beliefs that people inherently wanted to do a good job. He had expanded upon Mazlow's ideas of satisfying basic needs to obtain a happier and better performing employee. If you worried less about health and home, you could do an even better job.

"Go big! Go little, I don't care! Just go, w-witch!"

"They are playing your song," Mr. P chuckled.

Heather wouldn't have noticed the music, if he hadn't mentioned it. The intercom system softly played The *Purple People Eater*. Like all dealers, she was in uniform, decked out in a dark lavender velour vest and bow tie.

As Heather dealt the next card, she sensed a commotion, but she couldn't look away, riveted by her luck. The appearance of the five of diamonds threw her table into a state of shock. She fought to hide her smile, but she was full of an overwhelming sense of triumph.

"A nine card twenty-one. Impressive. Do you realize, Dick, if you had not doubled down, you would have had twenty, and she would have gotten the ten of clubs, giving her a plain old four card seventeen?" Mr. P asked.

Heather believed in miracles. Whether they seemed great or small, they happened every day, mostly in unexpected ways.

Shouting profanities, the drunken brute lunged across the table. Dick seized her by the throat and clamped down, choking her with both hands. He shook her once, violently hard, shocking her blind as he tried to snap her neck. Then it suddenly lessened, as if he had been held back at the last instant.

When she could see again, she stared dully through a red haze into the eyes of murderous hate. She panicked, because she saw he was drunk enough to kill her. Mr. P and others wrestled with the brute, barely keeping her alive by prying at his arms.

She desperately jabbed for his eyes. Her nails fell short, tearing into his cheeks. The sight of blood made matters worse, sickening her and adding to her lightheadedness. She tried to think critically, but her body's fight and flight mechanism overwhelmed her.

The table protected him from taking a knee in the testicles. She tried falling back, but he had her like a puppet in a vise grip. Desperation assailed her. She was going to die. Oh, Skyler. I love you. Mom . . . .

Out of the corner of her eye, she saw something blur. The overhead awning swept down. Its frame struck the brute, catching Dick in the temple. Stunned stupid, he released her.

Seeing red with black bubbling spots, Heather fell back, gasping for breath. A miracle!

Somebody strong caught her, grunting before gently lowering her to the floor. "Relax. I have you" the man said, sounding pained. "Look out!"

Heather glanced up, seeing a thrown playing card skip off the murderous brute's brow. It sliced flesh and bled into his eye, making him pause. the cashier's cage and the casino bank.

The sorting room was unoccupied. At an empty table, she collapsed into a folding chair. With the peril past, her adrenaline had ebbed, leaving her exhausted.

WILLIAM HILL WRITING WORKSHOPS

A fifteen year resident of Northern Nevada, William Hill writes fantasy and supernatural thrillers for young adults and the young-at-heart. Readers of all ages have enjoyed his novels. Some are part of school reading programs. Tales include: *Dragon Pawns: Jules and the Runt Dragon, The Magic Bicycle, Chasing Time, California Ghosting, Wizard Sword, The Vampire Hunters,* and *Vegas Vampires,* among others. See www.fantasyhill.com

William thinks writing should be fun. He aspires to entertain, educate, and provoke thought. He has a passion for imagining and storytelling, so through workshops he likes to share the magic. His goal is to inspire creativity, the pursuit of dreams, and better readers and writers.

In his workshop, he uses a Socratic dialog approach for brainstorming and group creating. He offers a Power Point presentation combined with stage magic and interactive exercises.

The Four Sessions of a Writing Workshop:

The Importance of Words. (Why Do I Need A Good Vocatulary?)

I relate variations of words with similar meanings to color, in this case different shades of green, drawing from the big box of 120 crayons instead of a box of 8. I show a blank drawing, then add just green to the forest scene with green apples, a bucket, and car, and then use the many shades of green to make it look more realistic, detailed, and varied. I stress the importance of word selection by showing that choices are made based upon the character's or narrator's voices, as well as the target audience's reading level. We expand on words to show how synonyms have different hues and feels (denotations/connotations) whether someone is thin, scrawny, or lean, or the opposite, as in hefty, rotund or plump. Writing exercises can include word selection and comparative description.

Where Do Ideas Come From?

I use real world examples from Ben Franklin, Philo T. Farnsworth, who invented the TV, and various authors (audience dependent): Jerdine Nolen, Donald Cruise, Bill Watterson (Calvin and Hobbes) Robert Munsch, HG Wells, JRR Tolkien and CS Lewis. I show how their lives and what happened in the world affected their writing. For younger audiences, I perform a magic trick to show something can be created from nothing, if it is an idea put under creative pressure.

Recipe of a Story:

Just like chocolate chip cookies, we are cooking up stories, so we need ingredients. Together we choose a target audience, a genre, and create a beginning, body, and resolution. We discuss the purpose of each character, their goals, weaknesses, the setting, the conflict, tension, pace, and theme. We do a short 'Show, Don't Tell' exercise about character. I perform magic to support the unity of theme idea, bringing the dots together, and a trick to show how suspense and tension work to keep readers interested.

Rewriting/Editing/Perseverance/Tips

I discuss helpful hints, such as eliminating adverbs and using strong/descriptive verbs (strolling vs. trudging, vs. waddling) and shortcuts, as well as inspirational stories of Dr. Seuss, Richard Bach, and others.

Writing Workshop Praise:

I highly recommend a visit from Mr. William Hill. Our teachers are very impressed with his natural rapport with students and his knowledge of writing. They will never look at writing the same. 10/06 Pat Mace, Librarian, Pottsboro MS, TX.

Thank you very much for your wonderful presentation. I thought it was excellent in getting the students to really understand the elements of good writing. 9/06 Maureen Moffet, Librarian, St. Anne's Catholic School, Bristol, VA.

I learned a great deal from your presentation. 9/06 Gary Campbell, English III Teacher, Ed White HS, Jacksonville, FL.

I want to say a personal thank you for your visit. It is people like you who actually touch the world with their writing that makes what I teach come to life. 10/06, Charlotte Strahan, 10th grade English, Pottsboro HS, TX.

Your book talk presentation was excellent. Thank you so much for helping motivate middle school students, 1/06 Michele Collins, Principal, Cynthia Reed, Librarian: Swope MS, Reno, NV.

The presentations were very energetic and down-to-earth, allowing student interaction. It encourages to 'just do it'. 11/05

Tom Cllickner, Librarian, Yorba Middle School, Orange, CA.

It was great. Right on point, so the students can understand writing. 9/06, Deborah Minor, Media Specialist, Pittsboro MS, NC.

What a learning experience and such a treat for the kids. 11/05, Robert Cornman, Librarian, Yerington MS, NV.

This is exactly what our kids needed to hear. 10/05, Librarian, Cathy Ventner, Lemmon Valley Elementary, NV.

The students commented afterwards that they felt it had been beneficial and enjoyable. Quite a few indicated that they wanted a copy of their work back so they might continue working on their pieces. 11/97 Beverly Sizemore, Asst. Coordinator UNC Chapel Hill Pre-College Program.

Now they are willing to rewrite their work. 9/05 English 6th and 7th, Joanne Robb, N. Chatham k-8, Chapel Hill, NC.

Your visit to Baldwin Middle-Senior High School was an absolute success. Our students are still talking about the interactive lesson you presented that challenged them to design an original story line. We teach and talk about these same concepts in our classrooms, but hearing it from the POV of a real life author was motivating and fun. 4/05 Nancy Rhoden, Reading Coach, Baldwin, FL.

He reinforced the skills that I teach my students throughout the year. 4/05 Betty DeFratus, Language and Reading Teacher, Pottsboro, TX.

If you're interested in a workshop or author visit, contact Mr. Hill at otterpress@aol.com

Workshops presented to students at:

ELEMENTARY SCHOOLS:
Alta Vista,, Auburn, CA
Edmondson, Loveland, CO
Fair Oaks, Auburn, CA
Foothill, Pittsburg, CA
Haynesfield, Bristol, TN
Holston View, Bristol, TN
Incline 3-5, Incline Village, NV
Lemmon Valley, Reno, NV
Meneley, Gardnerville, NV
Minden, Minden, NV
Poetry Community Christian School, Poetry, TX
Sacramento Country Day, Sacramento, CA
Scarselli, Gardnerville, NV
St. Anne's Catholic School, Bristol, VA
Big Thompson, Loveland, CO
Tonopah, Tonopah, NV
Warner, Reno, NV
Valley View, Austin, TX

MIDDLE SCHOOLS:
Billingshurst, Reno, NV
Cain, Auburn, CA
Carson Valley, Minden, NV
Cerro Villa, Orange, CA
Cookman Magnet, Jacksonville, FL
El Rancho, Anaheim, CA
Harrison, Pittsboro, NC
Horton, Pittsboro, NC
Incline, Incline Village, NV
Kingsbury, Roundhill, NV
Mammoth, Mammoth Lakes, CA
McPherson Magnet, Orange, CA

N. Chatham k-8, Chapel Hill, NC
O'Brien, Reno, NV
Pau-Wa-Lu, Gardnerville, NV
Pine, Reno, NV
Portola, Orange, CA
Pottsboro, Pottsboro, TX
Swope, Reno NV
Yerington Intermediate, Yerington, NV
Vance, Bristol, TN
Yorba Academy, Orange, CA

HIGH SCHOOLS:
Baldwin Middle-Senior, Baldwin, FL
Douglas, Minden, NV
Galena, Reno, NV
McQueen, Reno, NV
Pottsboro, Pottsboro, TX
Whittell, Zephyr Cove, NV
White, Jacksonville, FL

PUBLIC LIBRARIES:
Alainte, N. Las Vegas, NV
Bristol, Bristol, VA
Douglas, Minden, NV
Sparks, Sparks, NV
NW Reno, Reno, NV

THE NOW AND FUTURE AUTHOI

William Hill is a naturalized Northern Nevadan, a native Indianapolis, Indiana and a product of many places and stories. first learned to read through super hero comic books, then spy thrille Sci-Fi and finally fantasy novels, tucked in among the required clas readings.

Bill has lived in many places, including Prairie Village, Ks., Brisi TN; around Dallas and Denton in Texas; and in south and north Lá Tahoe, and currently in Gardnerville, NV. Bill has a 'serious' degi from Vanderbilt University in economics and an MBA from t University of North Texas, as well as certifications in outdoor emergen care and licenses in insurance and securities.

Since realizing that writing was his best talent and a gift, B escaped the restrictive drudgery of the corporate world to craft I tales. Along with working in human resources, Bill has been employ as an 'alchemist' in South Lake Tahoe, a ski patroller at Diamond Pe in Incline Village, NV, and a sports official in Douglas County. Ov the last year, Bill has enjoyed making writing presentations at schoc around the country.

The Vampire Hunters Stalked is Bill's tenth novel. Bill, his lovely wii Kat, and their eight year old son, Brin, live in the shadow of the Easten Sierra. Bill intends to write imaginative fiction and fantasy until dirt shoveled upon his coffin.

He is currently working on a sequel to *Dragon Pawns -Jules and tl Runt Dragon.*